A Malignant Mind

Jackson Hunter

Published by Jackson Hunter, 2024.

Also by Jackson Hunter

BATTLE TO OWN THE FUTURE

PROLOGUE

"The paradox of vengefulness is that it makes men dependent upon those who have harmed them, believing that their release from pain will come only when their tormentors suffer."
-Laura Hillenbrand

. . . .

THE CROWD HEARD JACK Baron's entourage before they sighted it. A lone bagpiper strode directly in front of Baron, his red cheeks ballooning as he breathed life into his bagpipes with all the gusto he could muster. He was a hulk of a man with a wild and wiry red beard, yet his fingers nimbly played the chanter to create a hypnotic celtic melody. The shrill primal wailing filled the arena as hot breath blown into the bag was forced through reeds within the chanter and drone pipe. It was a sonorous melody that aroused deep-rooted ancestral feelings in some of the listeners. Bagpipers traditionally led the Scots into battle to terrify their enemies and fortify the clan's courage to face their foe. Here the piper served to both announce half of Baron's ancestry, as well as his challenge. The bagpiper was dressed in regimental gear. Looking positively majestic, he wore a tall jet black feather bonnet made from ostrich feathers, a kilt, doublet embroidered jacket, plaid, horse hair sporran, tartan hose, and spats.

Next to the bagpiper strode a single heavily tattooed Maori warrior. His most noticeable feature was a full facial moko (tattoo) that depicted his lineage, Waikato-Tainui tribe, occupation, mana, and deeds. He was bare to the waist, wearing nothing but a traditional flax skirt that slapped at his heavily muscled thighs. Energized and enjoying the moment of the spectacle, he waved the New Zealand flag with its Union Jack and four stars of the Southern

Cross, from side-to-side high above his head. The piper and warrior striding side by side represented the two lineages of Baron's family going back hundreds of years.

The entourage continued to make its way down the aisle through the throng of thousands of noisy spectators towards the brightly illuminated boxing ring within the otherwise dimly lit arena of Madison Square Garden, New York City. Baron was a tall man. His head was visible above the canopy formed by those of his coaches, supporters, and the venue's security guards. The crowd cheered as they caught sight of the boxer now entering the arena. Cameras in hand, their photography caused the arena to briefly brighten with momentary flashes of brilliant white star light. Some in the crowd stood and rhythmically chanted out the fighter's name "Baron" over and over again.

Exactly when and how the Baron family acquired their family name was a mystery. Family records indicated the New Zealand Barons were partly of Scottish descent. That one of their male ancestors, a giant of a man, had fought beside the great warrior King of the Scots, Robert the Bruce, at the Battle of Bannockburn in 1314. Their man had distinguished himself during the battle where Bruce's army achieved victory over the English and restored Scottish independence. The King showed his gratitude by granting their relative a barony. It is believed that for whatever reason the family on migrating to New Zealand wished to remain anonymous while starting a new life in a foreign country. In recognition of their title they changed their surname to Baron.

Jack Baron wore a Korowai over his broad shoulders, a cloak that is skilfully woven from harakeke (flax). It was adorned with the finest feathers of kiwi and the now extinct huia that had been regarded by Maori as tapu (sacred). To Maori, the Korowai was a taonga (treasure) that signified the prestige and mana (power and rank) of the wearer. Jack had worn the Korowai with pride at all of his previous professional fights. The cloak had been lent to him for such events as a mark of respect by the elders of the Waikato-Tainui iwi (tribe) whose ancestors formed many of the hapu (subtribes) in the Waikato and neighboring regions of the North Island of New Zealand (Aotearoa).

The sacred Tainui waka (canoe) had brought Jack's Maori ancestors to subtropical New Zealand from the more tropical, coconut palm decorated, shores of Hawaiki (Polynesian homelands) over six hundred years ago. Jack Baron was forever bound to the Waikato-Tainui tribe through the marriage of his great grandfather, a tall and fearsome Scot from Aberdeen, to the daughter of one of the tribal elders. The children (tamariki) they bore were raised by the tribe on ancestral land. Jack's subsequent descendants had either married other members of the tribe, or British settlers to New Zealand who worked as sealers, whalers, farmers or gold-diggers, or in the burgeoning flax/timber industry. Baron's father Dirk was a tall dark-haired man of similar stature to his youngest son. Through struggle and plain hard work, he had obtained the freehold to land previously owned by the Crown, which the family now farmed in the rich lands of the Waikato in the centre of the North Island of New Zealand. Dirk and his elder son, Josh, had ringside seats. They waited patiently for Jack and his entourage to arrive. Baron's mother Vera, a fine-looking woman of Scottish descent, could not bear to watch the fight. She waited anxiously at their hotel close to the venue, praying her son would return to her unharmed.

Baron and his entourage made it to ringside, and two team members prized apart the taut ropes of the boxing ring to enable Baron to step up into the ring.

The announcer shouted into his microphone once again.

"And now making his way to the ring, the reigning and defending WBC heavyweight champion of the world Francisco F-r-a-n-k-i-e B-l-a-n-c-o."

Once again the crowd went wild with excitement as they glimpsed the other fighter and his entourage now making their way to the ring. The Latino American boxer was wearing a shiny gold hoodie that hid his head. He was tall, but not as tall as Baron. Two skimpily clad vivacious coffee-coloured Latino women danced energetically in front of the boxer, one waving their national flag. Blanco temporarily stopped at a podium on the walkway to allow fans and representatives of the press to take photographs. In a display of his skill, he hit out energetically with his fists at an imaginary opponent, ducking and diving like a shadow boxer. Eventually, Blanco and his entourage also made their way to the ring.

The two fighters moved to their respective corners. Cutmen frantically dabbed colourless petroleum jelly on exposed points of each fighter's face that were at risk of bleeding after being constantly and mercilessly pounded. The announcer called for quiet from the crowd as the national anthems of the countries represented by the two fighters were sung. There would be twelve rounds of boxing for the WBC world heavyweight championship. The announcer introduced the time-keeper, judges, and referee. Finally, he shouted into his microphone in a deliberately long-drawn-out drawl.

"L-e-t-s g-e-t r-e-a-d-y t-o r-u-m-b-l-e."

He then introduced each of the two fighters, detailing their vital statistics.

"It's undefeated champion versus undefeated champion. Fighting out of the red corner wearing black, standing six feet eight inches, official weight two hundred and sixty-three pounds, a professional record of twelve fights by knockout, the undefeated heavyweight champion of New Zealand, J-a-c-k B-a-r-o-n."

The crowd cheered wildly in response, with some again taking up the "Baron" chant.

"His opponent fighting out of the blue corner wearing gold, standing six feet two inches, official weight two hundred and ninety-four pounds, a professional record of twenty-two wins by knockout, Olympic gold champion, and reigning and undefeated WBC heavyweight champion of the world F-r-a-n-k-i-e B-l-a-n-c-o."

The crowd cheered again, even louder this time, with many standing and clapping. Some of the spectators could be seen hotly discussing and comparing the vital statistics of each boxer, arguing over who had the best odds of winning. Many considered the young New Zealander to be far too inexperienced, and very lucky to have secured a fight with Blanco, the current holder of the WBC world heavyweight belt. He was an upstart, who surely was about to get his comeuppance.

The boxers disrobed, stripping to the waist to reveal their very different body types. To any unknowledgeable observer, it looked like a bad mismatch. Baron at twenty-six years of age had the lean and muscled body of a Greek God. He was a picture of fitness with visibly impressive rock-hard muscles tethered to his tall frame. In every way, he resembled the seasoned champion of a gladiator pit. He didn't appear to carry a single ounce of fat. He was known to be an athletic boxer capable of generating exceptional speed and power. His boxing style was suggested by some boxing enthusiasts to resemble that of the great Mohammed Ali.

In marked contrast, the shorter Blanco at thirty-two years was flabby and appeared to be completely out of shape. Seasoned spectators who had seen Blanco fight before did not underestimate the man. He had been an Olympic champion and had won all his previous professional fights by knockout. They recognised his outward appearance was a disguise. He represented the shorter hulkier boxer who harbours a powerful inner physique. His powerful musculature was hidden beneath a thick layer of protective fat. He reminded some of a beachmaster elephant seal. These powerful goliaths with their extraordinary layers of blubber and muscle rule the beach, and are happy to fight to the death to preserve the right to mate with the female seals in their harems. Likewise, Blanco had gained the right to rule the boxing ring, and take on all contenders for the WBC belt. But would that right be taken from him tonight? The spectators had paid handsomely to attend the fight. Were they going to witness an upset? Would the reigning world champion be deposed? It was ordained that one of the contestants was about to undergo something he had never before experienced. For the first time in his career, he was going to lose.

The two fighters met in the middle of the ring, touched gloves, and briefly eyed each other nose-to-nose in a stare-down. The referee met the eyes of each boxer in turn and reminded them he wanted a fair fight. The boxers returned to their respective corners to receive last-minute encouragement and instructions from their coaches. The bell rang to sound the start of round one, and the fighters advanced to the centre of the ring. Blanco immediately charged Baron, his fists flying with dizzying speed defying his enormous size, aiming to take Baron by surprise and club him senseless. Baron, with the advantage of his superior height and longer reach, simply pushed his gloved right hand against Blanco's head, keeping him at a distance, and rendering him harmless. Without warning, and at lightning speed he let fly a powerful left jab, catching Blanco in the neck. Blanco's body shuddered. The protective layer of fat quivered in shock. Several of the spectators rose to their feet and screamed with delight. Immediately, in retaliation Blanco charged again, leaping up and lunging with his fist to reach Baron's head. Baron leaned back, avoiding the blow, and countered by hitting Blanco heavily in his large central mass. The blow would have cracked several of a normal man's ribs, but appeared to have no effect against Blanco's considerable blubbery armor. The fight continued like this for a further eight rounds, with Baron dancing around Blanco, avoiding most of his mighty punches, and using his superior height, speed, agility, and reach to reign potentially damaging blows on Blanco's body and head.

When the bell sounded for the tenth round it was clear that Blanco's support staff had been unable to effectively treat the cuts that had opened above their fighter's eyes. Blood was streaming down Blanco's now swollen and badly battered face. The odd metallic-tasting droplet of blood mixed with sweat made its way to the fighter's mouth. For the first time in his boxing career, Blanco could taste defeat. He had been skillfully out-boxed. He was breathing heavily now at the end of each round as the fight took its toll. He had been told by his corner that he could no longer win the fight on points. He would have to go all out to win by knockout. Blanco was a man enraged. He had never been defeated. Defeat was unthinkable.

Immediately after the bell sounded, Blanco charged at Baron like an enraged beachmaster, aiming to bluster his way past Baron's defenses to land the decisive blow. Instead, Baron side-stepped, and hit Blanco hard in the side of his unprotected head with all the considerable force he could bring to bear. It was like being hit in the head with a sledgehammer. Blanco's brain with its soft cheese-like texture was thrust violently sideways against his hard bony skull causing blood vessels to rip apart, and leak. Filmed in slow motion, Blanco's lights went out at that moment. Blanco staggered backward and fell heavily against the ropes. The ropes upheld his outstretched arms, and he hung there, his huge body crucified and lifeless on the side of the ring. The crowd went crazy, cheering wildly as they witnessed the violent spectacle. Many spectators stood up clapping vigorously or could be seen throwing their arms up in the air in excitement. In the heat of the moment and fuelled with a hot mix of testosterone and adrenalin, Baron also threw his arms up, repeatedly punching the air with his right fist to signify his victory. This fuelled yet a further frenzy from the spectators. The referee rushed forward to the stricken man, his arms moving rapidly from side to side like windscreen wipers in a violent rain storm as he gave Blanco the mandatory eight count. But the referee soon realized Blanco was unresponsive, unconscious, and possibly in need of urgent medical attention. He immediately turned and looked towards Blanco's corner and to medical staff, waving to them for assistance. Blanco's coach and supporters were already rushing towards their man. The spectators suddenly went deathly quiet as they realized they might be witnessing a potential tragedy unfolding.

Blanco's supporters untangled their fighter from the ropes and gently laid him down, as medical staff rushed to help. The ring announcer quickly, and with no pomp and ceremony this time, declared Baron to be the winner and the new holder of the WBC heavyweight belt. There was no cheering now. The crowd remained silent as a mark of respect. They had got more than what they had paid for and quickly departed the arena while medical staff frantically worked on Blanco's prone body. The still unresponsive fighter was placed on a stretcher and quickly carried to an awaiting ambulance. There was no post-fight press conference, and the media did not attempt to interview the boxing teams as they left the arena.

That same night as Baron, his coach, supporters, and family dined out in celebration of their success they learned that Frankie Blanco had died in the ambulance from a traumatic brain injury on his way to the hospital. The news hit Jack Baron like a tonne of bricks as he was forced to accept the fact he had killed a man with his hands. It was just the one punch to the side of the head that had done the damage. He felt wretched and sick inside. "What was it all for?" he asked himself "Should someone have to die for the sake of entertainment?" "When all said and done, boxing is just a game. It is not worth anyone losing their life over." "Is this the sort of spectacle people had come to see?" He sat dejected at the table, holding his head in his hands.

Jack's coach, a hard man with a soft centre, who had experienced life more than most, had taken the call.

Jack had heard him end the call "Please give Blanco's family our sincerest condolences. No one wanted the fight to end like this."

Jack's father Dirk stood up sombrely, and held and squeezed his son's shoulder.

"It wasn't your fault son," he whispered. "He knew the risks. We all do."

"That's right Jack. It was a fair fight. You have absolutely nothing to be sorry for," agreed his coach. "Take a break for a few weeks. You'll need some time to recover. We'll be waiting back at the gym to get you back into shape whenever you are ready. We need to start planning your defense of the belt."

"I could do with a hand on the farm. Come and stay as long as you like," offered Dirk, quickly changing the subject.

The international media were waiting as they left the restaurant. The press had eagerly waited to hear whether Blanco would regain consciousness. Instead, they had learned that he had passed away in the ambulance before he had even reached the hospital. They were merciless, constantly posing questions as the Baron family and team made their way to their transport. The security staff did their best to keep them away, but the media were relentless.

"Don't you have anything to say, Mr. Baron? Did you want to kill him?", "Do you think it was a mismatch?", "Do you think boxing should be banned?", "Shouldn't boxers who kill get a prison sentence for manslaughter?" "What's it feel like to kill someone with your bare hands, Mr. Baron?" "Are you going to defend your title?"

"Take no notice of them, son," advised Dirk, as he sought to protect his boy.

Flying into Auckland Airport on the journey home to New Zealand, the family and team were once again assailed by the media. This time, however, an honour guard of Jack's Maori tribe and extended family kept the media at bay, while others in the tribe performed a traditional haka to welcome home their distinguished iwi member.

The routine of farm work was exactly what Jack needed to take his mind off the fight. The four hundred acre Waikato farm had four hundred jersey dairy cows that needed milking before sunrise, and again in the afternoon. There were gorse, thistles, dock, and other weeds to be tackled, crops to be weeded and watered, and fences and equipment to be mended. It was long back-breaking work, but Jack was used to it, having been raised on the farm. You could say he was designed for it. His father was the same. Neighbours and town folk warmly referred to Dirk and Jack as the county's strongmen. Their physical abilities were legendary. Dirk could often be seen grasping a twenty-five kilogram hay bale in each of his large hands at haymaking time. He would effortlessly and simultaneously toss both bales onto the tray of the hay truck. He would carry the largest timber fence posts around as if they were matchsticks. He could work like this for hours on end, never seeming to tire. In his younger days and just for fun, Dirk would sometimes compete at the local Highland Games at Te Aroha or Paeroa. There he would impress Vera by easily winning the "tossing of the heavy hammer and highland stone" to the delight of the crowds who would gather to witness his feats of strength.

The county folk had eagerly waited to see whether Dirk Baron's offspring would inherit their father's incredible physique and strength. They were severely disappointed when the first offspring, a boy named Josh, took after his mother's side. Josh was a strong healthy boy who loved farm work, but his physique wasn't a patch on his father's. The neighbours and town folk became excited once again when Dirk's wife Vera fell pregnant for the second time. This time the county folk struck gold. They ogled and marvelled at the visible musculature of the newly born baby boy named Jack, resulting from the second pregnancy. Miraculously, the boy could stand and support himself just two days after he was born. Baby Jack was a constant source of gossip for ladies in the neighbourhood.

"I heard that Jack can do pull-ups now. It's amazing given he is only eight months old", and a month later "I heard he can climb the stairs now."

Some of the parents were stunned, but at the same time concerned, when they witnessed ten-month-old Jack effortlessly performing iron-crosses and chin-ups in the local pre-school playground. They took their concerns to the senior staff demanding to know whether it was right that a boy as powerful as Jack should be playing with their children. He could seriously hurt them, they warned. But they soon came to appreciate that Jack was a gentle boy. He never used his strength in anger at preschool or throughout his schooling. He would step in to stop fights between children, never to start them. He would watch over the children to protect them from harming themselves or others.

The staff of the pre-school were initially amused that the family would fill a backpack with extra food for Jack to eat during the day. They developed a routine where Jack was fed something from the backpack every hour. As advised by Jack's parents, and as witnessed themselves, the boy had to eat throughout the day or he would begin to feel unwell. If kryptonite was superman's weakness, then Jack's hungry metabolism was his weakness. As an adult he had taken to devouring several energy and protein bars, most also packed with carbohydrates, throughout the day. Despite his considerable appetite, Jack never became fat and overweight. Quite the opposite. All the extra food he ate appeared to grow skeletal muscle. At just four years of age, he already had a six-pack, and clearly defined biceps, triceps, pectorals, and deltoids. As a teenager, he was the ultimate athlete, combining strength with speed and balance. In high school, he won every event he entered, be it the long jump, high jump, sprint, shot put, discus or javelin, and consequently was a school celebrity.

Jack slept in his old bedroom during his stay at the family farm. The bedroom had been left untouched since the day he departed for University in the South Island. The walls were almost completely covered with the ribbons and medals he had won at school sporting events, and at regional and national sporting events. Cups and other trophies for the most prestigious wins were proudly displayed in a large glass cabinet in his parents' lounge. It would be a decade later that the latest medical science would provide an explanation for Jack's unique physique.

It was now four weeks since the fight. Jack, dressed in overalls, black plastic apron, and gumboots, had just finished hosing down the milking yard and shed when his brother Josh suddenly appeared. Jack took off the apron and hung it on a hook in the milking shed. As they walked back to the house for breakfast Josh recalled the fight.

"It's not just me Jack," stated Josh, "everyone has noticed you've lost your spark since the fight. We don't like to see you like this. It wasn't your fault Blanco died. Other boxers have died in the ring. It's a risk that all boxers accept when they step into the ring."

"That's easy for you to say. I am the one who killed a man with my bare hands. Look at me, Josh. Sometimes my strength scares me, the damage I could do if I became really angry."

"Jack, your body is a gift. Your physique is the envy of every man. I know, I've heard the endless comments about you from my male friends. They hold you in awe. I know you, Jack. You never strike out in anger. You are the last person to want to deliberately hurt someone. Give yourself a break."

"To tell the truth, Josh, I'm over it all. As a kid, all I wanted was to make Mum and Dad proud of me, to make the community proud of our family. I never expected it would all lead to this. I'm over the constant attention of fans and media, of always being in the spotlight. Of always being expected to be on the winning side. I want to do something "real", something tangible to help people with their lives."

"Why don't you stay here? Mum and Dad aren't getting any younger. We could share the farm and the farm work once Mum and Dad retire?"

"I am truly grateful for the offer Josh, but I need to get away from New Zealand for a while. I haven't told anyone yet, but I've applied for a job in the UK."

The brothers took off their gumboots and opened the back door to the house. As they walked through the door into the kitchen, Vera stepped forward.

"This letter came for you Jack in yesterday's mail. It's from the UK," exclaimed Vera holding out the letter.

"You two happy with fried bread, bacon and eggs, and baked beans?" asked Vera, observing the gloomy expressions on her two boys' faces. Dirk was already at the breakfast table devouring a large plate of food. The boys both nodded in response. Josh looked at his brother with a questioning look, wondering whether the letter was about Jack's job application.

Jack and Josh took their places opposite their father at the large pinewood breakfast table. Jack quickly inspected the letter and placed it in his pocket. He would open it later when he had some privacy.

"Who's your letter from Jack?" asked Vera sensing something wasn't quite right while placing large plates of food in front of her sons. "Anything interesting? Go on open it up. Don't keep us all in suspense, Jack."

Jack already knew who the letter was from. He took it out of his pocket, tore the end off, and extracted the letter. The letter was from Human Resources, Scotland Yard, London, United Kingdom (UK). He had been expecting a rejection letter, but instead as he read he learned they were offering him a junior constable position. In his mind, he had already accepted the position. How was he going to explain his imminent departure to his parents? He knew the news was going to hurt them, and that was the last thing he wanted.

He looked concerned and deep in thought as he looked up at his parents after reading the letter. Dirk and Vera, looked at one another, uncertain, half expecting bad news.

"I've given it a lot of thought and decided I'm not going back in the ring. Blanco did not deserve to die like that. I don't want to be responsible for crippling or killing another boxer," blurted Jack to his parents.

"C'mon son, it wasn't your fault. Bad things happen. You've worked hard to become a professional boxer. You have real talent. It's not the time to throw in the towel," reasoned Dirk.

"I'm sorry Dad, but I'm tired of using my skills just for entertainment. There has to be more. You know it was never about the money. I have other options."

"Jack is right. I don't want him killing another boxer. Besides, he might be the one who is killed next time," said Vera who had never liked the career path Jack had chosen.

"What are you saying? What are your options? Do you think maybe you can get a place back with the All Blacks? Rugby was always your second favourite sport," asked Dirk, looking perplexed.

"I don't want to use my skills just for entertainment anymore. Besides, there is no longevity in careers in boxing and rugby. As you well know, life at the pinnacle of contact sports is vanishingly short. I would soon be defeated or replaced. I want to make a tangible contribution to peoples' lives, to keep people safe, not batter them to death. I enjoyed my short stint with the New Zealand Police, and now I want to work towards a career as a detective."

"But Jack, isn't detective work just as dangerous?" asked Vera.

"Sure it's dangerous, but I've decided that's what I want to do with my life. With my skill-set, I think I'm pretty well suited to the job. If I am going to batter someone to death, then it's going to be some evil bastard who bloody well deserves it, pardon the language."

"Well, if that's what you want," conceded Vera looking glum.

"I don't think there is a good time to tell you this, but I've just been offered a junior constable position with Scotland Yard in London in the UK. That's what this letter is about. They were actively recruiting for more staff, and I applied for a position three weeks ago. They liked that I had previously worked with the New Zealand Police, and were impressed with my academic and sporting achievements. I start there in four weeks. I intend to work my way up from detective constable. I'm tired of all the attention that comes with being a celebrity here in New Zealand. I will be fairly anonymous in the UK. You could say, I'll be a little fish in a big pond. I can start afresh."

Dirk and Vera looked wide-eyed at each another, clearly startled by the big announcement.

"What sort of work will you be asked to do?" asked Vera.

"I'll be working in the Criminal Investigation Department, initially on burglary, domestic abuse, and hate crimes, but as I get more experience I'll be put on sexual assaults, serious violence, and fraud."

"I see," said Vera, looking even glummer if that was possible.

"Don't worry Mum, you know I can handle myself," responded Jack with a grin after noting her reaction.

Josh was also dumbfounded by the latest news, but patted Jack on the back and said "Good on you Jack. I'm sure you'll do well over there."

Eyeing his mother he continued "Come on Mum, you know Jack can look after himself. If he can't, then who can?"

Neither Dirk nor Vera wanted their youngest son to leave New Zealand. It had been hard enough when Jack had left to study at the University of Otago, but at least he was still in New Zealand, albeit on a different island. They had held high hopes that when he returned from University study he would settle for good somewhere in the North Island within driving range, marry a good woman, and raise a large family. Now their hopes and dreams of a life shared with their youngest son had been shattered. When would they even see him again? Secretly they were proud of their boy and his achievements. But they would worry constantly, not knowing the challenges he would be facing on the other side of the world. All they could do now was to tell him he was loved and to wish him well.

CHAPTER ONE

Jack Baron, dressed in a dark-blue pin-striped suit and tie, was seated in his office in an over-sized brown leather chair overlooking an expansive view of the Thames River, and the Southbank. He was devouring a large chocolate-coated energy bar and thinking about all that had happened since he had left New Zealand. It was ten long years ago since the night he had killed a man in the boxing ring in front of thousands of enthusiastic spectators who had cheered as he battered his opponent senseless. The effect on him had been overwhelming. You could say life-changing. He enjoyed playing sport as he enjoyed the challenge of pitting his physical skills against capable competitors. Also he could see the enjoyment in the faces of the spectators. Throughout his life he had always viewed himself to be a sportsman, an entertainer, and a protector; but never a killer. He was more than happy to punish vicious criminals who needed to be punished, but the innocents, well they needed his protection. He felt he had made the correct decision in leaving professional boxing and New Zealand. The crushing pressure of being a top New Zealand sports celebrity had been lifted from his shoulders. Sure, there were boxing and rugby enthusiasts who still recognized him on the crowded streets of London, but the average Londoner had no idea who he was or his history. They only took the time to comment on his exceptional size. He had heard all the usual wisecracks before many times over.

"How's the weather up there buddy?" "You're a big fella, aren't you?" "Bet you play basketball, don't you?" "Wow, how do you find clothes to fit?" "What's your shoe size?" "Are all Kiwis as tall as you?"

Jack would just smile, and leave them wondering.

Every second year Jack had spent his annual winter holiday in the Southern hemisphere on his family's farm. It was great to get away from the bleak northern hemisphere winter and to catch up with family and friends. On his first visit back the media was waiting to pounce at the airport, positively salivating and eager to learn whether he was returning to take up professional boxing or rugby again. They were sadly disappointed when he told them he had no ambition to take up professional sport again. But now he was only a distant memory to them, and the rest of the New Zealand population.

There was haymaking, milking the cows, crops to be weeded and watered, and fences and equipment to mend. Jack relished the physical work. But he was saddened during his last couple of visits to see just how much his parents had aged. The relentless passage of time had taken its toll. It was now Josh who managed the family farm. Jack and his older brother had always had a good relationship. The future of the family farm was discussed at the breakfast table during the last visit. It had been decided that Josh and his wife Raewyn would inherit the farm, but Jack would receive a portion of the yearly profits. Josh and Raewyn had been childhood sweethearts and had married early. They had two boys and a girl. Jack thought their children should be enough to satisfy his parents' longing for grandchildren. Of course, Jack's parents secretly wished he had remained in New Zealand, married a nice Kiwi girl, and raised several grandchildren for them. They would never tell Jack that though.

"We're proud of you, son," Dirk would say when Jack left each time to return to the UK.

"You sure there isn't a girl waiting for you back there?" his mother would ask each time.

"Don't worry, you'll be the first to know if I'm getting hitched," Jack would reply.

"Stay safe, we miss you," Vera would say, holding back the tears that she would quietly shed later when she was alone.

Jack felt satisfied at having reached the rank of Detective Chief Superintendent in the Metropolitan Police Service (MET). He had

had no desire to climb further up the ranks, despite constant suggestions and pressure from his superiors to apply. He had enjoyed his time in the MET. It had been both physically and mentally demanding. The people of London deserved the right to feel safe in the streets and in their homes, and hopefully, he had helped in some way to achieve that goal. But the cliché, "crime never sleeps" was as true now as it ever was. For Jack, the senior rank he held within the MET had left him seeking more hands-on involvement. So with some trepidation, he had recently established his own Baron & Associates Private Investigators agency in Aldwych, not far from the MET. Diana, his secretary at the MET, happily joined him. He recruited two staff members principally because of their multi-linguistic abilities, but also because they had worked in Private Detective Agencies in other countries. There was Aiko Saito, a quiet and reserved Japanese woman, who was fluent in Japanese, Mandarin, and Cantonese, and capable in several other Asian languages. She was a martial arts expert in karate and judo. There was Stefan Kovacs, a boisterous, likeable, and extroverted young man of East European descent. Impressively, he was fluent in French, Italian, Spanish, Polish, and Russian, plus smatterings of other European languages. He had dabbled in UFC mixed martial arts and was skilled in the use of various weapons including firearms, which made for an impressive skill set.

It had been all hands on deck during the first week to establish the new agency. Jack set himself up in one of the two offices, while Aiko and Stefan shared the other office. A tiny room was dedicated to the storage of hard copies of files and other paraphernalia, though most of the records would be stored electronically on hard drives, and in the Cloud. The reception area where Diana sat at a large desk had a couple of plush leather settees expressly meant for clients. Diana adorned the room with tasteful paintings and flora. The agency shared kitchen and toilet facilities with other companies in the building.

Diana had advertised the agency's services on several social media networking sites such as Facebook and in local and national newspapers. As Jack sat behind his large oak wooden desk he pondered who would be his first case to step through their door. Would he be approached by the wife or husband of a murder victim, by a man or woman concerned their partner was cheating, by a victim of theft or fraud, or perhaps someone whose life was in danger? He would not have long to wait.

CHAPTER TWO

Two burly and unkempt men in their mid-forties wearing faded blue jeans, thick grey woollen pullovers, and grey flat caps approached the entrance to Holborn Underground Station in the heart of London. They carried a small battered wooden wardrobe between them. It was 11 pm and the train station was almost deserted. On entering, they were spotted by an elderly Station Supervisor, who stepped forward and challenged them.

"Whoa! Where do you think you are going with that?" he asked gruffly, trying not to feel intimidated by the two heavily built men.

"Please guv. It's a present for my gran. It's her ninetieth birthday, bless her. She lives not far, on Holloway Road actually. Take the northbound Piccadilly do we?" responded the burliest of the two men, with a distinctive East European accent.

"Suppose it's OK. Lucky for you there are hardly any passengers at this time of the week. Just be careful though, especially on the escalators. I don't want that thing falling on other passengers. Yes, that's right, take the northbound Piccadilly line. Holloway Road is one stop after Caledonian Road," advised the Station Supervisor.

He watched as the men passed through the ticket barrier, lifting the wardrobe above their heads to prevent it from damaging the metal barrier.

"Bloody foreigners, always taking things a step too far," he thought to himself, shaking his head in exasperation. "Weird that they asked about the route," he pondered. "You'd think they would have known the route to gran's house if she was so precious."

One man whispered to the other in Romanian as they approached the top of the escalator.

"The old gent was lucky to be so agreeable. Thought for a moment there I might have to pop him one."

The two men carefully made their way down the escalators and stairs, and onto the platform of the southbound Piccadilly line. The platform was deserted.

"Why did it have to be bloody Holborn Station?" grumbled the smaller of the two men. "I heard it's one of the deepest stations on the network. It's like going down into the bowels of the earth."

They carefully lowered the wardrobe and positioned it in the middle of the platform adjacent to a row of seats fixed to the platform wall. They had accessed the CCTV coverage of the tunnel from the previous three nights and had observed that their target was a man of habit who always sat on the same seat. Luckily there was no one else sitting on his seat. Both men looked up and down the platform to confirm there were no other passengers on the platform. One of them then knocked gently thrice on the outside of the wardrobe with the knuckle of his index finger. Three stifled knocks were received in return from inside the wardrobe. On hearing the reply, the two men immediately departed. They made their way out of the station, this time ensuring they were not seen by the Station Supervisor.

CHAPTER THREE

A short, plump, balding man in his early seventies dressed in a worn grey corduroy jacket and black pants walked briskly along the southbound platform of the Piccadilly line, in the dimly lit tunnel beneath the Holborn Underground Station. It was now just after midnight. The platform was deserted save for a large rat that scurried about searching for morsels of food dropped onto the electrified tracks. The man of habit took a seat in the middle of the platform beside a battered old wardrobe that had been discarded by some very hopeful passengers. He was amazed by the items some passengers endeavoured to transport on the London Underground. He had even witnessed a family of immigrants loading a refrigerator onto a subway train.

Close friends and relatives of the man knew he was paranoid about the open platforms of the London Underground and deliberately avoided the rush hour. During the rush hour, jostling travellers were pushed closer and closer to the edge of the platform next to the electrified tracks. He'd heard anecdotal stories of fatalities. But he was too cheap to take a taxi. Who knows who you'd get as a driver? As for buses they were plain unreliable and were often crammed with drunken young late-night revelers. He spent the time reading a few of the catchy billboards placed on the wall of the tunnel while he waited for the southbound train to return to his hotel in Knightsbridge after a late-night meeting. The billboards advertised everything from marketing and weight loss solutions, and mortgage deals, to the next amazing electronic gadget. The man had made the same journey at the same time for the past three nights, always taking a seat in the middle of the platform.

The man didn't have long to wait for the train as soon a rumble could be heard in the distance. Then a warm wind rushed from the tunnel entrance signalling the arrival of the train. Shortly after, two bright headlights appeared out of the darkness of the tunnel. The train burst into the station and roared towards the platform.

The man's eyes were now intently focussed on the approaching train. He stood up and quickly made his way to the edge of the platform. He failed to notice the door of the wardrobe opening behind him. A small dark hooded figure climbed out of the wardrobe and strode quickly and stealthily forward behind him. The noise of the train blocked out the sound of footsteps. Had the man turned he might have had time to see his assassin, but he would not have recognized him. He was initially roughly pushed forward to the edge of the platform, and then a final vicious shove was aimed at his lower spine. He arched his back in the hope the blow might be cushioned, and he might yet retain a foothold. Instead, as in his worst nightmare, he was catapulted upwards and over the edge of the platform. The train driver gasped in horror at the realization of the impending tragedy. There was nothing he could do. The man fell the full five feet onto the electrified tracks below and was struck and killed by the train.

There had been no time for any utterance. The only sound now was the grumbling of the train as it stood motionless and impatient at the platform. The dazed and shocked train driver was left to assess the gruesome scene. Had there been one or two people on the platform? The driver could not be certain. The CCTV coverage when checked later was found to have been mysteriously deleted. This by itself might have been reason for an investigation. However, suicides on the train network were not uncommon in the populous city, were rarely investigated, and often went unreported. On this occasion, a small article appeared on page three of the "Times" newspaper the following day. The heading read "Eminent scientist commits suicide at Holborn Underground Station".

The battered wardrobe left at the scene was an oddity. The Station Supervisor arranged to have it removed the next day. He was perplexed why gran was not going to receive her present. He puzzled over why the wardrobe had been discarded on the southbound line when gran lived on the northbound line? Perhaps the two men had got lost, and became tired of carrying the wardrobe? This recent interaction had not improved his opinion of foreigners.

The killer had been wearing a body cam attached to his chest, the type typically worn by police for personal security. Footage of the killing was sent within the hour via a private VPN internet connection to a man who was eagerly waiting to receive it. The recipient grinned as he played the footage in graphic detail on a large screen. As he watched, he re-enacted the murder as if he was the killer, holding his hands out and pushing at the appropriate time. It felt good, very good.

CHAPTER FOUR

Professor John Kearney exited Holborn tube station and was immediately assaulted by the cold air outside. He turned sharply left onto the crowded Kingsway, passing by newsagent and flower seller stalls. They were doing a brisk trade with the rush hour foot traffic. He walked briskly along the tree-lined broad pavement, as he had done countless times before. It was a typical grey day, the biting cold filtering through his thick wool-lined Aberdeen overcoat. He was late for a meeting and keen to reach the sanctuary and comfort of his laboratory, a refuge from the biting cold of the damp early April spring morning. A mixture of mist and smog enveloped the city, blocking out the paltry sunlight.

Professor Kearney was not a native of Britain. He was a colonial and London was a world away from his birthplace in the Wairarapa plains of the North Island of New Zealand. His parents still worked a dairy farm in the western Wairarapa, which tended to have high fertility and rainfall. That said, when John had first walked amongst the stately buildings of London, taken a ride on a double-decker bus, and had his first drink of ale at a local pub, it was as if he had been a Londoner all his life. He put this down to being thoroughly exposed to British literature and history during his childhood education in one of Britain's former colonies. Later this exposure to British culture was reinforced by British films that played frequently in the cinema and on television.

Kearney turned left into Sardinia Street and on past the Old Curiosity Shop, believed to be the oldest surviving shop in London. He hurried on not wanting to meet the gaze of an old tramp wearing a thick World War 2 army greatcoat, who was huddled over the heating vent of a nearby building to keep warm. His destination was the Imperial Institute for Genomic Sciences (IGS). It was sited on the edge of Lincoln Inn Fields, the largest public square in London, composed of a small park and tennis courts. The park was a tiny fleck of green in an otherwise conglomeration of massive concrete buildings. The IGS building was not out of place with the character of the city, which had in recent years embraced modernity whilst still retaining its beautiful and stately historical elements. Built at the turn of the millennium, the IGS stood twelve stories high, a tower of gleaming glass and steel. It was a testament to the country's commitment to health research and human well-being. It was a magnet for the brightest scientific minds from all corners of the earth. It was perhaps a fitting place for a modern medical genetics institute, being sited next to several of the foremost patent law firms in Europe, and close to the Inns of Court. Great medical discoveries often had great value and had to be protected by the filing of patents, which were often vigorously challenged by competitors.

Professor Kearney climbed the stairs from the pavement and entered the reception area of the IGS building. He was immediately greeted by the familiar voice of Tom Grainger, one of two security attendants posted to greet and if necessary interrogate guests of the Institute.

"Cold enough for you Doc?" chirped Tom.

John Kearney shivered involuntarily in response to the question. He immediately removed his heavy overcoat to adjust to the warm central heating.

"At least Spring is here. The daffodils are in bloom. They always give a bit of colour to the place," he replied.

"Diplomatic answer, Doc," replied Tom with a broad grin.

John didn't see any point in discussing the extremes of the English climate. He resented the intense cold of the English weather. The cold had a way of penetrating even the most protective clothing, rekindling his longing for more temperate climes. He detested the English winter, not so much for its intense coldness, but for its almost complete absence of colour, and lack of light. When he looked out on an English field in winter all he saw was the black skeletons of dormant trees contrasted against a pitiless dull grey sky. Black crows screamed their high-pitched harsh nasal calls, like witches in a Roald Dahl storybook. John felt so deprived of colour and light that he teared up with emotion upon spotting the first daffodil in bloom after his first English winter.

In sharp contrast, the riot of colour in early Spring was truly a spectacular sight to behold. It was well worth the wait. To John, it felt almost as if the land had been reborn. England was once again transformed into an idyllic garden of Eden. He made a mental note to himself to visit the inner city parks before all the springtime flowers were gone. There were few better pills for improving mental health and well-being than a stroll through St James's Park in early Spring.

John took the lift to his office on the tenth floor of the IGS. His office was in sharp contrast to his tidy two-storied maisonette in Hampstead. Wall-to-floor shelves were laden with books, theses, journals, and piles of xeroxed copies of manuscripts, reporting on decades of research from himself and the biomedical research community. He placed his coat on a hook at the back of his office door. Near the far wall of the room was a large desk, the top of which was partly hidden by a pile of paperwork. There was just enough space remaining for his laptop. He took the laptop out of his backpack and positioned it on his desk. He connected it to the Institute's LAN network, his gateway to the global science community. He then scurried off down the corridor to Room 102, which served as a seminar and meeting room. On entering he was presented with fifteen fresh-faced young men and women, sitting around a large table, chatting noisily amongst themselves. They were all of different ages, experiences, and nationalities.

John took great pride in the fact that he had attracted and maintained such a large group of able scientists and students to his research team. This was in part due to the quality of his research, but also his tenacity in applying for and obtaining research grants from many national and international agencies. It was also due to the international reputation of the Institute. What young scientist wouldn't want to work at one of the foremost research institutes in Europe? He took his place at the table and invited the team to raise any concerns over lab and institute management issues. Then each team member in turn gave an update on the progress of their research, usually by PowerPoint display. Other members would pose questions, provide information, or offer suggestions to brainstorm experimental problems, or other approaches.

John couldn't help noticing that Takashi Masuda appeared agitated. He seemed overly anxious to finalize his presentation and did not join in group discussions, which was out of character. Tak was a graduate of Kyoto University. He had undertaken post-doctoral research work at the Dana Farber Cancer Institute in Boston, before venturing to London. He was an immensely capable yet reserved scientist. John knew very little of his private life, save for the fact that he lived alone quite close to the Institute. John was aware he was a talented sportsman who held a black belt in martial arts, as was frequently discussed by some of the students. As the group separated to return to their laboratory benches and resume their projects, Tak delayed and asked for a private meeting with John.

"Take a seat," said John as they stepped into his office. "Is there a problem Tak?"

Tak sat down clutching his lab workbook and looked up after opening the book.

"It's the latest results on gene product TERT2, John. I show you. See here. As you know I give fifty micrograms of the product or placebo each week to year-old mice. The mice have been monitored for almost a year now. See, I am now sure mice are not aging as quickly as their control littermates. No chronic illnesses, and less lipofuscin in cells as a marker of aging."

John stared hard at the data, looking for a mistake or a simple explanation. He maintained an outward calm appearance, but already his mind was racing, weighing up the possibilities.

"It's interesting the trend has continued Tak. You'll first need to show the results are repeatable. Let's not jump to any conclusions just yet. Let's see just how long the mice live for, and whether any particular illnesses appear," said John wanting to impart on Tak the need for rigour.

"Is there any sign of tumours as the mice age?"

"No John, not at this stage."

"Please regard the results as preliminary, and keep them confidential. Report further results to me personally, and don't discuss them with anyone else, or at lab meetings."

"Yes, John."

"If we don't keep the results strictly confidential then they won't be patentable and commercializable. All your hard work would be rendered worthless. Do you understand? I hope you haven't already discussed the results with anyone else?"

"Yes John, I understand. I mentioned them to Katia yesterday. She told me to see you. I hope that was OK?"

"Yes, that's fine. That's good work, Tak."

Tak went back to his lab bench to continue his work. John remained at his desk to devise potential future experiments required to analyze, confirm and extend Tak's findings. It was while analyzing and screening DNA sequences adjacent to the TERT gene that John had first identified the sequence for a short peptide. John recruited Tak to work on identifying the function of the short peptide. Tak's early work under John's direction revealed that the peptide was able to regulate the expression and function of the telomerase enzyme complex, a complex which prevents cell aging. If John's predictions were correct, the short peptide he had identified could one day be developed into a pill to control aging. The implications for society would be profound. Human life could potentially be lengthened to an average of 120 to 150 years, extending human well-being and productivity. The potential financial rewards for the eventual development of the resulting pharmaceutical would be in the billions of dollars. The discovery would cement his standing in the field, and bring acclaim to the Institute.

Dr Katia Westbrook was John's most senior lab member, which is why Tak had approached her. She was a stunningly attractive woman in her late thirties with silky maroon hair, full lips and long eyelashes. John tried to avoid eye contact with her during their frequent meetings lest he became captivated and become distracted. Her eyes were soft brown pools that could draw you in, and from which you might never escape. Her skin had that smooth unblemished olive complexion that invited a caress. She was very curvaceous and flirtatious. She had an equally stunning IQ to match her exquisite beauty. After graduating cum laude from the Genetics Department at Harvard University, she had pursued postdoctoral positions at the EMBL labs in Heidelberg, and the National Institutes of Health (NIH) in Bethesda.

Katia had joined John's lab two years ago and had become irreplaceable. John was not always readily available to the rest of the team. He had to spend time abroad at conferences, meeting with international collaborators, lecturing, and continually lobbying for research funding. In John's opinion, Katia could have established her own team and run her own lab. He often puzzled over this and just presumed she preferred a less complex, less demanding, and less politically complicated life assisting other researchers to reach their research goals.

In his private life, John was a desperately lonely man. In stark contrast, he had had a whirlwind social life as an undergraduate at

Otago University in New Zealand. All-night parties involved the downing of copious quantities of alcohol, often ending in passionate trysts. Work hard, play hard was the term used at the time by his era of students. Then quite unexpectedly John had fallen in love. It had come as a slow realization that he could not bear to live without Helen, a fellow student studying toward a double major in law and arts. Helen had qualities that perfectly complemented his own. However, the relationship was cruelly cut short. Helen was diagnosed with an advanced highly malignant form of melanoma. There was no chance of a cure. John could only watch as the love of his life withered over several months and then died. Distraught he absorbed himself totally in his studies, achieving first-class honours, and then a doctoral degree in genetics.

To further his career he obtained a post-doctoral fellowship abroad at the University of Oxford Bridge, Oxford, in the Department of Physiology, Anatomy and Genetics, which was headed at the time by Professor David Corbyn. After a very successful fellowship, he was appointed as a junior Faculty member. His latest appointment was a senior scientist position as Lab Head at the IGS in London. Since his arrival in England, he had committed himself entirely to his research work. "Work hard, play hard" was the motto students of his era had lived by, but it no longer applied as it had become just "work hard". As time passed there had been fewer opportunities to develop a new relationship. His research laboratory grew and he took on more and more responsibilities. Trips abroad to conferences and meetings, where researchers gathered to present and discuss their work in an informal setting, had provided some opportunities to find a life partner. However, John had deliberately avoided subtle advances made by female attendees. Further, he had never been tempted to try an online dating site. He didn't have the time and didn't want to risk another relationship in the event it also ended in pain and loss.

John was approached by Katia in the late afternoon.

"I hope you don't mind that Tak discussed his recent results with me. They look very promising."

"Yes, that's fine. I reminded him to keep the results confidential. Did Tak seem a bit out of sorts to you?"

"Yes, he's normally cool and calm, but he seemed quite ruffled and irritable. It's not like him at all."

"As you know, I'm not very good at that touchy-feely stuff. Let me know if you find out what's troubling him."

"Of course, John," replied Katia with a smile.

John shut down his computer at 7.00 pm and walked to the Holborn tube station to take a train to Tottenham Court. He then took the Northern line to Hampstead. As usual, the train carriages were overcrowded with weary travellers going home from work. There would only be standing room for at least the next four stops.

"Excuse me guv, ya couldn't spare me a quid?" asked a slightly dishevelled young man who pressed up against John.

"Sorry mate, I don't carry cash," replied John who relied mostly on bank cards.

The pimply-faced young man, who was covered in tattoos, frowned and grunted his disapproval, and immediately pushed his way across to the other side of the carriage to find a more receptive good Samaritan.

The train duly arrived, and John climbed the stairs out of Hampstead Station. It was a brisk five-minute walk to his maisonette. His mind had been very active during the journey. Tak's results had huge implications. Great care would be needed to ensure the results were made available to the right people, and only to the right people. The Director would be the first to be approached. Still, it was all a bit preliminary. The results would need to be repeated to ensure their authenticity, which would take at least another year. A lot could happen in a year. Would the results be repeatable? Would other researchers make the same discovery? Would the results be leaked? So many possibilities; it would be a long year.

John reflected on what the biomedical research community had to offer society. He was living through exciting times. As the new millennium progressed, who would have dared to believe the breathtaking progress being made? Technologies so powerful had been created that the human genome, the "blueprint" for life, had been completely unravelled. Three thousand million pieces of information that from the moment of conception determined or influenced one's physical appearance and ability, personality, intellectual ability, and disease susceptibility had been decoded. The future course of human history had been changed irrevocably forever. Genetic diseases that had plagued humankind for thousands of years could now be unmasked and eradicated forever, just as smallpox had been conquered by the pioneering scientist Edward Jenner two hundred years earlier. John took great pride in being one of the champions of modern genetics. With society and science walking hand-in-hand, utopia was just around the corner.

John reached his house and settled in for a quiet night. He was sitting at his dining table reading the "Times" newspaper on his iPad when his eyes were drawn to the headline "Eminent scientist commits suicide at Holborn Underground Station". He was very skilled at quickly scanning the major newspapers for the few medically-related articles they sometimes published. More often than not they were sensationalized out of all proportion. This time it was an obituary rather than an announcement of a major medical discovery. He clicked on the link that took him to the article.

John stared in disbelief as he quickly read the notice. The name of the man killed at the station was David Corbyn. John felt an immediate sense of shock. David had been his Head of Department while at Oxford Bridge University. He had been an immensely energetic man with a razor-sharp mind and wit. Sometimes, too much wit, John thought. He had devoted his entire life to his profession. More recently, David had participated in the human genome project, joining the company Xerxes in Munich. They had met and caught up with one another occasionally at conferences. David's work and life appeared to be going well. It was unthinkable that he had committed suicide. Why had his life taken such a tragic turn?

CHAPTER FIVE

The couple were making love on the luxurious king-sized bed. The woman's rhythmic sighs were in time with her partner's urgent thrusts. Her head was bent back, gasping for air, as her body worked hard in heightened sexuality. His hands were pressed firmly beneath her buttocks. He was taking deep urgent breaths which turned to groans of ecstasy as he climaxed again and again. Her orgasms came with a ripple of sighs, her face flushed pink in rapture. Satiated, they stayed pressed together for a while. Then they rolled apart. She smiled and cuddled up to him. She pressed her head onto his expansive chest.

Life had been good to Richard Bentley. From an early age, he had realized women were attracted to him. Needless to say, he was very attracted to them. He worked hard to keep his body trim, toned and attractive. Only his ego outweighed his vanity. He was ruggedly handsome with a dark complexion, full symmetrical lips, dark eyebrows, and lashes, dazzling bright green eyes, high cheekbones, and prominent lower jaw and chin. He had a full head of thick dark wavy hair. He usually kept his jet black beard trimmed back to heavy stubble, as he knew that style was sexually attractive to women.

He had invited Amy, an attractive brunette, to join him at Keystone as soon as he was asked to be the keynote speaker at the 5th International Conference on Genome Research. Richard had been born with an IQ that any member of Mensa would envy. He had flown through his studies at Yale in record time, moved to England for post-doctoral work at Oxford Bridge University, and taken a junior Faculty position there. He had then moved back to the States and been appointed a full Professor of Genetics at Harvard University at the young age of just thirty-two.

Richard lifted the silken bed sheets and walked stark naked to the floor-to-ceiling window of the luxury condominium. The window was misted due to the intense cold outside. It had just stopped snowing. The ground was carpeted in a deep layer of clean white powdered snow, perfect conditions for the experienced skier. Amy observed him closely from the comfort of the bed. She knew she was just one of his several girlfriends, but this was of no concern to her. She knew he was unique, and treasured his company for however long their relationship might last. She marvelled at his toned body. Everything was in perfect proportion from his broad shoulders to his firm perky bum and muscled thighs. He made Michelangelo's marble statue of the Biblical hero David look almost positively second class. He was certainly more well-endowed. The sight of his naked body never failed to stir her. She only wished he would return to the bed. Richard, however, had other ideas.

Richard was an accomplished skier and took great pleasure from pushing his finely muscled body to ever-increasing feats of skill and heights of endurance. The conference presented the perfect opportunity to renew his passion for skiing. It would be difficult for him to find another time to go skiing before the season was over. Today he had chosen go heli-skiing. He loathed the confinement of the well-worn and overcrowded paths of the ski resorts. The joy in skiing came from traversing virgin slopes and testing one's skills against unexpected obstacles and challenges. Most of all he reveled in the total isolation of man against the mountain. He thought to himself as he stood at the window that perhaps this was why he had taken up science. It presented seemingly insurmountable challenges that he could pit his intellect against. Richard not only relished being alone on the mountain, he also needed it to recharge his excitement for life.

Richard appreciated that with a bit of luck and playing his cards right, there was money to be made from biomedical research; and glory. And Richard had played his cards right. Early on he realized that academia was a bottomless pit of personal sacrifice. It held little tangible reward except for lofty meaningless titles. He saw his professorial position at Harvard University as just a stepping stone to greater rewards. He had constantly been head-hunted by large biomedical companies. When a very lucrative offer came from the company Biodas based in Boston he had accepted it without hesitation. The employment package had included an executive salary, shares in the company, bonus incentives, and most importantly a small royalty on all commercial discoveries. Importantly he could keep both his positions. He would retain his Professorial position and status at Harvard University, and therefore still be able to carry out academic research that was not subjected to the restrictions of commercial endeavours and free from interference by the executives at Biodas. He grinned as he scanned the perfect snow conditions. Oh yes, things had gone very well for him.

Despite all the commercial incentives, working with a large biomedical company did have its drawbacks. Scientific endeavour was no longer the activity of a boffin working in isolation. As head of the Molecular Biology Division of the pharmaceutical giant Biodas, he was responsible for directing and managing four large research teams comprising forty scientists and support staff. He found the paperwork and administrative responsibilities that went with the position suffocating. He preferred to direct the overall programmes by close contact with the appointed heads of each research team. Being able to get away at times for a bit of R and R was precious.

Richard's cell phone rang, reminding him that work was still just a phone call away. He connected the call to hear the voice of the Head of his Division at Harvard University.

"Richard, it's John Fallon here. It's just a reminder about the undergraduate and postgraduate lectures you are down to give next month."

"Hi John, yes I have them on my "to-do list.""

"I know you are a very busy man. I was sure you hadn't forgotten. I heard you are at the International Conference on Genome Research in Keystone. How's it going?"

"I think my keynote address was well received. I've made a few useful contacts. Right now I'm looking forward to a bit of skiing in the San Juan mountains before I head back. There is a superb layer of soft powder on the mountain ranges. You should be here."

"Ahh, that's a nice thought, Richard, if I only had the time. Make sure you don't come back with any broken bones. You'd be a hard man to replace," joked Professor Fallon.

While appreciative of Fallon's last comment, Richard swore under his breath. "Bloody Fallon, always checking up on his staff, the pushy git. He was only ever good for administration. Though how he managed to get a Head of Division position beats me. Never liked him as a colleague at Oxford Bridge, and like him even less now."

Richard's thoughts turned back to work. The discovery had been serendipitous. Richard remembered the day when Dr Phil Basten, the head of the Growth Regulation group had come to him in heightened excitement. Phil had shoved copious research results forward onto his desk and blurted out garbled sentences of explanation. When he had finally managed to understand the nature of Phil's excitement, he had frozen to his seat unable to speak. The joyfulness of this time had been shattered when both Phil and the senior technician who had assisted him in the work had died in tragic circumstances. What would have made the promising technician commit suicide by plunging from a road bridge following a late-night stint in the laboratory? Phil's case was even more tragic. He had been killed in a hit-and-run accident only a few hundred yards from his home where he lived with his wife and three young children. Richard attended both funerals, which were sad affairs.

There had been a police investigation, but the culprit was never identified.

On a brighter note, Richard could now take more control of the discovery and be seen as its rightful champion. He had already collected Phil's workbooks and data and had accessed those of Phil's staff. On his return to the Institute, he would interview potential applicants to continue the work. After completion of animal studies, and successful human trials, patents would be filed, likely worth hundreds of millions of dollars. The inventions would be licensed to Biodas as the vehicle for their commercialization. He would receive handsome royalties following their commercialization.

Richard was brought back to reality by Amy's gentle pleading.

"Richard, come back to bed darling."

"Why not come skiing with me?" suggested Richard.

This was not the reply Amy was hoping for. She wanted Richard back in her bed. But if that wasn't possible she preferred to hang out with men in the ski lodges who would be more attentive. The thought of endurance skiing high up on the mountain slopes in unknown backcountry territory was not at all appealing.

"No, I'd rather not," came the terse reply. "You know I prefer skiing on the groomed slopes with other people around."

Richard had anticipated her rejection and was already hurriedly donning his ski wear. He wasn't going to let Amy dictate the terms of his precious break away and spoil his opportunity to go skiing.

"See you about five o'clock then. I'll take you out for a delicious meal when I get back," yelled Richard as he picked up his skis, poles, and boots, and opened the door to the frozen wonderland.

Richard climbed into the helicopter.

"Am I still dropping you off at the site we agreed upon when you booked yesterday?" asked the pilot, a no-nonsense fit-looking man with a swarthy complexion.

"Yes, thanks. The snow's looking great today. I'm really looking forward to it."

"The forecast is for good weather for the rest of the day. You're lucky. The weather has been pretty poor recently," informed the pilot.

Neither the pilot nor Richard had taken any notice of a young Japanese man who had patiently waited next to John while he had made his booking the previous day. The young man subsequently arranged a helicopter flight the next day to the same site in the mountains with a different pilot. However, he had planned to arrive half an hour earlier than Richard.

The helicopter pilot was in no mood for further conversation. This did not bother Richard as it allowed him to take in the stunning mountainous Colorado terrain, as they flew southwest for about an hour from Keystone. The region of the Rockies he had chosen in the Sneffles Range of the San Juan mountains, around twelve thousand feet high, was particularly rugged and challenging.

Richard instructed the pilot to land the helicopter on a promontory overlooking a valley, at the site they had previously agreed upon the previous day. As they descended the copter's blades fanned the powder snow creating a whirling blizzard. Having landed, Richard grabbed his gear and dived out into the maelstrom. He sank into the powder snow, crouching low as the pilot twisted the throttle to provide lift and thrust. The helicopter rose skyward fanning the snow into an even greater frenzy. The helicopter was soon just a distant speck in the dazzling blue cloudless sky. It left a deafening silence in its wake. The silence of the high mountains never failed to amaze Richard. It was so foreign compared to the continuous background noise he was used to in the city. Every slight noise seemed to be absorbed as if in a vacuum.

Richard carefully placed his skis into the snow and slipped his ski boots into the bindings. He brushed the fluffy snow from his overalls, repositioned his ski goggles, grasped the handle of a ski pole in each hand, oriented his skis, and glided effortlessly downhill. He was in his element speeding across the snowy terrain. The sharp edges of his skis sliced through the snow, as he leaped over moguls and knolls with practiced ease. Every nerve and every sense was alive anticipating the unexpected, the misplaced rock or fallen partially hidden log that could spell disaster if not navigated correctly.

Richard could see the tree line in the distance. It was a curious line that marked the uninhabitable and living areas of the mountain. The pine tree branches were laden down with a heavy coating of snow. He skied to a halt, resting on his ski poles whilst he caught his breath. He surveyed the slope ahead to determine which path he might follow. Instinctively, he turned around and faced upwards to view the track he had taken. Strange, he thought for a brief moment he had glimpsed a small dark object moving rapidly against the white background. He paused several more minutes scanning the area for a sign of the object. Nothing. He thought to himself he must have just imagined it. He shot off again leaning hard onto the edges of his skis. The only sound was the swishing of skis on snow and his exaggerated breathing. All of a sudden a steep escarpment appeared to loom out of nowhere, and he veered sharply to the left to avoid it.

Sharp tandem cracks echoed around the valley, an alien noise that split the deathly silence in the mountains. The two bullets failed to hit their mark, namely the centre of Richard's body mass, due to his sudden and abrupt change of direction. Nevertheless, one stray bullet tore through the flesh of Richard's upper left leg. Richard careered down the slope, swaying like a rag doll on one ski. In desperation he steered his body in the direction of the escarpment he had hoped to avoid, in order to escape an imagined third lethal gunshot. He toppled over the edge of the bluff, then tumbled over and over, and fell into a bed of deep soft powder snow. When he regained his senses and sat up, he discovered he was perched high on a ledge beneath an inverted cliff face that surrounded him on three sides. Fortunately, the deep soft powder had cushioned his considerable fall. Nevertheless, his whole body felt bruised and battered. The snow around his left leg was stained bright crimson red. Blood oozed from beneath his overalls. He pulled his ski pants on the affected leg up to his thigh and pressed his scarf into the open wound. He realized his body was probably in shock. Hypothermia would soon set in if he lay too long on the snow.

Luckily one of his ski poles was close by. He crawled in pain to recover it. The boot on his right leg was still attached to its ski. Using the ski pole as a crutch he managed to push himself to a standing position. He limped very slowly to the edge of the ledge. The way down was less steep than the vertical cliff faces surrounding him. He decided that he would toboggan on his back with his crippled and bloody leg bound to the other for support, and the ski strapped beneath. It was only when he turned to make the necessary arrangements that he noticed a rope being lowered down the cliff face behind him. Whoever had shot him had decided to trapeze down the cliff face to finish him off.

Richard reached into his jacket pocket and grasped his trusty Beretta M9. He always carried the weapon with him into the mountains to ward off mountain lions, and predatory grey wolves. These predators were reported to be slowly making a comeback in Colorado. For a moment he toyed with the idea of attempting to shoot the assailant as he approached the edge of the bluff. But he had second thoughts. He realised the pistol and his aim would only be effective at close range. Instead, he slowly lay down again in a foetal position next to the crimson-stained snow. He positioned himself to face his assailant, who he hoped to surprise by feigning death. He removed his glove and firmly gripped the pistol against his water-shielded goose-down-filled ski jacket to keep his hand and fingers warm. If they froze he wouldn't be able to hold the weapon and pull the trigger. He turned his head in the direction of the cliff face. He kept his eyes half-closed in a pretense of unconsciousness, and to better visualize the approaching figure against the bright sunlight. The figure dangled very briefly at the top of the cliff, looking for signs of movement and life. Seeing none it very quickly glided down the rope reaching the ledge with apparent ease. A semi-automatic Browning rifle was strapped to its shoulder.

On reaching the ledge, the attacker crouched low, inspecting the scene, looking for any signs of life. It crept stealthily forward, the automatic weapon held forward in a firing position. Richard waited patiently for an opportune moment. The figure momentarily looked downwards to avoid an exposed rock on the ledge. Richard took his chance, quickly stretching out his arms with his hands clutching and steadying the beretta. He fired three shots at the figure. At first, the figure stumbled forward firing the automatic weapon in erratic abandon, the .308 bullets making harmless shallow streaks in the snow before becoming forever embedded beneath the powder. It then slumped backward and crumpled slowly into the snow. With an intense effort, Richard rose to a standing position. He slowly hobbled over to the fallen figure, holding his beretta out in front and scanning anxiously for any sign of movement. He bent down and carefully removed a black woolen balaclava covering the face of his attacker. He stared a while at the face of the young Asian man whose lifeless eyes were transfixed at the sky. He felt certain he had never met the man before.

CHAPTER SIX

O n most Friday afternoons the Kearney lab congregated in the White Horse Inn at the end of the working day. It was a convenient pub as it was just a convenient stone's throw from the Institute. It was a cold wet Friday night and the Inn was packed with workers socializing with work colleagues before departing their various ways for the weekend break. The casually dressed Institute members stood out from the suited brigade made up of the solicitors, barristers, and accountants from the nearby Inns of Court, and city offices.

Graham Clark took hold of the jug of bitter passed to him by a barmaid and sat down at a table with six of his work colleagues.

"No Fosters?" smirked Stephen Crampton, a tall, mischievous, and likeable English PhD student.

"I thought I'd try a different pommie bitter this time, mate. Can't say I've found one I fancy, but that isn't going to stop me trying," replied Graham with a broad smile.

Graham was a young Australian clinician who'd obtained his medical qualifications and PhD degree at Sydney University. He'd ventured to the United Kingdom principally because of the outstanding medical research being conducted there. At the same time, it gave him the opportunity to gain insights into his ancestry. He was proud of the fact that his great grandfather was a convict deported to Port Phillip in 1837 for stealing a loaf of bread to feed his growing family. His descendants had prospered in their new country. Graham had followed in his father's footsteps, his father being a surgeon at Prince Alfred's Hospital, Sydney. He would chuckle when his English friends constantly referred to Australia as the "lucky country". This was in reference to the colossal amounts of gems, ore, and minerals the country mined and exported globally to build its attractive fast-growing economy. Graham had joined the Kearney lab a year ago to undertake post-doctoral work.

"Did you hear about old Prof Corbyn?" inquired Stephen.

"Yes, wasn't he John's Head of Department at Oxford Bridge University in his early days?" questioned Graham. "I met him once at a genetics conference in San Diego. It was a forgettable experience as I think I was a bit low down the pecking order for his liking."

"Crazy that he would want to top himself," said Stephen.

"I guess you just never know what is going on in other peoples' lives," suggested Graham.

"He lost his son to cancer five years ago, which might explain it," said Emma Brooks, a bright-eyed young PhD student from Yorkshire.

"Say, has anyone seen Tak in the past couple of days?" asked Stephen addressing the group.

"He said he would give me some of that new polymerase agent he'd ordered. But I haven't seen him in the lab for at least two days which is not like him," replied Graham.

"I saw him the day before yesterday," responded Emma. "He mumbled something about having to take an urgent flight to visit his sick father in Tokyo. He seemed pretty agitated and distracted, so I didn't probe him further."

"I wonder whether he informed John that he was taking time off?" asked Stephen.

CHAPTER SEVEN

Richard reached into his jacket pocket and retrieved the GPS-enabled satellite phone he always carried whenever he ventured into the mountains or at sea. He made an emergency call by pushing the SOS button. A satellite in geosynchronous equatorial orbit about twenty-thousand miles above the earth's equator immediately alerted emergency services. He received a call from an emergency operator almost instantly. He gave the relevant details and was advised that a rescue helicopter would be dispatched straight away to collect both him and the body of the unknown assassin.

Richard carefully slid down the narrow slope until he was clear of the surrounding cliff faces. He wanted to ensure he was exposed in the open to be more easily spotted by the helicopter crew. He was relieved when he eventually caught sight of the rescue helicopter. At first, it was just a small black dot on the distant horizon against the dazzlingly blue sky. Soon it was hovering above him flailing snow into the air. With the last of his remaining strength he used his ski poles to position himself to a standing position. He was secured with a harness by one of the helicopter crew who had been winched down onto the snow. The duo was then slowly winched aboard.

"Where's the body?" the rescuer requested once Richard was settled on board. "Are you sure the guy is dead?" he asked anxiously.

"He's lying a bit further up there on the ledge," pointed Richard. "I can assure you he is very dead."

The rescuer advised the pilot, and was again winched down onto the snow, but this time with a stretcher. The body and weapon were recovered and brought out into the open. The body was tightly bound onto the stretcher and then winched up into the cabin of the helicopter, followed by the rescuer. A paramedic on board confirmed that the young Asian man was deceased. He then tended to the wound on Richard's damaged leg and gave him some painkillers.

"You were very fortunate," he declared. "Lucky for you the bullet passed straight through and didn't hit a bone or an artery."

"I reckon it was pure luck that I am still alive. I heard two shots. I was aiming to dodge that bluff and dodged a bullet instead. Unfortunately, I collected the second bullet," explained Richard.

"I'll clean and bandage your leg wound, but you should get it checked out at the medical facility when we reach Keystone."

The helicopter crew was apprehensive, not knowing exactly what had transpired on the mountain. They were now having to care for a "killer" who sat at arms' length amongst them. One of the crewmen carefully searched the dead man's clothes in the hope of making an identification.

"Strange," he replied. "The guy isn't carrying any ID. You didn't remove it?" he accused Richard.

"No, and I've no idea who he is or why he attacked me," responded Richard angrily, offended by the suggestion.

"Would you mind handing over your weapon, just for the trip back?" requested one of the crewmen.

"Sure, no problem," responded Richard handing over his gun.

"I see your attacker is wearing a chest-mounted GoPro action camera. If it was working at the time of the attack it could be used to verify your account. I know sportspeople wear them to record their ventures, but it is an odd thing to wear if you are going to kill someone. If it is still functional, then the footage could be used as evidence," said one of the crewmen. "We'll be handing it over with the body to the Summit County Police, just so you know."

On the journey back to Keystone, Richard sat disconsolate, recounting to himself the details of the attack. The painkillers had started to take effect, and he was feeling tired and light-headed.

On reaching Keystone he was immediately taken into custody by the local Summit County Police.

CHAPTER EIGHT

Sheriff Baden from Summit County was a huge, red-faced, fair-haired, barrel-chested, middle-aged man with a booming voice. He wore a large droopy mustache that some said reminded them of the American frontier lawman Wyatt Earp. He interrogated Richard Bentley for almost two hours. He had played back footage recorded by the GoPro camera that had been attached to the dead Asian man and decided Bentley was telling the truth. He released Bentley from custody with a warning that he should not leave the country until further advised. He cautioned him to take extra care in the event he was the intended victim of an unsuccessful contract killing. This he said was based on the fact that Bentley had not recognized his attacker, and had no explanation for a possible motive.

On the flight back from the mountains, Richard had tried to picture the face of the young Asian man he had killed. He was certain they had never met before. He asked himself the proverbial question, "why me"? Was the jealous boyfriend of one of his lovers seeking revenge? Had he been the victim of mistaken identity? More importantly was he safe now? Was his assailant acting alone, or would whoever was responsible try again? Why was the attacker wearing a body cam? Was it to record the killing for playback later, or simply to record the skiing and scenery. If it was the former, then the assailant or whoever had hired him had to be some sort of psychopathic maniac.

Richard checked into a medical centre on arrival back at the Keystone Village.

"That paramedic did a good job cleaning and bandaging your leg. I'll just give the wound a reclean, stitch it, and rebandage it, and you should be fine to go on your way," stated the attending physician, a thin lanky man with ginger hair in his early fifties.

"I could do with some more painkillers. I fell over a bluff and have a few good bruises."

"I'll give you a prescription for those. You'll need the use of a crutch for a while until you can place all your weight on that left leg. You're very lucky the bullet didn't damage an artery. That would have been a very different story."

Amy became all motherly when Richard returned to the hotel, sporting a heavily bandaged leg, supported by a crutch. She ordered him rest up and wanted to attend to his every need.

"Ohh...Richard. What have you done to yourself?" she cried. "You need to rest on the bed and keep that leg raised. Let me look after you."

Richard lied about his injury, describing a heavy fall after skiing into a hidden rock. He also lied when he told her that he had been asked to be a keynote speaker at a biomedical conference in San Diego in a few days.

"Don't fuss. It's nothing. I just fell heavily onto a rock. Look, I'll rest up in bed for a couple of days. But then I have to attend a biomedical conference in San Diego."

"You never said anything about that before?"

"It's a late-minute arrangement. I prefer to be alone as I'll need to rest and prepare for the Conference. I'll arrange for a shuttle to take you to Denver, and then you can catch a flight back to Boston."

Richard had no intention of travelling to San Diego. Instead, he had decided he would take immediate leave from work. He phoned his secretaries at the Division of Human Genetics at the Harvard Medical School and Biodas to inform them of his decision. He advised his Harvard secretary that his lectures would have to be rescheduled. Fallon wouldn't be pleased, but who cared what he thought. He was very careful not to mention his travel plans. He had decided he would go into hiding for a while, at least until law enforcement could explain to him why he had been attacked and if he was still in danger. He was scared for his life, especially given the caution from the Summit County Sheriff. He had given it careful thought and had elected to hide out at his sister's cabin at Lake Tahoe. It was his first choice, given its remote isolation in the wilderness of the Eldorado National Forest, within the central Sierra Nevada mountain range. Also, his sister had accepted her husband's name in marriage, and the cabin was in his brother-in-law's name. Someone would have to delve deeply to make any connection between him and the cabin. Importantly, none of his colleagues knew about its location.

Richard spent the next couple of days recuperating without Amy, mostly in his hotel room, together with a further visit to the Keystone Medical Centre to get his wound cleaned and rebandaged. As he sat looking out of the window at the spectacular scenery he contemplated the dreadful month that had passed. Just four weeks ago, Jackie, one of his conquests and a femme fatale had become pregnant and demanded that he support her and the baby when it was born. Richard had demanded a prenatal DNA test to prove paternity. She had willingly obliged, and to his horror, he had discovered he was about to become a father for the first time.

"I suppose it had to happen sooner or later," he thought to himself. "He would be happy enough to provide the child support payments, which wasn't a problem. But would she allow or even expect him to have visiting rights?"

Importantly, did he want any involvement with the child? He had no fatherly feelings whatsoever, and couldn't imagine his life being burdened by a dependent child.

Richard's thoughts quickly turned to work. He remembered Fallon's reminder. He would update his undergraduate and post-graduate lectures to meet his University obligations.

"What a bore, and waste of my time and talent," he thought to himself.

"At least I managed to get permission to deliver the lectures in a block, rather than piecemeal throughout the academic year. That would have been truly disruptive."

He used to enjoy lecturing and showing off his intellect to young students who would soak up his words like a sponge. Another benefit was the opportunity to bed one or several of the attractive young female students who took an interest in him. But nowadays the students looked more and more like children, and he was certainly no pedophile.

While hiding out he would take the time to look over his recent conference invitations and choose only the most luxurious locations and those where he'd been invited to give the keynote address. He remembered only too well the appalling Conference venues in third world countries he had attended as a junior staff member when he was given little travel funding in support. Discomfits included having to share a room with people who snored louder than a jumbo jet, beds that were harder than concrete, cold showers with no rose and no curtains, unrecognizable food, and local taxi drivers that took every opportunity to rip off their passengers.

His mind then wandered to Leon Gruber, a young scientist from Austria. Leon had filed a provisional patent application for his invention just before he had left his start-up company in Austria. The company had gone belly-up like many start-ups. With Richard's help, Leon was hoping to be able to continue with his findings and commercialize his patent in the USA. Richard was delighted when Leon had written to him requesting his help. He had helped the young man get a visa to work at Biodas.

"What a gullible young man. Easy pickings," Richard had thought to himself at the time.

Richard lapsed the provisional patent Leon had filed. He filed a new application based on Leon's additional work at Biodas. He filed the application in his own name as the inventor, with Biodas as the applicant. Leon's name was omitted, leaving him with no claim to inventorship, recognition, or reward. Leon had complained bitterly and threatened Richard and Biodas with court action.

"Does that novice think he can threaten me?" thought Richard to himself smugly.

"Let him go to the courts. He doesn't have the funds to put up a decent fight."

Richard's mind then turned to the exciting research projects being undertaken in his labs at the Harvard Medical School and Biodas. He began working through in his mind what further work had to be done to bring some of the key results to fruition. Soon he had temporarily forgotten all about the hassles of the past month, even including being shot at and almost killed.

CHAPTER NINE

On the day of his departure, Richard hired a Chevrolet Tahoe four-wheel-drive SUV and drove with some discomfort due to his leg injury to Salt Lake City where he stayed overnight. He switched vehicles there in case he was being tracked. He returned the SUV to a local company representative and hired a Jeep Grand Cherokee from a different local firm. He drove to his sister's cabin located at the Southern edge of Lake Tahoe set amongst a wood of Ponderosa and Sugar pines.

He walked carefully with the aid of the crutch through the slushy snow onto the cabin's porch. He opened the front door of the cabin and was immediately confronted by the smell of stale air. A cabin in name only, the place was impressive. Two stories high, it housed five bedrooms, two large lounges, and an impressive farmhouse-style kitchen with all modern appliances. The lounge was decorated with the heads of mule deer, Rocky Mountain elk, bighorn sheep, pronghorn antelope, and mountain goat that his brother-in-law liked to hunt in the woods surrounding the lake. Every couple of years or so he had holidayed with his sister and brother-in-law at the cabin and joined in their hunting trips. The twelve-point antlers of a monarch bull elk he had killed took pride of place on one wall. In recent years the cabin was rarely used as his sister had accompanied her husband on a diplomatic posting to Switzerland.

Most importantly a state-of-the-art security system had been installed, with motion alarm systems in each room, and surveillance cameras sited at key positions in and around the house. Richard had direct access to the cameras via his computers and cell phone. He switched on the air-conditioning system. Then he dropped the crutch and his belongings in the main lounge and headed for the basement which housed his brother-in-law's impressive collection of hunting rifles. He selected an AR15 semi-automatic rifle and opened a drawer full of ammunition. He grabbed a box of ammunition for the rifle, and a box of nine millimetre ammunition to refill his beretta. Then he walked to the kitchen where he loaded the weapons with the ammunition.

Richard wasn't certain how long he intended to remain in the woods. It would be at least as long as it took for his leg to heal sufficiently. And for Sheriff Baden and law enforcement to work out who his attacker was, and whether he was still in danger. He took comfort from the fact that he was familiar with the cabin and its immediate surroundings.

He had plenty of paperwork to keep him busy. He limped to the kitchen and made himself a coffee. As he sat at the kitchen table he reminded himself that there were several papers for publication that needed polishing off, and grant and patent applications that needed to be finalized. He pictured each of them in his head and placed them in order of priority.

The thought of the unfinished papers caused his mind to wander to recent events, in particular his involvement with his old colleague Simon Jackson. Richard recalled his recent visit to Simon's laboratory at Johns Hopkin's University. Simon had him meet with several of the lab's post-docs and students, suggesting he offer them guidance and encouragement. He had done so as he felt somewhat grateful to Simon. Simon had devised a scheme to inflate the numbers of their publications in high-ranking journals when they were both junior Faculty staff in the same Department at Oxford Bridge University. In the science and medical research world, publications were the currency of productivity and success. The more publications you had, especially in high-ranking journals, the more successful you were deemed to be. The more successful you were the better the chances of promotion and the more likely you were to get the choice positions. Many senior scientists take on roles as subeditors of journals that report research findings in their field.

Simon had devised a scheme in collaboration with David Corbyn whereby a small group of Heads of Lab would select certain manuscripts submitted for publication to the high-ranking journals they each edited and reviewed. The manuscripts were carefully selected on the basis that they reported on exciting novel research, and were submitted by scientists with little or no international reputation. Simon and David and their schemers would drastically slow the manuscript review process, sometimes requesting an array of difficult experiments be performed before the manuscript could be considered for publication. In the meantime, they would get their most able senior research fellows to replicate the results in record time, and publish the same or similar results in the journals they edited. They would eventually reject the original manuscript they were asked to review, forcing the authors to submit it to another journal, further delaying its publication, and destroying its novelty. Several other members of the Department had been invited to join the group, but they had declined.

"What did those morons say? Oh yes, now I remember. They said they thought it was unprofessional and disgraceful," Richard recalled, feeling agitated just thinking about it.

"More fool them. In the words of the great English poet Percy Bysshe Shelley, just "let anyone look upon all my works now, and despair.""

"Jackson's scheme was certainly better than the one devised by Corbyn. As Head of the Department, he had insisted on being a coauthor on everyone's publications despite having absolutely no input. That greedy bastard exploited all of his Department's staff."

It is a pity I couldn't get the same scheme going here at Harvard, thought Richard to himself.

Richard's mind turned to the dinner that night with Simon after the lab visit. Simon Jackson was a deeply religious man. It had always mystified and somewhat annoyed Richard how an intelligent man like Simon had wholeheartedly succumbed to religion. Almost immediately an array of his dislikes of religious beliefs and traditions popped into his head.

"Did he have to insist on saying grace before the meal? Who does that in this day and age? He knows I am not religious. How presumptuous of him. It is appalling that the religious want to drag us back into the dark ages instead of forward into the modern age of enlightenment."

Richard immediately put such thoughts aside when he remembered the most recent interaction with Simon. His face contorted in anger. He remembered opening and reading an e-mail he had received from Simon one month after visiting his lab. The e-mail had accused him of misdirecting the research of one of Simon's students during his visit.

"What rubbish. The student was plainly stupid and had obviously failed to comprehend his sage advice," he thought to himself. "Simon is a right nutter. Does he assume everyone is a sinner apart from himself? The sooner he seeks medical help the better."

"For a religious man, Simon has some pretty undesirable characteristics. What about the commandment "you shalt not covet your neighbour's house?" He was always a green-eyed monster when it came to money, possessions, and success. He certainly made sure he did the best out of the shared publication scheme he devised. Everyone needed to watch out if Simon thought someone was getting paid more than him, that's for sure."

Richard had also resented Simon's unrelenting questioning of his employment conditions at Biodas.

"What a bore. If Simon didn't have the talent and drive to find a lucrative position with a commercial company, what right did he have to resent anyone else from doing so?"

Putting such thoughts aside and having drunk his coffee, Richard moved through to the study, taking his laptop and satchel which was filled to the brim with papers. It was a massive workload that he had to undertake, but now it seemed he had all the time in the world.

CHAPTER TEN

John Kearney had just consumed a large mug of black coffee at his desk at work when his phone rang. He was surprised when the American-sounding caller with a booming voice introduced himself as the Sheriff of Summit County. After explaining his credentials, the caller asked

"Do you know a young Japanese man named Takashi Masuda?"

"Yes, I do. He is a member of my research team here at the Imperial Institute for Genomic Science in London. Why are you asking?"

"Then I'm sorry to inform you he was killed yesterday while skiing in the San Juan mountains near Keystone, Colorado. His body is being held in a morgue in Keystone awaiting a coroner's examination."

John could scarcely believe what he was hearing.

"That can't be right. Are you sure you've made the correct identification?" he asked in shock and disbelief. "Tak was here at work only a couple of days ago."

"Yes, I'm certain we've made the correct ID. Look, we need someone to formally identify the body. I've attempted several times to contact his folks who live in Tokyo, but I've had no luck in making contact."

"Tak never mentioned taking leave. I couldn't imagine him taking a holiday now anyway as he was very committed to his research project. His project was producing some pretty exciting results."

"Look, since we can't locate his next of kin, I was kind of hoping you would be willing to fly over to make the ID, and answer a few questions."

"I see. Yes, of course. I'll catch a flight over as soon as possible."

"I'd like to learn what you know about Mr. Masuda. There is no need to elaborate now, but there is something very odd about his death."

John took a ten-hour flight on a British Airways plane from Heathrow to Denver. Both the airport and the plane were packed with passengers. There were long queues and noisy passengers at customs. He was very tired by the time he left the airport. He then hired a 4WD Lincoln Continental sedan for the one-and-a-half-hour drive to Keystone via the Loveland Pass. Luckily the road had mostly been cleared of Spring snow. During the drive, he pondered why Tak had decided to take a holiday now without giving any notice. And what had the Sheriff meant when he said there was something very odd about Tak's death? He also pondered what Tak's loss would mean for the progress of his project on aging. He would need to recruit another capable post-doc and bring him or her up to speed as soon as possible. Katia would be invaluable as she was familiar with the project. She could troubleshoot any problems as the new research fellow came to grips with what was required. John eventually reached the picturesque village and ski resort of Keystone and found a carpark outside the Keystone Medical Centre where he had arranged to meet Sheriff Baden. The Medical Centre specialized in handling and treating skiing casualties, including those more unfortunate who were pronounced dead on arrival.

"Good morning, Professor," greeted Baden who had been waiting patiently for the Professor to arrive. He held out his large leathery hand as John stepped into the foyer of the Medical Centre.

"D'you have a good flight over? How was the drive?" he asked as the two men briefly shook hands.

"It was a smooth flight. Clear air all the way," replied John. "The countryside is certainly very beautiful here in Colorado."

"Glad to hear you appreciate our fine scenery. Sorry to ask you over here in such tragic circumstances. Well, we might as well get it over with, first thing. If you would just follow me, I would be hugely grateful if you would ID your fellow for us," instructed the Sheriff.

The Sheriff led the way to a cold room at the far end of the building. A part of one wall was made up of tiers of stainless steel draws. The Sheriff pulled on one draw revealing a black body bag inside. He unzipped the front of the bag, exposing the face of a young Asian man lying on his back. John stared awhile at the lifeless face, seemingly lost in thought.

"Always a shock when you see the dead body of someone you know. Can you confirm this is the body of the man you know as Takashi Masuda?"

"Yes it is," came the barely audible reply.

"Then I'd like you to ask you a few questions if you will," instructed Baden.

"Yes, of course," replied John in a daze.

"We can use the meeting room here at the Medical Centre. Save us having to make the drive to my office in Breckenridge."

The Sheriff led the way to the meeting room, making small talk to ease the situation. Once seated, he again expressed his appreciation.

"Much obliged that you took time out to make the ID," he said with gratitude. "Reckon we'll only need an hour or so of your time, then you'll be free to go. Any other plans while you're here Professor?"

"No, I have to get back to work as soon as possible. You know, grants and papers to write, meetings to attend, students, staff, reports. The work never ends," mumbled John who was still feeling badly affected by the sight of his lifeless Research Fellow.

"I find your young man's death to be a somewhat puzzling case. I'd be grateful if you would fill me in on everything you know about Mr. Masuda."

"Of course, I'm more than happy to answer any questions you might have".

John recounted Tak's background, academic record, and general personality.

"He was a pleasant young man and an invaluable member of my research team. Outside of work, he was known to be an excellent sportsman and an expert in martial arts. He was also an accomplished skier, which makes it hard to understand why he had a skiing accident, especially a fatal one."

"By any chance, do you also know a man named Richard Bentley? He says he is a scientist, like you."

"Richard Bentley? Well now, I haven't seen him for more than five years. He and I were junior staff in Professor David Corbyn's Department of Physiology, Anatomy, and Genetics at Oxford Bridge University more than fifteen years ago. Why do you ask?"

"What sort of man is Bentley?" asked Baden, completely ignoring John's query.

"Surely he wasn't involved in Tak's accident?" asked John, taken aback by the new line of questioning.

"I'd like you to tell me what you know about Bentley. You've worked with him in the past, and spent time with him then. What's your opinion of the man?"

"We both received tenure at Oxford Bridge University at the same time. We both took it up and established research teams there. But after a while, I sensed that Richard had become bored with academia. Being an American he decided to return to the States to pursue his career there. Frankly, I was never certain that Richard was cut out to be a dedicated academic scientist. He seemed far more interested in commercializing science and its potential monetary rewards. Has Richard got something to do with Tak's death?"

"From what you have told me you might be shocked to learn that Professor Bentley is claiming he was shot at by Dr Masuda while skiing in the San Juan mountains not far from here. Bentley suffered a flesh wound to his leg from a bullet. He claims your Dr Masuda pursued him to finish him off. He said he had no choice but to kill the young man in self-defense."

"That's outrageous, surely not! I can't believe that. Why on earth would Tak have anything against Richard Bentley? I don't think they even know each other for goodness sake. Besides, Tak is not the type of person who would deliberately kill anyone," retorted John feeling his blood pressure beginning to rise.

"I'm afraid we have good evidence that your Dr Masuda did attack Professor Bentley. Your young man was wearing a body cam at the time. I have since viewed the footage, and Professor Bentley's account of the attack has been confirmed. Masuda did shoot Bentley. You mentioned that Dr Masuda was a martial arts expert. Martial arts are intended to kill or maim people, aren't they? Could Masuda have been a trained contract assassin?"

"That's ridiculous. His expertise in martial arts came about from an interest in his Japanese culture. I'm sure he only intended to use his combative skills in self-defense and to keep fit."

"Look, Professor Kearney, you appear to be a link between Dr Masuda and Professor Bentley. Can you assure me that you know nothing about this case, and are not involved in some way yourself," probed the Sheriff.

"That's a preposterous suggestion! I came all this way to be of assistance. If you carry on with this line of questioning I will be heading back to the UK immediately, and all correspondence will be made through my lawyer."

"Calm down Professor, calm down, I had to ask, it's my job."

"I give you my assurance that I know nothing about this case. I am as bewildered as you are. To tell the truth, I am shocked by what you have told me."

"Just to recap then, do you know any reason why a member of your staff would want to kill a fellow scientist? Was there competition for research discoveries for instance? Can you tell me what Dr Masuda was working on?"

"He was working on a potentially very valuable project involving life extension. The results, if reproducible, would have profound implications for humanity."

"I see...there you are. Is it possible that Dr Masuda had discovered that Bentley had made the same discovery, and wanted to shut down Bentley's research?"

"Has he? If so, I am not aware of it. In any case, scientists don't murder each other over their discoveries. Any disagreements are handled by a court of law."

"I'm just putting this up as a possible motive for the attack on Bentley."

"As I've said, Tak is not a killer."

"Then how do explain the fact he was carrying a semi-automatic hunting rifle, and deliberately shot Bentley? Bentley says he had never previously met Masuda."

"Perhaps he needed the rifle for protection from predatory animals. We hear all sorts of stories about Americans being attacked by wild animals in the wilderness. Perhaps Tak was trying to protect himself from Bentley. Truly, I can't explain any of this. It all sounds so out of character and implausible."

"So do you think Bentley is a killer, and deliberately sought to kill your young fellow, who retaliated?"

"Again that seems highly unlikely. There must be some other explanation."

"That's just it. There isn't."

The Sheriff questioned John further regarding Tak's interaction with other staff and his general behaviour.

"Did Dr Masuda show any signs of unusual behaviour in the past week?"

"I can't say for sure, but I and others of my team felt that Tak was agitated when he was last seen in the laboratory."

After further discussion, the Sheriff and John came to the opinion that there was nothing they knew of that could account for the situation that had unfolded. After the questioning the Sheriff cautioned John.

"One of my investigators came across an article published in the "Times" newspaper. It reported that Professor Corbyn, who you mentioned, committed suicide recently on the London Underground. Could that be more than mere coincidence? The attack on Bentley was in the same week as Professor Corbyn's death? I caution you to take extra care of your safety given that you know all three of these individuals and are connected to their past. I will be passing on what I know to the Federal Bureau of Investigation (FBI), who will likely take charge of this case. I see no reason to detain you further, but either I or the FBI may want to question you again."

The Sheriff asked Kearney to promise to keep in touch should he learn anything connected to the case. John did his trip in reverse, mostly in a daze. He found it hard to concentrate on anything other than the shocking deadly account of what had taken place in the otherwise beautiful and pristine Colorado mountains.

CHAPTER ELEVEN

John Kearney assembled his research team upon returning to his laboratory. He realized Tak's continued absence would soon raise a lot of questions. But more importantly, he wanted to learn whether anyone in the team could shed light on Tak's actions. He relayed some of what he had learned from his trip to Keystone to his team. He deliberately omitted Tak's attack on Richard Bentley. The details would eventually be released by the American press, but for now they had best be kept secret.

"Some of you might have noticed that Tak hasn't been in the lab for a couple of days. He never informed me, but apparently, he went overseas on a skiing holiday. Did he tell any one of you about his travel plans?"

"He told me he was making an urgent visit to his sick father in Tokyo. He seemed pretty upset, I recall," responded Emma.

"Thanks, Emma, but that doesn't fit with what I am about to tell you. Unfortunately, I have some tragic news. Regrettably, Tak was killed while skiing in a mountain range near Keystone, Colorado," he informed the gathered team.

His announcement was met with gasps of disbelief, followed by a hushed silence. Then almost immediately there followed a noisy exchange between the team members.

"I just can't believe it," said Katia with emotion. "Tak was such a superb athlete and an accomplished skier. What happened? And why did he lie to Emma about his whereabouts?"

"Maybe he wanted to break his trip to Tokyo with a stopover in the States to go skiing. It looks like he just pushed the boundaries too far," blurted Stephen. "Skiing is a pretty unforgiving sport if you happen to make an error. Though I read somewhere that you have only one chance in a million of being killed while skiing, so I guess he was just incredibly unlucky."

"I don't know the exact details about his accident," John lied.

"I think the Institute should hold a memorial for him, so we can formally say goodbye," suggested Emma.

"Yes, I second that," said Graham.

"I will discuss your suggestion with the Director," replied John.

John doubted the Institute would want to hold a memorial for a potential murderer. But his lab would hold its own memorial for Tak in any case.

"Does anyone have any other relevant information about Tak's sick father, or anything that might shed light on why Tak chose to stop-over in the States to go skiing?" he asked.

His request was returned with blank stares.

"He'd been looking very haggard recently and was grumpy. Perhaps he was just tired of lab work and wanted a breakaway?" offered Emma.

"Yes, that was probably the reason," replied John, trying to look convincing.

John ended the meeting, leaving the team members to talk amongst themselves. He asked Katia to walk with him to his office.

"Take a seat Katia. I would like you to take over Tak's work on the TERT2 lifespan extension project. Progress on the project must not be interrupted."

"That's fine John. As you know, Tak had been keeping me informed of his results, and I've been tending to the mice in his absence."

"I'll apply for funding to recruit a Research Fellow to work on the project, but it will take me up to six months to obtain the required funds."

After discussing the project details and plans with Katia, John sat alone at his desk contemplating his action plan. Uppermost in his mind were Sheriff Baden's cautionary words. Was his own safety really at risk? Richard and David had been members of the same

Department at Oxford Bridge University, but was that just a mere coincidence? Why would Tak attempt to kill Richard, a man he supposedly had never met? Was Richard working on a life-extension project in competition with Tak? Tak may have had a mole at Biodas or Harvard Uni. The mole might have relayed progress indicating Richard's research teams were going to scoop Tak's findings. That all sounded so implausible. Tak just wasn't materialistic or egotistic, which would rule out these as motives for the attack on Bentley.

On the other hand, did Richard deliberately kill Tak, because of his research results? Perhaps Richard was on his way to kill him. That seemed equally implausible. Whatever the answer, there were several irrefutable facts. Tak had left the lab without notice, travelled to the United States, and had acquired a powerful semi-automatic rifle. These facts alone indicated he was the likely aggressor. Tak's name was not present on the list of attendees at genetics conferences being held in Keystone, so there was no particular work reason he should have been there.

CHAPTER TWELVE

It had been one week since Baron & Associates Private Investigators had opened for business in Aldwych. Nobody had walked through the door seeking a service. Diana kept herself busy setting up filing systems and searching for free internet sites, social networks, and newspapers in which to advertise the agency's services.

"I'm getting worried. I've never been in a job that pays me for doing nothing," mused Stefan, eyeing Aiko with a twinkle in his eye.

"Ssshh, remember patience is a virtue. All good things come to those prepared to wait," responded Aiko quietly with a cheeky grin.

"Why, look at you getting all proverbial. I'm not necessarily expecting a juicy murder case. Even a missing person would do."

"You know, there are about two thousand crimes carried out each day in London, and there are more than five million per year if you count all of England and Wales. They are positively piling up. Crime is big business."

"I'm here ready and able, let the party begin," grinned Stefan, twiddling his pen.

That night as Jack Baron returned to his house in Aldgate he heard his landline phone ringing as he approached his front door. He quickly unlocked the door and dashed to the phone.

"Hi, Jack here," he gasped into the phone.

"Jack, it's Mum. I've got some news that may be of interest," said his mother sounding excited, but at the same time somewhat apprehensive.

"What is it? Has something happened?" replied Jack, worried that one of the family might be sick.

"It's Raewyn," came the reply.

Jack's heart sank, expecting the worst.

"She found an interesting, though now dated, article in an international newspaper. The article described a medical discovery.

It was all about a young German boy. I swear he was just like you when you were young, Jack. You know, all muscly, and hungry most of the time. The medical experts say one of his genes is faulty, making him extra strong. I'm not saying you should, but maybe you could get yourself tested to see if you're the same as this boy. I asked Raewyn to e-mail the article to you."

Relieved it was nothing serious Jack replied "I'm sure it's just a coincidence. Anyway, thanks, Mum. I'll think about it."

"Your father thinks I'm loopy. He said I shouldn't mention the article to you, but it could explain the way you are. Dirk says he doesn't care to know for himself. He says God made him that way, and he doesn't need to know why."

Jack hung up after a long conversation about the family, what the grandchildren were doing, and how things were progressing down on the farm. He checked his e-mails and sure enough, there was an e-mail from Raewyn. Jack made himself a coffee and sat at his dining table staring at the iPad he held in his oversized hands. Did he really want to know the reason for his unique physique? If he had the faulty gene would he be seen as some sort of deviant, a monster to be feared or even ridiculed? Then again, scientists might have come to know more about the condition. What were its downsides? Certainly, his huge appetite was a pain in the arse. He asked himself, what did he have to lose in getting tested for the faulty gene?

Jack opened the e-mail and clicked on the link to the newspaper article. The article reported that a genetic mutation had turned a four-year-old boy into a "superboy" having superhuman strength. Just two days after he was born he could stand upright and support his weight. The child had muscles twice the size of other children his age, and half the amount of body fat. As Jack read, it was like all the pieces of a puzzle coming together. The article was an accurate description of himself as a young boy. It mentioned the boy was hungry for a full meal every hour due to his rapid metabolism.

"Don't I know that feeling," sighed Jack.

The boy could eat six full meals a day, but still struggle to gain weight.

"That fits me to a tee," thought Jack.

DNA sequencing had revealed the boy had a mutation that blocked the production of a protein called myostatin that limited the growth of skeletal muscle. Blockade of myostatin released the body to produce more skeletal muscle. The resulting condition could be summarized as an overgrowth of skeletal muscle. Those affected had incredible strength, tremendous agility, lightning-fast metabolism, and minimal body fat. One commentator said it was as if nature had chosen a few lucky persons to be sculpted in the form of Greek Gods.

Jack had no doubt the findings would eventually spur the spread and use of myostatin blockers by unscrupulous athletes. Perhaps it was happening even now. Then again he wondered whether those with natural forms of the condition might be outlawed from competing in sports events due to their natural advantage. Surely not? On a more positive note, it was mentioned that myostatin blockade could be used to combat muscle-wasting diseases. So maybe something good would come about from understanding the condition. If he had the condition then he could be studied, and the results could potentially help others.

Jack searched the internet and located a genetics testing service not far from the agency. He was lucky enough to get an appointment the next day. On arrival, he was greeted by a young woman physician. He explained to her the reason for his visit, mentioning the newspaper article.

"We have six hundred genetic markers we normally screen for, but I'm sorry myostatin is not one of them. Myostatin mutations are exceedingly rare, maybe as few as several hundred affected people in the entire world," mentioned the physician, eyeing Jack up and down with interest.

"I see, then I'm sorry to have bothered you. It would seem I've made a pointless journey," responded Jack.

"Look, I am fascinated by the prospect that you might just have this gene mutation. I'll see what I can do, but I'll need some convincing first," clarified the physician.

"I may have inherited the condition from my father. He has the same physique," replied Jack in support.

"Do you mind taking off your shirt? I have never examined a person with a myostatin deficiency before."

"Sure, no problem," said Jack, unbuttoning and removing his shirt.

"Good gracious, you do have an impressive physique," whispered the wide-eyed physician, who reached out and squeezed Jack's left pectoral muscle.

"And you don't take anabolic steroids to enhance your muscle mass?"

"No, I don't. What you see is all-natural."

"Hmmm... interesting."

Jack put his shirt back on.

"Well, you've certainly convinced me. It will be extra work for us to do the analysis, but we'll sequence your two myostatin genes for you to determine whether they harbour a mutation. My nurse will take a blood sample from you, from which we'll extract the DNA for the analysis. We should have a result for you within a couple of weeks."

CHAPTER THIRTEEN

John Kearney scanned through various online directories and located the phone number of Baron & Associates Private Investigators. He had learned via old friends back home that Jack Baron had recently left the MET to establish a private detective agency. He phoned the firm, gave his name, and made an appointment to see Jack Baron the following morning. Baron & Associates was located at Aldwych, just a short half-mile walk from the IGS past the London School of Economics. John walked straight to the firm the next morning, after spending a couple of hours working at his desk at the IGS. There was only light rain falling, with a peek of grey sky showing through the blanket of dark grey cloud. Baron & Associates was accommodated on the upper floor of a stately building close to the River Thames. On entering the reception area John was greeted by a middle-aged primly-dressed woman.

"No need to keep you waiting, Jack will see you now Professor Kearney," she stated with a broad smile.

She opened the door to an expansive office with large windows that provided a magnificent view over the South Bank and the River Thames. The only traffic using the river this morning was a small number of ferries carrying tourists on river cruises. Nevertheless, several million tonnes of freight are transported along the River Thames each year helping to reduce lorry movements on London's congested roads. John considered it would be a pleasant view to have while working, no doubt. Jack Baron rose from his substantial brown leather chair, smiled, and leaned forward to greet John.

Jack Baron was exactly as John remembered him, though a touch older with the first signs of greying hair. Jack was literally a man mountain, standing six foot eight inches tall, and weighing at least two hundred and fifty pounds. He had a ruggedly handsome face. Completely dwarfing John, he extended his huge hand the size of a baseball mitt. They briefly shook hands. Jack was a fellow countryman. The two men had first met at Otago University in the deep south of New Zealand. They had quickly become friends. They had both come from farming backgrounds, which gave them something in common. John remembered that Jack's family operated a high-value dairy farm in the Waikato in the centre of the North Island of the country. The Waikato region is characteristically flat or rolling land with high annual rainfall. It has long sunshine hours, and a temperate climate that allows grass to grow nearly all year round, all of which creates the perfect conditions for dairying.

John remembered some of Jack's previous history. Jack had undertaken a Master's degree in Applied Science, specializing in forensic science. As a first year student he had taken a room next to John's room at Knox College, a historic University student hall of residence. They had immediately struck up a friendship. They had moved out of the College in their second year to different student flats. But whenever they happened to meet they would catch up with each other and discuss their recent experiences. Jack had worked undercover for the police in his last two years of study. He had policed non-students supplying and selling illegal drugs to students. This had been a prelude to his career in fighting crime.

John appreciated that Jack Baron was talented, both academically, and as an athlete. A supreme athlete, he had represented the University's highly successful rugby team. On completing his Master's degree he had temporarily worked for the New Zealand Police and had played two seasons for the New Zealand All Blacks rugby team. The "all Blacks" were to become one of the most successful sports teams in the world. Jack had helped them to secure the Rugby World Cup for the second time. He was truly a fearsome vision of manhood whilst performing the "haka" with his team. The "haka" is an intimidating Maori war dance, traditionally used on the battlefield. It precedes all international All

Blacks rugby matches. John remembered that Jack was also a talented boxer. Jack had given up rugby to become a professional boxer to the dismay of many of his countrymen. He had defeated several up-and-coming pretenders to heavyweight titles and had won the coveted WBC belt in a controversial boxing match where he had, unfortunately, killed his opponent. The fight had made frontline news in New Zealand newspapers and those around the world, with many commentators arguing that the pugilistic sport of boxing should be banned. Then all of a sudden Jack vanished altogether from the limelight. John had contacted the Baron family and discovered that Jack had surprisingly emigrated to the United Kingdom to take up a junior post at New Scotland Yard.

John was not surprised to learn that since joining the MET, Jack had been rapidly promoted up the ranks to the position of Detective Chief Superintendent. During his time at Scotland Yard, he had gained a fearsome reputation amongst the criminal gangs of London. John had read various newspaper articles citing Jack's work with the MET. His physicality had been tested time and again. He bore several visible scars as evidence. John tried to avoid staring at a prominent scar that ran like a coiled rope down the side of Jack's face.

"It's great to meet up with you again after all these years, John. How many years has it been?" asked Jack in his deep gravelly voice.

"It's been a while," John replied with a grin.

"I must say I am curious as to what brings you to see me. Is it business or friendship? It's a shame we haven't kept in more frequent contact. A busy work life has a way of robbing time for socializing."

"I'd heard you'd left for London. We've moved in different circles since. I've read the odd newspaper article about your exploits when you worked in the MET. I don't know if you are aware, but I moved from Oxford Bridge University to a research institute in Holborn. Our places of work are just a stone's throw away from each other.

Academia is very absorbing, and there never seems much time for anything else. Are you married, any children?" asked John.

"No, I never married. Never came close to it. I live a demanding life, and wouldn't want to leave some poor woman a widow," responded Jack.

He'd given the same pat explanation countless times before when asked the same question.

"Neither am I. Look, Jack, I think I might need your help, or at least your opinion and advice."

John recounted the strange events of the past few days, ending with the caution from Sheriff Baden.

"I am concerned for my safety, Jack? I don't understand how my Research Fellow Tak became involved with Bentley? As far as I know, they didn't even know each other. Perhaps Bentley is a killer and maybe I should be worried that he'll come for me next?"

"Hmm... I'm not sure how to advise you," replied Jack, rubbing his bristled chin in thought. "What you've recounted to me is certainly puzzling. It's far too premature to make any conclusions based on what you've told me. You have got me interested, though. It's certainly very intriguing. I'm happy if you want me to undertake a preliminary investigation on your behalf. If that's what you wish?"

"In that case, I'm happy to hire you to find out whether I am in danger, or not. In particular, I'd like to know how Tak was involved. When you run a research lab, students and staff become like family. I would like to be able to provide closure for Tak's family. It's curious, though, that his family is missing and can't be contacted. Needless to say, I am mostly worried about my safety."

"My advice to you is not to take any chances. Advise your Institute that you are taking a month's leave. I have a property in outer London I maintain as a safe house. You can have it at a peppercorn rent for however long is necessary. Go home and collect what you'll need. Meet me at this address," said Jack handing over a card containing the address.

"Be sure to leave your laptop and cell phone at work. They could be traced. Take extra care when using the Underground or other forms of public transport. Check constantly to make sure you are not being followed."

After the meeting, John advised the Institute that he was taking leave. He also advised Katia of the same so that his team would not become concerned. His lab would be in safe hands with Katia during his absence. He took a bus to his maisonette in Hampstead. He filled a suitcase with several changes of clothes, toiletries, work documents, and a couple of novels. He took buses to Theydon Bois, north of Hampstead Heath, checking constantly to see if anyone was deliberately following him. He already felt like a fugitive. He would stop walking and pretend to look in shop windows while taking the time to observe pedestrians in the vicinity. He would regularly cross the streets to see if anyone made similar movements. He was certain nobody was following him.

The safe house was a two-storey maisonette overlooking the Theydon Bois golf course. As John approached the house Jack appeared from around the back section. He signalled John to accompany him. They entered the building from a raised patio at the back of the property overlooking the golf course. The inside of the house was very Spartan. It was obvious it was only used as temporary accommodation. Jack had filled the pantry and refrigerator with food supplies to last a couple of weeks.

"Stay inside, and don't go walkabout," ordered Jack. "I've placed a pile of burner phones and SIM cards in one of the kitchen drawers if you need to get in contact. You can contact me by phone. Use each phone just once and discard it afterwards."

"You know, I did think seriously about contacting Richard Bentley. I thought I should tell him that I did not know of Tak's intentions, and had nothing to do with the attack on his life. As he was a previous colleague I felt he deserved that assurance. But I had second thoughts as he probably hasn't been advised of the identity of his attacker. If he has then he might think I was involved in some way. Besides for all we know Bentley may be the killer. If he deliberately killed Tak, then I might be next on his hit list. I hope Sheriff Baden has made some progress."

"Yes, that was wise," assured Jack. "As soon as I have any useful information I'll message you on one of the burner phones. I'm sure you'll want to get all this sorted so you can return to work as soon as possible. You said Sheriff Baden had failed to locate Tak's relatives. I have a bad feeling about that. Contact me if anything else comes to mind."

When Jack returned to his flat in Aldgate he found a letter from the genetics testing service had been slipped through the letterbox of his front door. He took the letter through to the lounge and sat looking at it for what seemed like an eternity, asking himself again whether he wanted to know his results. Having decided he did want to know, he ripped the envelope open and extracted the letter. Luckily he had taken several undergraduate science papers at University, so the medical language was not entirely foreign to him. The result was there in black and white. Jack Baron carried a mutation in the myostatin gene which rendered the molecule dysfunctional. He told himself to remember to phone his parents early the next morning to inform them of the results of the test.

CHAPTER FOURTEEN

J ack Baron was somewhat bemused that his first client had turned out to be a former friend and fellow countryman. Seeing John again had rekindled all the happy memories he had of his time as a young student at Otago University. John hadn't given him a lot to work with, but there was no doubt in Jack's mind that John's Research Fellow Tak Masuda had become swept up in something very sinister. The question was "was Tak a born killer, or had he become ensnared in something beyond his control?"

Jack Baron took a British Airways flight to Tokyo, accompanied by Aiko Saito. Jack had earlier contacted the Criminal Investigation Bureau within the Tokyo Metropolitan Police Department located in Kasumigaseki, central Tokyo. He had explained the reason for his visit was to contact Dr Masuda's parents and to pass on his sincere condolences on behalf of Professor Kearney. And to learn as much as he could about Tak Masuda, and understand his motive for attempting to kill Professor Bentley.

Jack and Aiko were met in the arrivals area of Haneda Airport by one of Chief Superintendent Yamada's junior staff, who had been deliberately chosen because he spoke English fluently. He had been holding up a card with Jack Baron's name neatly written on it. But he had recognized them instantly from afar, and had walked to greet them. Jack Baron had earlier advised Superintendent Yamada that he could be readily recognized by his large size. Jack towered over the small Asian passengers that had also alighted from the plane, and were scurrying to the various exit points to book taxis, shared-ride shuttles, buses and trains. They had politely avoided gazing at him, but they would surely have viewed him as a curiosity.

"Welcome to Tokyo," greeted the young Japanese man, stepping forward and bowing deeply as Jack and his staffer entered the arrivals hall. Jack bowed slightly in return. Aiko bowed appropriately low.

"Thank you for meeting us," said Jack. "I'm so glad you speak English. But in case there is any misunderstanding, I've brought my staff member Aiko Saito along with me. She is fluent in both Japanese and English."

They were led outside of the airport to a late model Nissan car, parked not far from one of the main exit points.

"I have been told to take you to the Police Department to meet with Chief Superintendent Yamada. As you know, Sheriff Baden from Summit County in the United States had rung the Department seeking Dr Masuda's parents for identification of the body. Unfortunately, as of today, we have not been able to locate the parents. I am sure you will want to find out if there are any updates regarding their whereabouts. Dr Masuda has one brother and one sister. Unfortunately, we also haven't been able to contact either of them."

Driving along the multi-tier highways of central Tokyo reminded Jack of a futuristic science fiction movie. It was a metropolis of forty million people housed on land no larger than the Isle of Wight. Yet it had an order that a worker bee would surely admire. The complete absence of graffiti was in stark contrast to the graffiti-laden streets and buildings back home in London. They finally arrived at their destination and were driven to an underground carpark beneath the Police Department. The group took a lift to the Criminal Investigation Bureau on the sixth floor. The driver had phoned ahead to announce their arrival. Six of Chief Yamada's staff were patiently waiting in a meeting room immediately opposite Yamada's office. Chief Yamada suddenly appeared.

"Konnichiwa," said Aiko, bowing low again, while Jack bowed slightly in return.

The Chief introduced each staff member in turn, accompanied by more bowing. Jack was advised that only Inspector Akimoto, his second in command, and the driver who had since left, had a reasonable command of English.

"Welcome to Tokyo, Mr. Baron," said the Chief. "We will do all we can to assist you and American law enforcement in locating Dr Masuda's parents. Inspector Akimoto, please update Mr. Baron with the information we have to date," ordered Chief Yamada.

"We located the Masuda's house in the Chiba prefecture, east of Tokyo. The neighbours confirmed they hadn't seen the parents for more than one week. A search of the house didn't reveal anything unusual. But the couple have not used their credit cards or made any bank transactions since their disappearance, which is highly suspicious. A neighbour reported that a black panel van had been parked next to the house about the time the couple was last seen. We traced the owner of the van from the number plate. The owner reported that the van had been stolen about a week ago. Unfortunately, we have not been able to ascertain who had possession of it at the time of the Masudas' disappearance, and have not been able to locate it since. Just as worrying, we also haven't been able to locate Dr Masuda's brother and sister."

"Mr. Baron, as you can see, we are having difficulty locating Dr Masuda's family. Would you kindly describe what you know about this case, as it may help us with our ongoing investigations," requested Chief Yamada.

Jack spent the next fifteen minutes describing what he had learned from John Kearney. After considering what he had been told, Chief Yamada was just about to launch into a discussion of his plans to investigate the Masuda family's disappearance. Instead, he was interrupted by the arrival of a slightly built Japanese woman. She scurried into the room, bowed low, and spoke quietly at length to Chief Yamada. Jack turned to Aiko, hoping she might understand what was being said.

"I'm afraid there has been a significant development," pronounced the Chief Superintendent first in Japanese, eyeing the assembled team with a concerned expression on his face, and then in English to the two visitors.

All eyes were now intently focussed on the Chief Superintendent.

"A farmer in the Saitama prefecture has discovered four bodies in a deserted farmhouse. They are a middle-aged couple, and a young man and woman. Their ages fit the description of Dr Masuda's parents and siblings. It is quite clear from the scene that they were murdered. The smell coming from the farmhouse had attracted a neighbouring farmer, who went to check and came upon the tragedy."

The Chief Superintendent drove Jack and Aiko out of Tokyo to the crime scene in his GT-R Nissan car. Key members of the rest of his team followed closely behind in an identical Nissan car. The snow covering the frozen ground had started to melt. Soft pink blossoms were just starting to emerge on the rows and forests of cherry trees, heralding the beginnings of Spring. It took thirty minutes to reach the isolated farmhouse, which looked run-down and derelict. A member of the local police force and the farmer who had discovered the bodies were waiting in front of the farmhouse. They looked very sombre. They bowed low when greeting the newcomers. The Chief reminded everyone present that it was a crime scene. Nothing was to be touched or moved.

On entering the farmhouse the group was confronted by an awful stench. The front door led directly into the kitchen. Seated around an old wooden table were four bodies slumped in their chairs. Their hands had been tied behind their backs with nylon cable ties. The ties had cut into their swollen wrists. Their feet had been bound together with nylon ropes. Their heads were slumped forward and not immediately recognizable. Each head was enclosed in a clear plastic bag. Each bag had been fastened at the neck with silver-coloured duct tape. There were signs of asphyxiation including pallor, cyanosis, and small red and purple splotches on the victims' faces and necks. There were no signs of a conflict before the victims had been restrained.

The observers stood awhile in silence, seemingly in a mark of respect for the victims seated at the table. Jack spoke first.

"It looks like an execution scene. The victims presumably had no idea they were going to be murdered."

"It would have taken more than a single killer to subdue or terrorize the entire family," suggested Chief Yamada.

"I agree," replied Jack. "It would take at least two or more likely three men."

"We have photos of the parents and siblings so we can make a preliminary ID. But we will need to get a relative or work colleagues to make the formal ID," announced Chief Yamada. "I'll have my forensics team go over the crime scene for any physical evidence that might tell us who the killers are."

"Did Dr Masuda ever mention his family to Professor Kearney?" asked Chief Yamada, directing his question to Jack.

"John Kearney emphasized to me that Dr Masuda had on occasion talked lovingly of his family. He owed them a lot. They had supported him greatly while he was a student, both financially, and with visits."

"Do you have any idea why anyone would want to kill Dr Masuda's parents?" asked Chief Yamada.

"I think these killings provide us with a clue as to potential scenarios. Perhaps Dr Masuda was the subject of blackmail over competition between him and Bentley regarding research results. Masuda's family could have been held hostage by Bentley until Tak Masuda sabotaged his own research. This would give a motive for Masuda's attack? Dr Masuda may have hoped to kill Bentley before he could attack his family. Bentley would have realized his demand was not being met after Masuda attacked him so true to his word he ordered hired killers to execute Masuda's family. I don't know the details, but Professor Kearney told me that Dr Masuda's research could potentially be worth millions of dollars. In another scenario, Masuda may have been blackmailed by a third party to kill Bentley. But what the motive of the killer is would be anyone's guess."

"That first scenario is interesting," responded Chief Yamada, "but do you really believe a distinguished university Professor would be responsible for mass murder? In any case, he would have needed accomplices. If the second scenario applies, then you will have a lot more work ahead of you to resolve this case."

CHAPTER FIFTEEN

Jack Baron left Aiko with Chief Yamada's team at the farmhouse to continue their investigations. He drove back with the Chief to Tokyo and booked into a hotel close to Narita International Airport. He was shocked that the case had quickly turned so sinister. It was one thing to have two academics attempting to kill each other, but quite another to have a family of supposed innocents being executed in cold blood.

The next person on Jack's list to question was Professor Richard Bentley. Would Bentley be able to explain why Masuda had attacked him? The following morning Jack consumed a hefty breakfast after an uncomfortable sleep on a bed that was never intended for a man of his size. He had wolfed down a large assortment of buffet foods he barely recognized. They were nevertheless very tasty. Other hotel guests were clearly amazed at the amount of food he consumed, but were very careful not to stare in his direction. After checking out of the hotel, he took a taxi to the airport, and a Delta Air Lines flight from Narita International Airport to Logan International Airport, Boston. He rented a bright red V8 Chevrolet corvette from a car rental agency at the airport. Jack loved to drive powerful American cars. He never understood those big men who squashed themselves into under-powered sardine cans. Jack had earlier phoned the biomedical research company Biodas, hoping to arrange an appointment to meet with Professor Bentley. He was put through to Bentley's phone, but got his answerphone, so he left a message. Instead he phoned the receptionist at the company who informed him Bentley was not available, and was advised to try the Division of Human Genetics at the Harvard Medical School. He decided to visit Bentley there in person, and if he was not available then he would arrange to speak with one of Bentley's senior colleagues. He drove to the Longwood Medical Area of Boston to the Harvard Medical

School. The School has more than ten thousand faculty members on its campus and across the metropolitan area at fifteen affiliated hospitals and research institutes. It was renowned as an outstanding biomedical research centre. He approached a receptionist at the reception desk and asked her to page Professor Bentley.

"Who should I say is calling?" she asked.

"Jack Baron. I've made a special visit from London."

After a short period during which the receptionist talked with several other staff, she replied.

"I'm sorry but Professor Bentley was recently involved in an accident. He has taken a leave of absence. And before you ask, I am not authorized to give out the addresses of our staff."

"In that case, I would like an appointment with the Head of the Division of Human Genetics, a Professor John Fallon, I believe," requested Jack, who had researched the staff list online before his visit.

"Yes, that is correct. Professor Fallon is Head of the Division of Human Genetics here at the Medical School," confirmed the receptionist. "Can I ask, what is the nature of your visit?"

"I am an investigator associated with Scotland Yard, the Metropolitan Police Service (MET) in the United Kingdom. I was hoping Professor Bentley might be able to help me in respect of a crime we are investigating," Jack explained, holding up and displaying his law enforcement badge from his days in the MET.

"Given that Professor Bentley is not available, I am hoping that Professor Fallon can provide me with some of the information I am seeking."

After phoning the Head's secretary, the receptionist replied "Professor Fallon is available to meet with you in his office this afternoon at 4.00 pm."

Jack had a couple of hours to kill before he was due to meet with Professor Fallon. He used the GPS on his mobile phone to locate a cafe with free WiFi reception not far from the Medical School. He took a table out of the way at the back of the cafe. He used the time to research Bentley after logging onto the network. It soon became clear that Bentley was not listed in any public phone directory. He tried various people search apps and public records searches which provide street addresses and other personal information. He managed to put together a brief profile of Professor Bentley. Bentley was a wealthy Republican, aged in his early forties. He owned a maisonette in Charlestown, Boston, and a holiday house at Newport Beach, Los Angeles. He had no recorded past felonies, bankruptcy, or points of note that might mar his copybook.

Jack walked back to the Medical School and was signed in by the receptionist. Fallon's secretary greeted him at the reception desk, and escorted him to the correct floor, then ushered him into the Professor's office. A tallish man with volumes of early greying hair stepped from behind a large oak desk. After shaking hands, Professor Fallon offered Jack a seat and grinned as he stated

"My secretary tells me you are from the Metropolitan Police Service in the UK. I've had many distinguished visitors in my office, but never a man from Scotland Yard. I am intrigued to learn the reason for your visit."

Professor Fallon's large office was situated on the top floor of the Medical School and had an attractive view over the QUAD Lawn, a little piece of greenery in an otherwise expanse of concrete.

"You have an attractive view from here," responded Jack looking out the window, and ignoring the request. He took time to compose what to say. Eventually, he replied.

"Professor Fallon, I appreciate your willingness to meet with me like this at such short notice. I am a private investigator from Baron & Associates in London, and a former Inspector at Scotland Yard. I have a client who has hired me to investigate the attempted murder of one of your staff, a Professor Richard Bentley. I had wanted to speak with Professor Bentley in person. But I have been informed he has taken leave. That's understandable in the circumstances, as I understand he was wounded in the attempt on his life."

Professor Fallon stood staring up at Jack for several minutes, clearly sizing him up. He was considering the fact that Jack had lied about his credentials. Mr. Baron had originally stated to the receptionist that he was currently employed by the MET. But this was an obvious lie to exaggerate his self-importance to gain an appointment. Fallon's eyes were penetrating.

"Professor Bentley informed me of his accident. I can confirm that he requested extended leave to recover. I can assure you that the Institute is very concerned about these unfortunate events. We will endeavour to do our utmost to assist law enforcement in this country with their investigations. It is my understanding that Richard was very lucky to escape with his life. His assailant was not so lucky, however. Are you able to tell me the name of your client? What is his interest in these unfortunate events?"

"I'm afraid I'm not at liberty to say," responded Jack, citing client confidentiality.

"Then I'm not sure I can be of any help to you," countered the Professor. "It seems unbelievable that anyone would want to harm one of my Division's distinguished staff members. As his manager, I am very concerned. Could other members of my staff also be in danger? Could I be in danger?"

"I can't say. I can assure you, however, that I will do my best to determine whether anyone else is a potential target. You may be aware that Professor David Corbyn, who I understand was your and Richard Bentley's former Head of Department, was killed on the London Underground. While his death has been attributed to suicide, at this stage I am treating it as a possible murder. I came to see you in person to ask whether you would be willing to provide a character reference for Professor Bentley, as his line manager. Has he recently done anything out of character?"

"What are you suggesting? All of our senior staff in the Division of Human Genetics have impeccable records. Richard is one of our most talented researchers. He heads the Advanced Genetics Group, which is undertaking stellar research."

"Would you call him a hyper-achiever? Could he be overly competitive? How does he get along with other Heads of Labs, both here and at other Institutes? I understand he also has commercial involvements at the research company Biodas? Does he have any enemies you know of that might wish him harm?" asked Jack.

"I don't like the inference I think you are making," barked Fallon, becoming red-faced and agitated. "There is always competition in biomedical research, but a lot of effort goes into making sure everything is fair and above board. We do our best to negate conflicts of interest. Scientists are human when all said and done. Other researchers might likely envy Professor Bentley, but scientists don't go around killing each other over envy. I might add that Richard has been somewhat lucky. Nature has given him extraordinary talents, including a brilliant mind. That said, I'm keen to support him, and to ensure that whatever he is involved in doesn't bring this Institute into disrepute."

"Do you think Richard Bentley is capable of murder?" probed Jack further.

"That's preposterous. Richard was the one who was attacked, not the other way round. He was the victim. If you don't have anything that might shed light on these recent events then I would like to end this meeting. I have urgent business to attend to," declared Professor Fallon who didn't appreciate Jack's latest line of questioning.

Jack realized he wasn't going to be able to extract any useful information. It was clear Professor Fallon was representing his Institute. He didn't want it or his staff becoming tainted or associated with what he viewed as unsavoury events. Jack decided he would have to meet with Professor Bentley in person. Only then could he gauge his true personality, and get a first-hand description of the reported attack on his life.

CHAPTER SIXTEEN

Many years earlier in the winter of 1968 the East European bloc experienced a particularly cold and bitter winter. The repressive leadership of Romania, a country with extremes of poverty, had outlawed abortion and contraception. "Sex police" were created to intimately examine women to ensure they weren't having abortions or using contraception. This created a problem for many young married poverty-stricken couples with young children who were forced to eke out a meagre existence. They could not afford to raise their children. As a last resort, their child or excess children were reluctantly given up into the care of the State. The hope was that they could be reclaimed later when they were old enough to earn a living to support their families.

So it was that a diminutive and dishevelled young woman, single, homeless, and unemployed, approached the steps of the main orphanage in Cajlia in northwest Romania, near the Hungarian border. In her arms she cuddled a small bundle wrapped in a clean and warm blanket. She and her late older husband had named the three-month-old baby boy Nicolae after their great leader. The mother slowly climbed the concrete stairs at the front of the building. She hesitated for just a moment, but on reaching the top of the stairs she knocked on the heavy wooden door of the orphanage. She hugged and kissed her baby boy on his forehead one last time. Then she passed him over to the caregiver who had arrived. The mother was hoping the boy would have a better life in the hands of the State than the life of extreme poverty she had to offer him. At least he could be expected to be kept warm and well-fed, something she could no longer offer. She took one last look at her son, then walked back down the stairs weeping silently. She had no idea that she had just committed her cherished son to systemic institutionalized neglect, and physical and sexual abuse.

Yet, Nicolae proved to be a capable and resourceful boy, and a survivor. After eight difficult years of appalling conditions at the orphanage, he had grown into a tall and lanky boy. Nevertheless, he was incredibly thin by normal standards due to years of constant physical and nutritional deprivation. He had survived the appalling conditions because of his natural intellect and cunning. In contrast, around half of the orphanage children died each year due to disease, extreme cold, starvation, brutality, and a complete absence of duty of care. Nicolae had learned from an early age not to antagonize his caregivers. As a young boy, he had a slightly feminine look which had attracted one of the high-ranking supervisors, named Gheorghe. Once Nicolae reached the age of four, Gheorghe would escort him to his office after the rest of the children had been sedated before bedtime. There he would sexually abuse the boy, damaging him for the rest of his life. Other caregivers knew well not to interfere. In any case, they had their own perversions and sadistic predilections they would inflict upon the children.

The caregivers fostered violence to belittle and control the children. As punishment, they would get the older children to hit the defenseless younger ones. The harder the better. Fists were used to create bruises. Nicolae suffered fewer beatings by carefully cultivating friendships with the caregivers. Gheoghe would keep watch over his favourite Nicolae to ensure the other workers didn't beat him too hard. He would slip him extra food and the odd item of clothing. Those children who were not favoured by any of the staff received regular daily beatings. They suffered badly due to brutality and neglect. Some became disabled, both mentally and physically; forever "irrecoverable".

Nicolae was a born leader and formed a gang of boys of similar age and health who swore to protect one another. Even older children lived in fear of retribution from the gang should they assault Nicolae and his gang members too harshly. The children constantly fought over food, mainly bread, diluted soup, and stews. Here again, the gang proved useful in ensuring all members got their share of the left-overs of the caregivers. They would scavenge and fight for clothing from children who had recently died. They needed it to combat the terrible cold of winter. Temperatures often plummeted below zero degrees celsius. There was no heating.

It was only in 1989 that representatives of the Western media gained access to orphanages across Romania. The images revealed starving, malnourished, and half-naked children in overcrowded rooms that reeked of urine and bleach. The Western world was in shock at the extent of the neglect. There was an outpouring by childless or well-intentioned Westerners including American and British citizens who sought to adopt the children. But it was years earlier in 1976 when a resourceful English couple made an application to the Romanian authorities. They visited the orphanage at Cajlia, hoping to adopt a child. They identified a young eight-year-old boy, named Nicolae. With a suitcase full of money, cigarettes and toiletries to bribe the authorities and staff of the orphanage, they departed Cajlia with Nicolae.

Nicolae proved to be a very bright boy as his parents had hoped. At the end of his formal education, he was awarded a hard-won scholarship to attend University. He became quite wealthy while still a relatively young man. Around that same time, the Romanian media reported that the bodies of several elderly caregivers had been found in Gheorghe's office at the orphanage in Cajlia. They were bound by their hands and feet, propped up against a wall. The head of each battered victim was covered by a plastic bag sealed at the neck with duct tape. If a coroner's report had been written, it would have concluded that the victims had died of asphyxiation. Gheorghe himself was found to have had the end of a broken wooden broomstick repeatedly shoved up his rectum before asphyxiation. He was found sitting in a corner of the room in a pool of blood naked from the waist down.

CHAPTER SEVENTEEN

B entley had been easy to track down with mini real-time GPS trackers implanted in his shoes, and shirts while he was recuperating at the conference in San Diego. Marius Borza grinned as he hacked into the home security network of Richard Bentley's cabin in the woods. His supposed safe house. It never ceased to amaze him how supposedly smart people placed so much trust in technology. As a young man, Marius's computer hacking skills had caught the attention of a gang of Russian "black hat" hackers, and they had invited him to join them. Members enjoyed living in luxurious homes in different countries as they plied their illicit trade of hacking into computer systems all over the world. They would deliver ransomware to extort huge ransoms or obtain credit card and bank account information to fund their extravagant lifestyles. They used the "dark web" in multiple nefarious activities including human trafficking.

Mar, as he was called by his colleagues, had come to California to pay back a debt to Nicolae. Besides, Nicolae was paying him handsomely for his work. All he needed was an Iridium satellite phone, a laptop, and a technique commonly referred to as "credential stuffing", and he could hack into any electronic network from anywhere on the planet. The internet reached into every home and business like a spider's web. Mar had been handsomely paid by Nicolae over the years for his hacking skills. He had hacked into the servers of grant funding agencies, and universities to obtain all sorts of documents, including reviewers' reports on grant applications and manuscript submissions, grant assessment recommendations, and references. All that kind of work was bread and butter "easy-peasy" to a pro like Marius.

Mar was sitting comfortably in the back seat of the SUV his accomplices had stolen. He soon had access to Bentley's security camera network. He showed the laptop screen to Pavel Covaci, the senior member of the group, sitting beside him.

"He's alone," said Pavel, smiling and nodding to two other comrades in the front seat.

Mar and Pavel watched the laptop screen as Bentley was seen walking unsteadily with a limp from the downstairs lounge to a bedroom on the upper floor of the cabin. He was carrying an AR15 rifle. They watched as he entered the bedroom and laid the rifle on the floor just under the right side of the bed. He reached into his jacket and placed what looked to be a small gun under his pillow, and put his cell phone on the bedside table. He undressed to his underwear, got into bed, and switched off the lights.

The wireless alarm system was even easier to disable than taking control of the camera network. It relied on radio frequency signals, which Mar jammed using a special device to send out radio noise. The noise prevented the signal from getting through from the sensors to the control panel. He would permanently disarm the alarm system once they got inside the house. Bentley's supposed high-tech security system would soon be out of action. Bentley would be a "sitting duck".

The five intruders gave Bentley half an hour to succumb to sleep. They then each donned night vision goggles, gloves, special sanitized suits, and shoe covers, walked out of the woods and climbed silently up onto the porch. Each man held a Tavor assault rifle, the successor to the famous Uzi assault rifle. Pavel had been fascinated, when using the internal security cameras to monitor Bentley's movements, by the sight of the numerous stuffed animal heads that decorated the lounge. It was time for the mighty hunter to become the prey, he mused. One of the men bent down and quietly picked and opened the two front door locks. The five men entered the house. One, a lightweight, who made his living as a thief was given the task of recovering Bentley's weapons. He stealthily climbed the stairs to the upper floor and quietly opened the door to the bedroom in which Bentley was sleeping. Without making a sound he approached the bed in which Bentley slept oblivious to the intruders. He carefully picked up the AR15 rifle from under the bed and extracted the beretta from under the pillow. He collected Bentley's mobile phone which had been left on the bedside table. Bentley slept on, none the wiser.

Nicolae had blackmailed Dr Masuda into killing his colleague Richard Bentley. He had been furious when his plot to use Dr Masuda as an assassin had been foiled. In a rage, he had immediately ordered the execution of Masuda's family, which had been held hostage until the blackmail request was fulfilled. The gang members promptly dispatched the Japanese family, whom they had kidnapped and held as prisoners for several days. They had quickly left Japan after the killings as they had no desire to remain any longer in a country so foreign and unfamiliar to them. In contrast, they were all very familiar with America, and they all spoke English, though not perfectly.

The intruders had earlier decided amongst themselves to have some fun with their intended victim, given the hassles he had caused Nicolae. They had been instructed by Nicolae not to kill him outright on capture, just to wound him if necessary. He was to be "contained" and "spoken to" before his execution according to "Cajlia" rules. All five men were well aware of those rules.

The men took up positions at or near the points of possible escape, namely at the bottom of the stairs, outside the upper bedroom windows, and entrances to the front and back doors, and basement. They knew their target already had a leg wound and wouldn't be highly mobile. The man by the front door opened the door and fired off several volleys of gunshots into the air. The sharp explosive sounds cut through the stillness of the night. That should wake the prey he thought to himself. The hunt had begun.

Richard awoke with a start and promptly sat up in bed. His slowly awakening brain told him it was rifle fire that had awoken him. It was close by. Too close. He instantly grabbed for his beretta beneath the pillow. Finding it wasn't there he urgently fumbled with both hands around the top of the bed in case the gun had been misplaced. Not being able to find it he panicked and rolled off the bed onto all fours. He lunged for the AR15 rifle under the bed. It also wasn't there. Scrambling, he searched the top of the bedside table for his cell phone. Would he even get reception? Phone coverage was erratic around the Lake. But the phone also wasn't there. Damn, he had left his satellite phone outside in the rental car.

"What the hell is going on?" he asked himself. It slowly dawned on him that he had an intruder. The intruder must have entered his bedroom, and removed his weapons and mobile. The direction the rifle shots had come from suggested the intruder was now downstairs, possibly just outside the house.

"Who or what was he shooting at? Should I switch on the lights?" he asked himself, beginning to sweat profusely with fear. "No, I would make an easy target," he told himself.

Instead, he crouched still in the darkness listening intently for any sound. There was only deathly silence except for the faint tooting and whistles of a great horned owl way off in the woods. Becoming quickly accustomed to the dark room, he scanned his bedroom for signs of an intruder. Finding nothing, he stood up and quickly limped to the bedroom door. He placed his head just outside the opened door and anxiously scanned the stairwell landing and stairs, listening intently for any sound. There was no sign of an intruder.

"Why didn't the alarm system go off," he asked himself.

He wondered why the intruder had disarmed him, yet not attacked him while he slept. Had the intruder left, or was he still in the house playing some sort of sick hide and seek game? He tried to dispel the horrifying thought that he had become prey to be hunted down like an animal by some lunatic madman. He had seen the film "Deliverance" where backwoods madmen terrorize vacationers in the woods. The movie had sent chills down his spine.

Richard calculated he had three choices. He could remain in the bedroom to draw the intruder to him and hope to overpower him. Or, he could escape through the bedroom window. Third, he could dash down the stairs to the basement to get hold of a weapon. He decided the latter two choices were too difficult or risky. All the windows in the house had safety stays, and couldn't be opened fully. The stays allowed the windows to be left open in the summer for air circulation, without letting destructive raccoons, pine martens and bears gain access. The windows were made of toughened glass, and would be difficult to smash. Besides the resulting noise would be a dead give-away. If a window could be broken, there was still nothing to hold onto to break his fall. His prior injury was going to prevent him from running anywhere. If he became further injured and disabled he would be an easy target. He reasoned he would also be an easy target if he tried descending the stairs to get to the basement.

So his only option was to stay in the bedroom. The intruder would have to come to him. He grabbed the heaviest object he could find in the room to be used as a weapon. It was a large and heavy metal ornament depicting a bighorn sheep. He positioned himself just to the side of the door, aiming to surprise the intruder as he entered the room. He would remain there for a couple of hours if necessary to be sure the intruder had left.

And so the hunters and their prey remained stationary in their respective positions, each listening for any signs of activity. The hunters were the first to tire from all the inactivity. Their prey was just not playing their game. It wasn't fair. It made them angry.

"I'm tired of waiting for Bentley to make a run for it. I'm going to flush him out," whispered Pavel at the bottom of the stairs to the others, using a two-way walkie-talkie for communication.

Pavel ascended the stairs and quietly made his way to Bentley's bedroom door. Inside the bedroom, Bentley could just make out the soft footfalls of the intruder on the stairs.

"The bastard is back," he thought to himself.

He steeled himself, tightening his muscles in readiness to strike with his weapon. He stilled his breathing so as not to give his position away.

Pavel correctly reasoned that Bentley was hiding just to the side of the door, but which side? He didn't relish the idea of being clubbed to death from behind as he opened the door. Instead, he decided to take a couple of pot shots at waist height through the bedroom wall. If he was lucky he'd just wound the guy. He held his Tavor rifle at waist height, calculated where the target might be hiding, and fired a shot at either side of the door. He heard a suppressed cry of pain, indicating one of the bullets must have found its target. Then he heard the sound of a body slumping to the floor. He cautiously opened the door and found it to be partially blocked by Bentley's body laying prone on the floor. He shoved harder on the door to push the body aside to gain entry. Fortunately, the target was still alive, but blood was seeping from his pyjama pants onto the floor. As he entered, Bentley, now wracked with pain, looked up at the intruder.

"You bastard," was all Bentley muttered.

"I need some help carrying the target downstairs. I'm in his bedroom," said Pavel speaking into his walkie-talkie to his accomplices.

The other four men abandoned their positions and made their way to the bedroom. They lifted Bentley off the floor, carefully avoiding the blood, and carried him between them, down the stairs to the kitchen. Bentley made an effort to fight them off, but they were far too strong, and he was in no condition to put up much of a fight. They sat him down on one of the chairs at the kitchen table.

"Who are you? What do you want? I need urgent medical help, please..." Richard begged in a faint voice.

The men ignored him. Marius positioned an iPad Pro on a stand on the table directly in front of the wounded man. Through a veil of pain Richard immediately recognized the face and voice of the man who appeared on the screen.

"Well hello, Richard. It's judgement day. It's time for payback. You were lucky on the ski field, but you're not going to escape me this time" said the man on the screen, grinning from ear to ear.

"Why, why are you doing this?" Richard begged his tormentor.

"Come now, Richard. You can remember what you did to me, and might I add, probably to others. You are a narcissist, and some might say a sociopath. You really don't belong with the rest of humanity. It is time for you to be punished."

"I don't know what you are talking about. I'm begging you, please, you need to get me to a hospital."

"I don't think so, Richard. We are going to treat you ourselves instead, right here. Unfortunately for you, our treatment will be terminal. Time to go. Just so you know, we're going to record the proceedings so I can replay them again at my leisure for my pleasure."

"You bastard, let me go," were to be the last words Richard Bentley ever uttered.

Richard's tormentor nodded his head, which was a signal to the others. Pavel stepped behind Richard, reached into his jacket pocket, and extracted a plastic bag. One of the other men handed him a roll of duct tape. Two men stood on either side and held Richard firmly by his upper arms. Richard fought to free himself, but he was now very weak. Pavel placed the plastic bag over Richard's head and sealed the bag around his neck with duct tape. Richard had a strong will to live. It was at least two minutes before he drew his last breath, his body shaking in uncontrollable spasms as it was deprived of life-giving oxygen.

All the while the man in the screen looked on, smiling as he witnessed the killing of a man who had tormented him and ruined his life. He was willing to accept the possibility that Richard had no real appreciation of the pain he had caused so many. But that was one of the character flaws of psychopaths and sociopaths.

CHAPTER EIGHTEEN

Jack Baron had a dilemma. He urgently needed to interrogate Bentley in person. Only Bentley might have information as to why he was attacked by Masuda. Bentley had to be anxious about remaining safe? But Jack didn't know Bentley's exact whereabouts. He needed to employ research and guesswork to determine where Bentley would choose to hide out? Bentley's holiday house at Newport Beach was beachfront property. It was crammed cheek to jowl with other houses along the outstretched beachfront. Only a narrow path separated the beach from the house. Thousands of holiday-makers walked, roller-bladed, scootered, or cycled along the path each day. This surely had to be an unlikely refuge.

Perhaps Bentley had chosen to hide out with a relative, or better still at a relative's holiday house or vacant property. Jack researched various genealogy websites. Thanks to an unknown relative with a passion for genealogy he soon discovered that both of Bentley's parents were dead. They had been killed in a car accident a couple of years earlier. Bentley had just one sibling, a sister Katherine who currently lived with her diplomat husband in Switzerland. Jack searched various property record websites for properties owned by either the sister or her husband. He discovered the couple resided in Bern in a house owned by the Foreign Buildings Office of the Department of State. It would be an unlikely hide-out. The husband was on the title of two properties, one on the shores of Lake Geneva, and another in the woods on the Californian side of Lake Tahoe. Jack hazarded a guess that the latter was the most likely place for Bentley to hide out.

Jack decided to take a flight from Logan Boston Airport to Sacramento International Airport and drive to Lake Tahoe from there. His journey to Sacramento was uneventful, with the plane only half full. He rented a Ford Explorer SUV at the Sacramento

International Airport and decided to spend the night at one of the cheaper big chain hotels close by in North Natomas before heading east. After booking in and showering he walked to a tidy restaurant located not far from the hotel. He sat down at a table up against the back wall. The position gave him a good view of anyone coming into the restaurant. It was clear from the number of diners that the restaurant was popular with the locals, which was a sign the food was probably of a high standard or plentiful, or both.

"Have you had a good day?" questioned the waitress who suddenly appeared to take his order.

"Can't complain," replied Jack.

"Where are you from? You don't look and sound like you come from around these parts."

Jack smiled in return.

"I'm originally a Kiwi from New Zealand. But I've lived the past ten years in the United Kingdom," he replied.

"New Zealand? Where is that? Is that part of Canada? Are all people from New Zealand as big as you?" asked the waitress.

"No, it's a smallish country in the South Pacific ocean. The next stop is Antarctica, you know, where penguins live. Did you ever see the films "Lord of the Rings" or "The Hobbit"? They were filmed in New Zealand. It is a very beautiful country. You should visit sometime."

"I heard about those films, but never saw them. Gee, I thought they were made out in the mountains of Arizona or Colorado. It will take years before I can save enough for an overseas holiday from working in this joint." After a pause, she asked, "What's a kiwi?"

"Kiwi is just a nickname for a New Zealander. The name is taken from a small flightless bird that is native to the country."

"I haven't heard of a kiwi bird before. Bird that can't fly, huh. What sort of bird is that? I've eaten a couple of those kiwifruits though. They're those brown furry fruits with the tasty green insides."

"That's right. New Zealand grows and exports a lot of those."

The waitress noticed her manager giving her a glaring look from spending too much time with one customer. She quickly took the order, scribbling the codes onto a small pad, and scurried off to the kitchen. She soon returned and delivered the order. Jack ate two large fillet eye steaks with four eggs, fried tomatoes and mushrooms, two servings of fries, and salad, and downed a large black coffee. He left a hefty tip and walked out onto the street. That tip might assist her holiday ambitions he thought to himself.

They were eagerly waiting for him. Four men with menacing looks were leaning against Jack's car looking cocky and sure of themselves. Unfortunately for them, Jack Baron was not the type to be intimidated. He sized each of them up very quickly. He identified the leader, who was the first to approach him. The man looked lean and fit and was positively boiling with toxic masculinity. He had a toothless grin and was holding up his two bony fists to display sets of nasty-looking ebony knuckle dusters. The second man, smallish and wiry, then stepped forward. He had wild eyes and gripped a long menacing hunting knife. He rapidly tossed the knife from one hand to the other in a show of dexterity. He grinned and continually exposed and retracted his snake-like tongue like a reptilian creature straight out of Jurassic Park. The third man to step forward was at least as big as Jack, but was fat and out of shape, and looked a bit clumsy and simple. The fourth man held an aluminium baseball bat. He appeared more cautious of Jack's size and took up a place behind the other three. None of them spoke. But it was clear they meant business. They were not going to give Jack access to his car. Instead, they were intent on delivering grievous bodily harm.

Knuckle dusters were designed to increase tissue disruption. They would fracture a victim's bones on impact. The aluminium alloy baseball bat enabled faster bat speeds during swings. The result was greater velocity and greater injury. As for the hunting knife, that was a killing machine, pure and simple.

The four men completely encircled Jack as he approached his car. The situation that presented itself left no opportunity for a polite discussion of right and wrong, or a compromise, or an agreement. Deep inside Jack's head, the primitive reptilian part of his brain responsible for his body's physical needs, self-preservation, motor control, and balance surged into action. It funnelled its primitive instructions at lightning speed into a body that bore exceptional muscle power, capable of generating tremendous speed, agility, and force. Without pre-warning, and at lightning speed, Jack lunged forward and let fly a massive blow to the sternum of the leader. The man's rib cage cracked, ramming bones inward, and piercing lungs. He crumpled to the ground clutching at his chest as he suffocated in excruciating agony. In a flash, the second assailant lunged forward with his knife. Jack had already anticipated his move and quickly side-stepped. At the same time, he directed his considerable weight and massive fist combined with overwhelming force to the neck of his assailant. The heavy blow crushed the man's larynx, severing his spinal cord. He was dead even before he hit the ground. The cautious man fled with his baseball bat leaving the simple giant to his fate. Jack briefly toyed with the giant, expertly fending off the big man's wayward blows. He hit the giant heavily in his voluminous stomach with a non-lethal punch. The big guy buckled over. Supporting himself with his hands on his knees, he stood there wheezing and fighting for every breath. He then very slowly righted himself, swore something uninterpretable in a foreign language, backed away, and fled in the direction of his companion.

Jack momentarily considered chasing after the fleeing assailants to apprehend and question them. It would have been extremely useful to identify the person who had hired them. But he decided against it in case he would be walking into an ambush. Instead, he dashed to his car and accelerated in the opposite direction to his intended route. Once he was certain no one was following he headed back on the route to the Interstate-80 E which would take him to Lake Tahoe. The drive to Lake Tahoe gave him time to think and consider the assault. He did not recognize any of the assailants. Only the giant had spoken. He had blurted out a swear word in a foreign language that sounded distinctly European. It confirmed his impression that the men were of east-European origin. Working in London he had experience with criminals of many different nationalities. There was something in the facial features of east-Europeans that gave them a distinctive look.

The adrenalin rush that accompanied the fight had left Jack light-headed and tired. He recognized the signs, as they had always followed each of his boxing matches. Although he could not be sure, he was certain he had killed two of his assailants. He felt no sense of remorse over their deaths, or feelings of guilt. The killing was certainly not for anyone's entertainment. There was no audience cheering him on. It was either his survival or theirs. Better to take such filth off the streets before they killed again, he told himself.

Jack was tired by the time he reached Lake Tahoe. He pulled over into a vacant lot in Tahoe City, snacked on a box of energy and protein bars, pushed back his driver's seat, and got a couple of hours sleep in his car. Upon waking, he visited a roadside café to load up on more food and coffee. He put Bentley's cabin address into his GPS. After driving down the Californian side of the lake he was soon outside Bentley's large two-storey house. He noticed a Jeep Grand Cherokee and two Chevrolet Suburban SUVs parked in or near the driveway. He assumed at least one of the vehicles must belong to Bentley. It was an encouraging sign. Jack gave the place a quick recce before walking to the porch. He knocked on the front door. When the door opened he had expected to see a man. But he was surprised to be standing face to face with a very attractive-looking woman. Disconcertingly, she was pointing a Sig Sauer pistol directly at his chest.

"Whoa, there is no need for the gun," blurted Jack in surprise. "I just want to talk with Professor Bentley. This is his sister's residence, isn't it?"

"Who are you? Why do you want to speak with Richard Bentley?" the woman demanded in a husky voice, looking suspicious, and eyeing him up and down.

"I'm a private investigator. I'm representing a client in the UK. He thinks Professor Bentley may have information useful to him."

"Let me see some ID," came the terse reply.

Jack slowly took out his UK Security Industry Authority Licence from his jacket pocket. He held it up so that the woman could easily view it.

"I once held a senior position at Scotland Yard, until I went private," Jack added in support, holding up his old law enforcement badge.

The woman appeared to relax somewhat. She holstered her weapon. She held out her hand, which Jack reluctantly shook.

"I'm Special Agent Donna Collins of the FBI. I'm afraid you've had a wasted trip. You're also a bit out of your jurisdiction, aren't you?"

"Is the Professor not here?" asked Jack somewhat puzzled.

"Oh, he's here all right. He's in the kitchen. But he's not up to having a conversation."

Agent Collins led Jack through to the kitchen. She introduced him to two of her colleagues Tim O'Connor, and Sam Callaghan who were busy investigating the scene. A man was sitting at the kitchen table, his body slumped forward. His head was covered with a plastic bag. Beneath the chair was a large pool of partially congealed blood.

"It's Professor Bentley," said agent Collins. "He's been shot in the side of the stomach, then suffocated with a plastic bag. Hell of a way to go. He's probably been dead for no more than a few hours."

"I've seen that asphyxiation MO quite recently," added Jack. "An entire Japanese family was killed by the same method just outside Tokyo. It seems unlikely to be just an incredible coincidence. It's the same type of bag and tape."

"It's a first for me. It appears Bentley was initially mortally wounded in the upstairs bedroom by a gunshot wound to his stomach before being asphyxiated down here in the kitchen. Our weapons expert suggests the cartridge was a 9 mm Parabellum, likely fired by a Tavor bullpup rifle."

"I'm not surprised. It is the most popular and widely used submachine gun cartridge."

"He would have been in no position to put up any resistance. There are a couple of bullet holes on either side of the bedroom door, and some blood on one side just inside the bedroom. It looks like he was hiding just inside the door, hoping to surprise his attackers. Instead, he was shot there before being carried down to the kitchen and murdered."

"Yes, it looks like the killers may have played a game of cat and mouse with him. What brought you here to Bentley's cabin?"

"We were alerted to the fact that an East European criminal gang had illegally entered the country by ship a week ago. We have been trying to track and locate them. The trail led here, on the east side of the Lake. We visited multiple dwellings up and down the Lake hoping to locate them. In that process, we came upon Bentley's cabin, and the rest is history. We have no idea why the gang entered the country and what their plans are. We can't be certain they are responsible for killing Bentley, but they're our number one suspects."

Jack recounted the assault in Sacramento.

"Coming here I was assaulted in Sacramento by four men that looked distinctly east-European. One of them had wanted to stab me to death with a knife. The other three were intent on bludgeoning me to death. If it's the same men who killed Bentley, then you missed them."

"Crikey, I'm amazed you're still here to tell the tale. We can't be certain just how many gang members entered the country, but it's certainly more than four," stated Collins.

Jack breathed a sigh of relief. He knew now that his assumption had probably been correct. Had he chased after his assailants he would likely have run into an ambush. The outcome could have been very different. He recounted the details of the case he'd been asked to investigate to Agent Collins. He mentioned the attack on Bentley by Dr Masuda, and described the execution of Masuda's family near Tokyo.

"Not sure whether it's also connected, but two of Professor Bentley's staff working on a promising area of research were killed recently. Also, there is a Professor Corbyn, an Emeritus Professor who had worked at Oxford Bridge University together with Bentley several years ago. Recently, he either committed suicide or was murdered on the London Underground. I suspect the latter. Someone or a group of criminals could be targeting particular academics and their support staff who worked at Oxford Bridge University at the same time as Bentley and Corbyn. And before you ask, I don't have any idea of a potential motive."

"As we say in the FBI, it's who had the means, motive, and opportunity. Do you want to fill me in on the details over dinner?" asked Donna.

Jack was starting to feel decidedly hungry after the long drive. Besides, what man could turn down an invite by such an attractive woman?

"There is a diner called the Fork and Spoon in Tahoma about twenty miles north of here," suggested Agent Collins. "I'll leave you here with Tim and Sam. I need to question a neighbour located two miles west of here. He may have heard a gunshot or commotion in the last few hours."

"Fine, I'll meet you there at 7.00 pm. But first I'd like to check over the crime scene if that's OK with you?"

"Yes, sure, I've already done my inspection. I've notified the local Sheriff. He and his team will be here soon to conduct a forensics examination. They'll collect the body. I shouldn't have to tell you that nothing should be touched or moved. Tim and Sam, keep an eye on Jack here to make sure he doesn't mess up the crime scene," she ordered.

Jack took the time before the Sheriff arrived to carefully examine the crime scene. There was a trail of blood leading from the bedroom, and down the stairs to the kitchen. The Professor appeared to have been shot just inside the bedroom door. Fatally wounded, he must have been dragged or carried from the bedroom to the kitchen while still alive. The killers had sat him in a chair. In a macabre execution, they had placed a plastic bag over the wounded man's head to finish him off. There were no tyre marks outside the house other than those of Jack's SUV, Bentley's Jeep, and the FBI agents' two vehicles. The attackers must have parked out of sight and walked to the house at night. They must have experience with electronics. They had permanently disabled the house's sophisticated electronic security system. Jack's thoughts immediately turned to his friend John Kearney. Nobody knows his whereabouts, Jack assured himself.

The Sheriff and his team arrived just as Jack was leaving. The Sheriff was a big, strong, barrel-chested man with a rosy face. Why do all American Sheriffs look the same, thought Jack to himself? Jack stepped forward, and they shook hands in greeting.

"Agent Collins tells me you've come over from London. Hope you can combine your efforts to catch the killers. It's a pretty gruesome way of dying," said the Sheriff, eyeing the body seated beside the table.

"There have been other killings with the same MO. They may involve a gang of East Europeans. The killers appear to be targeting a group of distinguished research scientists and academics with a common history. Just why is a mystery we'll need to solve. I'm just off now to discuss the case with Agent Collins. As you say, hopefully, two heads will be better than one. I'm guessing several lives may depend on the progress we can make."

"Good luck to ya. I'll go and see how Collins' FBI colleagues are getting on. You'll probably pass the forensics team on your way out. Maybe they can provide you with a few clues."

CHAPTER NINETEEN

Jack met Agent Collins at the Fork and Spoon restaurant in Tahoma overlooking the lake. She was dressed in tight-fitting blue jeans, a white shirt, and a black suit jacket. She was sitting at a small round table at the back of the restaurant. Upon sighting Jack she partly stood and signalled him to join her.

"D'you have any trouble finding the place?" Agent Collins asked.

"No, my trusty GPS showed me the way as always," Jack answered.

"What's your take on this case?" she asked after Jack had settled into his chair.

"I haven't the slightest idea," replied Jack, being honest. "I can summarise for you what I do know, or think."

"Yes, I'd be grateful for your information and your thoughts on the case."

"As we discussed previously, I'm guessing that a Professor Corbyn was murdered on the London Underground, and his death is somehow related to the killing of Bentley. The link here is that they had been colleagues back when they were starting out on their careers," said Jack.

"You say probably? So it could have been suicide? What's the evidence that it is one or the other?"

"There is no evidence. That's the problem. The train driver can't be sure there was more than one person on the platform at the time. There is no CCTV coverage. The CCTV recordings had been deleted."

"Well that's convenient, and might I say highly suspicious."

"As I've mentioned previously, we have Dr Masuda's attack on Bentley."

"Yes, I've since been in touch with Sheriff Baden from Summit County. He is equally baffled by Masuda's attack on Bentley, and has decided to leave it in the hands of the FBI unless something related happens in his County."

"We also have Masuda's family being executed by asphyxiation at an isolated farmhouse outside Tokyo. Also as we've just witnessed, Professor Bentley has subsequently been murdered by a gunshot wound and asphyxiation at his sister's Lake Tahoe cabin."

"Two attempts at murder. Someone wanted Bentley dead that's for sure. That person could have blackmailed Dr Masuda to kill Bentley. He probably told Masuda "you kill Bentley, or I'll kill your entire family"."

"I think you are probably right. But why choose Masuda? That can't have been a random choice, but I can't explain it?"

"Perhaps he conveniently found one in Professor Kearney's research team to blackmail. Maybe he had seen Masuda at a science conference. Masuda had all the skills of an assassin, if not the desire to be one. Surprisingly, and it seems mostly by good luck, Masuda didn't manage to kill Bentley so the killer was as good as his word. He killed an entire family of innocent people in revenge."

"Also, two of Bentley's staff died under puzzling circumstances. Was that just a coincidence, or was the killer trying to stymie Bentley's research?"

"How did they die?" asked Agent Collins

"One jumped off a road bridge, and another was the victim of a hit-and-run accident near his home."

"Typical MOs for contract killings wouldn't you say?"

"Maybe. And as you know, we have a group of recently arrived East Europeans potentially involved in some of the murders."

"If they're the same ones that attacked you then at least two of them are no longer among the living, according to you."

"They seem hell-bent on impeding our investigation. I'd certainly like to know how they identified me as a target."

"There has to be someone you've met since that knows you are researching the case. Or they had the crime scenes under surveillance, and identified you? Crikey, they may even have been watching us at Bentley's sister's place. They may even have tapped Bentley's work phones?"

"Damn, you're probably right. I phoned Bentley at Biodas and left a message, including my name, and credentials. That would have been enough to make the connection."

"I'm certain there is an electronic expert amongst the killers. They had no problem shutting down the sophisticated surveillance and alarm systems at Bentley's cabin."

"I'm concerned that Bentley's other colleagues including my client back in the UK are potentially in danger. Corbyn and Bentley have a common history from working at Oxford Bridge University, which is probably not a mere coincidence."

"Possibly, but Bentley's death could just be a one-off."

"I have an uneasy feeling that it may be just the beginning. I followed up on Masuda's attack on Bentley by talking with a Professor Fallon, Head of the Division of Human Genetics at the Harvard Medical School in Boston. He line-managed Professor Bentley. He knew him from his Oxford days. Fallon was shocked by the attack on Bentley, but couldn't provide any insights into the reason for the attack. He seemed mainly concerned that the Institute should not be tainted by what he viewed as unsavoury events involving one of his senior staff. I had hoped to talk to Bentley himself, but we know how that ended."

A middle-aged waitress approached their table bearing a pen and pad. Agent Collins ordered steak, eggs sunny-side up, fries and salad, and black coffee. Jack asked for a triple helping of whatever Agent Collins had ordered.

"I don't mean to be picky, but you sure have a hell of an appetite," stated Donna once the waitress had left to fill the order.

"That's because I'm such a large unit. No, actually I have this genetic condition that gives me a rapid metabolism. I need to eat a lot of food to get enough fat, as my body keeps converting all my food into skeletal muscle. I was raised on a farm and my family grew most of the food we needed, but now I have to purchase it worse luck. Gets to be an expensive habit, eating that is," explained Jack.

"Well, all that eating doesn't seem to be doing your body any harm. Just to let you know I did a background search on you just before coming here. It goes with the job," stated Donna with a wide grin.

"Don't believe everything you read," countered Jack, returning the smile.

"New Zealand's golden boy, the newspaper articles said," smirked Donna. "You played for the New Zealand All Blacks rugby team."

"Yes, I was lucky enough to play a couple of seasons for the All Blacks."

"I'd say the All Blacks were lucky to have you. I've heard about rugby, but don't know anything about the game myself. I understand it's a bit like American gridiron, but without all the protective gear. Is that right?"

"It's only vaguely similar. Rugby was invented in England in the first half of the nineteenth century. Over the years it became New Zealand's national sport. There are fifteen players on each team in rugby. There are only eleven in gridiron."

"What position did you play?"

"Big guys like me make up the forwards. Smaller, nimbler, and speedier guys make up the backs. Being so tall I played as one of two locks that form the engine room of the scrum. A scrum is like a pack where teams compete for the ball after restarting the game due to an infringement."

"Now you've got me confused."

"I confess, New Zealand is a sports-mad country. It's not just renowned for rugby, you know. It is also highly regarded for rowing and yachting. I forget how many times New Zealand has won the America's Cup yacht race."

"I also read you're pretty handy with your fists. A New Zealand heavyweight boxing champion, and winner of a world boxing championship belt, no less. What aren't you good at?"

"That was quite a few years ago now. I was in the flush of youth then. I've mellowed a lot since. I'm a lot older and a lot wiser. See, I even have the odd grey hair," said Jack grabbing a handful of hair.

"Tell me, why did you give up on professional boxing? It could have made you very wealthy. Was it because the last fighter you boxed was killed in the ring? It wasn't your fault you know. Everyone knows it is a dangerous sport. It seems you haven't forgotten your fighting skills given the way you must have handled those East European thugs."

"I figured I would have a much longer more rewarding career as a detective. Surviving a street fight is just a matter of knowing the most effective places to hit an attacker to permanently immobilize them as quickly as possible. It takes a lot of practice to respond on instinct at speed, especially when your life is at stake. I've had a lot of practice."

"I read in the press about a couple of the cases you solved while you were at Scotland Yard. The Jack-the-Ripper look-alike case five years ago in London was viewed on this side of the Atlantic as a pretty impressive piece of law enforcement work."

"Enough of the flattery, you'll make me blush. Tell me about yourself. How long have you been with the Bureau?"

"I've had ten years as a Special Agent. I'm a trainee out of Quantico. The job suits me fine. I'm too risk-averse to do what you do. I like being a cog in a wheel of a bigger organization. I've got a guaranteed income, free health insurance, paid vacation, paid sick days, and a full retirement plan. I get to work all over the world. I enjoy protecting my nation against crims and terrorists. I guess the only downside is I get to meet lots of people, but mostly bad ones. It's a lonely job. It's hard to form a lasting relationship. I'm always travelling. Anyway, for me the upsides beat the downsides every time. You married?"

"No, like you, married life never suited the job. Wouldn't want to leave some poor woman a widow," he said giving his pat explanation.

Special Agent Collins looked deeply into Jack's eyes with a hopeful questioning look, and then she smiled.

"It's pretty cold out tonight. Want something to keep you warm?" she said huskily lowering her head.

"Yes, I'd like that. Thanks for the invitation," smiled Jack, taken by surprise and immediately feeling a stirring in his groin.

Having eaten, the newly met couple drove in Donna's SUV to a nearby hotel. Neither had had sex for what seemed like an eternity. On entering the privacy of their room, they began tearing off each other's clothes. Donna was part Latino with silky smooth, soft-tanned skin, and long dusky hair. She was athletic and strong. They made passionate love for an hour. Then they lay spent, contently coiled together in the spooning position. Without realizing it they soon drifted into a deep sleep. Seven hours later they awoke and showered together. They agreed to take breakfast at the local diner within walking distance of their accommodation. Both had a full breakfast of eggs, hash browns, bacon, pancakes, and black coffee, while they discussed how to progress the case. As usual, Jack had a double helping.

"I'm going to have to return to the UK," stated Jack. "We need to find out who else has a history with Bentley and Corbyn and could be a target. Perhaps there is some sort of historical grievance between academics who spent time together at Oxford Bridge University."

"Yes, I agree that's a distinct possibility. Maybe there was competition for intellectual property, for instance."

"I'd certainly like to know more about that gang of East Europeans. Why on earth would a gang of criminals want to kill a distinguished University professor? What do you know about them?"

"Not much. My colleagues in Europe tell me they are involved worldwide in money laundering, extortion, computer hacking, theft, people smuggling, and murder. You name it, they're involved in it. Nice bunch. They have considerable funds, are ruthless, and are impossible to track down. If they are involved, then I'm guessing someone must have hired them."

Donna looked at Jack as if pondering an idea.

"Why don't I join you on your trip back to the UK. We could also fit in a bit of R and R at the same time," she said smiling at Jack.

"Sounds like a good plan to me," he grinned.

CHAPTER TWENTY

Jack and Donna travelled separately from Lake Tahoe in their two cars in close convoy, with Jack intending to return his rental car upon reaching Sacramento. From there they would travel together to San Francisco in Donna's Chevrolet Suburban SUV. They took the Interstate-80 W, which would take them to Sacramento in just over two hours. Traffic was light, the weather was fine, and there was only a very light dusting of fresh powder snow on the freeway. They had just traversed over the Donner Summit when two Chevrolet SUVs appeared seemingly out of nowhere. They swiftly pulled up directly alongside Jack's SUV. The leading SUV sped up and immediately turned sharply in front of Jack's car. The other SUV took up a position immediately adjacent to Jack in the second lane of the three-lane highway. Jack was now hemmed in by Donna at his rear and by the two SUVs side and front. The lead SUV began to rapidly decelerate, causing Jack and Donna to brake. At the same time, the windows of the SUV directly adjacent to Jack's car were lowered. Disconcertingly, two occupants in the passenger seats raised what looked like assault rifles to the windows. Donna reacted by instinctively pumping her brakes savagely to slow her car down to help Jack escape backward from the imposed car cage. She then stomped savagely on the accelerator. At the same time, she swerved dramatically to bring her car behind the SUV carrying the gunmen. Her aim was to drive her car like a battering ram into the back of the assailants' vehicle.

She was too late. She heard the sickening sound of the assault rifles spitting sprays of bullets that peppered and punctured the side of Jack's car. The bullets left strips of neat holes along the sides of the doors. She watched helplessly as she witnessed Jack's body jerk repeatedly as some of the bullets hit his large body mass. Jack's car careered out of control, swerving erratically down the highway until it came to an abrupt halt after hitting a large boulder on the verge. Steam instantly rose from the car's damaged radiator like an erupting geyser. The inside of the car rapidly filled with smoke from the airbags, which had exploded on impact. The assailants, having accomplished their deadly assault, sped up and away. Donna slammed on her brakes and brought her car to a halt on the verge several yards in front of Jack's car. She dashed back to Jack's car, and opened the driver's door, fully expecting the worse. Jack was sitting upright amongst the white smoke-like powder residue released by the exploded airbags, his head tilted back on the seat. His eyes were closed shut. As she looked at him he slowly opened one eye and grimaced.

"Ughhh... it hurts," he cried out, opening both eyes. "But I'm OK, don't worry. I'm lucky you persuaded me to wear a Kevlar vest this morning," he croaked.

"Ohh... Jack, I thought you were dead for sure. Don't scare me like that."

"I'll have a few bruises and maybe a cracked rib or two, but I'll survive. I'll be a bit sore for a few days, that's all. Are you sure those jackasses are not hanging around somewhere?"

"The shooters high-tailed it at speed. I'm only worried about you. We should get you some medical attention as soon as possible."

"Don't worry about me. I have a guardian angel looking after me."

"Oh yeah, who's that?"

"Well, you of course."

"Well, I haven't done a very good job so far. We should return to Lake Tahoe to get you checked over ASAP. We can catch a flight to San Francisco from there. I don't want to drive and accidentally bump into those shooters again."

Donna assisted Jack out of the car. They waited until the road was clear. Then they slowly walked and staggered to Donna's car.

Donna assisted Jack into the passenger seat of her car, and they headed off on the I-80 E back to Lake Tahoe. Donna phoned her FBI colleagues to give details of the assailants' SUVs. She gave their direction of travel but held out little hope of the attackers being apprehended. Jack and Donna called in at the Incline Village Community Hospital in North Tahoe. There Jack had an X-ray scan which revealed he had two cracked ribs. He was given ice packs to place on the cracked ribs, and on five large angry purple bruises where bullets had made an impression.

"You some sort of bodybuilding type; hope you don't mind me asking? Make sure you don't overdo it on the steroids," commented the attending physician, a tall lean white-haired man with wrinkles, wearing a white coat and stethoscope, after examining Jack's naked torso.

"No, it's all natural," replied Jack, but he could tell the physician wasn't convinced.

The physician had seen the results of too many homicides in his long career, which was one of the reasons he'd left his big-city practice for the village life.

"I'm not going to ask how you got these wounds," said the physician. "There is far too much gun violence in this country. I see you have a couple of old wounds on your chest. Are they also bullet wounds?"

"Yes, picked them up last time I was States-side about five years ago. Lucky for me they were hard-point bullets from a handgun. Luckily they just happened to miss my vital organs."

"That sounds like a lot of luck you've had son," commented the physician.

"Unfortunately I wasn't wearing a Kevlar vest on that occasion. I've got my guardian angel here to thank for wearing my bullet-proof vest today," said Jack looking at Donna.

"What weapon made those other wounds to your stomach and face?"

"You Americans have a monopoly on gun violence. In the UK where I mostly work the main assault weapon is the knife."

"I wouldn't want your job even if you paid me twice my salary. I've prescribed you some painkillers. You'll need them, believe me. You take care of yourself, you hear," said the physician shaking his head in bewilderment as he exited the room.

CHAPTER TWENTY-ONE

D onna and Jack drove to Reno-Tahoe International Airport, and took a United Airlines flight to San Francisco. They then took a British Airways flight from San Francisco International Airport to Heathrow, London. On arriving at Heathrow they took the Underground to Aldgate and then walked to Jack's semi-detached house in a street of identical semi-detached houses. They showered after the long trip, Jack snacked on a load of energy and protein bars, and they slept for two hours. On waking, it was early afternoon, and they chose to eat out at one of the many bars located on Old Street. The dim lights and dark brown-stained wood of the bar and furniture, and the hushed conversation of the patrons had a soothing effect on Jack.

"How are you feeling now?" asked Donna.

"I'm fine, just a bit sore, and a bit woozy. Just don't expect wild passionate sex from me for a day or two."

"I think I can wait a day or two," responded Donna, winking at him with a smile.

"I've got a few matters to attend to at my office tomorrow morning. It's not far from here in Aldwych. You can come along if you like. From there we'll head off to Oxford. We'll take my car. I think I'm capable of driving."

"Sounds good to me."

"I'll phone my secretary now. I want to find out who we should meet at the University tomorrow."

Jack took out his cell phone and dialed Baron & Associates.

"How was your trip? Where are you now, Jack?" asked Diana, Jack's secretary.

"Not far away. I'm having lunch in Old Street. I'll be back in the office early tomorrow morning and can fill you in on the trip then. I take it Aiko is back from Tokyo? She can fill me in on the

Masuda murders. Look Diana, can you find out who is currently in charge of Professor Corbyn's Department of Physiology, Anatomy and Genetics at Oxford Bridge University. Can you make an appointment for us with whoever it is sometime tomorrow?"

"Sure, no problem. Who might I ask does the "us" refer to?"

"I have Special Agent Collins with me from the FBI. It will be just the two of us."

"That's fine. I'll make the necessary inquiries and get back to you shortly."

Diana rang back thirty minutes later with the requested information.

"I've arranged an appointment for you with Professor Jonathan Collingwood. He heads the Division of Medical and Health Sciences at Oxford Bridge University. It includes the Departments you mentioned. I've also arranged an appointment with Professor Robert Brown. He has taken over the headship of the Department of Genetics from Professor Corbyn. The meeting with Collingwood is at 11.30 am, and the one with Professor Brown at 1.30 pm. I've e-mailed you a map of the University, and marked the buildings where you'll find the Professors' offices."

"Thanks, Diana. That's excellent work as always," replied Jack, who ended the call and placed his mobile phone back in his jacket pocket.

Jack and Special Agent Collins spent the rest of the afternoon reminiscing over old cases. That night they snuggled into bed together. They engaged in very tender sex so as not to aggravate Jack's wounds too much. His wounds were already rapidly healing due to his incredible constitution and physique. Jack normally rose early at 6.00 am out of habit. Every morning, he would snack on several energy bars and normally spend about thirty minutes undertaking high-intensity circuit and weight training, and cardio exercises. However, this morning his exercises were significantly tempered because of his wounds which were still painful when he moved. After breakfast when Jack again astounded Donna with the amount of food he could consume, they briefly visited Jack's office. Jack introduced Donna to the three members of his team. They were each concerned for Jack's welfare after hearing about the assault on his life.

"Are you sure you don't want me to accompany you as your bodyguard?" asked Stefan Kovacs, cheekily.

"I'll consider your offer, but I think you have more important work here" replied Jack smiling.

Jack learned that Aiko and her Japanese colleagues had made no further progress in identifying the Masuda family killers. The killers had taken great steps to ensure that they had left no physical evidence that could identify them.

Jack felt some relief, having been assured the office was operating well with Aiko and Stefan having each picked up several minor cases that were keeping them busy. Jack and Donna travelled the ninety-minute journey to Oxford via the M40 in Jack's late-model black Range Rover Sport. Jack parked on the grounds of the hospital associated with the University. The grounds housed the Medical and Health Sciences Divisional Office. They made their way to Professor Collingwood's office on the third floor and introduced themselves to his PA. After a brief wait, they were ushered into the Professor's office.

"Take a seat Mr. Baron, and Agent Collins. Mr. Baron, your secretary mentioned you were investigating a case that involves the deaths of two of the past staff of this Division. Is that correct? If so, I'd like to know how I may be of service?" said Professor Collingwood, pointing to the seats arranged in front of his desk as an invitation to be seated.

"That is correct. I am representing Professor John Kearney, one of your past staff members, who has some concerns about his safety.

He now works at the Imperial Institute of Genome Sciences in London."

"Yes, I know John Kearney."

"You will no doubt be aware that Professor Corbyn who formerly headed the Department of Physiology, Anatomy and Genetics was reported to have committed suicide on the London Underground. You may have seen his recent obituary in the "Times"."

"Yes, everyone here is aware of Professor Corbyn's death. We were all very saddened to hear he committed suicide."

"This may surprise you, but we have good reason to believe that Professor Corbyn did not commit suicide. We think he was murdered."

"Really? Surely not? Why would anyone want to murder an elderly University Professor?" asked Professor Collingwood, looking very concerned. "Professor Corbyn was very close to retiring."

"I'm sorry to have to tell you that Professor Bentley, also a past member of the same Department, was recently murdered at his sister's cabin at Lake Tahoe in California. Bentley had held joint positions at the American biotech company Biodas and the Harvard Medical School in Boston after leaving Oxford."

Professor Collingwood took a while to grasp the enormity of what he had just been told, then replied somewhat sheepishly.

"I suppose you are now going to tell me that the murders of two Professors from the same Department is not a mere coincidence?"

"That is correct. We have reason to believe their murders are not a coincidence. We think the murders have something to do with the time the Professors spent here at Oxford Bridge University. There is the possibility that two of Bentley's staff at Biodas were also murdered, though this has yet to be proven. Professor Bentley was killed using a somewhat unique modus operandi. Further, he had earlier been attacked by someone, a Japanese man, known to

Professor Kearney. The man's Japanese family was killed using the same MO used to murder Professor Bentley."

"Are you saying Professor Kearney is involved?" asked Collingwood looking incredulous.

"No, not at all. We think he is a potential victim like the others. Our best guess is that one of Kearney's Research Fellows, that is the young Japanese man, was blackmailed into killing Bentley. The blackmail attempt having failed, the blackmailer or his contracted killers subsequently hunted down Bentley and murdered him."

"What was this unique MO, if you don't mind me asking?"

"The victims were all asphyxiated with a plastic bag."

"Ohhh... that's dreadful. Surely this must be the work of more than one killer."

"Yes, we believe the killer has hired a group of East-European criminals to assist him. I have to inform you that we hold grave concerns for the safety of an unknown number of other past or current Departmental staff members. They may be future targets. Our best guess at this stage is that the killer and his targets share a common history. Something happened when they worked together in Professor Corbyn's Department of Physiology, Anatomy and Genetics that has led one of them to seek revenge.

"But that would have been some fifteen years ago. Why should the killings happen now, so many years later? Bentley was a Senior Research Fellow in the Department of Physiology, Anatomy and Genetics at that time. The original Department has since been split, with each of the three disciplines having its own Department. The original Department was quite large fifteen years ago with around twenty Heads of Laboratories, which the University calls Principal Investigators. There is now thrice the number of staff. It was a time when there were several fledgling laboratories. The Senior Research Fellows who headed them were aiming to grow their research teams, and establish an international reputation in their respective fields."

"I see. That would have been a stressful time for them I suppose. A bit like fledgling birds learning to fly the nest for the first time."

"Yes, that's a good analogy."

"Look, we would appreciate it if you would provide us with a list of the senior staff who were employed in the Department during the years that Professors Corbyn and Bentley were there."

"That's easy. My secretary will get copies of the University calendars from our library. The calendars contain lists of staff for a particular year. She will photocopy the relevant pages, and e-mail them to you. Can I have an e-mail address? I'll just speak with her now."

Jack handed Professor Collingwood his business card, and the Professor immediately left the room to advise his secretary, then promptly returned to his office.

"Can you remember any animosity between the senior staff at that time?" asked Jack.

"I was only appointed as Head of the Division two years ago. I was an outside appointment from University College London. It was well before my time here. I suggest you contact Professor Robert Brown. He now heads the Department of Genetics. He was a senior member of the original Department at that time, and knew each of the researchers personally."

"Thank you for the suggestion. We have an appointment with him later this afternoon."

"You mentioned that some of my current staff may be in danger. The University has security staff. But they are only here to protect students and staff while they are on the University campus. Has the Thames Valley Constabulary and London Metropolitan Police been notified?"

"At present there is no evidence that an actual crime has been committed on UK soil."

"But you said you believe Professor Corbyn was murdered."

"Correct, but as yet there is no actual evidence that he was murdered. The subway CCTV record had been deleted, there were no witnesses on the subway platform, and the train driver can't recall the sequence of events."

"Oh, I see."

"Special Agent Collins and her FBI colleagues in the States are investigating the death of Professor Bentley. Hopefully, together we will eventually identify and apprehend his killers."

"I will have to inform the Vice-Chancellor that the safety of University staff may be at risk. Your best bet is to speak to Professor Brown if you want to learn about the history of individual staff members."

Jack and Donna thanked Professor Collingwood for his time. They decided to walk to the River Cherwell, and have lunch at the Boathouse restaurant before their next planned meeting. As they sat on the river bank several couples and families could be seen leisurely punting gracefully upstream to the beautiful rural countryside, or downstream through the lovely picturesque University Parks.

"I'm amazed by the number of tourists here," exclaimed Donna. "They're everywhere you look. How do the locals cope?"

"Yes, you don't notice the tourists so much in London except at key tourist sites. Here they stand out and congregate like ants. I'm sure the locals involved in the tourist industry greatly appreciate the business, but other locals probably not so much," responded Jack.

"It's such a beautiful city. I'm not surprised it attracts so many tourists," replied Donna.

"The Victorian poet Matthew Arnold named Oxford the "City of Dreaming Spires," for obvious reasons. A fitting description don't you think?"

"Definitely an apt description."

After lunch, they ambled back to the University. They reached the new four-storey Department of Genetics building, sited next to a University park, in time to meet Professor Brown. Brown's PA came down to collect and escort them to the Professor's office. It was an average-sized office overlooking several of the city's pretty spires. On the way, they passed several swish laboratories separated by clear glass walls that housed state-of-the-art scientific equipment. Senior researchers and students, each dressed in a white lab coat, were busy at work undertaking experiments of some sort or other. When invited to, Jack and Donna sat down at Brown's small meeting table. Professor John Brown was considerably older than Collingwood. He had that down-trodden time-weathered look and a constant brooding expression. Jack would not have been the least surprised had Brown been considered but overlooked for the position of Head of the Division.

"I received a call from Professor Collingwood about your visit this morning," stated Professor Brown, speaking slowly and deliberately with a slight lisp. "He said you think Professor Corbyn may have been murdered on the London Underground?"

"Firstly, thank you for meeting with us Professor Brown. We appreciate it. Yes, I am sorry to say that is correct. We believe Professor Corbyn was likely pushed in front of an oncoming train."

"That's truly ghastly if true. Professor Collingwood also said that Richard Bentley had been murdered in the United States. Who would do such terrible things, and why?"

"Bentley's murder is one of the reasons why we believe Corbyn was likely also murdered."

"I see. Of course, I am happy to assist in any way I can. I was one of the senior Heads of Labs back in those days. You could say I'm a spent force now, only useful for administrative purposes. It's just too hard chasing research grants at my age. Still, I very much enjoy my position guiding new staff and students and assisting them to reach their personal goals and their full potential. Professor Collingwood asked me to put together a list of staff who worked in the Department fifteen years ago in case the list in the University Calendars wasn't wholly accurate. Here it is," said Professor Brown handing Jack a page of A4 paper.

"Thank you for that. Appreciated."

"Is that all you need?" said Brown eyeing the page.

"We would be grateful if you would paint a picture for us of the Department when Corbyn and Bentley worked at Oxford Bridge University. Your list shows there were around fifteen Heads of Labs at that time," said Jack after quickly scanning the page.

"Was there any animosity amongst the senior staff? In your opinion was there any particular individual amongst the senior staff who you think might be capable of murder?"

"No..., wait a minute. They are all committed senior scientists you're talking about. Why does one of them have to be the murderer? All of our staff were committed to spending their entire lives in understanding and finding cures for diseases that afflict humanity. There are few nobler causes."

"We appreciate the work that was being undertaken. But we are working on the theory that the killer is a past member of the Department who bears some sort of a grudge. Surely you can appreciate why we are asking these questions?"

"Yes, of course, I understand. Of course there was animosity between some of the staff. We are all human whatever our talents and foibles. Our staff members compete for research funding. Their careers, livelihoods, and families depend on their funding success. Most senior staff sit on granting body assessment panels deciding those of their peers who will receive funding, and those who won't. In essence, they control and determine each other's futures. You can say they control each others lives. Under such a scenario how can there not be animosity at times? But to suggest that such a form of governance would lead to murder is, well, just a step too far in my opinion."

"Can you provide any examples where inter-collegial animosity might reveal itself? Did you ever witness any open aggression for instance?"

"Well, of course, when grants were being assessed there was obvious animosity. It was mostly in University committees where the committee members personally knew each other and the applicants. Especially if they were either from the same Department, past students, or who were past or future collaborators. Committee members would sometimes try and support those applicants they considered friends or colleagues who could potentially help them in return in some way. *Vice versa*, colleagues they didn't like were sometimes harshly criticized. I witnessed this time and again. All sorts of criticisms could be leveled at an applicant. For example "He took my job", "he got my promotion", "he only wants the money", "he has already received enough funding" and "he stole my idea" are criticisms I've heard myself and were given as reasons for why a particular applicant should not be awarded a grant. Such criticisms had nothing to do with the actual grant applications and often went unverified. When you're there in the meeting it's like one of the committee members is tossing all their dirty washing all over you. The criticized quickly become one of the "untouchables" and their grant applications destined for the discard pile. Forget about considerations of conflict of interest. Many turn a blind eye in these meetings."

"I see, but I thought conflict of interest was something the Universities and granting agencies took very seriously."

"Yes, supposedly. But I've even been a member of assessment committees for small local granting bodies, where each member of the committee has submitted their own grant application for consideration. Any applicant who is not a member of the assessment panel has little to no chance of having their grant application approved. The committee members fight it out at a meeting, and often those with the loudest voice or longest or strongest records of success are declared the winners."

"You make it all sound very political."

"It is, I can assure you. That said, generally the grants finally selected are amongst the best. But in most years there is only enough money to fund the top five to ten percent of grant applications. Since the top thirty percent of applications are good enough to be funded, you can see that there is going to be a great deal of bitterness from those whose grant applications end up not being funded. Each grant application may have taken the researcher three to six weeks to write, and a group's success and the livelihoods of its members may depend on it being funded."

"Are there any other circumstances that might reveal animosities between researchers, particularly between investigators belonging to the same department?"

"Funnily enough, it is supposedly friendly social occasions like end of the academic year functions, or get-togethers at conferences where resentments bubble to the surface. Sometimes alcohol may have been consumed and lubricated tongues. Skits are mostly funny, but a few portraying staff are intended to hurt and humiliate. In my opinion, some of the senior staff go too far. You are probably aware of the kind of things I'm talking about. It might involve a portrayal of a scientist who had been very successful and acquired several major research grants as being lazy because he didn't do enough teaching. One scientist may accuse another of being overpaid, or acquiring an undeserved early promotion or a choice position, or membership of an influential committee. Someone may accuse another of being too commercially orientated rather than bound to academia. The list of umbrages is as long as a piece of string. More often than not these accusations are based on ignorance, jealousy, greed, or just plain malice or mischievousness. It is the green-eyed goblin acting in some of these skits. I guess for the aggressors involved it is possibly a release valve for their insecurities. The aggressors are generally the senior staff who sometimes co-opt unknowing junior staff into the skits. They can hardly refuse, can they? From what I've heard these hijinks go on not just in Universities, but also in companies both large and small, law firms, schools...you name it. Heck, politicians slang each other off almost every day. They have made a profession out of it. You have to be pretty thick-skinned to survive politics. Some people think it should be accepted practice and think nothing of it. I'm not one of those. But most young scientists venture into a life of research in the hope of making novel useful discoveries. And not to be beaten down by politics. That said, most people don't commit murder after being harassed. They simply move on and get a job elsewhere."

"Yes, I appreciate all that, but was it the same parties each time, or did everyone participate?"

"It was mainly the same culprits year on year. A bit like what happens in public school systems. The bullies would excuse themselves by saying it was all just a bit of fun. But to those targeted it was seldom funny."

"If the aggressors were the same year on year, did they target a particular individual or individuals? Did you ever witness any head-to-head animosity?"

"Yes, there were particular individuals who were regularly harassed. Successful staff who were not favoured by the bullies were often targeted to cut them down to size. The tall poppy syndrome comes to mind. Other targets were those with particular backgrounds, or awkward mannerisms or behaviours that made them stand out."

Jack noted Brown's marked lisp and wondered whether he might have been a target of ridicule.

"I rarely witnessed head-to-head animosity. I'm guessing it happened, but if it did, it was behind closed doors. Those targeted rarely openly objected or made a scene."

"You would say then that fights over success in acquiring research grant funding were a normal part of academic life?"

"Yes, of course. I'd say it was the main cause of contention. Bullies were often exposed when the outcome of major grants was announced. It was rumoured that those who had failed to be awarded a grant would sometimes hunt down someone they disliked who had received a grant. I heard that the unsuccessful would hurl a tirade of abuse at the awardee. It was either in the victim's office or any other isolated place where the aggressor's atrocious behaviour would not be witnessed by a third party. I never witnessed this myself, and it never happened to me. If it had, I would have reported it to a Harassment Officer straight away. That type of behaviour is close to schizophrenic, as far as I'm concerned."

"Do you not think that repeated bullying like this might lead to murder?"

"In all my years closeted within academia, I've never heard of an academic rivalry that has led to murder. Though I did hear of a case where one staff member reported that another staff member declared "he would destroy him". I can report that it came to nothing. I think a lot of it is just hot air and frustration. Whether the aggressor truly meant it at the time, who can say? I'm sure these disgusting types of behaviours occur in all professions. But it is particularly rife in academia where there is a close-knit interdependent community of high achievers."

"I am particularly interested in Dr Richard Bentley. He is the only staff member we know for sure was murdered. Would you say he was likely to bully other staff, or more likely to be a victim?"

"Oh, most definitely the bully. He was a very arrogant chap as I remember. Very bright and super ambitious. He excelled at everything, and beware anyone who got the better of him. He had a cruel streak. Never showed any empathy. If I remember correctly, he was an actor in some of the Department's skits that I think went too far. Everything was about him. I was very pleased when he eventually returned to the United States."

"Would you be able to add to this list?" said Jack holding it up. "Could you add those who had aggressive natures, those who have been potential targets, those who flourished during their time in the Department, and those that didn't for whatever reason."

"Certainly. I will have to read through old Departmental annual reports. It will take a while. I'll also have to ask and phone around regarding individual personalities, and potential animosities. It is bound to raise some sensitivities, you understand. It was a long time ago and a lot has probably been forgotten. Looks like you are asking me to become your deputy, detective," smiled Brown

"Yes, I think I am. It would be particularly helpful if you could add where each past member of staff currently works. Could you also provide a map showing the laboratory spaces occupied by each Lab Head at the time? I would be grateful if you could provide this information as soon as possible as I do believe more of your colleagues' lives are possibly at stake."

"You can take Drs Williamson and Davis off the list. They both died of cancer several years ago. So you think some of us are at risk of being targeted? You don't think I am in any danger do you?" asked Professor Brown suddenly appreciating the reality of what he had just been told.

"We can't rule out that possibility. But you might wish to consider whether you made any enemies during that time. In the meantime, maintain your guard at all times, and take normal safety precautions. You know, keep your doors locked, tell someone if you are going to be away for some time. Try not to be alone."

"Ohh...I see. It will take me a week or thereabouts to get all the information you want."

"Any help you can give us would be much appreciated," replied Jack handing over his business card.

"I almost forgot to ask. One last thing. Would any of the staff from that time have an East-European connection, either current or historical?"

"The Heads of Labs at that time originated from the UK, America, and the Commonwealth. Though students and Research Fellows which make up the majority of the Department originate from all parts of the world, including Eastern Europe. Could the killer be a disgruntled student or junior Research Fellow from that time?" asked Professor Brown with a puzzled look on his face.

"That's a definite possibility, but for the time being we'll be concentrating our efforts on the senior staff," replied Jack.

Jack and Donna strolled back to the parked car. Once seated inside they examined the list that Professor Brown had given them. There were sixteen staff members listed after discounting the two who had died of cancer. They recognized five names on the list, namely Professors Corbyn, Fallon, Kearney, Bentley, and Brown. Two of those were now deceased. That left eleven unaccounted for senior staff members who had been Heads of Labs.

Jack took out his phone and rang Diana.

"Hi Diana, I've got another job for you. I'm going to e-mail you a list of eleven Heads of Labs who were employed at Oxford Bridge University fifteen years ago. I need to know their current positions and whereabouts, including whether they are still alive or deceased. I asked Professor Brown for the same information, but you might be able to find it more quickly as I've loaded him down with extra work."

"Sure no problem. I'll get onto it ASAP and get back to you," came the matter-of-fact reply.

Jack and Donna booked into the Cotswold Lodge Hotel. It was just a short walk north of the Division of Health and Medical Sciences. They had a lengthy and satisfying dinner at the hotel while they waited to hear back from Diana. The e-mail response was received later that night. Jack forwarded a copy to Donna. Diana had prepared two lists based on those staff members still living in the UK, and those who had taken up positions elsewhere. Of the six remaining in the UK, one was no longer engaged in academic or scientific research. Instead, he had opted early on to go into politics and public service positions. He seemed an unlikely target or suspect, hence was discounted.

That left five still in the UK with three remaining within the Division together with Professor Brown. Just one of those, a Professor Harry Moore, had moved to the new Genetics building. The two who had not remained in the Division had taken positions outside Oxford. Graham Campbell was Head of Genetics and Epigenetics at the Winslow Genetics Institute in Cambridge. Susan Jones was the Head of the Faculty of Medical Sciences at University College London. Of the five who had left the UK, one had taken up the position of Dean of Medicine at the University of Otago, Dunedin, New Zealand; one was now the Vice-Chancellor at Monash University in Melbourne, Australia; another named Jim Dalton was the CEO of a company called GenomeIt based in San Diego; Simon Jackson was the Head of Genetics at Johns Hopkins Institute of Genetic Medicine, Baltimore, Maryland; and the fifth was Peter Singer, a Senior Scientist at the Institute of Molecular and Cellular Biology (ICMB), Singapore.

Looking over the list, Donna commented, "Wow, that's impressive, so much talent spawned by a single Department."

"I read somewhere that the Division of Health and Medical Sciences at Oxford Bridge University is ranked number three in the world for biomedicine after its older sister Oxford University, so perhaps it is not surprising. If you spend time there you automatically become hot property for recruitment elsewhere. Some believe that the biomedical ranking of Oxford Bridge University may even eventually surpass that of Oxford University. Did you know that Oxford University is the oldest university in the English-speaking world? It's almost one thousand years old. I read that it has produced almost seventy Nobel prize winners. Now that's what I call impressive. Though, I guess I should mention that Cambridge University has produced around a hundred and twenty prize winners."

"That's interesting. Explains the age of most of the buildings in Oxford. We don't have anything comparable age-wise back in the States. I believe Harvard University is our oldest, but it is just a baby in comparison. I shouldn't brag, but I learnt recently that it has produced one hundred and sixty Nobel prize winners. Looks like we're pretty even in brainpower, wouldn't you say?"

"Looks like it. Anyway, getting back to the case, we'll have to cross-check Diana's findings with those of Professor Brown. Let's hope Brown can give us clues to any further potential targets. Bentley's lab may have been adjacent to the killer's lab, and there could have been antagonism over laboratory space allocation. As I understand, space is critical as it can dictate whether a research team has room to grow. Though resentment could be due to anything I suppose from scientific espionage, fights over authorship or intellectual property rights, suppression of promotion, harassment, conflict of interest, extortion, exploitation, insults, intimidation, public ridicule, or the lot. You name it; I've heard that all these happen in those places of higher learning and major companies and organisations where the pecking order is sorted out by peers, often in the absence of any real form of independent governance or policing. I'm convinced one of the members of the original Department is our killer, but who it is, just what their motive is, and who is the next target, if there is one, is anyone's guess."

"You also have to ask, what is a University Professor doing associated with a group of East-European criminals?" mentioned Donna. "He must have grown up on the wrong side of the tracks, that's for sure. I'll phone my contacts now and see if there is any update on the whereabouts of that gang."

Donna rang off five minutes later, a concerned look on her face.

"Seems there was a skirmish between East-European and Hispanic gangs at Venice Beach, California. The Hispanics were probably just protecting their turf. The skirmish left two of them dead. I'm concerned, if it is the same gang then they're still in the States. Doesn't one of the Professors on Brown's list work near San Diego? That's not that far south from Venice Beach."

CHAPTER TWENTY-TWO

Professor Carlos Vaquero was working late at night in his office writing a manuscript for submission to the journal Proceedings of the National Academy of Sciences USA. He was deep in thought when there was a knock on the door to his office. Professor Vaquero was a handsome, charming, and well-respected man in his late thirties. For the past five years, he had held a Chair in Biomedical Engineering at an Ivy League research university in Ithaca, central New York.

"Come in!" he yelled, all the while remaining absorbed in his work.

The door slowly opened. In walked Nataliya Yurkovich, one of his five PhD students, formerly from Ukraine.

"Would you have time to discuss my recent research findings?" she asked meekly and somewhat tentatively, unsure whether the Professor would want to be distracted from his work so late at night.

"Certainly, take a seat," replied the Professor, finally looking up from his work.

The Professor had always sought to make himself available to help and advise his young students, whatever the time of day. Nataliya was a stunningly attractive woman in her mid twenties with a quiet and reserved personality. She had earlier taken one of the Master's courses taught by the Professor. She had always sat in the front row of the class, where she stood out from the other students. She was voluptuous with long blonde hair and unblemished smooth fair skin. She was an excellent student academically. Thus Professor Vaquero had been delighted when she requested to undertake the research part of her Master's degree, and subsequently a PhD in his laboratory.

When Professor Vaquero eventually looked up from his work he was intrigued to see that Nataliya was not dressed in casual clothes which she normally wore while working in the laboratory. Instead, she was wearing an incredibly flimsy, short, almost see-through turquoise party dress. The low-cut dress was held up by the thinnest of shoulder straps. The flimsy dress exposed most of the upper half of her gorgeous body. It accentuated the shape and fullness of her figure. Nataliya sat down and began discussing her findings, referring to the lab book she had placed on the Professor's desk in front of her. She kept her head lowered the whole time while focussing on her results. To Carlos, it was almost as if she was inviting him to inspect her gorgeous body without challenge or recrimination. Anyway, that was certainly Carlos's opinion.

The Professor was a happily married man with three young children. He always felt guilty whenever his eyes strayed to view another attractive woman. That said, whilst feeling ashamed, he could not resist taking up Nataliya's imagined offer. Whilst remaining attentive to what she was saying, he took the time to gaze at her breasts. He imagined what they must look like when fully uncovered. How they would feel to his touch and caress. He was caught slightly off-guard when she finally looked up at him the first time to gain his opinion. He could feel his face becoming slightly warm and flushed with embarrassment. But after he had responded appropriately to her questions, she lowered her head again and continued to discuss the latest results in her lab book. In turn, he returned to his gazing and fantasizing while remaining attentive to what she was saying. Eventually Nataliya looked up and declared she had nothing further to report, and after a further discussion declared she was happy with his advice.

"Why are you all dressed up? Are you going to a party?" asked Carlos, intrigued because he had never seen her so spiffed up before.

"I'm glad you noticed. Now and then a girl likes to dress to impress. You like?" she asked.

"I'm sure you will be the belle of the ball," offered Carlos smiling, and dodging the question.

"What does that mean? Is it good?" she persisted.

"Oh, yes, it means every boy at the party will want to dance with you."

"Would you like to dance with me, Professor?"

"Yes, of course. If I was going to the party, it would be an honour to dance with you."

"The problem is, I don't know how to dance. I was never taught. I am not even sure how to hold my partner. I was hoping you might be willing to show me," urged Nataliya in a pleading voice.

Carlos immediately wondered whether Nataliya was being genuine. Had her visit been to seek research advice, or was it a ruse to flirt with him? Most of all he was worried that he couldn't trust himself with this gorgeous creature. With three children, his wife had little time for him of late. He often fantasized about what it would be like to be a bachelor again. On the one hand, he was angry with Nataliya if she was flirting with him. She knew he was a married man. On the other hand, he wished his fantasy would come true, so long as it could be kept forever a shared secret. He longed to explore every curve of her gorgeous body. He stood up from his chair and walked around to the front of his desk.

"Can I have this dance?" he asked smiling, holding out his left hand.

Without speaking Nataliya stood up from the chair. She smiled at Carlos and offered him her right hand. He took her hand in his left palm. He placed his right hand in the small of her back and pressed her tightly to him. He could feel the warmth of her body against his and was immediately aroused. They took a couple of dance steps. Without warning, Nataliya suddenly leaned forward and kissed Carlos on the lips. It was a simple peck. But when he didn't resist her or reprimand her, she kissed him again. But this time it was a wet, sensual open-mouth exploration. The phrase "I did not have sex with that woman" played repeatedly in Carlos's head. Nataliya drew back, looked into Carlos's eyes, and smiled. She slowly walked to the office door and locked it. Then she slowly raised her hands behind her neck and undid the shoulder straps of her dress. She let the dress fall to her waist, exposing her naked generous breasts. Carlos stood gazing wide-eyed at the most beautiful pair of breasts he had ever seen. He reached forward and cupped each breast in his hands, feeling their softness, and weight. He caressed both breasts, and licked, tasted, and teased the nipples. He buried his face between the breasts, pressing them against the sides of his face, feeling their softness and warmth. He breathed in slowly and deeply, smelling and luxuriating in the fragrance given off by Nataliya's warm body. All the while, she purred while he caressed her, and in return, she adeptly unzipped the fly of his trousers, put her hand inside, and caressed and stroked him.

"Don't you have to go to your party?" whispered Carlos in a hoarse voice, his face now flushed with lust.

"What party was that?" replied Nataliya with a grin, sliding the flimsy dress over her curvaceous hips, letting it fall to the floor.

The Professor always informed Nataliya when he would be working late in his office. The two of them continued their secret affair for several weeks. Until the day it abruptly ended. Nataliya had taken the afternoon off to search for a new place to rent. The owner of the current place she rented had given her notice. Carlos had told her earlier that day that he would be working late, which was a signal for her to come to his office that night.

Nataliya entered the laboratory. She could see the light under the door of Carlos's office. She knocked on the office door. There was no answer. She opened the door expecting to see Carlos at his desk, absorbed in his work. Indeed, Carlos was at his desk, but he was not working. He was sitting at his desk leaning backward. His bloodied head was covered by a plastic bag secured at the neck with tape. Nataliya immediately raised her hand to shield her eyes from the gruesome sight of her damaged lover. She felt a sharp pang in her chest as if someone had stabbed her. She stumbled backward holding on to the door frame to prevent herself from falling. After a moment she regained her senses, and slowly closed the office door. She ran out of the laboratory and out of the building. Once outside the University grounds she dropped to her knees and began to shake and weep uncontrollably. Professor Vaquero's body was found by a cleaner early the next morning. The NYPD was alerted, and the office was cordoned off as a crime scene.

CHAPTER TWENTY-THREE

The company GenomeIt was located in Torrey Pines, La Jolla, just a few miles north of San Diego. It was a gleaming tower of glass and steel overlooking the cobalt blue expanse of the Pacific Ocean. Its founder and CEO Jim Dalton was a charismatic Englishman. He was an attractive man of average size, with a full head of fair hair, and freckled fair skin. He was one of the first to realize there was low fruit to be picked upon completion of the sequencing of the human genome, a milestone in human history. The human genome was proving to be a portal into understanding ancestry and disease risk. GenomeIt was one of the first companies to offer complete genome sequencing to interested members of the public. The DNA sequence information was valuable not only to the client but it could be passed on with consent from the donor to major pharmaceutical companies. They would use the information to pinpoint disease-forming genes from which they could develop powerful drugs to combat both common and rare diseases that afflicted the human population.

Professor Jim Dalton was sitting in a plush black leather chair next to his huge highly polished ponderosa pine desk. He was looking out through the gigantic glass wall of his office over the Pacific Ocean to San Clemente Island. It had been a huge struggle to get where he was today. His most urgent pressing problem was whether he would be able to hold onto control of the company he had established. The company had gone public and had listed on the stock exchange five years ago. Dalton and his wife together held fifty-one percent of the shares. Following a bitter divorce, he had managed to retain a thirty percent shareholding. But every year he was having to sell off more and more of his shares to meet his wife's alimony demands. To make matters worse his ex-wife's new fiancé was very wealthy. He was buying GenomeIt shares whenever they came up for sale. Jim knew he would soon be at the mercy of his ex-wife and her partner, who would become the majority shareholders.

Jim's thoughts turned to his ex-wife Victoria. He wondered where it had all gone so wrong for them. He sorely missed her. They had both grown up in relatively poor families in Hackney, East London when it was one of the poorest boroughs in England. Against all the odds they had both won scholarships to Oxford University. He fondly remembered their first meeting in the Bodleian library while preparing for exams. There had been an instant attraction. Their relationship grew and they took a flat together, spending nearly all their time studying. They were both rewarded with First Class Honours degrees in their chosen subject of biomedicine. They spent much of the rest of their spare time in joyous sexual exploration. Victoria was both demanding, energetic, adventurous, and passionate. So much so that Jim often wondered whether he would always be enough to satisfy her.

They married on the eve of taking up doctoral studies at Cambridge University. On qualifying, Jim was offered a junior faculty position in the Department of Physiology, Anatomy and Genetics at Oxford Bridge University. Victoria, now pregnant with their first child delayed her career for full-time motherhood. On the birth of the child the family dynamics changed instantly and irrevocably overnight. All of Victoria's focus and attention was now on the growing baby. She took complete control of the family's purse strings, finances, and activities. There was always never enough money to go around. Every purchase was carefully scrutinized. Every extra penny was saved for emergencies and the family's future. There was rarely any spontaneity and joy. Jim worked longer and longer hours, seeking solace in his University laboratory. Here at least he was respected and had independence and control. The long hours he spent away from home caused Victoria to become increasingly resentful. She constantly criticized his absence, his fathering skills, and his value as a husband.

After the birth of their second child, any hope that Jim had of retaining a satisfying relationship, including intimacy with his wife, was dashed. It was as if a tap had been turned off. He lost count of the number of times Victoria uttered "Keep that dirty thing away from me," "I'm too tired," "I have a headache," "I've just had a shower", or "Wait till the morning, I'll be in the mood then." But Victoria was never in the mood. Reflecting on the past five years, Jim realized Victoria had never once initiated lovemaking, yet still, he had remained faithful. On the rare occasions she submitted to sex, she never participated or reciprocated, choosing to lie still and inert while he desperately tried to breathe life into her. Whatever he tried, however hard he tried, she was never moved. Further, their diminished sex life was made a taboo subject by Victoria. It was never to be discussed. There was no chance of counseling, no hope of recovery.

"What had happened to that vivacious and passionate woman he had loved to turn her into someone so dispassionate and cold?" he asked himself, with tears beginning to well in his eyes.

One day Victoria asked Jim to check her iPad, which was not holding its charge. He was shocked to discover she was viewing pornographic images and videos of naked men, and couples engaged in sex. Mostly they were younger men heavily endowed with buff bodies. He was hurt and crushed. "Wasn't pornography something only men indulged in?" he asked himself, despite being aware of research findings reporting that almost as many women as men enjoyed watching pornography. It dawned upon him that his wife had not lost her libido, just her interest in him as a man, and husband. He had clung on to the slim hope that she still loved him as she had stayed with him over the years. But she was clearly not in love with him. What's more, she obviously no longer found him sexually attractive. Not enough to even pretend she found him desirable. For Jim that was the final straw.

While Jim's personal life was a car crash, his research life had been going from strength to strength. He had not only discovered several new human genes but had shown they had potential clinical application. To his great dismay the University would not back his resulting patent applications, and the commercialization routes he proposed. He turned to his colleagues. He lobbied those he thought were wealthy enough to join him in establishing a fledgling company to commercialize his inventions. Despite his pleas, nobody in the Department would join him in his proposed new venture. In desperation, he reached out to businessmen in the United States. He discovered Americans were not as risk-averse as his colleagues, as testified by the thousands of fledgling biomedical companies up and down the western and eastern seaboards, each trying their luck in commercializing their inventions. Eventually, he found a backer. Together with Victoria and their two children, he immigrated to San Diego, California. He secretly hoped that the change to a different country and culture would rejuvenate his failing marital relationship.

Over time his company's focus changed to exploit the knowledge and information stemming from the Human Genome Project. The change of direction proved to be highly lucrative. Soon Jim was the founder, CEO, and the major shareholder together with his wife, of a multi-million dollar biotechnology company. After a while, much of what the company did became somewhat repetitive. Jim was released from a crippling workload. The children, now young teenagers, were spending increasing lengths of time with their friends. These changes left him alone at night with Victoria. This only served to cruelly expose their now completely broken relationship.

CHAPTER TWENTY-FOUR

Jack and Donna learned of Professor Vaquero's murder the next day when one of Donna's FBI colleagues contacted her. Donna conveyed the details of the conversation to Jack.

"Another Professor has been murdered. This time at a University in New York. It's the same MO, except the victim was hit on the head with a blunt instrument before being asphyxiated. It's even possible he wasn't conscious when he was suffocated. It's the first time we've had the murder actually inside the university grounds."

"Who is the victim?"

"The deceased is a Professor Carlos Vaquero. I've informed my colleagues we'll be over to view the crime scene tomorrow."

"That's fine," agreed Jack and continued. "I'll phone Diana and advise her of our plans. I'll ask her to obtain the victim's background. If it's the same MO then it's likely we are dealing with the same killer. Seems he and his accomplices have now moved to the eastern seaboard."

Jack and Donna drove to London Heathrow and caught the first flight out to John F Kennedy International Airport. They booked into a hotel in Downtown Ithaca near the University. Diana e-mailed Jack a file on Professor Vaquero that night. Jack summarized the information for Donna.

"Professor Vaquero was a local, raised in the state of New York. He was the son of a New York Congressman. He obtained a PhD in Biomedical Engineering from Cornell, then undertook post-doctoral work at the Massachusetts Institute of Technology in Cambridge, Massachusetts. He returned to New York and took up a faculty position at the University."

"What? What about Oxford? Didn't he work at Oxford Bridge University at any stage during his career?" asked Donna.

"Apparently not. I agree that's unexpected. Have we got this all wrong? Are the killings just random? Maybe the killers just have a hatred of intellectuals? You know, hundreds of thousands of the intelligentsia were murdered during the Spanish Civil war, mostly teachers, academics, artists, and writers," speculated Jack.

"Seems unlikely. Perhaps the killer met Vaquero at someplace other than Oxford Bridge University. The killer could have spent time at the Professor's university," suggested Donna.

"I'll get Diana to check whether any of the Professors from the Department of Physiology, Anatomy, and Genetics ever spent time there. I suppose they might even have met the killer at a conference and never got along for some reason, or maybe he was one of their collaborators. We'll need to check their scientific publications, just in case."

"Let's hope the crime scene can give us a few clues, as we don't have anything else to go on."

Jack and Donna rose early the next day, and Jack snacked on several energy bars. Jack's body was healing well. He demonstrated to Donna his usual suite of early morning exercises. He was impressed by her ability to repeat most of them. But then again she was very athletic. They showered, dined together, and then drove by rental car to the University. They were met at the foyer of the University building by the Deputy Inspector of the Crime Scene Unit (CSU), part of the NYPD Detective Bureau's Forensic Investigations Division.

"Howdy, I'm Justin Roper, Deputy Inspector of the CSU. I understand this case could be linked to other murders you are investigating here in the USA, UK, and Japan?" said Roper, shaking hands with Jack and Donna. Donna introduced herself and Jack, and displayed her FBI credentials.

"Yes that is correct," replied Donna, and continued. "The murders have the same unusual MO. The victims are asphyxiated with a plastic bag and duct tape."

"I've never encountered that MO before in my career," said Roper.

"Our thinking is that the murders are linked to University Professors who spent time together at a particular department at Oxford Bridge University in the United Kingdom over a decade ago. But this murder has put the kibosh on that idea. Professor Vaquero never worked at Oxford Bridge University, or anywhere outside the USA for that matter," mentioned Jack.

"I see. Anyways, I'll show you the crime scene, which is essentially Vaquero's office. There could be some physical evidence there to indicate whether it's the same killer or not. It's not a pretty sight," said the Inspector. He led Donna and Jack to the fourth floor of the building and into Professor Vaquero's office.

Jack and Donna eyed the scene dispassionately. They had been confronted in the past by countless dead bodies. The victims had been subjected to torture, and just about every type of brutality or indignity one could imagine. They were now immune to sights that would make your average layperson lose their stomach contents. Jack was the first to note the differences in the tools of asphyxiation. He distinctly remembered that the bags covering the heads of the Japanese family and Professor Bentley had no print on them. Also, the duct tape was silver-coloured, not brown. Jack pointed out this potential discrepancy to Donna.

"The plastic bag has got print all over it, and the duct tape is coloured brown. The bags in the previous murders had no print, and the duct tape was silver-coloured."

"Maybe the killer is the same, but he just happened to buy more plastic bags and duct tape at a different store? Do they necessarily have to be the same?" questioned Donna.

"The facts just don't seem to fit the previous murders. This Professor never worked at Oxford Bridge University. The bag and duct tape are different. What's the chance this is a copycat murder?"

"Bloody hell! Are you telling me there could be a whole series of copycat murders up and down the country awaiting us?"

"Let's hope not. A graphic description of Bentley's killing was plastered all over the front pages of every national newspaper. The media coverage may have inspired someone to commit murder using the same MO to pin the crime on our killer."

"I've asked the University's custodian to let us take a look at the recordings from CCTV cameras installed in the corridors of the building. Unfortunately, there are no cameras installed in the laboratories or offices," declared the Inspector.

Jack and Donna followed the Inspector to the ground floor where the custodian's office was located. A short balding overweight man in his early fifties beckoned them to his desk. The group stared at the computer monitor on his desk. A video was playing which showed a young muscly man, possibly in his thirties, wearing blue jeans and a white muscle-T shirt. The young man was walking down the corridor towards Professor Vaquero's laboratory. It was early evening around the time the murder was presumed to have taken place.

"I've checked our records. There is no one fitting this young man's description in our Department," stated the custodian looking concerned.

"How did he get into the building then?" asked Jack, and continued. "I note that every research floor requires a swipe card for entry."

"The electronic records show he used the swipe card of Ms. Nataliya Yurkovich. I understand she is one of Professor Vaquero's PhD students," answered the custodian.

"You've got to be kidding me," exclaimed Donna, eyeing Jack, her eyebrows raised high.

"No, that is correct," assured the custodian.

"Perhaps the student was unhappy with her supervision and hired someone to teach the Professor a lesson, but things got out of control?" suggested the Inspector.

"I've never heard of that happening before. It's more likely that the Professor and his student were having some sort of dalliance. Perhaps the student hired someone to teach the Professor a lesson because he had ended the affair. I understand the Professor was married."

"I think the NYPD can handle this from now on. I'll pass on the information we have to the Homicide Squad. We'll work on identifying the suspect in the CCTV recordings. I'll arrange for Nataliya Yurkovich to be taken into custody and questioned. I expect we'll have some answers for you very soon. I'll contact you as soon as we have made an arrest," declared the Inspector, seemingly confident of the outcome.

"We appreciate your relieving us of this case. Your killer appears to be an amateur. Our killers are professionals. They would have deleted any CCTV evidence or any other physical evidence."

Donna and Jack thanked Inspector Roper. He escorted them out of the University building. Donna and Jack decided to stay in New York to await the outcome of the NYPD's investigation. Donna showed Jack some of the sites of New York and the State over the following two days. They attended a New York Yankees game, visited the 9/11 museum, the Empire State Building observation deck, the Statue of Liberty, Times Square, and even took a trip to Niagra Falls. On the morning of the third day, Inspector Roper rang to say that an arrest had been made. He suggested Donna and Jack meet him at the CSU to discuss the case.

"As we thought, it turned out to be a rather straightforward case," said the deputy Inspector, and continued. "The man seen in the corridor, our major suspect, was Nataliya's boyfriend. He is a fellow Ukranian. He was supporting Nataliya financially by working as a restaurant hand while she did her PhD. She was to be his ticket to wealth and happiness. It seems she wanted to short-cut the process by aiming to marry the handsome and wealthy Professor. One of Nataliya's girlfriends rang the NYPD not long after our meeting. Nataliya had confided in her that she was having an affair with the Professor. She told us that somehow the boyfriend had found out about the affair and was incensed. We questioned Nataliya about her relationship with the Professor. At first, she denied the affair, but she finally admitted they were lovers. I think she had fallen in love with the Professor. Her boyfriend also initially denied all charges. But he finally confessed under the weight of all our evidence. He will serve a lengthy jail sentence before being deported back to Ukraine."

"How did he manage to get access to Nataliya's university swipe card to enter the upper floors?" asked Donna.

"He stole Nataliya's university swipe card while she was out looking for a new rental. He did the deed and returned the card before she was any the wiser. The number of each Professor's laboratory and their office is posted on a board just outside the lift. He would have had no problem finding his way. He admitted he had read a newspaper article describing Professor Bentley's murder. He hoped to lay the blame for Vaquero's murder on your killer. I'm sorry, but this case has been a red-herring for the two of you."

"I imagine the press will have a field day with this case. I can just see the headline now "Congressman's son killed by angry boyfriend following sordid affair with young student."

"We are very grateful that you and the NYPD managed to solve this crime so quickly. I fear our case is not nearly so straightforward. It involves more than a simple menage-a-trois gone wrong."

"Then I wish you both the best of luck with your investigations," replied the Inspector, showing them to the door.

CHAPTER TWENTY-FIVE

The naked couple were having sex. It was not for procreation, nor from any sense of duty, or conjugal right. It was for the sheer joy of a sexual relationship, to feel those intense and sumptuous sensations that only close intimacy can conjure. The attractive red-haired fair-skinned woman in her mid-thirties was responding to his every touch. The couple orgasmed simultaneously in the throes of ecstasy, and after recovering they rolled on their backs onto the bed thoroughly spent and satiated.

As the couple lay there gently panting, they were shocked to hear the swishing noise as the bottom edge of the bedroom door brushed over the long-pile carpet, indicating the door was being opened. Then suddenly there she was. The Dalton's cleaning maid Maria was standing in the middle of the bedroom doorway near the end of the bed. Her large doe-like brown eyes were wide open and her mouth was agape as if she had been caught in the headlights. She stood completely immobilized in shock by the scene that confronted her. The naked couple immediately scrambled into action. They began tearing and grabbing at the bedsheet to cover their exposed nakedness.

"I apologize, Mr. Dalton, sir. But Mrs. Dalton asked me to clean the house today instead of tomorrow," stammered the maid in a hurried and pitiful squeaky voice.

"Get out!" shrieked the naked women.

"So sorry, sir," mumbled Maria still in shock with her head bowed.

Maria did a one-eighty turn, ran out of the bedroom, down the stairs, and out of the house. That night she discussed the incident with her husband.

"We need the money you get from housekeeping. Tell Mrs. Dalton you felt sick, and couldn't complete the work on that day," he advised her, then continued "Go to work next week as usual, but don't mention to Mrs. Dalton what you saw."

However, as a devout Catholic Maria felt she had no choice but to resign her position. She wrote a letter of resignation. It included an explanation stating "the reason was that Mr. Dalton had been unfaithful, which is a sin according to God in my religion." She slipped the letter under the front door of the Dalton's house the following day.

Victoria was the first to discover the letter. To say that she was fuming after reading the letter would be an understatement. The discovery boiled inside her all day, and that night she challenged her husband when he returned from work.

"You fucked our maid, you bastard!" she screamed, shoving the letter in his face as evidence.

"No, of course not. Maria caught me in bed with another woman," explained Jim sheepishly, his face turning bright red from embarrassment.

"In our bed?! Who was it?!" shouted Victoria.

"No one you know," replied Jim, lowering his head in shame. But then he continued indignantly "Did you think I was going to remain celibate for the rest of my life?"

"What are you getting at?! You always were a lousy lover!" yelled Victoria.

"Well, you grew into a cold heartless bitch!" shouted Jim back in anger, and continued "Fucking you was like fucking a bloody cadaver! If you want to jerk off to images of naked young men that's your choice, but I prefer something alive, warm-blooded, and responsive, which isn't you!"

"You can sleep on the couch tonight....no better still, you can leave the house, and don't come back!" screamed Victoria, her face bright red with fury.

That was the last time the family was together. Not long after, Victoria sued for divorce and gained custody of the children. Every day she and her new man were getting closer to taking control of the company Jim had founded, and grown each year through his blood, sweat, and tears.

Jim's thoughts turned back to what he had achieved over the past few weeks. He had travelled to key Universities, research institutes, and companies across America, the United Kingdom, and Europe. He had hoped to secure their collaboration to develop new therapies for common and rare diseases based on the huge genetic datasets the company was developing. He was very excited that five new partners had come on board.

He had written two large programme grants to the NIH requesting several million dollars to fund research to unravel gene associations with particular diseases. He loved expressing his ideas in grant applications. But he loathed all the accompanying compliance paperwork.

He had drafted two patent applications that covered the clinical application of mutations in two genes from screening clients' DNA. Legalese was something he was not familiar with and always represented a challenge.

"Why would anyone want to be a lawyer?" Jim thought to himself. "Legal jargon and written expression were stupefying in their repetitiveness, complexity, and length. Why write single sentences that run for half a page in length? Why repeat sentences endlessly, shaping a patent application into a thesis from an initial draft of just a few pages? Did lawyers have an answer for this type of behaviour? How many patent applications in the biomedical field are finally issued and protect inventions that eventually see clinical application? No more than one in every twenty, that's how many. How can anyone work in such an occupation, knowing that almost all of your work is destined for the rubbish bin?" No, he would never have entertained the thought of becoming a patent lawyer. But he accepted someone had to do it. Poor bastards. But then he remembered that Einstein started his distinguished scientific career as a patent examiner in a Swiss patent office, and immediately felt less repelled by the thought.

Jim's thoughts turned back again to Victoria. He wondered whether Victoria was really happy with her new man. How could she not be? He was a true man's man, an excessively wealthy adventurer who had explored breathtakingly beautiful places all over the globe. The type who would make the final ascent of Chomolungma (Everest) in the early dawn with no oxygen, with his less able companion strapped to his back, then sit on the roof of the world watching the sunrise over the Himalayas before safely returning to base camp. How could he compete with that. He couldn't.

"Would her new relationship last?" he wondered to himself. "Was it his or was it her fault that their marriage had failed so miserably? Perhaps it had always been destined to fail."

CHAPTER TWENTY-SIX

Professor Jim Dalton lived in a sprawling two-storied property on La Jolla Shores Beach. It was just a short drive from his company. He drove home after a busy day courting new investors and preparing the talk he was to give at the upcoming International Conference on Genomics being held in his hometown. He was looking forward to a swim and relaxation around the pool. He had phoned his latest woman friend. She said she'd come over later that night. He pulled into his driveway and clicked the remote to activate the garage roller door. The door opened and he drove his Tesla Roadster into the awaiting space in the garage. He went to shut down the security alarm for the house before it became activated. It was only then that he realized something was amiss. The alarm system was not active. He shrugged his shoulders and made a mental note to contact the security firm that had installed it.

Jim Dalton was struck hard from behind as he stepped through the inner doorway of his garage to the house. He crumpled onto the soft mat covering the marble floor. When he awoke thirty minutes later, he had a throbbing headache. That was the least of his worries. He discovered he had been bound by his feet and hands and was sitting propped up on a chair next to the dining room table. Panicking, he immediately attempted to stand but found he was firmly bound to the chair. At that moment a figure with an unfamiliar face strode into the room. Strangely, his hands were gloved, and his shoes were covered by disposable plastic shoe covers.

"Who the hell are you, and what is going on?" asked Dalton, still struggling to release himself from his bonds. "Untie me. Are you crazy?"

Another man appeared from behind, and quickly placed an iPad Pro on a stand on the table directly in front of him. A face suddenly appeared on the tablet's screen. It looked somewhat familiar, albeit older than he remembered.

"Hello, Jim. It's good to see you again after all these years. It's time for some payback!" barked the man in the screen, with a smirk written on his face.

"What do you mean? I don't understand. I haven't done anything to you. Payback for what? Why are you doing this?" cried Dalton, desperately trying to free himself of the ties.

"I'll give you a minute to think about that," scoffed the man.

During that minute the man looking out from the screen took the time to remember the reasons he had judged Jim Dalton worthy of his attention. Dalton had harassed him for months to establish a company to commercialize Dalton's research results. He had declined Dalton's offer and explained to him that he simply did not have the money to invest. Jim just wouldn't accept his explanation and had set out to destroy him in retribution. Dalton trashed his grant applications, impeded his approval of ethics applications, ridiculed him in public and private, and damaged his chances of promotion. He hijacked several of the original ideas his students were working on. He had evidence that Dalton had colluded with others to damage his reputation.

Meanwhile, Dalton stared at the face in the screen, desperately trying to understand the reason for the predicament he was in.

"Payback for what?" he asked himself over and over.

The man with the familiar face steered directly into Dalton's eyes for exactly one minute without blinking, all the while grinning like a Cheshire cat. Dalton continued to beg for his life. His pleas fell on deaf ears. After one minute was up, the man in the screen nodded his head, which was the signal. One of the intruders took a plastic bag and duct tape from his jacket pocket. He opened the bag, walked behind, and placed the bag over Dalton's head. Dalton began to struggle furiously, but the intruders forcibly shoved the chair into the table pinning their victim. One intruder then unwound some duct tape and carefully taped the opening of the plastic bag to Dalton's neck. The Professor's struggling only served to hasten his demise. The man with the familiar face continued to stare with satisfaction directly into Dalton's eyes. The victim's eyes were now bulging with fear as he furiously sucked in and out to glean the remaining oxygen from the bag. His whole body began to shake. The blood vessels in his head bulged. His face colour darkened. His eyes became glassy. He urinated with the urine soaking his pants and wetting the floor. Finally, the eyes in his purple head remained unmoving and open. Jim Dalton stared sightlessly at the face of his accuser with shock written all over his face.

Dalton's woman friend duly arrived later that night to find all the house lights turned off. The house was locked, and no one was there to answer the doorbell.

"He's bloody well stood me up, the bastard!" she cursed and did an about-turn.

It was the Latino maid who normally cleaned the house twice a week who found the body bound to the chair. She screamed when confronted by the gruesome sight. Holding her phone with trembling hands she rang her husband to ask what she should do. He advised that she should immediately leave the house without touching anything, and then phone the San Diego County Sheriff's Department. That is exactly what she did.

CHAPTER TWENTY-SEVEN

Donna Collins received news of Professor Dalton's murder from her colleagues the next morning. She passed the news on to Jack.

"Same MO. The same type of plastic bag and duct tape. Has to be our killer this time," said Jack. "That leaves just five Professors left from the group who secured positions overseas."

"That sighting of an East-European gang at Venice Beach, just a stone's throw from San Diego, may have been no coincidence," suggested Donna.

"We should place Professor Fallon at Harvard Medical School, and Simon Jackson at Johns Hopkins University under our protection. They're the only potential targets left now in the States."

"I'll have my FBI colleagues watch their houses, and track their movements. We'll tap their phones. I don't think we should warn Jackson though. He might do a runner, and then we wouldn't be in a position to help him?"

"Not sure I'm happy with that, but it's your jurisdiction. In any case, we can't rule out the possibility that either Jackson or Fallon is the killer rather than potential victims," responded Jack.

"We need to check where each of the people on Brown's list was at the time of each of the murders. I'll pass that job onto my FBI colleagues," suggested Donna.

"Sure, but for the UK professors, you'll need the support of the MET as the FBI has no jurisdiction in the UK. I can arrange that."

"The problem is the killer may have contracted out the killings to a gang of criminals. All the while he could be hiding blamelessly in his University or Institute office. Bentley's murder and the slaughter of Masuda's family were clearly carried out by a group of killers," reasoned Donna.

"Yes, I think you are right," replied Jack looking somewhat despondent.

"Where to now do you think?" asked Donna, looking equally downcast.

At that moment she received a phone call from one of her FBI colleagues. She signed off and turned back to Jack.

"Damn, the forensics on the Dalton crime scene are clean. There's no physical evidence. Just like with Bentley's murder. The killers are meticulous. We just can't get a break."

"Let's hope Brown's research turns up something," said Jack.

Jack picked up the list of staff members Brown had given him and inspected it carefully.

"We need to get back to the UK to question the other five Professors on the list who still work in the UK. There's an Associate Professor Gail St Johns from the Department of Anatomy, Professor Dick Richards from the Physiology Department, Professor Harry Moore from the Department of Genetics, Professor Graham Campbell from the Winslow Genetics Institute in Cambridge, and Professor Susan Jones from the Faculty of Medical Sciences at University College London. Let's try our luck for meetings without first getting appointments. We don't want to scare any of them away."

Jack and Donna took a British Airways flight direct from John F. Kennedy International Airport to London Heathrow. They travelled from London to Oxford on the M40 motorway in Jack's Range Rover, making good time due to little traffic congestion. The original building that had housed the Department of Physiology, Anatomy and Genetics now housed just the Department of Anatomy. It was an old brick building that had been affectionately renovated inside to a modern open plan design, which was now all the rage in offices and research institutes all over the world. Jack and Donna introduced themselves at reception. Jack asked whether A/Professor St Johns was available to meet with them. The receptionist made a phone call and told them that the Professor was available. A short time later a middle-aged woman with a large mop of unruly greying hair arrived. She wore thick black-rimmed glasses that gave her a rather stern appearance, and a jet black suit. After everyone had introduced themselves, she escorted them to a nearby meeting room on the ground floor of the building.

After they were all seated, Jack explained the reason for their visit, namely to understand the dynamics of the original Department fifteen years ago. In particular, they wanted to know what she thought of the three murdered Professors Bentley, Dalton, and Corbyn.

"I'm not sure I can be of any help. I wasn't on the same floor of the Department as them. Their research interests were very different from mine. My interests lie in anatomy, theirs was genetics."

"Nevertheless, you may have heard things. Was there anyone in the Department who might have held a grudge against them?"

"Not that I am aware of," came the reply.

"How was lab space allocated?"

"Each of the three disciplines occupied different areas of the building. When a Head of a Lab left the Department, the empty lab was filled by the new replacement. The replacement could be someone in the original lab who was senior enough to assume the Headship or another deserving Principal Investigator who needed a laboratory to expand his or her team. Or more often it was an outside appointee. It was often just good luck and timing if you managed to acquire a lab of reasonable size in an ideal position."

"I see," said Jack. "That makes sense."

"Did you ever attend any functions or meetings where frustrations or antagonism between colleagues may have crawled out of the woodwork?"

"Certainly not at the Anatomy and Physiology groups' functions and meetings. Each of the disciplines held its own functions and meetings. The Anatomists and Physiologists were in the minority. We stuck to ourselves. I can say now though, several of us thought the Genetic groups contained some big egos, so we avoided close association with those types whenever possible."

"Professor Corbyn was Head of the original Department. Would you say he was popular?"

"He wasn't well-liked by the Anatomists and Physiologists. Most of the money he acquired for the Department went on the Genetics research groups, or more often than not his own group. He hardly bothered to recognize the Anatomy and Physiology research groups. He treated us as outsiders, almost as if we were inferior, and had nothing substantial to offer. Splitting the Department based on the three disciplines has been a godsend. At least we are now getting our fare share of the University's block funding, and have been able to grow. Corbyn was a misogynist, like many men of his age and era. I wouldn't be surprised if he blocked my advancement when I first applied for promotion."

"I see...well, thank you for your time, Professor. We appreciate you being so frank," replied Jack.

"Hope I've been of some help," said Professor St Johns, smiling, and grateful to have been appreciated.

She escorted them outside the building. They met later with Professor Dick Richards from the Physiology Department. But he also had no personal knowledge of the history of staff in the Genetics groups. He was equally critical of Professor Corbyn."

"I don't think there is much point questioning anyone who didn't belong to one of the Genetics groups in the original Department," sighed Jack. "I'm guessing our killer was the head of one of those Genetics groups."

"Let's hope Professor Moore can provide more useful information," responded Donna.

They walked to the new Department of Genetics building, a short distance from the building that had housed the original Department. The attractive Department of Genetics building was state-of-the-art, built of steel and glass. Unfortunately, luck had abandoned them. The receptionist informed them that Professor Moore was away on conference leave. He was not due back until later in the week.

"Can I ask which conference he is attending," requested Jack, slightly disheartened.

"Certainly, he is attending the 10th International Conference on Genomics in San Diego. He is a plenary speaker there," she replied.

Jack immediately looked over to Donna, raising his eyebrows. Concern was written all over his face.

"Can we make an appointment to see him as soon as he returns? It's rather urgent."

"I'll ask the Department secretary to arrange it. She'll get back to you."

Jack handed the receptionist his business card, and they left the building. They strolled to the River Cherwell, and took a seat on a bench in a meadow of bright yellow daffodils near the riverbank. They relaxed and spent the time discussing the case.

The secretary phoned an hour later to confirm the appointment at 3.00 pm in four days time.

"I don't like it Jack," mentioned Donna. "Moore could have important information. He's in San Diego, close to where Professor Dalton was murdered. Perhaps we should get him protection. Or at least advise him he may be in danger."

"He's due back soon. I've heard these conferences have thousands of attendees and high security. He is hardly going to be in danger given all the potential witnesses. Let's look over that list again. I want to refresh my memory of who was in the Genetics cluster when Bentley and Corbyn were members of the

Department," said Jack extracting the list from his jacket pocket and unfolding it.

"Just to recount, there is Fallon now at Harvard Medical School and Simon Jackson at Johns Hopkins in Baltimore who are both currently under FBI surveillance. There is Brown, who is the current Head of the Department of Genetics. Kearney, who is under my protection. Moore, who is at that conference in San Diego near where Dalton was murdered. There is also Professor Graham Campbell from the Winslow Genetics Institute in Cambridge. A Professor Susan Jones from the Faculty of Medical Sciences at University College London. Finally, Professor Singer at the ICMB in Singapore."

"What about the two Professors who moved to Australia and New Zealand?" asked Donna.

"I think we can forget about them. One was a physiologist and the other an anatomist.

"Who of the Professors we know about so far do you think could be the killer?" asked Donna.

"Fallon and Brown seem unlikely killers. Jones is a woman and therefore statistically less likely to be the killer. So we are left with Moore, Campbell, Jackson, and Singer who we haven't yet met. I bet all four will be attending that Genetics conference in San Diego, given their interest in Genetics. I'll get Diana to check whether they are all delegates at the Conference," said Jack.

CHAPTER TWENTY-EIGHT

The 10th International Conference on the Human Genome was being held in the San Diego Convention Centre. The Centre is a massive construction on West Harbour Drive close to the shore. Its distinctive fibreglass sails reflect the maritime history of the region. The Centre is so large it can house more than one hundred thousand delegates.

Professor Graham Campbell was a short, bearded man, with bright penetrating eyes. He had longish fair hair that he let wash over his forehead. He was a family man with two energetic teenage boys. His young wife was used to him attending meetings and conferences all over the world. Nevertheless, she always worried about him while he was away. The boys were some comfort and a distraction. Professor Campbell had been invited to give one of the main plenary talks in the large ballroom of the Convention Centre. His talk was to be delivered as part of an international award he had recently received for his outstanding research work.

Professor Graham Campbell was a graduate of Edinburgh University. He had taken up a junior faculty position in the Department of Physiology, Anatomy, and Genetics upon graduating. He had been very successful at Oxford Bridge University, in part because of his talent and drive. But also by being part of Simon Jackson's scheme of exploiting their position as editorial board members. He subsequently secured a senior position as the Head of Genetics and Epigenetics at the Winslow Genetics Institute (WGI) in Cambridge. This was a highly sought-after position at a prestigious Institute that had envious levels of funding. Campbell realised early on that investigating genome variation was a "big boys" endeavour. Such studies had to be carried out at a scale that was not available to small lesser funded biomedical laboratories. Few Institutes worldwide could compete with the WGI for scale.

Campbell was a canny man who knew exactly how to grease the wheels to gain choice positions, promotions, and valuable collaborations. Whilst still only a junior Faculty member at Oxford Bridge University, he had purchased a house close to the residence of the Director of one of Britain's major medical research funding agencies. He would often bump into the Director at the local alehouse and coffee shop. Whether this was purely by chance or engineered, who can say? But having the Director's "ear" had its rewards. Soon he was Chair of the agency's grant assessing committee that made the final decisions as to who was to receive major funding in the field of Genetics. Where previously his research grant applications had just an average success rate in being funded, they were now always successful. And always fully funded. There is an old saying "don't bite the hand that feeds you". Potential grant applicants knew only too well the cost of harshly criticizing Campbell's grant applications. For it was Campbell who held their fates in the palms of his hands.

Graham Campbell was brought up in the highlands of Scotland. His father was the ghillie for a Laird who owned a large country estate north of the Cairngorms National Park. He had often accompanied his father on shooting parties to stalk red deer stags on the estate. It was his father's job to attend to the Laird whenever he ventured on a hunting or fishing expedition. Graham renewed his interest in the sport of hunting after discovering that the Director of the WGI was a passionate enthusiast. Graham was often included in shooting parties with the Director. Whether this was by chance or by good fortune, who can say. Sometimes he just happened to meet up with the Director at the lodges afterward. Some of those overlooked for the position of Head of Genetics and Epigenetics at the WGI were somewhat surprised at how young Graham was to be invited to the position. They were equally perplexed why Graham and the Director got along so well when they were not even relatives. It was often said of the man, in quiet places, that he made friends with nobody except those who could advance his career.

The ballroom was packed with four thousand attendees. Campbell's talk was being simulcast onto three large projection screens. The lights of the room had been dimmed considerably to intensify the coloured images he was showing on each screen. Campbell was a confident, engaging, and experienced speaker. He was in his element. He enjoyed being the centre of attention. The award he had received was nothing more than what he deserved. He was nearing the end of his one-hour lecture. He had introduced the audience to the Winslow Genetics Institute (WGI). He had described its goal which was to understand genome variation in humans and other living creatures. The results were expected to provide insights into evolution, acquired mutations, and their biological consequences. The massive scale of their work involved the sequencing of the genomes of tens to hundreds of thousands of individuals. Such a feat was well beyond the capability and resources of almost all other research centres in Britain. Research in genetics had been forged by early pioneers working in near isolation in small laboratories. In a relatively short timespan, it had evolved into an undertaking almost unparalleled by any other modern-day industry in terms of size, cost, and complexity.

Campbell proceeded to list the future goals of the Institute. The audience was spell-bound, listening intently to every fact and detail in case they happened to miss something. All eyes were fixed on the big screens. Nobody noticed the slight ruffle of the curtain at the front side of the stage. Protruding from the curtain was the end of a silencer attached to a Smith & Wesson pistol. Yet again, Graham Campbell was part of a hunt, only this time it was different. This time he was the prey. Only those seated at the very front heard the soft sound as the two jacketed soft-point bullets left the barrel. But everyone to their horror witnessed their impact. Campbell was leaning on the lectern staring out at his audience as the bullets entered his brain, blasting away the left side of his head. The impact exploded bones, blood, and brain material all over the floor. Immediately, there was widespread panic. Attendees at the front of the room dropped to the floor in front of their chairs. Those at the back made a frantic dash for the exits. Two security guards positioned at either side of the room dashed through the terrified crowd as best as they could to get to the curtain where they thought the shooter had been. But they were too late to see the killer quickly slip away.

A GoPro camera had been mounted on the barrel of the silencer, which captured the killing in exquisite detail. Footage of the killing was sent within the hour to a man who was eagerly waiting to receive it. The man grinned as he watched footage of Campbell's head exploding all over the stage. He took time to remember all the grievances he held against Graham Campbell, including personal attacks by Campbell in reviews of his unsuccessful grant applications, being deliberately omitted from e-mails announcing important meetings, being told by other staff that they had heard Campbell slagging him off to influential people, having insults hurled at him in his office by Campbell after success in obtaining a research grant, and these were just a few of his grievances.

The grievances were many and varied. In particular, he remembered the time Graham begged him for a novel gene his laboratory had just cloned. Before he gave Graham the gene he had made him solemnly promise he wouldn't undertake the same work being undertaken by Lucas, his PhD student. The student had been working for two years on the novel gene, but was making slow progress. He had received the promise verbally but never sought the same in writing. Graham colluded with Jim Dalton, and together they put their two best post-doctoral research fellows to work on the novel gene. They published the results in just six months, destroying his PhD student's efforts, as his work was no longer publishable or original which is a prerequisite for doctoral studies.

"This one's for you Lucas" he whispered, as he replayed the footage of Campbell's exploding head.

CHAPTER TWENTY-NINE

Professor John Fallon made inquiries and had soon obtained the cell phone numbers of his former colleagues Professors Simon Jackson and Harry Moore. Using the phone in his office at the Harvard Medical School, he first phoned Simon Jackson.

"Simon, it's your old colleague John Fallon here. Look, I've just heard through the grapevine that Graham Campbell was shot while delivering his plenary lecture at a conference in San Diego. Maybe you haven't been keeping up with the media releases, but Richard Bentley was murdered just days ago in the woods at Lake Tahoe. And David Corbyn recently committed suicide on the London Underground. The murders of two and maybe three of our colleagues can't just be a coincidence, can it? Should we be worried?"

"Hello John. You're one of the last people I'd expect to hear from again. I'd heard you had moved to the Harvard Medical School. I am currently attending the Conference you just mentioned. I witnessed the whole ghastly affair. Graham was nearing the end of his award talk when some maniac shot him in the head in front of everyone, right there on the stage. His brains and blood were splattered all over the place. I can tell you, I'm pretty shaken up. The local police are here in force, so it should be safe enough now. Yes, I'd seen the news coverage of Bentley's murder. Look, I'm not all that surprised that Bentley and Campbell were murdered. They were obnoxious and probably had made plenty of enemies. I understood from the press releases that Corbyn had committed suicide, poor bastard, so you can count him out?"

"I had a visit here at the Medical School from a detective over from the UK who said he was treating Corbyn's death as a probable murder. I read an article in the "Boston Globe" which mentioned that Bentley's killing was believed to be the work of a group of

177

professional criminals. I have to admit I'm scared. Do you think we could be the killers' next targets?"

"What nonsense. Face it, Bentley and Campbell were a couple of sinners. There's no doubt about that. They got what they deserved. It's probably just a coincidence they were murdered a week apart. I don't think we should be worried at all."

"You're not involved in the killings are you Simon?" asked Fallon, sheepishly.

"How dare you suggest that! Of course I'm not, what an idiotic suggestion. I've got to go. I've got better things to do with my time. There's a lecture about to get underway that I'm interested in attending."

Outraged at Fallon's suggestion, Simon Jackson placed his cell phone back in his jacket pocket.

"It beats me how that prick managed to obtain a senior position at Harvard University. The bastard likely bought his way in. If I had my way he'd be cleaning the bogs in the municipal toilets," he mused, smiling to himself at the thought.

John Fallon next phoned Harry Moore. He repeated what he had told Simon Jackson.

"I just spoke with Simon Jackson, who's at the same conference you're attending. He said he wasn't worried. He told me that Bentley and Campbell probably deserved to be murdered, that they were being punished for some sin they'd committed," said John Fallon sounding concerned.

"That's a dreadful thing to say. That's typical of Simon. He always believed he was "holier than thou". I'm sure he would have loved a job as a hanging judge, so he could deliver guilty verdicts upon all the defendants. I was also at Graham's lecture. It was absolutely shocking. He never deserved to die like that. These murders are too much of a coincidence, aren't they?"

"I had a visit from a detective over from the UK who thought Bentley may have been involved, but he can't be the killer as he's dead. The news coverage I've seen says law enforcement suspects the killer is in control of a group of criminals. More to the point, they suspect the mastermind behind the killings is one of our Oxford colleagues. I can't believe it, can you? Who do you think it could be?" asked John Fallon.

"If you ask me, Simon has to be the most likely candidate. He's always so full of religious vindictiveness. But then again we all treated Peter Singer badly. I wasn't the worst. Corbyn treated him as if he was dirt. I'm amazed Peter stayed at Oxford Bridge for as long as he did. He moved to Singapore, didn't he? I read a press release that said the men that killed Bentley were suspected East Europeans, and not Asians, so that doesn't fit. I don't mind admitting I'm scared. What do you think we should do?"

"Just between us, I'm going to take leave from the University immediately, and hide out for a while until the mastermind and whoever else is involved is apprehended. What about you?" asked Fallon.

"There are police crawling all over the conference venue. I'm going to ask them for protection, at least until the conference is over. Then I'm going to get out of here on a plane back to the UK as fast as possible."

"Good idea. I'd be grateful if you would phone me if you learn anything about the murders. Here's my phone number."

John Fallon and Professor Moore exchanged contact details and wished each other well.

CHAPTER THIRTY

D onna received news of Professor Campbell's murder from her FBI colleagues and passed it on to Jack.

"Shit!" exclaimed Jack, annoyed. "We are in the wrong bloody country. Damn it, we thought they'd be safe being surrounded by thousands of delegates. We should have offered all of them protection. We should have pulled them out of there, out of harm's way, consent or no consent. Let's catch the next flight to San Diego. It seems we have a conference to attend."

"In the meantime, I'll get my colleagues to keep an eye on the four Professors attending the conference. At least we can now eliminate Campbell as a suspect. This is getting a bit like playing dominos. One by one they fall like in an Agatha Christie movie."

Jack and Donna took the non-stop Heathrow Express from Paddington to the airport, a journey of just fifteen minutes. There they caught a British Airways flight bound for San Diego. Packing light, they took a Yellow Cab taxi from the San Diego airport and were outside the Conference venue on West Harbour Drive within an hour of landing. Donna's FBI colleagues had advised her that they had Professors Jackson, Moore, and Jones guarded by Agents at the conference. Singer though was still in Singapore with no intention of attending the Conference, and Fallon was at the Harvard Medical School, taking care of his Division's business.

Jack and Donna were exhausted after their flight and now were faced with having to avoid the usual groupings of street vagrants outside the Convention Centre. Upon entering the Convention Centre, they were overwhelmed by what they saw. The Centre was crammed wall to wall with at least fifteen thousand attendees, all busy socializing with one another.

"Thank goodness your men have our three guys under surveillance. Otherwise, it would take far too much effort to find them amongst this horde?" exclaimed Jack.

Donna immediately rang Agent Pitt who had Professor Jackson under surveillance.

"Is there any useful intel on Jackson's recent movements?"

"Sorry boss. There has been nothing unusual about his activities, and phone calls. He'd been at work at Johns Hopkins before coming here. He can't have killed those other three Professors," replied Agent Pitt.

"Where was he when Campbell was murdered?"

"He attended Campbell's plenary. But it just wasn't possible to track him with the lights so dim, and the packed-out audience. He could have slipped out, or even shot Campbell for all we know."

"He could still have contracted the criminal gang to murder the other Professors, and shoot Campbell. Where is Jackson now?"

"He's currently in the Exhibit Hall at ground level checking out the industry booths. He's a tall, reasonably overweight, loud-mouthed guy. You can't miss him. Right now he's with the Illumina display checking out the next generation of DNA sequencers. It's booth number 214. You should see how much each of those machines costs. Only the size of a suitcase, but damn near costs the price of my house."

"Have you learned anything about him?"

"He's a family man, loves his wife and three kids, a boy maybe fourteen, and girls about ten and six. He's always phoning them."

"Make sure he doesn't leave there. I want to speak with him."

Jack and Donna found their way to booth 214 among the thousands of attendees, and Pitt pointed out Professor Jackson. He was still talking with the Illumina representatives in their booth which displayed DNA sequencing machines and microarray technologies. As described by Pitt, Jackson was a tall, overweight man, with a head of thick ginger hair. He was wearing brown corduroy pants held up by braces, looking like a figure out of the seventies. His voice was very loud and demanding. He could be heard several booths away. Jack stepped forward behind him and gently tapped him on the shoulder. Jackson turned to face Jack, looking decidedly annoyed to have his conversation with an Illumina representative interrupted.

"Yes, what do you want?" he shouted harshly after turning around to face Jack.

"Professor Jackson, we need to talk with you urgently. My name is Jack Baron. I am a private investigator, previously from Scotland Yard in the UK. This is Special Agent Collins and Agent Pitt of the FBI," said Jack pointing out his colleagues. "We have reason to believe you are in grave danger."

"What? Poppycock!" shouted Jackson, laughing heartedly at the suggestion.

"You do realize Professor Campbell, a previous colleague of yours, was shot and murdered yesterday right here at this Conference?"

"How could I not know? Everyone at the Conference is talking about it. I was at Campbell's talk and witnessed the whole affair. The poor man had his brains blasted all over the stage. Grisly spectacle. But look at this place now. It's like Fort Knox. It's crawling with police and security guards everywhere you look. Besides I can't help it if Graham upset someone enough to get himself killed. If you ask me he was always bound to make enemies."

"We have good reason to believe that someone is systematically executing certain former members of your old Department at Oxford Bridge University. Did you know Professors Corbyn, Bentley, and Dalton?"

"Yes, of course, they are all former colleagues of mine."

"Well, they have all recently been murdered."

"I read the news coverage on the killing of Richard Bentley, and the suicide of David Corbyn. But you're now saying Jim Dalton has been murdered?"

"That's correct. He was killed yesterday at his home just north of here on the La Jolla Shores Beach. News coverage about the killing will likely be released soon."

"What? That's appalling. So my Oxford colleagues are being deliberately murdered, one by one, you say. Do you know who the killer is? What are you doing to catch him?"

"We don't know who is doing this, but we're hoping you might be able to help us in that regard. We don't want to ruin your conference, but we'd appreciate it if you could make time with us later today to answer some questions."

"You can't possibly think I'm involved?" exclaimed Jackson looking distinctly indignant.

"We have reason to believe that the same killer or killers who murdered Professor Campbell may still be at large at this venue. You could be in grave danger, despite the heightened security. You and your former colleagues Professor Harry Moore and Susan Jones, who are also attending this conference, could be the killer's next targets."

"That's crazy. I don't have any enemies," blurted Jackson. "Or none that I know of," he said more meekly and beginning to sweat profusely.

"That may well be the case, but for your safety, you should not leave Agent Pitt's side."

"Agent Pitt will guard you during the rest of your attendance at the Conference," stated Donna. "We would be grateful if you could name a place and time that are convenient to meet with us to answer a few questions. Think about it and pass the details on to Agent Pitt and he will contact us."

Donna pocketed her cell phone after speaking with Special Agent Bergman who had Professor Moore under surveillance.

"Moore is in the Sails Pavilion on the upper floor checking out some of the industry displays. I'm told he's at the GeneScript booth number 94 looking at something called CRISPR genome editing reagents. Bergman says CRISPR technology is so amazing it can be used to permanently change your genes," reported Donna.

"Sounds like science fiction come true," replied Jack.

Donna and Jack took the lift to the upper floor of the building. They found their way to Booth 94 by reading the signage at the ends of the aisles of booths, much like you'd see at the end of supermarket aisles. Professor Moore was standing near Agent Bergman. Moore was a metrosexual-looking man of small stature. He was immaculately dressed, his trousers and shirt carefully pressed, and his hair precisely coiffured. Donna introduced Jack to Agent Bergman.

"What do you know about Moore's movements?" Donna asked Bergman quietly.

"We co-opted the help of the Met in the UK. They tapped Moore's phone. There's been nothing suspicious about his phone calls and movements since the killings began."

Jack and Donna walked over and introduced themselves to Professor Moore, and explained the situation.

"You're frightening me. So you think I am in danger? What are you going to do about it? A former Oxford Bridge University colleague John Fallon rang me just a few minutes ago. He said he'd heard about the news of all the killings and was frightened for his safety. He told me he was going to hide out somewhere until the killers were caught. Are you going to protect me? I require somewhere safe to stay under your protection. You know, like a safe-house ... maybe," stammered Professor Moore, being flustered and anxious.

"Special Agent Bergman will continue to guard you while you are at the conference," answered Donna, pointing out the Agent.

"No, that just won't do. A single man against an army of killers," pleaded Moore, almost out of control.

"If you look around you will see that the conference organizers have recruited the assistance of a large number of officers from the San Diego Police Department. Likely, the killer or killers will have since fled the scene," replied Donna, giving Jack a look of uncertainty.

"Well then, Special Agent Bergman I am expecting you to protect me," declared Moore, looking unhappy.

Donna gave instructions to Bergman, and she and Jack walked to the nearest police officer.

"Is your Chief here?" asked Donna, holding out her FBI badge for the officer to inspect.

"He's probably in the Conference Manager's Office on the ground floor, Agent Collins, working on security options."

Jack and Donna took the lift to the ground floor and located the Manager's Office. Jack knocked on the door. The door was opened by a tall, swarthy, powerfully built man in his mid-fifties wearing the uniform of the San Diego Police Department. Donna stepped forward and held out her FBI badge, and introduced Jack.

"What can I do for you? I am Chief David Strong of the San Diego Police Department. This is Ben Lewis who manages this site. Is this to do with the killing yesterday?" queried the Chief.

"We believe the murder of Professor Campbell yesterday is connected with the recent murder of Professor Jim Dalton in La Jolla, and with the murders of other academics near Lake Tahoe, and in London," stated Donna.

"Do you have any useful information you can give us on the murders of Dalton and Campbell?" asked Jack.

"What I can tell you is that neighbours reported Dalton being visited by a woman of below-average height with short blond hair around the time of the murder. Dalton enjoyed the company of several women friends. He was a bachelor after going through what appeared to be a nasty divorce. Sightings of women coming and going from his house weren't unusual or unexpected. Unfortunately, forensics didn't find anything useful. The bag and duct tape used to suffocate Dalton were clean. They could have been purchased at any hardware or grocery store. As for Campbell, forensics is working on the wound ballistics, splatter pattern, and bullet fragments. The audience at the front of the room reported hearing two shots being fired in rapid succession. The shots were muffled, hence must have been fired from a silencer. The killer fired using a small-bore weapon, almost certainly a pistol, from behind the curtains at the side of the room. No shell casings were found. I'm afraid it's going to be tough to get anything useful. What I can say is that the killer must have been experienced with pistols. Getting a precise headshot with a pistol at that distance was impressive."

"Three colleagues of Dalton and Campbell are attending the conference. They are Professors Simon Jackson, Harry Moore, and Susan Jones. They are currently in the trade rooms on the upper and ground floors," offered Donna, handing over photographs of the three Professors.

"We think they may be the next targets if the killer is still here. That seems unlikely given the presence of your men. Having said that we can't rule out the possibility that one of the two male Professors is our killer. We have Special Agents Bergman and Pitt guarding them. Special Agent Rivera is guarding Susan Jones."

"I've positioned three hundred of my men from various San Diego stations at the entrances and exits to each room in the facility," said the Chief. 'I'll have some of my men keep an eye on your Professors, without crowding them. The men have been cautioned to watch for anything out of the ordinary. It's going to be a challenge. It's a huge site with fifteen thousand attendees, but we'll do our best."

CHAPTER THIRTY-ONE

Professor Susan Jones was being guarded by Agent Rivera in the Exhibit Hall on the ground level. She had been checking out the industry booths for the latest items of equipment and research tools that could be useful for her research work. She was now talking with an old colleague who had taken a position as a rep for one of the many pharmaceutical companies attending the conference. They were discussing their families and relationships when Jack and Donna interrupted their conversation.

"Can we have a word? It's important," requested Donna, holding up her FBI badge.

"Yes ... OK," replied Susan, taken aback by the sudden intrusion.

"We'd like to talk with you in private," clarified Donna.

"Ohh.... OK. Sorry Jane. Catch up with you later," apologized Susan to her ex-colleague, looking slightly embarrassed.

Susan's friend backed away, frowning, and looking concerned that her colleague was about to be questioned by an FBI agent.

Donna and Jack led Susan to a quiet area of the floor and introduced themselves.

"Is this something to do with the murder of Graham Campbell? I was there at his talk when he was shot. That poor man was a previous colleague of mine. You know he has a wife and two children. My sympathies go out to them."

"We don't want to unnecessarily frighten you, but there is the possibility you are also in danger. Three of your other colleagues from your days at Oxford have also recently been murdered. We believe Professor Corbyn did not commit suicide as reported in the press but rather was murdered on the London Underground. Richard Bentley was murdered at his sister's cabin at Lake Tahoe, and Jim Dalton was recently murdered at his home near San Diego.

187

"Oh my gosh! That's dreadful. Do you have any idea who is responsible?"

"We had hoped that you might have an idea. We believe the killer, who is somehow linked to a group of East-European criminals, is one of your previous Oxford colleagues. He's probably someone from one of the genetics groups. This person appears to be on some sort of personal vendetta."

"Oh, no...that can't be. No, I don't know anything about these killings, or who could be responsible. I'm telling you right now, I am not going to stay around here just to end up like Graham. I demand a police escort to the airport. Right now! I'm taking the first flight back to the UK. I'm not staying around here to be shot at."

"Please calm down. We'll arrange an escort for you with Chief Strong from the San Diego Police Department. He is here heading the police protection unit for the conference. We'll also be returning to the UK shortly. We may want to speak with you again. In the meantime, we ask you to give some thought as to anything you can recollect from your time at Oxford that may have a bearing on this case."

Donna and Jack led Susan down to the basement and introduced her to Chief Strong. The San Diego Police Department assumed responsibility for her protection.

Donna turned to Jack once they were out of earshot.

"Do you think the killer would murder a woman?"

"Remember the mother and daughter of that Japanese family were murdered along with male members of the family. The killers don't seem to care about gender. I'll arrange for the MET to provide protection as soon as Professor Jones arrives back in the UK."

CHAPTER THIRTY-TWO

A gent Bergman was now a fixture at Professor Moore's side, and San Diego police officers trailed the two men. Moore had visited most of the trade booths in the Sails Pavilion that interested him. He had discussed various items of equipment and reagents with the company representatives in charge of the displays. His energy levels were severely diminished from all the walking and talking. Moore was an alcoholic and was tired of all the business talk. He badly wanted a change of scene.

"I need a bloody drink, and soon," thought Moore to himself.

Moore's obsession with alcohol was by no means benign. After just two glasses of an alcoholic drink, his whole personality changed like that of Dr Jekyll and Mr. Hyde. He was transformed from a thoughtful, kind, and generous Irishman into an evil Mr. Hyde. Once inebriated he would spew forth venomous and crude insults at anyone who dared to associate with him. Insults would include anything from disgust at a reluctance to partake in his drinking binges, to your or your wife's perceived sexual proclivities. Anything was fair game. The cruder the better. Nobody, not even his closest friends chose to drink with the man. Even in the light of sobriety the next day, his opinion of you could have been irrevocably changed for the worst. He would have inflated any perceived slight to an act of war. For his colleagues, this meant trashing their research grant applications, submitted manuscripts, or applications for promotion, no matter how distant their relationship had become.

Moore was a graduate of Trinity College Dublin, Dublin University. He had a quick and sharp mind. He managed to hold down a job, despite his often degenerate behaviour. This was in part due to his incredible ability to metabolize alcohol. He would often be seen inebriated late at night. But by the following morning, his brainpower was as sharp as ever. The only giveaway of the previous night's activities was pools of blood in place of his eyes. He was tolerated at the Department of Genetics at Oxford Bridge.

Moore was very protective of his research on genetics to the point of being somewhat schizophrenic. He would challenge his colleagues if he thought they were undertaking similar research. He would threaten to destroy them if they were. In the dog world, he would be labelled as having "small dog syndrome". His alcohol-induced split personality would not have been tolerated in the corporate world. Fortunately, academia was far more tolerant. It appreciated diversity in all its forms. Moore's anti-social behaviour generated enemies, hence he struggled to obtain grant funding to pursue his academic research proposals.

Moore was still very anxious about his safety but was adamant that he was going to attend the lectures that interested him.

"There's a lecture by Professor Poyton I want to attend," he advised Agent Bergman. "It's in theatre 29D."

"Great," replied Bergman. "My chance to catch up on all the education I missed out on. Look, if it is going to be a long talk then I need to use the bathroom first."

They walked and located room 29D. Only a few people were milling around outside the room catching up with their colleagues. The lecture session wasn't due to start for another ten minutes. Most delegates were often tardy in getting back on time to the venues after lunch. A few San Diego police officers had shadowed Moore and Bergman and were standing close by. One happened to station himself across from the toilet next to the lecture room. Agent Bergman approached the officer.

"Can you make sure no harm comes to this gentleman while I use the bathroom, he is currently under FBI and police protection," he requested holding up his FBI badge and pointing to Moore.

"Certainly, no problem," replied the officer with a distinctive European accent.

"I shan't be long," Bergman advised Moore.

After entering the restroom Bergman positioned himself by the urinal. Looking around he could see there was nobody else in the restroom. As Bergman started to unzip his fly a San Diego police officer entered. The officer went to use one of the cubicles, but then suddenly turned and lunged at Bergman. He reached out and forcibly held a cloth soaked in an anaesthetic over the Agent's mouth. At first, Bergman struggled, but he was quickly overcome. He was dragged and unceremoniously dumped in one of the toilet cubicles. The officer exited the restroom and nodded to a colleague waiting outside with Moore.

"Our Chief of Police is very concerned for your safety. He wants to increase your protection. Please accompany us," the officer said to Moore.

"Well at last someone is taking my safety seriously. I still want to attend Poyton's lecture though," exclaimed Moore as he followed the two officers into a small meeting room, room 28A.

The room was not being used for the Conference. One of the two officers closed and locked the door as they entered. As soon as the door was locked, the other officer grabbed Moore from behind. He clamped Moore's wrists behind his back with handcuffs.

"What is the meaning of this?" protested Moore, struggling with the handcuffs.

"We have reason to believe you are the killer everyone is looking for," answered the officer with a wide grin, winking at his colleague.

He dragged Moore to one of the several chairs in the room and forced him to sit.

"That's preposterous. I am not the killer. I'm innocent. I want to see your superior immediately. Your job is to protect me!" shouted the agitated Professor indignantly.

"Now, now Professor. There is no need to get angry. We are only doing our jobs," said the officer winking again to his companion.

"Uncuff me at once. I want to speak with your superior," pleaded Moore.

At that moment one of the officers strapped a personal CAM to his chest. The other officer took a plastic bag and duct tape out of his pocket. Then he stood behind Moore and placed the plastic bag over their captive's head, and sealed it at the neck with duct tape.

CHAPTER THIRTY-THREE

"There is something wrong. Bergman is not answering his cell phone," shouted Donna to Jack.

"Get hold of Chief Strong. Tell him to get his men to search every room in the building for Moore. Tell him Moore was last seen on the upper floor. I'll start searching the east end there. You take the west end."

Jack and Donna took the lift to the upper floor. Attendees now coming back from lunch were starting to mill in greater numbers around the entrances to the lecture rooms. Jack raced around the east end of the upper floor looking for anything that looked out of place. He noticed that the door to one of the rooms was closed, unlike most of the rest. He tried the door, but it was locked. Inside the room the two men wearing police uniforms looked at one another, startled by the noise at the door. They ignored the interference, presuming it must be one of the attendees who had either got lost or was seeking out a quiet place to work. Instead, just a few seconds later there was a mighty crack as the door frame shattered and the door gave way to a charging two hundred and sixty-pound ex-All Black rugby forward.

Standing in the doorway, Jack was initially confused by the scene. Moore was sitting in a chair. His head was slumped forward covered by a plastic bag. In front of him was an officer of the San Diego Police Department. Jack failed to glimpse the other officer standing aside from the door opening. Both police imposters were big men. They'd had years of practice as enforcers in global crime. The officer standing by the door hit out with his clenched fist aiming for Jack's temple. Jack glimpsed the movement out of the corner of his eye. He instinctively pulled his head back just in time. The flying fist only glanced his head. Whilst the man was unbalanced, Jack slammed his right fist into the man's nose. The blow forced nasal bone, cartilage, and the lower frontal bone into the man's brain. He was sent crashing to the floor. He was dead before he hit the ground. The other officer quickly came to his partner's aid, slamming his fist into Jack's right kidney. Jack bent over, wincing with pain. He was about to strike back when the officer fled through the open doorway.

Instead of chasing after the imposter, Jack rushed to aid Professor Moore sitting slumped in the chair. He first removed the plastic bag from his head. He then picked the Professor up into his arms, and carefully laid him down on the floor face upwards. He immediately applied CPR, making chest compressions and rescue breaths for twenty minutes. Finally, after getting no response he admitted defeat. The man was dead, and there was nothing further that could be done for him.

Jack pulled out his cell phone and phoned for an ambulance. He then rang Donna.

"I found Moore in Room 28A at the far eastern end of the floor. I was too late. He's dead. I've rung for an ambulance. The police cordon has been compromised. Members of the east-European gang are posing as San Diego police officers. Tell Chief Strong to be on the lookout for imposters in police uniform. Jackson has to be the killer. He's the only Oxford Bridge University Professor left here. I'll meet you on the ground floor where he was last seen. You can arrest him, and read him his rights."

Jack dragged the dead bodies out of sight behind the lectern at the front of the room. He searched the clothing of the police imposter, but there was nothing to identify him. He took the lift down to the ground floor. He quickly explained to Chief Strong where he had left the dead bodies. He then headed for the commotion at the end of a row of trade booths. Donna, Agent Pitt, and three San Diego police officers had Professor Jackson surrounded. Donna had read him his rights. One of the officers handcuffed him.

CHAPTER THIRTY-FOUR

Simon Jackson was raised in the bible belt of America. His father was a man with a reserved nature, who preached as a Baptist minister in the small town of Lafayette in Tennessee. The family lived in a small wooden bungalow provided by the church. They were dependent almost solely on the salary the church provided, and any gratuities from church ceremonies. There were few if any luxuries, but the family was happy and fulfilled. They were community-spirited and would do anything they thought would improve the well-being of their fellow human beings, both at home and abroad.

As a young boy, Simon vividly remembered the day the evangelistic Southern Baptist minister Hank Rogers came to preach in nearby Nashville. The family all dressed in their finest clothes travelled to Nashville by car to attend the rally. It was the largest gathering of Christians Simon had ever seen in his life. More than one hundred thousand Christians had gathered to hear the great man preach at one of his "crusades". Simon was awe-struck when Hank Rogers stood up onto the podium to preach. A tall man, Hank Rogers, towered above the crowd. His booming voice reached out across the congregation imploring the attendees to Christian fellowship. All the while a choir, that sounded like angels, sang in the background. Young Simon decided there and then that he would take up his father's profession. But it would be with the evangelistic fervour of Hank Rogers that his father so palpably lacked.

If it hadn't been for a twist of fate, Simon Jackson would have followed in his father's footsteps. Instead his science teacher, in Simon's last year of high school, had taken a small group of the brightest boys to Vanderbilt University. The occasion was to hear a lecture given by Professor Julian Collingwood. Collingwood was a distinguished scientist who would later become Director of the

NIH and receive the Presidential Medal of Freedom. Simon was awe-struck by the man. Professor Collingwood expounded upon the idea of sequencing the entire human genome, the blueprint of life. More than that, he was outspoken about his religious faith, promoting the idea of theistic evolution, with science and faith in perfect harmony.

That night asleep in bed, God had come to Simon, calling upon him to study the DNA blueprint of life. God had designed human DNA as a vehicle for the creation and advancement of mankind. Simon Jackson was a very bright lad, as testified by his high SAT score at the end of his final year at school. He received offers from most of the Ivy League Universities. He chose to study at Johns Hopkins University in Baltimore, which has one of the top medical schools in the country. He obtained a medical degree there, followed by a doctorate in biomedicine. After excelling there, he went to Oxford Bridge University in the UK to take up post-doctoral study. This eventually landed him a junior faculty position in the Department of Physiology, Anatomy and Genetics at Oxford Bridge University.

Simon Jackson was appalled that less than half of the people in the UK had religious faith. Even worse, many of his fellow science colleagues had a complete disinterest in faith. He saw it as his duty to ensure that everyone knew about the biblical interpretation of evolution and the meaning of life. His evangelical fervour also extended to ensuring that everyone received their just rewards according to his interpretation of biblical scripture. He had taken after his mother's side of the family and had a stature similar to that of his idol Hank Rogers. He had a loud booming voice to match. He never failed to speak his mind. He was particularly zealous in his criticism of the wealthy, often reflecting on his own pious and frugal upbringing. He would often remind himself and others of the biblical saying that "it is easier for a camel to go through the eye of a needle than for a rich person to enter the Kingdom of God."

Simon Jackson railed against criticisms expounded by non-believers that God was not benign. Had they not heard of the eternal fight between good and evil, between God and Satan? It was Satan that slew the innocents. It was God who saved them. He railed against arguments that humans had no soul. One day science would be able to explain the ethereal composition of the soul. Even after the great scientific advancements of the past two hundred years by the likes of Newton and Einstein, physicists could still not explain the nature of gravity. They still couldn't explain the composition of dark matter and dark energy that make up most of the matter in the universe. They still could not explain how in quantum physics a single atom can exist in two places at the same time. They still could not explain why time stands still at the edges of black holes found in the centre of almost every large galaxy. How gravitational forces there are so strong that nothing can escape from them, not even light. Surely such extraordinary feats that defy the laws of physics are only possible by the hand of God.

Simon Jackson was a workaholic, aiming to prove to God that he was worthy of his favours, and hopefully worthy of entering the Kingdom of Heaven. He believed it was divine intervention that he had met Mary while they were both doctoral students at Johns Hopkins University. They had married on the eve of departing for Oxford. Most importantly, Mary shared his faith. She accepted that marriage to Simon would mean the end of her academic career. She was a buxom, motherly, woman who relished home-making and motherhood. Soon the couple had three children to nurture. Their roles in the family were pre-established according to scripture. She submitted to Simon, who was the leader and provider.

Simon would rise early each day and would expect Mary to have breakfast ready for him. He would work long hours from Monday to

Saturday, and expect his meal to be ready on his return home. Dinner was always followed by one hour of religious devotion, reading from various sections of the bible, and ending in prayers for the family, other important persons, and worldly causes. Simon would continue working from home until going to bed just before midnight. He would allow himself one night off from work on Saturdays. The children would be put to bed early, the couple would wash, and then Mary would give herself to Simon. The fulfillment of her own desires was never discussed or of any significance. She would aim to please Simon, as women have pleased men since the time of Adam and Eve. Sundays were always a day of rest and religious devotion. Simon and Mary attended a Baptist Church a stone's throw from their house. They liked the minister there. But Simon had to admit that he was a far cry from the charismatic and evangelical Hank Rogers.

CHAPTER THIRTY-FIVE

J ackson was bellowing like a mother cow for its lost calf.

"I'm not your bloody killer. Unhand me. I want a lawyer," he was hollering, breathing heavily, and sweating profusely.

"We'll take him to the holding cells downtown," said one officer.

"Wait, let me see your badges," the lead officer replied, eyeing his two officer companions with suspicion.

Each officer presented his badge.

"You might like to follow us to the station. You can interrogate Professor Jackson there," offered the lead officer, looking at Donna and Jack.

The three officers, Jack, Donna, and her FBI colleague escorted a still protesting Jackson to the underground car park to an awaiting all-wheel-drive Ford Interceptor utility vehicle emblazoned with San Diego Police Department lettering and the logo "To Protect and Serve". The three officers and Jackson climbed into the police vehicle and drove off. Jack and the FBI colleagues followed in a black FBI Chevrolet Suburban SUV, not emblazoned with any logos. Jackson had given up pleading by the time the leading car had passed two blocks. He sat sulking and uncomfortable in the plastic seat in the back of the vehicle. The cars slowed down and pulled up at a stoplight at an intersection. Reminiscent of a gangster movie sequence, the driver of the lead vehicle rapidly drew his revolver from its holster and shot the officer in the front passenger seat through his temple. He swivelled just in time to take down the lead officer in the back seat with a shot to his forehead. The stoplight turned green and the driver floored the accelerator causing the vehicle with its four-litre V6 engine to rocket forward into the traffic with tyres squealing. All the while Jackson was screaming in horror.

"Don't shoot me, don't shoot!" he screamed.

"What the hell! Who is shooting at who?" yelled Pitt who was driving the trailing FBI vehicle on witnessing the shootings in the car in front.

"Shit..., follow them!" shrieked Donna.

Pitt accelerated the five-litre V8 engine, forcing the occupants backwards into their seats. A desperate chase ensued. Time and again the Chevrolet almost caught up to the Ford Interceptor, weaving in and out of the traffic. The occupants were being flung around the interior of the vehicles like rag dolls. Then without warning the Ford Interceptor jumped across the median barrier into the oncoming traffic. It narrowly avoided hitting a large Freightliner. After completing a one-eighty degree turn, it accelerated out of sight.

"Damn, damn..., damn!" shouted Pitt, braking heavily and slamming both hands repeatedly against the steering wheel.

"There must have been a police imposter accomplice in the car. With his help, Jackson has got away!" Jack exclaimed, echoing everyone's thoughts.

Donna immediately put out an APB giving details of the police vehicle and its direction. The dejected Agents and Jack returned to the Conference centre where they met with Chief Strong.

"I've engaged a large portion of the San Diego police force to track Jackson and his accomplice to bring them to justice," said Strong.

"I'm returning to the UK tomorrow," replied Jack. We need to identify any other potential targets who spent time with Jackson at Oxford Bridge University. The key will be to try and understand his motive. I have a client in the UK who is under my protection. There is also a Professor Fallon, who is Head of the Human Genetics Division at the Harvard Medical School in Boston. He told Moore he was going into hiding until the killers were apprehended. Donna, you and your FBI colleagues will need to find him and place him under protection. There are other potential targets scattered further

200

afield including Professor Singer in Singapore. Chief, did you get an ID on the dead police imposter who killed Moore?"

"Sorry, only Moore's body was in the room," answered Chief Strong.

"Damn," exclaimed Jack. "Someone must have collected the body so it couldn't be identified."

"What about Professor Susan Jones? We'll need to talk with her. Did she get a flight back to the UK?"

"Yes, my men confirmed she left for the UK this afternoon."

Jack turned to Donna and was about to thank her for the help she had given so far when she blurted

"I'm coming with you."

"Fine by me," said Jack, smiling.

On the way to the airport, Donna received a phone call from an FBI colleague. She grabbed the cell phone from her pocket and swiped the answer tab. She listened intently for five minutes then pocketed her phone. She turned to Jack with concern written all over her face.

"It's bad news, I'm afraid. I've just been advised that Fallon has been killed. He had set off from Boston on a private jet headed for Argentina with refuelling stops in Florida and Colombia. He never made it. His plane crashed in a pretty inaccessible part of the Colombian jungle just after being refuelled. Observers reported there was a large plume of smoke seen from miles away."

CHAPTER THIRTY-SIX

J ack and Donna took a British Airways flight from San Diego International Airport to Heathrow. The flight touched down at Heathrow ten hours later. The travellers had left under a warm clear blue sky day in California and were met with a grey sky day, that was cold and rainy. They took the Heathrow Express and then the Underground from Paddington Station to Jack's house in Aldgate. After a rest and a quick bite to eat they drove to Oxford Bridge University in Jack's Range Rover. Their first port of call was to see Professor Brown in the Genetics Department.

During all the travel time, Jack had the opportunity to mull over their progress on the case in his mind. They had made little headway, and worst of all they had not been able to save the lives of Professors Campbell, Moore, and Fallon. In the case of Moore, it was despite being on-site and in the presence of a large contingent of the San Diego Police Department. "Daring and brazen" were the words that came to mind when he reflected on the killings. Perhaps understanding the collegial rivalry at Oxford Bridge University would provide the breakthrough they needed. Hopefully Professor Brown had made some progress.

"Welcome, take a seat," offered Brown. "It's taken a while, but I have completed the task you requested. I've included background checks on some of the more notable interactions of each staff member. I've checked all available University records. And questioned all relevant staff who are available, including University administrators who were employed at the time. Several had taken up other positions or retired."

Brown handed Jack a copy of his research, which was the size of a thesis.

"The document includes all the published papers, unsuccessful and successful research grant applications, fellowships and awards, committee and editorial memberships, and patents filed by each researcher in the Genetics cluster at that time. I've also included national and international conferences attended by each person during the time they spent in the Department. I've included a map of the old Department detailing the locations and sizes of each staff member's laboratory. Perhaps the most interesting is the summaries of conversations I had with various University staff including ex-colleagues, Research Fellows, students, technical staff, and relevant administrators."

"Wow, thank you for that. I apologize, I never fully appreciated the size of the task," responded Jack, feeling somewhat guilty about his initial opinion of Professor Brown. "This document is pretty weighty."

"I'm more than happy to assist if I can help you identify the killer and prevent further deaths."

"You may not know this, but Professor Graham Campbell was shot dead at the conference he and some of your current and former colleagues are attending in San Diego. Unfortunately, Professor Moore was also recently murdered at the same venue."

"Oh dear, that's awful!"

"We have reason to believe that Professor Simon Jackson may be the killer. He was apprehended at the venue but unfortunately escaped from police custody shortly thereafter. The FBI and San Diego police are hunting for him as we speak."

"I read a news article about Campbell's murder in the "Guardian" this morning. But Moore, he was such a debauched, but likeable rascal. I just don't understand it."

"Altogether, I'm sorry to say that five of your colleagues have now been murdered. We don't know the motive. Hopefully your document will give us the lead we badly need."

"I must say, I find it hard to believe that Jackson is a killer. He was always an obnoxious blowhard and bigot. But I never thought for one moment he was capable of murder. He was a such a religious man. Thou shalt not kill, comes to mind."

"I guess you never really know what a person is capable of. One thing I can't get my head around is the different modus operandi. Campbell was shot dead. Bentley was shot first and then asphyxiated. Moore and the Japanese family of the man that attacked Bentley were all asphyxiated. We believe Corbyn was deliberately killed on the London Underground. Why the different modus operandi? Perhaps we are dealing with different killers?"

Professor Brown lowered his head deep in thought, his forehead wrinkling. When he raised his head again and looked up at Jack, he offered a possible explanation.

"I know for a fact that David Corbyn was paranoid about the London Underground system. Over the years he had complained bitterly to Transport for London to have the platforms on the Underground incorporate platform screen doors. The Singapore transit system has them. It improves passenger safety by separating the platform from the train. Perhaps the killer enjoyed acting on one of David's worst fears."

"Thank you, Professor. That's very helpful."

Then the Professor had another thought.

"As for Bentley and Campbell, they frequently used to boast about their hunting prowess. They were often heard comparing the sizes or features of their recent hunting trophies. The rest of us found such talk abhorrent. Sounds cold, but it seems to me, the killer must have thought it was time for the hunters to become the prey."

"Yes, I see. You may very well be right. The MOs were specially tailored to each victim. Though the default seems to be asphyxiation with a plastic bag," offered Donna.

"We know Bentley's first assailant used a GoPro camera to record the attack, suggesting the other murders may have been recorded for posterity. It does suggest the mastermind behind the murders is collecting a record of your colleagues' deaths for his library collection," commented Jack.

"That's the work of a very sick mind," muttered Brown.

"I can't thank you enough for this weighty piece of research," said Jack holding up the more than two hundred-page document. "Perhaps it will provide us with the killer's motive. Don't hesitate to contact us if you have any further ideas."

CHAPTER THIRTY-SEVEN

Jack and Donna crawled back through heavy traffic on the M40 to London. After rising early the next morning, Jack snacked on several energy and protein bars. Jack and Donna completed their routine high-intensity workouts and showered together. Donna prepared them a healthy breakfast of oat-based cereal, avocado on toast with a poached egg, banana smoothies in Greek yoghurt, glasses of freshly pressed orange juice, and cups of hot black coffee. Donna smiled as Jack devoured extra helpings of everything.

Jack phoned a contact at the MET to inquire about Professor Susan Jones. He learned that she had returned to work, and was still under the MET's protection. Jack and Donna walked from Jack's flat to University College London, near Euston Square to meet with her. It was a short pleasant twenty-minute walk past the Museum of London. They located the Medical Sciences Building after asking a couple of students for directions. The receptionist contacted the Department secretary who came down to collect the two visitors. The secretary escorted them to Susan's office on the second floor of the building. They introduced themselves to a tall burly Sergeant from the MET who was standing guard outside the office door. The secretary then ushered them into the office.

"I hope your journey back to London was uneventful?" enquired Jack after taking a seat.

"Two of Chief Strong's men, personally escorted me to the airport. His men remained there until I boarded the plane. The Sergeant from the MET was waiting for me in the arrivals area. He has stood guard outside my door ever since. Needless to say, I am very grateful for the protection."

"Unfortunately, I can confirm we still have a serial killer at large. Just to bring you up to date, five of your previous colleagues have now been murdered, namely Professors Corbyn, Bentley, Dalton, Campbell, and Moore."

"Did you say Harry Moore is dead? But I saw him just yesterday at the Conference in San Diego?"

"Yes, I'm afraid he was murdered not long after you departed the conference building."

"Can I ask how he was murdered? Was he shot?"

"No, he was killed by asphyxiation using a plastic bag, which is the same MO as used on Bentley and Dalton."

"How awful!" exclaimed Susan, her face turning white with shock. "Thank goodness I left the conference straight away, or I might have been next."

Jack and Donna spent the next fifteen minutes describing the recent murders of the Professor's five colleagues in more detail than had been allowed at their first meeting.

"We still believe the killer is likely to be one of the remaining members of the genetics groups from the original Department. That now includes yourself, and Professors Jackson, Kearney, Brown, and Singer. We have only just learned that Professor John Fallon was killed in a plane crash while trying to flee to Argentina. However, his death has not been corroborated. It is unlikely to be as the plane crashed in a relatively inaccessible part of the Colombian jungle. The plane was likely incinerated on impact."

"Uhhh...no, that can't be.... how awful," gasped Susan, looking distressed.

Jack and Donna were surprised by the Professor's emotional response to this latest piece of information. She had immediately turned her back on them on hearing the news. When she turned back around a few seconds later they could make out tears welling in her eyes.

Susan Jones was of average physical attractiveness. She had been raised in London in a higher socioeconomic household. She had just reached teenagehood when her parents' marriage split apart. It was a familiar story. Her father, infatuated with his gorgeous young secretary abandoned his older wife and the family for his new love interest. The mother who gained primary custody of the children was transformed into a bitter woman who no longer trusted men. Susan was raised to believe that all men were weaklings controlled by what lay between their legs. They were all potential liars and adulterers. It forged a strong life-long drive in Susan to be as good or better at her job than her male colleagues. While completing her PhD in Genetics at University College London she fell in love with another doctoral student. He was a burly confident extroverted man who had an opinion on everything. They married, but over time they gradually grew apart. They grated, constantly arguing over just about everything, small or large. After four years and no children, Susan realized she had made a grave mistake in marrying the man. She left him to undertake a post-doctoral position at Yale, an Ivy League research University in Connecticut. After two years, and following a divorce from her husband, she returned to take up a junior Faculty position in the Department of Physiology, Anatomy, and Genetics at Oxford Bridge University.

In meetings of the genetics groups, she got to spend time with John Fallon. She liked what she saw. One year Susan and John just happened to attend the same conference in Vancouver, Canada. They travelled together on an Air Canada flight from Heathrow to Vancouver International Airport and were booked into the same hotel. They were both registered to give lectures at the Conference being held in the Vancouver Convention Centre. The night before John's talk they agreed to meet and have dinner together at the Five Sails Restaurant. The restaurant had sweeping views of the water and mountains. It was just a short walk from the Convention Centre and their hotel in Canada Place. They chatted about their work, and politics at Oxford Bridge University. They discussed what they wanted to see in Vancouver once the conference was over, with two days in hand before having to return to the UK.

Susan saw something in John that she was subconsciously drawn to, like a flying insect uncontrollably drawn to the bioluminescence emitted by a hungry glow-worm larva. He triggered a mothering instinct in her that had yet to be fulfilled. To her, John was like a lost boy who had never received the love he fully deserved. He radiated a certain vulnerability that she could sense. She longed to hold and hug him and tell him everything would be all right.

In the lift returning to their hotel rooms, she asked John if he would like to come to her room for coffee. John was flattered by the offer, appreciating that more than coffee was on offer. He was sexually attracted to Susan but didn't want the complication of a relationship. He politely made the excuse that he needed time to prepare for the lecture he was to present the next morning.

On returning to Oxford, Susan continued to pursue him. She ensured she met up with him at meetings, and at morning and afternoon tea breaks. Unfortunately for Susan it was to be unrequited love. She was heartbroken when John left to take up his new position at Harvard University. Despite his rejection she always supported his grant applications on the odd occasion she was lucky enough to be asked to review them.

"I find it difficult to accept that any one of my colleagues is capable of murder," commented Susan in response to the news.

"The current evidence suggests Professor Jackson may somehow be involved in the murders. He was apprehended at the conference venue in San Diego. Unfortunately, he escaped. He is being hunted by the San Diego Police as we speak," explained Jack.

"Simon Jackson is a self-righteous, condescending, churlish, judgmental, chauvinist, but I am certain he's not a murderer. For goodness sake, the man is a devout practicing Baptist raised by a Baptist minister."

"It is not uncommon for the religious to turn to killing as an act of retribution. They are human after all. Just look at the crusades, the Inquisition, the Middle East, and 9/11. Today's terrorists are mostly religiously motivated."

"The murder of my colleagues isn't a case of terrorism, is it?"

"No, of course not. I am just trying to make the point that the religious are not exempt from being capable of murder. Many wars have been fought over religion."

"I don't think Simon is so zealous that he would kill his colleagues. I don't for one minute believe he is involved."

"Well, that leaves Kearney, Brown, Singer, and Fallon."

"I thought you said Fallon was dead?"

"No, I said he has supposedly been killed in a plane crash. We have no actual proof he was on the plane at the time of the crash. He could still be alive for all we know. We don't have a body."

"How many people survive a plane crash? Zilch!" replied Susan sarcastically, and extremely angry to have been reminded of John's death.

"The FBI has thoroughly checked John Fallon's recent activities, and there is nothing suspicious to suggest he is the killer. He has been working at the Harvard Medical School the past week during the time of the murders, and there has been nothing unusual about his phone calls," explained Donna.

"What... you tapped his phone? That's unbelievable. That's a clear breach of privacy. Are you tapping my phone as well?" asked Susan, outraged.

"No, I can confirm that your phone is not being tapped. We don't view you as a suspect. To catch criminals we sometimes have to undertake measures that may seem distasteful to the public," explained Jack.

"In your opinion were any of the colleagues I just mentioned hard done by. Was anyone in the genetics groups overly harassed while at Oxford Bridge Uni?" asked Jack somewhat exasperated.

He continued. "It may have given the killer a motive for murder."

"Everyone gets harassed at some time or other. During school, on social media, by one's siblings, by your next-door neighbour, while playing sport, et cetera, et cetera. It's no big deal."

"Yes, but not systematically by your close colleagues. Not to the extent that it damages your career. Let's not forget that thousands of youngsters worldwide have committed suicide after being harassed on social media. Harassment is something that shouldn't be taken lightly."

"Well it was well known that Singer was abused by Corbyn. We all stood by and let it happen. The abuse became so bad that he left to take up a position in Singapore. Corbyn abused his position of authority. We all knew it. He treated Singer as if he was a junior Fellow in his own research laboratory. He stole Singer's consumables, for goodness sakes. He hijacked his research. He lured Singer's best staff to work in his own laboratory. He constantly ridiculed Singer in public. He insisted that he be included as the senior author on all of Singer's publications."

"I'd say that could be motive enough to commit murder if you were that way inclined. But surely the only target would be Corbyn? There's no reason to expect Singer would want to murder anyone else unless he thought you were all culpable. What about Brown? The killer doesn't necessarily have to be young. The killer appears to be associated with a vicious East-European gang of thugs who are doing the killing for him."

"Brown was already old when most of us joined the Department. He had had one or two research successes. But mostly he never achieved a lot in his career. You could say he just never had the drive.

He would never have thought of stepping over others to get to the top. He was just too nice."

"Could he have been resentful for an unfulfilled research career?"

"I think he was mostly happy with his lot. I just don't think he has it in him to be a serial killer. Thinking about it, I find the idea laughable."

"Well, that leaves Kearney and Fallon."

"Kearney did his best to keep clear of Departmental politics. As a Kiwi, he was always teased whenever England played New Zealand at rugby or cricket. We usually won the cricket and they won the rugby, so it was pretty much even-steven. It was all good-humoured banter. Kearney was a friendly enough person. He had a knack for avoiding being harassed, and was capable of fending off the bullies in the Department."

"And what about Fallon, would you say the two of you were close?" asked Jack, remembering Susan's surprising reaction to the revelation that Fallon had been killed in a plane crash.

"I admit I would have liked us to be closer, but John seemed to prefer his own company. He never got a break from some members of the Department. They were always bad-mouthing him to other colleagues, administrators, and visitors, at meetings, and Departmental functions. I felt sorry for him. He seemed vulnerable. He never fought back. Just took it all. I don't know why they did it. John was very wealthy which could have raised jealousies. Early on he went through a very successful period, raising lots of research funding. That enabled him to grow a large research team, while others struggled. I think there was pushback. Talk about the tall poppy syndrome. They wanted to cut him down in size. When he'd had enough he left to take up a senior administrative post at Harvard University. He probably hoped he could restart his research career without being harassed by his Oxford colleagues."

"Would you know whether he was resentful?"

"Hard to say with John. He never really showed his feelings. They say predated animals that are wounded hide their vulnerability, don't they?"

"Thanks, that's been very helpful. We'll be in touch again if we need further information. The Sergeant posted outside will remain there for your protection."

Once out of earshot, Donna commented "I wonder if she would have been so forthcoming if she didn't accept Fallon was already dead?"

Jack and Donna decided to return to Jack's place to read through Brown's thesis. They sat at the breakfast table, each with a large cup of black coffee. Jack took the document and divided it into two.

"Here," he said to Donna. "You read this half, and I'll tackle the other half. When we're both finished we'll swap, and then compare notes."

CHAPTER THIRTY-EIGHT

Nicolae had never flown in an aeroplane before, or even travelled by car for that matter. He sat in awe throughout the journey from the orphanage in Romania to Oxford in the United Kingdom. He did not communicate his wonderment at all the amazing sights he was feasting his eyes upon. How could he? The strange couple that had whisked him away from the orphanage spoke a language he could not comprehend. He was partly excited, partly apprehensive. Were the foreign couple taking him to a faraway land to be their slave? Or was he to be trafficked for sex? Why else would such rich people want a scruffy orphan boy raised in misery and squalor? To Nicholae the journey seemed endless. He had only been allowed outside the orphanage into the grounds on a couple of special occasions. His whole world had been very small, mostly an overcrowded room that reeked of urine and bleach. He had no idea the world was so big. He could not see an end to it when looking out the plane's window. He worried about how he was ever going to find his way back to the orphanage after he escaped. There were so many other planes on the ground when their plane finally landed. The place was crowded with so many people rushing here and there. He was very frightened and held on tightly to the woman's hand.

The strange couple led him out of the airport building to a large black car. A smartly dressed man with a peaked cap and black suit got out of the car and opened the doors for them. A slave perhaps, he thought? The couple got into the car and placed Nicolae between them in the back seat. The woman seemed friendly enough. She immediately gave him a bag of sweets of all different kinds and flavours to eat and tried to speak to him. The man appeared stern and silent throughout the journey, not bothering to interact with him at all. Nicolae was gobsmacked by the number of very fine houses they passed as they drove through the very strange green land.

Finally, after an exhaustingly long drive, the car approached a large entranceway. The massive gates guarding the entrance amazingly opened all on their own. Nicolae spotted a couple of men working in the gardens just inside the gates. More slaves perhaps. The driveway swept past several stands of trees and more gardens containing beautiful exotic flowers. Finally, they approached what looked to be a large castle. Nicolae thought to himself that this must be another orphanage full of children just like him. He had no appreciation that the large manor house was the residence of just a single-family. A family in which he was to become an integral member.

The car stopped outside the house. The man with the peaked cap got out and opened the car doors. The couple was met at the entrance to the house by a woman and a man, both in uniforms. More slaves perhaps, as they helped with the luggage. Nicholae was ushered through the large wooden doors of the house. The doors opened to reveal a huge entranceway, and an ornate sweeping staircase leading to another floor. Everywhere he looked there were delicate ornaments, fine furniture, and large paintings of people and country scenes. He was shocked to find the house was empty of people. Where were all the other children? The woman led him up the large sweeping staircase and down a long corridor to a bedroom overlooking the driveway and front garden. He was surprised to find the room contained just a single bed. The bed even had lots of blankets and huge pillows. In the orphanage, a room that size would have contained at least twenty cots and beds, a scarcity of blankets, and no pillows. The woman who had met them downstairs led him to another room. She undressed him and washed him in a large white bathtub with warm water and soap. She then dressed him in a set of brand new clothes. He was led back to the bedroom where he was allowed to play with an array of toys strewn all over the bed and the floor.

Later, the woman led Nicholae to what was the kitchen. A large plump woman, who giggled a lot, placed copious amounts of food in front of him on a large plate. He had never seen or did not recognize most of the food items. He nibbled at each unknown food item to see if he liked it, then gorged himself on the foods he liked. The two women looked on in amusement. Not long after he promptly vomited up most of the food he had eaten onto the polished white marble kitchen floor. He immediately shrank back like a wounded animal. He kept his head low, covering it with his hands, waiting for the punches and abuse to be delivered. But astonishingly one woman hugged him, and the other woman washed his face and cleaned up the vomit. That night alone in bed, missing his friends, he wept profusely. The woman who had taken him from the orphanage must have heard him. She came into the room, sat on the bed, and stroked his hair. She sang strange songs until he finally fell asleep.

CHAPTER THIRTY-NINE

The Ford Inspector emblazoned with its San Diego police logo sped away. Its siren blaring and red and blue light bar flashing, it caused traffic to give way. It turned sharply into a driveway, and both the siren and light bar were switched off. It then sped down a ramp into an underground car park. The driver got out of the car and opened the passenger door.

"Get out," he shouted menacingly, pointing his pistol at Jackson's chest.

"Don't shoot," pleaded Jackson, visibly trembling and shaken by the car chase.

"You make a move you'll be a dead man," said the driver.

He pushed Jackson roughly in the small of his back towards the elevator. Once inside, he pressed the button for the upper floor, thirty stories above. They exited the lift.

"Go left," said the driver shoving Jackson hard from behind.

Once outside room 3011, he demanded, "Stop here."

He knocked on the door. It opened and he shoved Jackson forward into the room. He closed and locked the door behind him. Then he grabbed Jackson, who was still handcuffed, by the shoulders and pressed him down into a chair by a small dining table. He took out ropes and bound Jackson's legs and arms to the chair.

The man who had opened the door quickly positioned an iPad Pro on a stand directly in front of Jackson. Almost immediately a vaguely familiar face appeared on the screen.

"Well, well, who do we have here?" asked the man in the screen, grinning from ear to ear like a Cheshire cat who had just got the cream. "You look vaguely familiar," he continued. "Somewhat fatter, and less hair, but still the prick I remember, I bet."

"Why are you doing this? I had nothing to do with the murders," blubbered Jackson.

"Of course you didn't Simon. I believe you totally because I am the killer they're looking for."

"No, you can't be. What did I ever do to you? Let me go. I'll do anything you want. Just name it. I can make amends."

"You are a bastard. You had me kill the only person I ever loved! The only person who ever loved me!" screamed the man in the screen, almost in a trance, remembering several of the precious moments he had spent with his adored mother June.

"No, that's not right. What person! What, who are you talking about?" stammered Jackson, hopelessly confused.

"Don't you remember the Departmental end of year function? Oh, how you loved to mock me. I bet you were all in on it. All your smug faces aren't so smug now, are they?"

"Which function? It was all just a bit of fun. There was never any harm intended."

"Never mind. It's a bit late now to say you're sorry. My mother is dead. It's time for payback. It's a pity I can't be there to suffocate you with my own bare hands, but I'll be recording your departure."

"Are you crazy? You won't get away with it. Please, I have a wife and children. Mercy, please. Remember the commandments say thou shalt not kill. Wrongdoers will not inherit the kingdom of God."

"Do you really think Saint Peter will allow a bigot like you to enter the Kingdom? Spare me your judgement. Prepare to meet Satan, you religious zealot. Your family, and your more deserving religious compatriots who actually follow their teachings will be well rid of you."

The man in the screen nodded to one of his accomplices. The man shoved the chair forward pressing Jackson hard against the table, pinning him to curb his struggles.

The other accomplice reached into his jacket pocket. He extracted a plastic bag and duct tape. He handed them to the other man. Jackson fought vigorously against the ropes and handcuffs to attempt to escape. He screamed as he spotted the man with the plastic bag,

"God, why have thou forsaken me? Save me! Save me, please! No, don't do this!"

But the man quickly and deftly opened the plastic bag and placed it over Jackson's head. Jackson continued to struggle, pushing away from the table with his legs. But his captor was too strong. The bag began to quickly fill with perspiration, making a crackling sound as Jackson sucked heavily in and out to get enough oxygen. His captor roughly taped the bottom of the bag under the chin and around the neck. The man in the screen gazed directly into the terrified and dying man's eyes as his body shook violently in its death throes.

"This is for you June," the man in the screen whispered to himself.

The two murderers vacated and locked the room once they were certain their victim was dead.

CHAPTER FORTY

A new man introduced himself to Nicolae on the second day in the big house. He spoke to Nicholae in his native Romanian tongue informing him that he was his teacher. He explained that the couple who had brought him to this faraway land called Anglia (England) were now his adoptive parents and guardians. He told him his name in this new country was John, not Nicholae. That his parents' names were John Senior and June. Several weeks later he learned that he had a second name that designated the whole family. His full name in Anglia was John Fallon.

For the next two years, John received personal tuition at home every day, with an emphasis on spoken and written English. He was also taught an array of standard subjects in the English school curriculum. John was fluent in spoken and written English by the end of the second year. Nevertheless, he still retained a hint of a Romanian accent.

June treated John as any mother would treat her son throughout the remainder of his childhood on the estate. She hugged him when he raged in frustration at having to cope with the accelerated learning. She hugged and quietened him, often in the middle of the night, when nightmares of the time he spent at the orphanage returned. Together they would sit watching John's favourite television programmes. She would read him stories from the great English writers and poets.

No expense was spared on John's education. Another teacher was employed for three months to teach John etiquette and manners befitting someone of the upper class. This learning was further reinforced when June travelled with John to London to a school that taught children courses in etiquette and manners including communication and social skills. Finally, after two years of intensive training and education, June knew it was time to introduce John to his peers. She drove him to the Oxford Summer School English language programme at Dragon School. She left him there to interact with similarly aged children of at least fifty different nationalities. John enjoyed that course so much that June enrolled him each year in the L'Oreal Young Scientist Centre courses in London run by the Royal Institution.

At the age of eleven, John was admitted to Magdalen College School in Oxford. It was one of the top ten performing private schools in the United Kingdom. By the end of the first year, John's speech was such that no one would doubt that he was a child of an upper-class family. It would take a trained ear to distinguish the remnants of his Romanian accent. At home he received personal tuition from an array of excellent tutors in different core subjects, soon placing him ahead of many of his peers. From the age of thirteen, John attended Oxford Royal Academy Summer Schools. He took an array of core subjects at Balliol College, Lady Margaret Hall, Yarnton Manor, and St Hugh's College, Oxford. John proved to be an exceptional student. In his final year of high school, he was awarded a scholarship to attend Oxford University. In the later years of his schooling, June accompanied John to cultural and tourist sites around the country, to shows in the West-end of London, to cricket matches at Lords, tennis matches at Wimbledon, and rugby matches at Twickenham. They travelled together during the school holidays to explore the major European capitals.

John Fallon Senior had never wanted children. He felt it was a "gift" that he had been born with aspermia. He would never father a child. There were few things in life that he loved other than wealth and power. His wife was one of them. He had witnessed how his wife mothered and fussed over her nephew and niece like a clucky hen whenever they visited. He recognized the immense sadness in her eyes when the children left to return home. Only then did he resent his infertility. He could not bear the thought of June's eggs being fused with another man's sperm. Of her being linked and beholding to a sperm donor, even if the donor had relinquished his rights as a father. As a compromise, he raised the idea of adoption, which June readily agreed to.

John Fallon Senior thought it would be an interesting experiment to raise a wretch from a poverty-stricken country into a world of wealth and privilege. If the child was bright enough, who knows, he could even be trained in the family business. The adoption of a British child was out of the question. He didn't want any adoption agency prying into his past. He didn't want them probing into what he got up to in his spare time while travelling overseas. John Fallon Senior spent nine months of the year overseas attending to his multiple business interests. There would be no scrutiny by prying eyes on the adoption of a child from one of the many orphanages in Romania. The child would occupy June's time when he was absent. The boy would satisfy her desire for motherhood. She would be happy. There would be less chance of her affections straying to another man.

When John Senior was home in Oxford he would take the boy to a sports or cultural event, often outside Oxford. He would book them into a hotel overnight, and give the boy a sedative before bedtime. He would then sexually assault him. For John Senior was a practicing paedophile, and had been so most of his adult life. He felt no remorse for his actions. After all, the boy was not his biological son. As he explained to June, this was an important time for father-son bonding. June readily encouraged their getaways, being completely unaware of her husband's betrayal of trust. When John Junior turned twelve his adopted father was no longer interested in him sexually. Now the boy was simply seen as a competitor for his wife's affection and attention.

CHAPTER FORTY-ONE

John Fallon was a high achieving student, obtaining a first-class honours degree in genetics due to talent and hard work. He completed a PhD in genetics and biomedicine at Cambridge University, before returning to Oxford to be closer to his mother, where he accepted a Research Fellowship in the Department of Physiology, Anatomy and Genetics at Oxford Bridge University.

Ten years later newly promoted Associate Professor John Fallon had just completed an experiment in his laboratory alongside a Master's student he was supervising. His life was busy and fulfilled. He had one of the largest research teams in the Department of Physiology, Anatomy and Genetics at Oxford Bridge University. He was very competitive in obtaining research contracts. The University administrators acknowledged his success and invited him to join the "Top 100 earners group". It was a group of research grant awardees that were the most successful in obtaining grants for their research. They would regularly meet to discuss new ways to bring money into the University.

John's private life was also harmonious. His parents had purchased a house in Summertown, North Oxford, the most expensive suburb in Oxford. He was allowed to occupy the house rent-free. They had loaned him a Bentley GT Continental sports car to drive. They had also provided him with a small income to supplement what they viewed as a comparatively paltry University salary. Thus while John himself personally owned nothing substantial he nevertheless lived a life of comparative luxury with sufficient income to enjoy life to the full.

John Fallon had essentially been raised solely by his adopted mother, whom he adored. As an adult, he still retained a strong and loving relationship with his adopted mother. His father was largely absent most of the time, managing the family's global business interests. He took little interest in John's adult life, except when necessary. It was an arrangement that suited both John Senior and Junior.

John was looking forward to spending a short break away with his parents sailing their yacht off the coast of Portugal and visiting many of the attractive seaside towns south of Lisbon. He had invited his parents to the Genetics groups' end of the academic year function the night before leaving on their holiday together. The function was to be held in a large restaurant near the University.

The Fallons drove from their estate on the outskirts of Oxfordshire to meet John at the restaurant on the night of the function. They seated themselves at one of the many white-clothed dining tables. Most of the Genetics groups were in attendance. Some members had brought along their partners or family members, including their parents and children. Most of the attendees were busy talking to others sitting at their table or close by. As with previous end of the academic year functions, the dinner was to be preceded by a talk from the Head of Department (HOD), in this case, Professor Corbyn. The HOD's talk was to be followed by skits by whoever wished to partake. The skits were usually light-hearted, witty, and sometimes even comical, and enjoyed by all. However this particular year the events proved to be anything but.

Professor Corbyn climbed up onto the stage overlooking the tables when the food had been consumed, and most of the diners had begun to relax. He began by thanking the administrative staff for their year's contribution. He gave a big bunch of cut flowers to his secretary. He thanked staff involved in teaching administration, giving them each a small token of the Department's appreciation. Once the formalities were over he declared "Let the festivities begin." This was the call to the staff to perform the skits they had prepared.

Dr Bentley appeared from the corner of the stage dragging a lectern which he positioned at the front of the stage. Leaning on the lectern he announced he was going to discuss some of the Department's research interests. Everyone immediately became attentive, believing he was about to deliver a serious, but perhaps humorous, lecture.

"Who studies epigenetics in our illustrious department?" he began. "Why that will be Dr John Fallon. Have you ever asked yourself why he studies epigenetics? Well, I'll tell you why. He wants to know how the severe neglect and abuse of infants leads to delays in their development, impaired cognitive ability, and failure to thrive. Now, let's ask ourselves what John actually knows about such things. I have it on good authority that little John received personal tuition, enjoyed the finest day and summer schools, and travelled to exciting European capitals during his vacations. And oh.., look at how that has affected him. He drives a Bentley GT continental, and lives in the poshest suburb in Oxford. My heart bleeds for him. So much abuse and neglect and failure to thrive. What grade should we give him for his research," asked Bentley cupping his hand behind his ear as if seeking an answer. "I give him the lowest grade possible, an E grade. On this occasion my colleague Dr Jackson has kindly volunteered to present John with his award."

A sizeable man dressed as a scary clown strode across the stage to the lectern. His face resembled a montage of the joker in the Batman series and a killer clown. His face had been painted white and bore thick bright red lips that extended to the edge of his face. His mouth enclosed an implant containing a cluster of sharp teeth. His eye sockets were blackened. His head was bald except for a few wisps of bright orange hair. A low murmur came from the staff and guests as they sighted the creature. They were expressing their surprise and uncertainty at being confronted by such a terrifying figure.

The killer clown announced in a booming voice "It is my pleasure tonight to present three awards on behalf of our august Department."

Though trying to disguise his voice, it was obvious that the scary clown was none other than Dr Jackson. His tall and flabby build, and booming voice, gave him away.

"The first award goes to Professor Brown for his wonderful speaking ability. I refer to his sloooww, and cumberrrson speech, and his lispyness. Of course "thith is thomewhat thubjective". How on earth the undergraduate students put up with such mangled speech beats me," pronounced the clown in a booming voice, laughing heartily.

The pronouncement was met with a few chuckles from those seated. Others who had any sense of empathy lowered their heads, not wanting to be seen to share Jackson's opinions. Professor Brown felt a flush of embarrassment and he immediately lowered his head, feeling decidedly uncomfortable.

"The second award goes to Dr Singer for being the worst "dreg" of the Department, like sludge at the bottom of your test tube. Is he a mouse or a man? Step on him and he doesn't squeak, so who knows he might even be human."

There were mumblings of displeasure from the audience. But Professor Corbyn could be seen chuckling to himself, clearly delighted by the description.

"However, the main award of the night is the Lord Silverbourne award which goes to Dr Fallon for being lucky enough to be born a billionaire. Why does he even bother to work when his supplementary income is over a million pounds per year? Why doesn't he pay for his own research and donate the money to us? If anyone here is short of a few bob I am advised that Dr Fallon will be more than happy to oblige by throwing a few thousand quid or more your way. That's chicken feed to him. Haha..., we have news for him. The rich like him shall find it very hard to enter the kingdom of heaven."

Several of the Heads of Lab including two at Dr Fallon's table glared at John. They bore wide smirks which mirrored their pleasure at seeing Fallon's discomfort. Suddenly across the stage came a female student pushing a large pram. A male student of small stature dressed in baby clothes lifted his bonnet-covered head from the pram, a large spoon jutting out of his mouth. Jackson leaned forward with his hand and extracted the spoon.

"Behold, little John and Lord Silverbourne's silver spoon!" he cried out in a posh accent, holding the spoon high above his head for everyone to see.

Mr. Fallon senior, assaulted by all these antics, briefly glanced at his wife. His face was fixed in a steely expression. He did not engage in conversation the rest of the evening. John Fallon junior could not bear to look at his father. He kept his head bowed for the rest of the evening, which fortunately passed without further insults. Mrs. Fallon conversed freely with others at the table. She attempted to cheer her son, who was feeling bruised by his colleagues, but with little success.

Mr. Fallon senior did not speak to his son upon returning to the Fallon's residence in Oxfordshire, other than to bark instructions while the family packed and prepared for their vacation. He held a vacant expression as if lost in thought. The Fallon family boarded a British Airways plane for the two-and-a-half-hour flight from Heathrow to Humberto Delgado Airport, Lisbon, located two-thirds of the way down the spectacular coast of Portugal. The plane was crowded with rowdy young holiday-makers, which did little to temper Fallon Senior's mood, despite his separation in business class. The family took a hire car north to Marina da Nazaré, less than a mile south of the beach resort of Nazare. Their yacht, an Amal 50 fifty-foot sloop, called Bluewater, was docked in the marina just as they had left it several months earlier. They boarded the yacht, and got ready for the sail down the coast to Sesimbra, just south of

Lisbon. There they would moor the boat, stay for a few days, and do some shopping and sightseeing. June stowed their provisions in the galley. John Junior stowed his luggage in the bedroom at the bow of the yacht, with his parents as usual occupying the larger bedroom at the stern.

Fallon Senior went to the helmsman's station and started the Volvo diesel engine. Once under power, the yacht glided gracefully out of the marina into the Atlantic swell. Fallon senior switched off the motor when they were away from the shore. He pressed the levers to employ the electric furling mechanism and winches to raise the sails. There was a light six-knot breeze. The breeze allowed the yacht to hold a steady five knots of boat speed. John went up on deck and lay down on a large foam sun lounger near the bow. He took in the smell of the salty sea air, and the deep blue sky. His mother began working downstairs in the galley, preparing for lunch.

John quickly fell asleep due to the warmth of the day, and the gentle rolling and rocking of the yacht. After about thirty minutes he was awoken by blustery winds. The air had turned decidedly colder. He looked at the helmsman's station, but Fallon senior was not on deck. His stepfather must have put the yacht on autopilot, and gone below. John walked past the helmsman's station. He was just about to descend the stairwell to the galley when he heard the raised voice of his father.

"That bastard of a boy is nothing but a loser. To think he turned down my offer of a prosperous career in our business. To do what? To join a mob of childish and churlish academics who have never achieved anything of real substance. Even his peers consider him a loser. Look at how they ridiculed him. All that money we spent on his education, and for what I ask? He's clearly been showing off with our money and made them all jealous. Did you hear what that ridiculous clown said about the support we've given him? Said we'd given him an allowance of one million pounds a year. From where on earth did he conjure up that ridiculous figure? From John's boasts, most likely. He made out John was more than happy to squander the money we'd given him. Did you hear that clown say John was born with a silver spoon in his mouth. Hardly. They sure know sod all. That boy has been nothing but trouble. He was born into abject poverty and can return to the gutter as far as I am concerned. I am cutting him out of my will and taking away his allowance. I want you to do the same. I'll have my lawyers draw up the documents as soon as we return to Oxfordshire. From now on he can fend for himself. Let's see him boast about that to his colleagues."

John Senior was incensed about what he had witnessed at the end of the academic year function. But really it was just the final straw of a deep-rooted hatred that had been bubbling to the surface. June had come to love the boy. She spent far too much of her time on him. The boy had replaced him in his wife's affections. He could not tolerate the situation any longer. He used the only weapon he had, namely to withdraw all financial support to drive the boy away.

June stood in silence, her head bowed throughout her husband's tirade. When he had finally finished, she burst into tears and ran to the bedroom. John was standing on the top stair of the stairwell looking down. His father's comments shocked and hurt him. He always knew that his adoptive father was indifferent to him, but never imagined his resentment ran so deep. He walked meekly back to the bow in a daze. He embedded himself into the large sun lounger there away from the strengthening wind and spent time pondering over what he could do. He had never boasted about the small allowance his parents had provided him. He didn't deserve to be ridiculed by his peers and be the subject of such outrageous lies. His colleagues had no knowledge of his early childhood years, and he would never enlighten them. Once again, protected from the cold wind, and feeling very sorry for himself, he soon fell asleep.

John was awoken by the wild rocking of the boat, and by the increasing chill and growing strength of the wind. It had become dark early, too early, with the daylight hidden by dark and menacing black clouds. His father was standing over him.

"The Coast Guard has warned there's an Atlantic gale, force ten, heading our way from the North. I'm plotting a course back to the marina. The holiday is over," barked Fallon senior. "You lower the genoa. I'll take the wheel."

John only half awake, stood up, in a daze. But now facing his father with the cold wind on his face he suddenly became animated. He was instantly consumed by an overwhelming feeling of anger and hatred at being abused for years as a child by this aging paedophile of a father. Of never being viewed as good enough. At having to watch his adoptive father verbally abuse and intimidate his adored adoptive mother. Now, this beast of a man was going to cut him out of the family altogether. It was all too much. As his father walked back to the helmsman's station, and in a moment of madness, John rushed at him from behind. He thrust his arms out in front and violently shoved his father over the side of the yacht into the raging sea. The yacht sped on in the strong wind quickly leaving John Senior well adrift of the boat. The last John ever saw of his adoptive father was of a man with his right arm raised high above his head, screaming for help as he was pounded by the raging sea.

To his horror, John turned to see his adoptive mother June standing by the helmsman's station. She had witnessed everything.

"You have to save him!" she screamed into the wind, shaking uncontrollably, and pointing at the rapidly disappearing figure of her husband. "Turn the boat around. Now. We have to rescue him!"

John quickly walked to where his mother was standing. Sobbing now, almost uncontrollably, he hugged his mother briefly to calm her and kissed her gently on the forehead. This diminutive woman who had raised and educated him, and loved him unconditionally.

She was the only person he had ever come to love. She was the only person who had shown him unconditional love in return. He whispered just three words to her.

"I'm so sorry."

He picked her up into his arms, walked quickly to the side of the deck, and hurled her overboard into the raging sea.

Night had come early. The sky was black and angry. The wind kept increasing in strength. The ocean swell was heavy, causing huge waves to crash right over the bow of the yacht. The Fallons' ocean cruising yacht was being tossed about uncontrollably in the maelstrom. With tears streaming down his face, and occasional sobbing, John steered the yacht back in the direction they had come and towards the coast. He waited until he could just make out the faint lights of houses and apartments along the shoreline. He then set the autopilot for the yacht to sail southwest away from the coast out into the open sea. He raced down the stairwell and opened all the watertight doors. He smashed the seacocks to allow water to flood into the hull. He quickly removed his shoes and most of his clothing. Then he raced back onto the deck and dived overboard head-first into the maelstrom.

John was a powerful swimmer. He figured he was about two miles from shore. He estimated it would take about an hour to reach the safety of land. The actual swim took twice as long. The waves continued to grow in size, tossing and pounding him unmercifully. His biggest risk was not sharks which head for deep water during such storms, but rather exhaustion and hypothermia. Now and then he had to stop, tread water, and look around to make sure he was swimming in the right direction. He was exhausted, both physically and mentally by the time he reached the shore. He had come ashore on a white sand beach at Sao Martinho do Porto to the south of the marina. He lay prostrate on the sand for several minutes to gather himself and then staggered, dripping, to the nearest bar along the beachfront. As he entered the bar, everyone stared at the sight of a near-naked man, surprised that any sane person would be walking outside unprotected in such atrocious weather conditions. But then, young English tourists were well known for their crazy escapades.

"Is there anyone here who speaks English?" he cried out shaking his wet hair and causing water to splash onto the floor.

"I do," yelled a man, who had just put down his drink and raised his arm.

"Please, you have to help me," he blurted out, breathing heavily, bent over, shaking. "Our yacht was damaged in the storm. I was swept overboard. My parents are still on board. You have to contact the Coast Guard to mount a search for them. Hurry, please."

The good Samaritan immediately phoned the Autoridade Maritima Nacional, the branch of the Portuguese navy responsible for coast guard activity, to report the tragedy. They in turn contacted the harbourmasters at Nazare and San Martinho do Porto. Both harbourmasters declared the weather was too atrocious to undertake a search and rescue operation. They confirmed they would mount a search once the storm had relented, which would probably be in the morning. But they stated it was likely to be a body recovery operation. As it turned out, neither the sloop nor the bodies of its owners were ever recovered.

CHAPTER FORTY-TWO

J ack and Donna had both finished their halves of Brown's lengthy document by mid-morning. They then swapped halves, taking notes as they read. By lunchtime, they had both completed reading the entire document. They stared across the table at one another recollecting what they had just read. Each remembering what Professor Susan Jones had revealed. Almost in the same breath they each declared "The killer, it's got to be Fallon."

"But Fallon was killed in that plane crash in the Colombian jungle. Nobody could have survived a crash like that," replied Donna.

"Yes, but was he onboard the plane after it refuelled? The killer has got to be either Jackson, Fallon, or Singer. I can vouch for John Kearney. He is an old University friend. I knew his parents well. Don't forget Kearney came to me for help, fearing he might be in danger. He brought the attack on Bentley to my attention. I think the killer has got to be Fallon, and he's still alive. He was doing spectacularly well for a while at Oxford Bridge Uni, presumably because he had the support of more senior colleagues in his field. But it looks to me that when those senior colleagues retired he was relentlessly targeted by some of his peers, or to be more accurate "bullies" in the Department. From then on his research career turned pear-shaped."

"Yes, and he even clashed with the Head of Department Professor Corbyn," said Donna.

"At some point, Corbyn and Fallon had a falling out over a paper submitted by Fallon. Corbyn insisted on being included as the senior author, despite not contributing to the research."

"If you ask me Corbyn appears to have been a grasping man who repeatedly sought to capture the hard-won research findings of others."

"I remember Professor Brown saying that most Heads of Labs are routinely invited onto the committees that decide the outcome of research grant applications submitted by their peers," added Donna.

"Yes, that puts them in a powerful position to influence the careers of their colleagues, wouldn't you say."

"The bullies would only have to trash Fallon's grant applications to starve him of research funding."

"They could also disperse gossip amongst the committee members to paint a negative picture of Fallon and his lab."

"Some of the administrators Brown interviewed said they'd heard some of the Heads of Labs state they wanted to destroy Fallon."

"It all seems to fit with why he was sometimes the object of ridicule at departmental functions."

"Fallon inherited quite a large laboratory space in a great location. Looking at the map Brown provided shows Fallon's large lab was located in close vicinity to the smaller labs of Singer, Jackson, Bentley, Campbell and Moore on the same floor. I wonder whether there were also grievances over laboratory space issues. A lab could not grow without sufficient space. It would restrict the Lab Heads' career prospects."

"But surely all this is not enough for anyone to consider murder? Especially a series of ruthlessly planned and executed killings. There has to be more," puzzled Donna.

"In my experience, a single insult is enough to provoke murder. In recent years there have been multiple mass killings of work colleagues by resentful employees. As you know Donna, it is an incredibly common crime in the United States. Even school children have got in on the act and must pass through metal detectors before entering school. Some have even turned into mass murderers killing both their fellow students and their teachers. Fallon was bombarded with insults and threats in abundance, so I'm not at all surprised it has led to this."

"I'm guessing Jackson is probably dead. We should contact Singer, and warn him."

"He's probably well aware of the situation if he has been following the latest press releases. He must be terrified."

"I'd certainly like to know how Fallon is connected to those East-European thugs."

"We might have to delve into his past to get an answer to that question."

"I'll post an all-points bulletin to all law enforcement agencies in the States to locate Fallon. I'll include the latest photo we have and a description of his last whereabouts. It could be San Diego if he was involved in the murders there. We'll have Fallon's mug shot on the Crime Watch Daily programme. I'll also reach out to Interpol to cover all airports and international borders. We'll freeze all his assets. We'll catch that bastard before he can kill again."

Fallon, unbeknown to Donna and her FBI colleagues, had already transferred his wealth to overseas accounts that were untraceable and untouchable.

CHAPTER FORTY-THREE

Professor Peter Singer realized he was a marked man. The death of Professor Corbyn and the murder of Richard Bentley seemed initially to be just a curious coincidence. He had followed the subsequent press releases describing the serial killings of his other former colleagues with increasing apprehension. Their systematic murder could not be coincidental. There had been no information released as to the identity of the killer. He presumed the killer was a psychopath they had all been associated with at Oxford. But who was it, and why carry out the murders now so many years later? It just didn't make any sense. The descriptions of how his colleagues had been murdered sent a shiver down his spine. He immediately broke into a cold sweat just thinking about it. What crime had he or his academic colleagues committed that could justify murder? There had been mention of East-European thugs. As far as he was aware, none of his previous colleagues had an East European connection.

Peter Singer had moved from his position in the Department of Physiology, Anatomy and Genetics at Oxford Bridge University to the ICMB in Singapore. He had been encouraged to do so by his Singaporean wife, who had witnessed first-hand Peter's declining mental health at Oxford Bridge University. Peter didn't take much persuading as he detested the English weather. But the main reason was that he loathed his Head of Department, Professor David Corbyn. Corbyn had singled Peter out as a weakling and took great delight in humiliating him in public. He was a leach who would frequently grab Peter's resources. He would encourage Peter's best students and research fellows to jump ship to his own laboratory. Corbyn thought nothing of advising his staff to pilfer Peter's chemicals and biologics if his own lab had run out of particular supplies. This was even though each of the labs was supposed to be financially independent. They were expected to secure their own resources through their applications for grant funding. There were times when Corbyn almost treated Peter's lab as his own. He could still vividly remember Corbyn approaching the very first technician Peter had appointed to his team. Standing directly in front of the man, and with a smug smile on his face, Corbyn had yelled

"You must be the laziest technician we have ever employed", despite knowing absolutely nothing about the recent recruit to Peter's laboratory.

The poor man had done nothing to deserve such a label. Not surprisingly, after repeated harassment from Corbyn, he resigned from his technical position just four weeks later, leaving Peter having to urgently search for a replacement. Peter appealed to the Vice-Chancellor to intervene in his one-sided relationship with Corbyn, but the newly appointed Vice-Chancellor offered no constructive help at all to Peter. Instead, irrationally he sought to attack Peter's credibility, and ease him out of the University.

The other reason Peter left Oxford Bridge University was that he had a tiny laboratory. There had been no sign that anyone in the Department would be vacating their larger laboratory any time soon. Fallon had the largest laboratory after Corbyn. Peter had attempted to deprive Fallon of research funding by damning his grant applications, as had others in the Department, hoping it might encourage Fallon to leave. But the process was taking too long. Fallon was hanging on like a limpet, submitting ever-increasing numbers of grant applications despite ever-diminishing success. Thus Peter had nowhere to grow his research team. In contrast, the ICMB was very welcoming. It offered him a suite of laboratories already fitted out with every piece of state-of-the-art scientific equipment he could ever desire or need.

Peter had chosen not to ask for police protection. Look at how that had turned out for Jackson and Moore. He realized he was an easy target in Singapore. It was a city state on a small island. Where could he hide? He had read the newspaper article reporting the death of his colleague John Fallon in a plane crash in the Colombian jungle. Was he killed fleeing to Argentina as the article had mentioned, he asked himself? His mind wandered to the great train robber Ronnie Biggs who escaped British justice by living in Rio de Janeiro. He also remembered the Nazi war criminals Adolf Eichmann and Josef Mengele who hid out in Argentina. It hadn't ended so well for Eichmann though. He was eventually found by Mossad and hanged. Perhaps no haven was truly safe if the hunter proved to be unrelenting, a prospect that made him shiver.

In recent years Peter had spent short sabbaticals at Universities in China. He had also attended conferences there. Harbin came to mind as a place to hide-out. Harbin, the capital of Heilongjiang in China's northernmost province, abutted the borders of Russia and Mongolia. It had a population of fifteen million. He had a close colleague at Harbin Medical University, who he could contact. His contact would arrange a place for him to stay. He wouldn't even need to take up a visiting position at the University. He would simply spend his time writing review papers and finishing off outstanding unfinished research articles. He would return to the ICMB once the killer had been apprehended. He felt a lot happier now that he had finally made a decision. He would take temporary leave from the ICMB without disclosing a forwarding address. He decided he would take a circuitous route by boat, car, and plane so as not to be tracked to Harbin. His laboratory would be left in the capable hands of his most experienced Senior Research Fellow.

That night Peter Singer packed a suitcase with everything deemed essential for the next couple of months in Harbin. He booked a charter boat heading for the small Malaysian island of Penang via the Malacca Strait. He kissed his tearful wife goodbye.

"Don't worry, my dear. I think it's best I don't tell you where I am going, for your safety. I'm guessing I'll be able to return shortly after the maniac responsible for the murders is caught. I won't be going far," he said in an emotional hoarse voice.

What Peter Singer did not know was that for the past week he had been closely watched. His phone call to the agency that hired out the charter boat had been intercepted. As darkness fell, Peter took a taxi from his apartment on Orchard Road to the marina at Sentosa Cove where the charter boat was moored.

The skipper, a large Asian man with a swarthy weather-beaten complexion, was waiting for him. The skipper welcomed Peter aboard with a broad smile.

"Welcome aboard, sir. I'm pleased you've chosen our charter boat. We aim to make your journey as comfortable as possible. Please don't hesitate to come and see me if you require anything."

The skipper introduced his first mate, a surly-looking fellow who remained silent. What Peter did not know was that there were already three other clients on the boat. They had paid handsomely for the voyage. They had no intention of travelling as far as Penang. Instead, they had instructed the captain to head east in the opposite direction towards the South China Sea, into the open ocean. The first mate showed Peter to his cabin, a tiny but well-fitted-out room with a bed and closet to store clothes.

"How long will it take to get to Penang?" asked Peter.

"The trip to Penang will take fifteen hours. Breakfast will be served in the dining area next to the galley at 0800 hours sharp. I'll knock on your door at 0730 hours in case you are not awake," informed the first mate.

Peter remained in his cabin as the boat, under the power of its big throbbing merlin engines, slowly cruised out of the harbour for the open sea. Exhausted by anxiety, Peter decided to get an early sleep. He was completely oblivious of the direction the boat was taking as it left the harbour. It seemed as if he had only slept for a couple of hours when he was awoken by a loud knocking on his door. Half asleep and in a daze, he stumbled out of bed and dragged himself to the door. It can't possibly be time for breakfast yet he thought to himself. He opened the door, and there standing in front of him was someone he vaguely remembered. The man had aged somewhat since their last meeting at a conference in Europe. But the person was unmistakably his former colleague John Fallon. He imagined he must be dreaming. John Fallon was dead, all the newspapers had said so. But he panicked when John Fallon stepped into the room pushing him aside to allow two burly men entry. The two burly men pinned Peter by his arms. John barked an order to the two men in an unrecognizable foreign language he'd never heard him speak before. The men manacled Peter's hands behind his back and forced him to sit down on the side of the bed.

"What are you doing here? The newspapers said you were dead. You were killed in a plane crash," stammered Peter. But Peter knew the answer to his question before he had even asked it. He fully realized the perilous nature of his position.

"Don't believe everything you read," sneered John Fallon.

"Was it you who murdered our Oxford colleagues? Are you the killer?" he asked despite knowing the answer. "Why did you do it? What have I done wrong? What did any of us do wrong? Please don't hurt me," he pleaded as he begged for his life.

John Fallon showed no reaction to his colleague's pleas. He just stood in front of his victim and smiled. Horrified by this complete lack of empathy, Peter turned to his last hope, the boat's crew. He screamed as loud as he could, over and over.

"Captain, captain, help, help!"

They were the last words he would ever speak. Help was never going to arrive. The skipper and his mate were lying face down on the deck. Their throats had been cut. John Fallon took a plastic bag from his jacket pocket and placed it over his victim's head. Peter struggled, tossing his head from side to side, but eventually, the bag was secured with duct tape.

Once Peter Singer was dead, Vasile Popescu, the burliest of John's accomplices, manacled the body to a bedpost. The boat was driven close to the coast of Sarawak, East Malaysia, and a zodiac tender boat lowered. Two of the men waited on the tender while Vasile scuppered the charter boat. The three men made their way in the darkness to the coast, where they sunk the tender. Then they walked overland to a remote airstrip serving an isolated rural community. A private jet was waiting for them as they made their way out of the jungle.

CHAPTER FORTY-FOUR

"Professor Peter Singer has done a runner. I just phoned the ICMB in Singapore. They told me he's taken leave from work. They either don't know where he's gone, or are not willing to say. I talked with his wife, but she said Peter wouldn't even tell her where he was heading. She said he'd read the newspaper reports of the murders of his colleagues and was frightened. She was very worried for his safety," reported Jack to Diana.

"I'm hardly surprised. Everyone of Fallon's close colleagues who has been following the news must be wondering who the killer is and whether they are next on his hit list. Singapore is an international airport hub. Singer could have flown to any destination on the globe from there. I'll contact Interpol to find out which flight he took."

Jack and Donna were at Jack's Aldgate house when Diana phoned. She reported that a charter boat out of a Singaporean marina had gone missing together with its crew of two.

"It could just be a coincidence, but I thought I should mention it anyway. There's a news brief about it on page three of "The Straits Times"."

"Thanks, Diana, you're the best," replied Jack.

Jack switched on his iPad and quickly had the article on the screen.

"Look at this, Donna. A charter boat and its crew of two have been reported missing in the Malacca Strait. The skipper's wife has been waiting two days for any news. Her husband always checked in with her each day. His absence is ominous. The skipper advised the Maritime Authority they were undertaking a fifteen-hour round trip to Penang. They intended to return the next day. Seems they never reached Penang. A search of the Malacca Strait by the Maritime Port Authority has been conducted. There has been no sighting of the boat or its crew. It has simply disappeared."

Later that same day Interpol reported to Donna that no person by the name of Peter Singer had boarded a plane leaving from Changi Airport within the past week. Further, nobody fitting the description of John Fallon or his accomplices had taken any form of public transport either into or out of Singapore.

"If this is down to Fallon, I'm impressed by how he and the thugs working for him travel the world so freely without leaving a trace. Law enforcement has made no sighting of him since the reported plane crash in Colombia. My guess is he's still in the States, or is using a private jet, and abandoned or remote airstrips. It is likely the plane's transponder is switched off. That way the plane can't be detected and identified by secondary surveillance radar. When the plane's transponder is switched off the plane becomes invisible to electronic surveillance."

"Bloody hell. You're saying this psychopath could be anywhere by now. Singer was either on that boat and has gone to a watery grave, or he is so well hidden that we'll never find him."

Just then Donna's phone rang. She took the ten-minute phone call. Afterward, she turned to Jack with a look of dread written all over her face.

"A detective with the Singaporean Police says one of Singer's neighbours spied a couple of foreign-looking men hanging around the neighbourhood. They were a couple of big white guys who stood out like sore thumbs, as European tourists do in Asia. They've been identified on the apartment block's CCTV surveillance camera. It seems they had Singer under surveillance for a few days before he did his runner."

"Well, that's that then. We may need to accept the probability that Singer is no longer amongst the living. There seems no point in us visiting Singapore."

"Just how many potential targets are there? Surely there can't be many left"

"We have to find out who was in charge of the grant application committees that assessed Fallon's grant applications after he moved to the States. Whoever it is could provide us with a list of reviewers who may have trashed Fallon's more recent grant applications. Those reviewers could be the next targets if there is some sort of chronological order to this. It may be our last chance to prevent more killings."

Donna phoned her FBI colleagues to make the request, with instructions to get back to her ASAP.

CHAPTER FORTY-FIVE

John Fallon boarded a packed commercial airlines flight to a small country in central Europe. The passport he was using identified him as Nicolae Alexandrescu, a Romanian expat. It was courtesy of one of his orphanage friends who went on to excel at forgery. John Fallon was unrecognizable. His short voluminous greying hair was now thinner and blonde. He had swarthy olive skin due to tanning cream that altered his naturally pale complexion. He wore trendy brightly-coloured clothes that a man much younger might wear. He was wearing the most fashionable Italian sunglasses. A newly acquired small tattoo was apparent on his neck and a pierced earring in his left ear lobe. He had never previously disfigured his body.

As he took his seat in the economy section of the plane, John felt a sharp excruciating pain in the left side of his head. The pain made him grimace, and he almost lost consciousness. He collapsed into his seat. It had only been six months since he had been diagnosed with inoperable glioblastoma. Glioblastoma was the most aggressive form of brain cancer and a certain death sentence. Typically, the tumour had proven to be resistant to chemotherapy, radiation treatment, and other forms of therapy. What's more, the primary tumour had invaded deep into surrounding regions of the brain. John had sought several second opinions from some of America's foremost oncologists. Their consensus, from multiple scans and biopsies, was that he had no more than eight months to live. Possibly as few as two months left, or maybe even a year if he was lucky. It was no more predictable than rolling the dice. One thing was certain. The headaches were gradually becoming more frequent, and more severe. He had already experienced nausea and vomiting, and blurred vision, despite being off treatment. He realised he was rapidly running out of time. He had passed through the four stages of cancer grief, namely denial, anger, bargaining, depression, and had finally come to accept his fate. He felt a sense of contentment when he reflected on the untimely deaths of his colleagues. He had given some of them just one minute to reflect on the value of their wretched lives. That was all those bastards deserved. At least he had had several months to reflect and do what had to be done. Strangely though, before receiving the cancer diagnosis he had had no compulsive urge to kill. Now though, the craving was like a raging hunger that had to be satiated.

For now though, he was going to make one last gesture to humanity. What is a wealthy man to do when he knows with absolute certainty that he has only a few months to live? He had sold everything he owned and inherited from his wealthy adoptive parents. He had laundered the money through foreign banks and businesses untraceable by the FBI. He was going to establish a new Foundation that would care for the orphans of Romania.

Nicolae had always felt he was different from other people. There was something cold, and unforgiving, yet needy, about his personality. He didn't have the empathy he saw others express. Yet he felt a deep-seated longing to be loved. His need had partially been quenched by his adoptive Mother June, but still, her love had come too late. In this respect, he told himself that he wasn't that far different from some of his academic colleagues who also lacked empathy. Perhaps their upbringing had rendered them different as well. As a biomedical scientist, he knew that there was a scientific explanation. People always marvelled at how identical twins dressed the same, talked the same, finished each other's sentences, and continued to grow alike into old age. Both in looks and interests. Yet when they didn't, people would just shrug their shoulders in puzzlement, and wonder why not. Were they never true identical twins in the first place, they would ask themselves?

John Fallon's life's work had been to understand this anomaly. He had been a pioneer in the comparatively new biomedical field of epigenetics. Science had shown that while identical twins are born with identical genes, the expression of their genes is influenced by their life experiences, particularly as newborns. The part of a gene that controls gene expression becomes modified, causing a gene to be either shut down, partially inhibited, or activated. The genes of children who are neglected, unloved, and abused are modified differently compared to those of children who are loved and nurtured. Epigenetic changes due to childhood neglect influence personality, and cause a failure to learn, adapt, and survive.

To this day, many of the children born and orphaned during the mid to late nineteen hundreds in Romania are damaged beyond repair. The orphanages were referred to as "the slaughterhouses of souls". John Fallon knew this. He had lived it. He knew his early childhood had scarred his genetic makeup, and irrevocably marred his personality. His life-long ambition had been to determine the genetic changes arising from childhood neglect and abuse. He had aimed to find ways to restore the normal activity of the genes affected. His Oxford colleagues through sheer malice had blocked his progress, even after he had moved to another country. He just couldn't escape their influence and maliciousness. Damn them. Now there was no hope of devising a therapeutic option. His last resort was to use his adoptive parents' money to raise the level of care and services for orphanage children. He would ensure that a least some of the children were cared for properly, and hopefully loved and nurtured. He was going to use his parents' wealth to deinstitutionalize the care of orphans in Romania.

CHAPTER FORTY-SIX

Donna received word that Jackson's body had been discovered. The rental apartment in which he had been murdered had been paid for using cash for one week. The body hadn't been discovered until the end of the week when the cleaner had arrived to prepare the room for the next guests.

"I sure as hell wouldn't want to have been that cleaner," declared Donna to Jack. "It was the same MO, you know the bag over the head."

"I think we are going to need to delve into Fallon's past. I have a gut feeling that something is hiding there. There has to be more to Fallon's connection to that east-European gang," suggested Jack.

"Perhaps the unusual MO for some of the murders can tell us something. Most murders involve stabbings, shootings, strangulation, or bashings. Have you previously come across any asphyxiations using a plastic bag?" asked Donna.

"I confess, very few. I'll ask a former colleague at Scotland Yard to do a worldwide search on any cases involving that MO. I suggest your FBI colleagues also undertake a search. They'll need to omit cases of assisted suicide involving plastic bags and an inert gas as a euthanasia device. They'll also need to ignore solvent abuse and sexual asphyxia. I suggest they search for serial or multiple killings using this MO," said Jack.

"What's the inert gas for?" asked Donna.

"It prevents the sense of suffocation. Hence it also prevents the panic and struggling before the suicider becomes unconscious. It wasn't used in our murder cases."

"What do you think about sexual asphyxia? I enjoy sex enough without having to resort to that extreme."

"Me too," replied Jack, grinning.

Jack and Donna spent the next few days at Jack's house in Aldgate. Occasionally they ventured to Baron & Associates in Aldwych to enable Jack to catch up on other cases with Aiko and Stefan. They would exercise together in the early morning, make love, shower, have breakfast, then walk along the Northbank from Tower Bridge to Westminster Bridge. It was one of Jack's favourite walks, taking in the riverside views, and majestic cityscapes. Then they would return to either Aldgate or Aldwych to work on the case. They searched the internet extensively for any cases of multiple homicides involving asphyxiation with a plastic bag. They came up empty. Then they received a phone call that would completely change the course of their investigation.

"Hi Jack, Brian here. How're things in the world of the private eye?"

"Hi, Brian. I can't deny it's a challenge, but I am up for it. I hope the Yard is treating you OK?"

"I can't complain. Look, Jack, John passed on your request. I got landed the job. I might have something of interest for you. The only mass or serial killing by plastic bag asphyxiation, apart from that Japanese family you mentioned, was at an orphanage in Romania. It happened more than twenty years ago."

"You're kidding?"

"I kid you not. A group of caregivers was found in an office on the orphanage grounds. Each caregiver had been suffocated by a plastic bag with duct tape secured around the neck. One poor chap had been sodomized with part of a broom handle. Looks like some sort of retribution killing."

"Were the killers ever caught?"

"No, the killers have never been identified. It was rumoured they were probably disgruntled orphans who'd reached adulthood. It's thought they'd chosen to exact their revenge on their caregivers. Can't blame them. Hell, the shocking photos I've seen of neglected and emaciated children dressed in rags left me feeling right sick. You know half the children there died of neglect."

"Yes, I remember hearing those stories."

"Once knowledge of those hell holes reached Western nations there was a lot of press coverage. Some of the luckier children were adopted by couples from Western nations, in particular from the USA and UK."

"Fact is, Romania isn't alone in their cruel treatment of orphans. In many Western nations, orphaned children were, and still are, placed into foster, state, church, and school care, and youth justice facilities where too many are systematically sexually abused, assaulted, and neglected by errant carers, and governments. Sometimes even children with loving parents and happy home lives are predated upon by paedophiles that secure jobs looking after or teaching children."

"Oh, I didn't know that. That's painful to hear. I can thank my lucky stars that I had a happy childhood. Anyway, I hope those Romanian murders have something to do with your case."

"You know what? You're a bloody star," exclaimed Jack. "Remind me to shout you a beer next time you're free. Thanks, Brian."

"No problemo. I look forward to that beer. I'll e-mail you the relevant documents I have right away."

Jack quickly explained the content of the phone conversation to Donna. She gave him a big smile and shook her fists defiantly in the air.

"Yessss..., at last, we have a real lead!" she shouted.

"I'll ask Diana to obtain a copy of Fallon's birth certificate. It's just possible he was born in Romania and was raised in one of their orphanages. We need to check whether he was subsequently adopted by the Fallons and whether they visited Romania sometime in the 1970s."

Jack and Donna went to lunch at one of Jack's favourite restaurants on the South Bank to celebrate the breakthrough. They waited impatiently for Diana's reply. Diana phoned Jack at home early the next morning.

"I think you've hit the jackpot," she declared. "Seems John Fallon was born Nicolae Antonescu in Ciumeghiu, Romania. He spent his early childhood at an orphanage in Cajlia, Romania. He was adopted at the age of eight by the Fallons. They visited the orphanage in mid 1970 and took the boy back with them to the UK. Fallon senior was a very wealthy industrialist, so the boy must have had a privileged upbringing from that point on."

"That presumably explains the presence of the east-Europeans he has been associating with. Do you think you can get the names of the children who were at the orphanage with Nicolae at that time? Ask Stefan to help you as he knows several European languages. We may be able to trace the children to the present day and track them down. Or at least get an insight into their history."

"I'll do my best. I'll e-mail the documents I have now."

"Thanks, Diana, you're amazing."

CHAPTER FORTY-SEVEN

Nicolae Alexandrescu, alias Nicolae Antonescu or John Fallon was seated across the table from two well-dressed men wearing tailored dark blue pin-striped suits. Nicolae's appearance had changed yet again. He now bore the appearance of a very wealthy benefactor. His thick jet-black hair was swished back from his face which bore fashionable rimless eyeglasses. He was attired in the finest Italian Brioni suit, white shirt, trousers, and shiny Italian black leather shoes. The two lawyers facing him had sensed money was coming their way when they were first introduced. They had smiled smugly at one another. Their expectations were not wrong.

"How can we be of service Mr. Alexandrescu?" probed Mr. Favre, the more senior member of the duo, who projected a broad smile revealing a perfect set of glistening white teeth.

"I wish to establish a tax-exempt charitable Foundation. I am a considerably wealthy individual. Not wanting to go into detail, the money I deposit with you must be untouchable by any international authority. It is to be invested in the Foundation and the interest payments released for the specific benefit of the orphans of Romania. Both present and past orphans to improve their condition. The charitable Foundation and the results it achieves are to be widely advertised so that additional funding can be accrued from international donors. I am to remain anonymous as the Foundation's founder. A Board will be established to govern the Foundation. At least one of you, or both if you wish, will have a place on the Board. You will be handsomely paid for this service. I will serve temporarily as the interim Chair. But I am a very busy man. You will need to quickly identify an individual to replace me. Whoever it is must be strongly motivated to pursue the Foundation's goals."

"Can I ask, what is the size of the investment?" interrupted Mr. Mueller, the other lawyer who was eager to know the amount of money being considered.

John considered the question. He was reluctant to provide an exact figure of his investment at this stage. Banks are required by law to know the provenance of a client's money to prevent money laundering. John had no worries in this regard, as he had receipts for all the sales of his parents' assets by John Fallon, and transfer of the funds to his alias Mr Alexandrescu as the broker. In any case, John had carefully chosen this particular bank as it was known to have profited from the flow of dirty money and could turn a blind eye to potentially criminal activities when required. It had been publicly fined twice for doing so. However, the legal requirement for the bank to obtain client identification and verification was something to be more concerned about. He would arrange for his expert forger to prepare his identity documents when the time was right.

"You will learn soon enough. As I have stated it is a considerable sum," replied Nicolae.

The two lawyers turned to each other and grinned, like hungry crocodiles upon seeing a fattened wildebeest approaching the muddy edges of a swollen river.

"And what are the specific goals of the Foundation?" requested Favre.

"Foremost, the Foundation will seek to deinstitutionalize the care of orphans in Romania. Orphaned children in Romania have been subjected to institutionalized neglect for decades. It has to stop. Funding and support will be provided to those families who wish to have their children returned. You have to understand that some children have been institutionalized so long that they are viewed as irrevocably damaged. Some families will not want to care for them. In this case, they must go into foster care within small family groupings where funding would be provided for specialist care."

"That sounds like a very noble cause, Mr. Alexandrescu. Do you have a name for the Foundation?"

"The Foundation is to be named "The June Foundation for Romanian Children," replied Nicolae.

"Does the month of June have some significance for you?" questioned Favre.

"Something like that," replied Nicolae, not wanting to explain the name's significance.

His stepmother June had shown him unconditional love. Now his parents' wealth would enable the orphaned children of Romania to receive the love and support they deserved. The love and support he should have had, and yearned for as a young child all those many years ago.

"I will transfer the required funding into your account today to get the establishment of the Foundation underway. I have to return to the United States today as I have important business there."

"We will start the process to register the Foundation once we receive the funds. We will make discreet inquiries as to who might be worthy of being appointed to the Board. Be assured, that we have your best interests in mind. We will provide you with the resumes of potential Board members so that you can make the final selection, including the Chair. How would you like the resumes delivered?"

"You will need to set up a unique DropBox account to store the files. You are to place all correspondence into this box. Here is the e-mail address to use to send me the shared link," answered Nicolae, handing over a piece of paper with an e-mail address.

"Certainly, as you say," responded Favre.

With that, the two lawyers shook Nicolae's hand, and he left the building.

CHAPTER FORTY-EIGHT

J ack and Donna were excited by the new revelations. Donna
conveyed the new findings to her FBI colleagues in Washington.
They in turn passed them on to agents at field offices throughout the
country. Jack passed the information on to his colleagues at the
MET.

"So John Fallon is still alive. That plane crash in Colombia was
likely a ruse," declared Jack, looking at Donna for her agreement.

"The big question is where is he now, and what are his
intentions? Has he finished with his killing spree? Or is some other
poor sod waiting to be asphyxiated?" asked Donna.

"He intends to kill all those colleagues he holds a grudge
against."

"If he is following some sort of chronological order, then maybe
he's finished with the Oxford Bridge colleagues. He might be about
to move on to anyone who insulted him or damaged his career after
taking up his position at Harvard University."

"I have to admit, I didn't understand the titles of Fallon's research
papers listed in Brown's report. His research is way above my
understanding and pay level. I gather it has something to do with
trying to figure out how a person's upbringing affects their genes and
personality."

"Certainly is a fascinating topic. From what I've learned he
would have obtained most of his latest research funding from grant
applications to the National Institute of Genetics (NIG), which
provides significant amounts of extramural funding, after he moved
to the States," added Donna.

"Yes, that's the genetics equivalent of our Medical Research
Council, the nation's major funder of medical research. I bet that
anyone who has maliciously critiqued his NIG grant applications
would likely be a potential target."

"I'll get my FBI colleagues to obtain the referee reports for all of Fallon's major NIG grant applications while working at Harvard University. That is supposing the NIG keep records."

"We can look for obvious signs of malicious intent. A personal attack on his integrity, ability, and record might give away a malicious colleague who holds a grudge and is a potential target."

"We need to check whether his Oxford Bridge University colleagues were asked to review his NIG applications."

"Yes, they may have even harassed him from across the Atlantic."

"We'll need to pass the reports by an expert in the field to decide if there is any unsubstantiated attack on Fallon's research grant proposals."

"I think we could ask Professor Brown."

"Agreed."

Jack rang Diana, who with the help of Stefan, had learned that the names of the children at the Cajlia orphanage had been recorded and the records maintained. The names and some details would be e-mailed from Romania in a few days after a small payment had been made.

Jack and Donna waited patiently for the information they had requested. They filled in their time visiting places in London that Donna had never visited before. They also took the time to catch up on their other cases. Eventually, Diana e-mailed the list of names of the orphans who'd been housed with Nicolae at the Cajlia orphanage, up to the time of his departure, and their current state of care. The list contained only the names of the boys. Almost half had died due to the atrocious conditions at the orphanage. That left thirty-five boys who could have formed a close association with Nicolae. Amongst fifteen boys of similar age to Nicolae, there were around eight survivors who would be classified "normal" and had left the orphanage and integrated into the community. The remainder could be classed as damaged, institutionalized, or "unrecoverable", and were still under state care. Diana had underlined the names of the eight boys who were now suspects in the serial murders of John Fallon's academic colleagues.

"Let's hope that some of the boys, now men of course, are still using their birth names," said Jack eyeing Donna.

Donna contacted her FBI colleagues to ask them to check the names with US Customs and Border Protection. This was not a trivial exercise as there are more than three hundred official ports of entry into the USA, including land borders, seaports, and airports. In turn, Jack asked Diana to check the same with UK Customs and Border Control.

"It's worth a try," said Jack trying to sound convincing.

He was only too aware that private planes, helicopters, ships, and boats can readily deposit illegal immigrants on unoccupied shores. And at sanctuary cities that fail to enforce immigration law because immigration checks are either absent or lax. John Fallon may even be wealthy enough to own a private jet.

"I've asked Diana to check the names of the boys against the list of known male criminals held by the General Inspectorate of the Romanian Police. Hopefully, at least one or several of the boys has previously been incarcerated for a crime," mentioned Jack.

"They might be able to produce a photo ID we can post. I've also requested the same from Interpol."

It took a full week before Jack and Donna heard back from their sources. Four of the boys were well known to the Romanian police. They had each progressed from small crimes such as pick-pocketing to extortion, drug trafficking, and money laundering. They had served jail time for different periods, but were currently out of jail. They appeared to have several aliases. Their movements had become increasingly difficult to monitor.

"The Romanian Police concede they can't confirm the whereabouts of any of the eight men over the past six months," mentioned Donna.

"That looks like a dead-end then," sighed Jack.

"Not quite. We now have ID photos of four of the men. If they cross any international borders we'll have them."

Diana e-mailed through a collection of referee reports for John Fallon's applications. They stretched back over the time he had spent at Harvard University. The title of the research topic and the name of the referee were listed at the top of the page. Jack e-mailed them to Professor Brown for his analysis. After a couple of days, they were returned with the analysis. Brown had highlighted in yellow sections or sentences that appeared to attack Fallon personally, rather than critique the actual research proposal. Fallon had submitted thirty major new and revised grant applications in the past ten years. Just one of the grant applications had been successful. Professor Brown had mentioned that normally ten to twenty percent of submitted grant applications are funded, depending on the level of NIG funding available from the United States Government in a particular year. But a very capable senior researcher such as Fallon might be expected to have better odds of success. Brown had mentioned that each application was reviewed by at least five external reviewers.

Jack and Donna spent most of the afternoon skim-reading around one hundred and fifty referee reports, and Brown's comments. Brown had done a thorough job in pinpointing comments that looked out of place. The grant that had been funded had received glowing reports from all five referees. The other grant applications had at least two damning reports, amongst otherwise very supportive reports. Brown had mentioned that just a single damning report was normally enough to cause a grant application to be declined. What was immediately obvious, and pointed out by Brown, was that the unfavourable reports were written by just seven individuals. It was as if they had been regularly singled out to provide unfavourable comments.

"Something is very odd here," exclaimed Jack. "The unfavourable reports are all written by just seven referees."

"Yes, they are all Fallon's old colleagues, Bentley, Campbell, Corbyn, Moore, Dalton, Jackson, and Singer."

"Don't you think it is extraordinary that the NIG chose to include his past colleagues? There must be numerous potential referees to select from worldwide?"

"I agree. I'm sure the NIG has rules about conflict of interest. Surely, close associates, either current or past, would normally be excluded. My guess is someone decided to break the rules," mentioned Donna.

"Who needs enemies when you have colleagues like that lot. Look at this comment. It says here that Fallon was only interested in getting the money. That he had no interest in the actual research."

"That's a weird comment. Very malicious. As I understand, the funding can only be spent on the research and is administered by the University. It can't be used personally. Anyway, Fallon was independently wealthy, having inherited a vast fortune from his adoptive parents."

"His colleagues seem hell-bent on attacking his integrity, that's for sure. This report states "why does he think he deserves such a large grant", "he's only interested in making money from his results", "he doesn't belong at the University and within academia", and "why doesn't he fund his own research", "there is no merit in this proposal or any other proposal I've seen from this particular researcher", "he's done nothing with his research results"."

"I can perhaps understand why Fallon's colleagues may have wanted to destroy his reputation while at Oxford Bridge University, but why continue with their harassment after he had moved to Harvard?"

"Can only be jealousy, or grievance for a past perceived injustice, or action, or a decision that Fallon had taken."

"Look at this further comment from Professor Brown. He says he forgot to mention a grant application Fallon had submitted to the UK Genome Research Foundation while at Oxford Bridge University. Seems the application received excellent reports from the external referees. It was approved for funding by the grant assessing committee. But the Foundation's committee in charge of allocating the funding decided not to fund Fallon. Instead, they gave the funding to a more junior researcher who'd gained a lesser score. The reason was "they felt that Fallon already had enough research money"."

"Who was the Chair of that Foundation's committee?

"Have a guess."

"Was it one of Fallon's Oxford Bridge University colleagues?"

"You guessed right. It was David Corbyn."

"I'm thinking whoever chaired the committee that assessed Fallon's NIG grant proposals, and rigged the reviews that damned Fallon's applications, could well be a target."

CHAPTER FORTY-NINE

D r Victor Luca had held the position of Scientific Review
Officer (SRO) at the Center for Scientific Review in
Maryland for the past fifteen years. His job was to process grant
applications involving genetics research submitted to the NIG. This
involved assigning reviewers for each grant application. It was also
his responsibility to select a distinguished individual to Chair the
grant application review panel. The selected panel members met in
person at the Center for Scientific Review to discuss and assess the
grant applications submitted in each funding round.

Victor Luca had been born into a large Jewish community in
Bucharest, Romania. He was a bright young man who went on to
obtain a PhD in genetics at a Russian University. He completed
post-doctoral positions at the University of Tokyo, and the NIG in
Maryland. He worked as an NIG scientist for many years before
taking up the position of SRO of the Epigenetics Study Section.

Victor Luca was now an elderly man with shock white thinning
hair, who on the outside seemed quite cheerful and content. But
within, Victor harboured many sad, dark, and painful memories.
Romania had been home to hundreds of thousands of Jews until
the Second World War. Victor's early childhood had largely been a
happy one. His father, a tailor, was both kind and generous. Victor
and his friends had access to many Yiddish books, and they attended
Yiddish theatres and movies for children. His family attended the
local synagogue on Shabbat together with the rest of the large Jewish
community. On rising every morning he would chant the Modeh
Ani, a traditional prayer to be said by children, with his mother who
worked with her husband in the family shop. He particularly enjoyed
the quiet times with his mother when she would read to him from
the five books of Moses (the Torah).

Victor's happy life changed dramatically when Romania signed the Tripartite Pact, allying itself with the Axis Alliance and the Nazis. Romania had joined the Axis Alliance in response to offers of economic and military protection by the Nazis. An ever-increasing number of laws and regulations passed by the Romanian Government specifically targeted Jewish-owned shops. Victor's father was forced to sell the family's tailoring business, and life quickly became a hand-to-mouth existence in a world of violence, misery, and mistrust. But no one could have dared anticipate just how bad life was to become. Victor's most vivid memory of the war and his childhood was the day his family, together with their Jewish neighbours and friends, were rounded up into a group in the centre of Bucharest by government forces. He could still vividly picture in his mind the horrifying scene that unfolded that day. He could still hear the screams. He could still see the falling bodies as they crumpled all around him when the government forces opened fire on his neighbours and friends.

He could still remember the blood-spattered dress of his neighbour, the mother of his closest friend. Worst of all, he could still hear the cry "Ima, Ima Ima!" of her son, his closest friend Ezra, as he cried out for his dying mother. He could still picture the scene as a stiff-backed jackbooted Nazi officer walked swiftly forward, and removed his Luger pistol from its holster. He pointed the weapon at Ezra and shot the young boy in the back of the head as he lay crying and clutching his prostrate mother. Bits of blood and brain splattered the officer's highly polished jackboots.

"Schweinhund, schmutzig Juden," swore the Nazi officer in a rage, who then proceeded to kick the limp dead body of the boy, causing him to roll off his mother. He then placed each boot one at a time on the thigh of the mother and used her dress to wipe the human remains off his boots.

Miraculously, Victor and his mother survived the mass slaughter. It was as if they had been especially singled out to bear witness to the atrocity. They would live to let other Jews know there was no place for them in the new Romania. Victor still harboured that awful nagging feeling of guilt that lone survivors endure. It just wouldn't go away.

"Why should I live when so many others died that day?" he would constantly ask himself.

After the thunder of gunfire had ceased, and there was just the two of them standing amongst the fallen bodies, his mother who was shaking hysterically, hugged him closely in her arms. She whispered to him not to be afraid as she would always protect him. Victor's father had not been so fortunate. He was no longer the family protector as he had been killed that day along with most of their neighbours and friends. The bodies of several of the victims were hung from meat hooks in the city square for all to see. They had been mutilated, and were unrecognizable. It was an atrocious act, which sought to deprive the victims of any last remaining dignity or humanity.

Victor also vividly remembered the day the Romanian authorities forced him and his mother into a wooden cart. They were transported like stock to a concentration camp at Pechora in the northeast, away from his home. The Jewish prisoners at this camp were not murdered in gas chambers like at other camps. Instead, thousands of Jewish prisoners imprisoned at the camp were systematically and slowly murdered by starvation, dehydration, brutality, and neglect.

Victor had painful memories of his mother, formerly a plump woman, being slowly reduced to a skeleton. She would visit him in the children's barrack, bringing him morsels of bread when she could. She was sacrificing her health to save his. Sacrificing her own life to save his. He remembered those days when she first failed to visit him. Victor later learned from other survivors that the extra rations of food his mother had brought to him had come at a heavy price. A particular guard in charge of her barrack had her submit to rape and gross sexual favours, almost daily, for the food that kept Victor alive. The guard had cold-bloodedly shot her in the head at point-blank range when he had grown bored with her. The man's name became forever engraved in Victor's memory. Dracul Antonescu, a Romanian, was a cruel young man feared by all the prisoners. They nicknamed him the "evil one". Each day the older children were forced to transport dead bodies from the barracks to mass grave sites on the outskirts of the camp. Victor would never forget the day he had to lift the body of his dead mother into a cart under the watchful eye of Dracul. He would never forget the smirk on Dracul's ugly face as he was forced to cart his mother away for mass burial. It was the day he vowed to stay alive to testify against the Nazi guards and their Romanian collaborators. At the end of the war, the concentration camp was liberated by the Red Army. Victor was a starving child of skin and bone, just barely alive.

It had been almost ten years since Victor had appointed Professor John Fallon to one of his grant assessment panels. Fallon's resume indicated he had been born and educated in the United Kingdom. But Victor was certain he could distinctly recognize a faint European accent, possibly Romanian. The accent intrigued him. He set out to research John Fallon's background and upbringing as a project of personal interest. Nothing in his resume indicated Fallon had spent time in eastern Europe. Victor had friends in Mossad and the Simon Wiesenthal Center, and had even been a Nazi hunter for a short time. He knew how to research peoples' identities. Victor would never forget the day he discovered that John Fallon had been born Nicolae Antonescu, a Romanian citizen, and the son of Dracul Antonescu.

Towards the end of the war, the fascist authorities were deposed. Romania abruptly switched sides by joining the Allies. Many Nazi collaborators were rounded up. They were convicted of war crimes, and either imprisoned or executed. Dracul Antonescu was ostracized by his community. He found it impossible to secure work. He and his young wife lived a meagre existence under the constant threat of reprisal. Dracul was murdered late one night while walking close to home. His killer or killers were never identified. His wife, now single, homeless, and unemployed, gave up her baby boy to an orphanage. She perished soon after from poverty and disease. Her boy Nicolae, who she never visited at the orphanage, was left forever an orphan.

Victor felt as if he had been given a "gift", a chance for retribution. He had within arms reach the offspring of the monster who had raped and murdered his mother, and many other women at the concentration camp. The offspring of the man who had so nearly starved him to death. It was monstrous that Nicolae Antonescu, alias John Fallon, had escaped and was living an incredibly prosperous and privileged life in America. Isn't it said that "the sins of the father shall be visited upon the sons?" Rightly so, but the modern legal system didn't allow for such justice. He had to be the judge, jury, and executioner. He decided to sentence John Fallon to a slow and miserable death. It was his duty. It was his right.

Victor invited John Fallon to serve as a reviewer at several grant application assessment panel meetings. He always invited John and a couple of other members of the group to his home for dinner. It had been so simple to contaminate John's food with a massive amount of polychlorinated bisphenyls (PCBs). This slow-acting poison has no taste and smell. It is almost ubiquitous in the environment. Everyone is contaminated with low levels of PCBs to some extent. Yet high levels of PCBs are a slow-acting poison known to cause cancer and increase the risk of heart attack, stroke, and diabetes. Befriending John had been a stroke of genius. He could invite John to Study

Group meetings, and poison him at the same time. He would ensure John's grant applications were unsuccessful. He gained a huge thrill from watching John struggle to obtain research grant funding from the NIG. He loved to mock the man, to see him deflated.

On every visit, he would state "I'm so sorry to learn your grant application wasn't successful in the last round. But you know the process is so incredibly competitive these days. I could help you write your next grant application to a different agency if you like."

All the while Victor had no intention of helping John Fallon. On the contrary, he would use all his guile and cunning to ensure John Fallon's grant applications were never funded. He intended to make John Fallon suffer slowly, and die painfully.

Victor had read countless reviews for hundreds of research grant applications his panels had to assess. He knew grant reviewers could be roughly classified into three different types. Some were not critical. They saw themselves as saintly and virtuous, generous and helpful, and would give glowing reviews for all grant applications they were asked to critique, especially the applications of people they knew. In reality, they were of little help to the grant application assessment process. Fortunately, the majority of reviewers were critical and constructive. They would highlight the good points and limitations of a grant proposal, within an overall positive frame of mind. They were generally the most helpful to the grant application assessment process, and gave sound advice to applicants that they could use for future applications. Finally, some reviewers were critical but destructive. Such reviewers only highlighted the limitations of a proposal. They failed to mention any good points an application might have. Often they would attempt to make subtle or blatant personal attacks on the applicant. Such reviewers could be said to harbour borderline schizophrenic personalities. They saw every applicant as a potential competitor, even though they themselves were often highly successful. Other such reviewers had become jaded and bitter by a lack of success. They saw it as a way of exacting their revenge, particularly upon applicants they knew who were successful.

For John Fallon's grant applications he always carefully selected two reviewers that would provide negative reports. He had noticed that several of John's previous colleagues from Oxford Bridge University were overly harsh in critiquing John's grant applications. He thought this was rather strange but very useful. He would include them as reviewers of John's grants, whenever possible. Nobody would have reason to suspect that such a distant colleague would represent a conflict of interest. In any case, he had formed the opinion that many scientists were not particularly honest about conflicts of interest. Some would relish getting one over on a past colleague they happened to dislike.

Victor's final ploy was his selection of a Chair for his grant assessment panel. He had come to rely on a fellow Jew, Professor Nathan Schuller. Schuller was a close friend whose parents had been murdered by the Nazis at the Auschwitz camp. Nathan Schuller was well aware of Victor's early life at the camp at Pechora, and his suffering at the hands of Dracul Antonescu. Together they made a pact to ensure that John Fallon was deprived of research funding, just as the Nazis and their Romanian collaborators had deprived them of any humanity. The Chair was like a judge. The Chair would summarize a panel's arguments and opinions. At the same time, the Chair could sway the panel's decision-making. John Fallon's grant applications would have little chance of being funded.

CHAPTER FIFTY

J ohn Fallon read the report from his lawyers. It updated the progress they had made towards the establishment of the June Foundation. The report included the names of several prominent individuals that had been put forward for consideration as board members. Their various somewhat lengthy resumes were included. John then read the cover letter accompanying the report. When he came to the end of the letter he was both perplexed and disturbed upon reading the final comment from Favre.

"We are sorry your father Dracul Antonescu was treated so badly by his countrymen. We congratulate you on your amazing turn of fortune."

John had presumed that the lawyers would be interested in the verification of his identity, as it is a legal requirement for the prevention of money laundering. Accordingly, he had arranged for his master forger to prepare his identity documents. Yet this final comment proved that the lawyers had taken it upon themselves to independently research his identity and history. Perhaps they had used some sort of facial recognition software that could see through his disguise. His face was on the internet, in University and conference press releases, and on the University websites. They would know his real name and his work history. But more concerning, they had used his real identity to delve into his past. John Fallon could feel his anger rising.

Presumably, they would now know the approximate size of his wealth, if they had researched the history of his industrialist stepfather. Thankfully though, they would not know of his recent activities. But, it was all just a matter of time. Nevertheless, the lawyers had raised his curiosity. Who was his father, this man Dracul Antonescu, and why had he been treated so badly?

Was the lawyers' comment a threat of some sort? Were they going to blackmail him, perhaps? Why specifically mention the name of his birth father? He had never bothered wasting his time tracing his biological parents. They meant nothing to him. He had no memory of them. They had deserted him when he was just a baby. They had never visited him at the orphanage. He had never wanted to be reacquainted with them, ever.

John Fallon gave a lawyer in Romania and one of his closest friends Power of Attorney to gain proof of his identity. Within a short time, he held a copy of his birth certificate. Dracul Antonescu was cited on the document as his father. Elena Antonescu was cited as his mother. Together with the birth certificate were the death certificates of both parents. John arranged for the same lawyer to discover whether any of his close relations were still alive.

It turned out that Dracul had a younger brother, Florin Antonescu. He was still alive, living in Oradea, a city just north of Castel Cajlia. John Fallon flew by private jet to a rural airfield in Romania. As the plane descended he had a magnificent view of the vast ancient woodlands of Romania, amongst the oldest forests in Europe. He then travelled by car to Oradea. It was one of Romania's larger and more prosperous cities known for its architecture dating back to the Austro-Hungarian empire. He located Florin in a run-down suburb in Bihor County. Everywhere there were large red brick houses in various stages of development. Most were in disrepair as if building contracts had simply dried up. Aging building materials were strewn everywhere. Lawns and verges were left unmowed and unkempt. Florin lived in one such house. Its red brick walls were plastered but left grey and unpainted.

Florin and his wife were now very elderly and frail. They stood on the doorstep with their white hair, leathery wrinkled skin, and sallow faces. They looked frightened and uncertain when confronted by the foreign-looking man who had knocked on their door.

"I'm searching for my Uncle, Florin Antonescu" said John in fluent Romanian, with a pronounced English accent.

Florin looked across to his wife, before nervously answering.

"That is my name, but who are you?"

"My name is Nicolae Antonescu. I have only just discovered that I am the son of Dracul Antonescu."

The elderly couple looked wide-eyed at each other, totally dumbfounded by the news.

"My only sibling Dracul had a boy. But as far as we know, he died in an orphanage not far from here," said Florin, who coughed up phlegm and spat it vigorously onto the doorstep after speaking his brother's name.

"I can see some resemblance in the face. Look at the shape of his nose and mouth. And the eyebrows," commented the old woman.

"Yes, it is possible," conceded Florin with a frown.

"What do you want? We have nothing to give you."

"I survived the orphanage, and was raised in England by my adoptive parents. I want to know about my father Dracul. What he did for a living. How he died."

"You'd better come in then. We can have some ceai (tea)," offered the old woman.

John was led into the kitchen. He was offered a wooden chair next to a large wooden table. The old lady, his aunt, placed a pot of water onto the coal range to make the tea.

"Your father, my older brother," said Florin, "was the black sheep of our family. He was a very cruel man. When we were children, he used to beat and kick me almost every day. He was lazy, and never helped with any of the household chores. He was still a teenager when he left home. He had jobs but they never lasted. On the railroad and in the fields. He hated Jews and communists. Anyone different. He and his friends used to harass our Jewish neighbours, sometimes bashing them unconscious. He joined the Iron Guard against our parents' will. He sought out a job as a guard at a concentration camp for Jews at Pechora, when Romania sided with the Nazis. No doubt he was cruel to the prisoners there. He was lucky to escape execution after the Allies won the war. After that, he found it difficult to get work. We gave Dracul and his young wife what we could, but times after the war were hard."

"How did he die?" John asked unemotionally.

"He was murdered late one night while walking home. He had suffered a massive head injury. Like someone hit him in the back of the head with a claw hammer. The murderers were never found and brought to justice. But it was rumoured that some of the Jewish survivors from the camp at Pechora were responsible."

"What about my mother? How did she die?"

"She had always been quite frail. After your father was murdered, she became very ill. We heard she died of consumption in a sanatorium."

The small family group spent two hours discussing John's birth parents and relatives. In return, John offered only vague references to his own history. When he left he thanked the elderly couple. He told them they were unlikely to meet again. He later instructed his lawyers to place a tidy sum of money in the old couple's bank account.

News that his father had been a vile man detested by his family and ostracized by his community meant nothing to John Fallon. He had absolutely no feelings for his birth parents. He had never known them. Only his uncle's face gave a glimpse of what his father may have looked like. His father could have been a mass murderer for all he cared. According to his Uncle, he probably was.

It was only when John was seated in a comfortable chair aboard his private jet on his way back to the United States, feeling sleepy, that he recalled something that potentially had grave implications. It was his father's loathing of Jews that triggered him to remember

Victor Luca, someone he called his friend or at least a close colleague. John knew Victor Luca was a Romanian Jew, but until now that fact meant nothing to him. John had never confided in Victor that he was also a child of Romania, preferring that no one knew about his impoverished upbringing. Likewise, Victor had never confided in John about the exact details of his Jewish upbringing in Romania. Was it possible that Victor's relatives were imprisoned at the concentration camp in Pechora, the same camp where his father had worked as a guard? The implications horrified John. He immediately began to have very dark thoughts about how his life had played out.

CHAPTER FIFTY-ONE

D onna's FBI contact rang to report that Dr Victor Luca was the SRO in charge of processing and assessing John Fallon's research grant applications submitted to the NIG.

"Do you have his address?" she asked.

"Yes. He has a house near his workplace in Bethesda just off Tuckerman Lane. It's a tree-lined street running almost parallel with the Washington National Pike. The Pike is adjacent to the NIG Centre for Scientific Review where Luca works. The house is a two-storied weatherboard, painted light green and white. You can't miss it."

The agent gave the exact address and signed off.

"What makes you so sure Fallon will make contact with Victor Luca?" asked Donna.

"I figure he'll want to know who reviewed his NIG grant applications. He's on some sort of vendetta, and those reviewers are all potential targets."

"But won't Luca claim that the names of the reviewers are confidential? Right?"

"He'd be right about that, but it will depend on how persuasive Fallon is."

"Help me with this. I can't understand why Fallon's former Oxford Bridge University colleagues kept popping up as reviewers of Fallon's NIG grant applications? Maybe Luca had worked out that they would trash Fallon's grant applications?"

"Yeah, it's almost as if Victor Luca was stacking the cards against Fallon."

"I agree. As far as we know the only connection between Luca and Fallon involves the assessment of Fallon's grant applications. Luca never worked at Oxford Bridge University or Harvard University."

"There has to be some personal reason why Luca would want to sabotage Fallon's success."

"I've got a bad feeling about this Jack. I think we should place Victor Luca under protection. The question is do we inform him that he is a potential target? He may do a runner like some of the others."

"Whatever we decide, we need to get back to the States pronto."

Jack and Donna caught a British Airways flight from Heathrow to Dulles International Airport, Washington DC. They booked into a hotel in Bethesda. On the flight over they had discussed whether to alert Victor Luca or not. They'd jointly agreed to alert him, especially since the alternative had not worked out so well for the previous victims.

When Donna phoned Luca and fully explained their concerns he immediately brushed them off.

"You are telling me Professor John Fallon is a serial killer, and I am his next target. I've never heard anything so ridiculous," declared Victor Luca.

"We have good reason to suspect John Fallon of the murder of several of his former Oxford Bridge University colleagues. We also have reason to believe that you sabotaged his research grant applications seeking funding from the NIG. For this reason alone you may be next on his hit list."

"Again, that's ridiculous. John Fallon's grant applications were always reviewed according to NIG's impeccable standards. I was in charge and can assure you of the integrity of the assessment process. We always ensure that grants are reviewed by credible notable researchers in the field. We rigorously seek to avoid any conflicts of interest. Besides, John Fallon and I are on the best of terms. Goodness me, the last time we met I invited him to my family home for dinner after my grant assessing panel had completed their assessments."

"Can you explain then why you often had Fallon's past colleagues at Oxford Bridge University review his applications? Weren't you aware that many of them disliked John, and wanted to damage his career?"

"I appointed them simply because they had the appropriate genetics expertise. It's been at least ten years since John had worked at Oxford Bridge University. There was no conflict of interest there. I confess I did have some affection for John. I expected his previous colleagues would feel the same and provide fair criticisms."

"But they didn't, did they?"

"I can assure you they were reasonable compared to some of the reviews we receive."

"Whatever, you are being placed under FBI protection for the foreseeable future. We advise you not to go anywhere other than to work and your home. Two Agents will be assigned to guard your home. Another two Agents will accompany you to work and remain posted outside your office."

Donna deliberately omitted the fact that two snipers would be placed in eyesight of Luca's house.

"This is all a bit over the top, isn't it? I can assure you, there is nothing to worry about," declared Victor Luca, sounding totally at ease.

Inwardly, Victor Luca was a frightened man, but at the same time fatalistic. He had been lucky enough to have escaped the jaws of death twice as a child. Many of his friends and neighbours had not been so fortunate. He was an old man now. He had led a full life. If his time was up, so be it. He pondered what he had been told. Was John Fallon a serial killer like his father? Was he really on his way right now to exact his revenge? Had he worked out that he had been betrayed all these years? No, John Fallon was not that clever. He had chosen to remain ignorant of his Romanian background. Why should he take an interest now?

CHAPTER FIFTY-TWO

The men had watched the house for three days. They concluded that the elderly man inside was alone and unprotected. They waited until nightfall. John Fallon stepped up onto the stone doorstep and pressed the doorbell. His two accomplices hid on either side of the door. They could hear footsteps coming down the hallway. Then the porch light went on. It provided a dim yellow light over the entrance to the house. The door opened slowly. An elderly man looked up and tried to focus on the face that presented itself. The face had had a makeover and was barely recognizable.

"Is that you John, you look different? It's good to see you again. It's getting quite late. Is everything all right?" said the elderly man after studying the face for some time.

At the moment he finished talking the three intruders forced their way into the house. They grabbed and restrained Nathan Schuller by his upper arms, shoving a cloth into his mouth to stop him from screaming. They removed the cloth once they had the old man back fully inside the house.

"What do you want? What on earth is going on?" yelled the old man, totally confused by the situation.

They half escorted, half dragged Nathan Schuller down the hallway into his kitchen. They forced him to sit on one of the kitchen chairs next to the kitchen table. The two accomplices stood on either side of him. John Fallon sat down on a chair on the other side of the table facing him.

"How long have we known each other, Nathan?" asked Fallon, with a hint of menace in his voice.

"About ten years, give or take" replied the old man shakily.

"You know, I've always considered you and Victor as friends. Do you think I was right to do so?"

"Of course John, of course, we are friends," replied the old man, his face starting to redden, and his brow glisten with sweat.

"Is there anything you want to tell me differently, Nathan?"

"Tell you what? What do you mean? I don't understand. What are you saying?"

"I mean is there anything you want to tell me about why you and Victor sabotaged the success of my NIG grant applications."

"What? No... we did no such thing," replied Schuller, appearing righteously offended by the mere suggestion.

"Yes, you did!" shouted John in a menacing voice, leaning over, and stamping his fist on the table. "I'm inviting you to confess! I want to hear your confession. This is your chance to cleanse your soul."

"No John, you have it all wrong. We did our best for you. We only processed your grant applications. We didn't review them. You know how hard it is to obtain a research grant these days. It's like a lottery. Everyone knows that."

"Yes, that is exactly what Victor used to say. But I've had enough of your lies. Let me help you with your confession. You and Victor are both Jews who suffered at the hands of the Nazis during the holocaust. Am I right?"

"Yes, that's correct," responded Schuller.

"Only, I've just learned that my birth father was a Nazi collaborator who was a guard at the same camp where Victor and his mother were imprisoned. You want to punish me for the sins of my father, a man I never knew. Am I right?"

"No John, I know nothing of this. You need to speak to Victor," lied the old man, his face now trembling with anxiety.

"Liar! Liar! Liar!" screamed Fallon, his face turning bright red with rage. "If you don't confess now I will hand your care over to my friends here. I can assure you, they can be crueller than the Nazis ever were."

Just then Fallon caught sight of family photographs proudly displayed on the kitchen wall above a shelf on which stood a beautiful golden menorah, a replica of the candelabra in the ancient Temple in Jerusalem.

"You have children and grandchildren. How nice for you," stated Fallon, directing his gaze to the photographs hanging on the wall. "I will gladly hand the care of your loved ones over to my friends here as well. Confess and no harm will come to them. You have my word," said John, now with pure menace in his voice.

The old man lowered and shook his head, accepting he was beaten.

"It was your accent that gave you away. Victor wouldn't let it go. He discovered your father was a guard at a concentration camp in Pechora. It is the same camp where he and his mother were imprisoned by the Nazis during the Second World War. Your father raped and murdered his mother and many other Jewish women at the camp. You know, Victor was barely alive when the camp was liberated by the Allies. He was just skin and bone. Yes, he wanted to punish you for the sins of your father. He was outraged that you had been adopted into such a wealthy British family to live a life of prosperity and advantage."

"May be you didn't know that I too suffered because of my father. I was given up to a Romanian orphanage as a baby. Have you heard about the conditions at those orphanages? They were as bad as the Nazi concentration camps. I was starved, neglected, and molested. I had nothing to do with Victor's suffering. Nothing you hear! You are both sick old men forever stuck with the memories of your distant past. I am not an animal like my father. I have worked hard to contribute to society. I had so much more to give, but you and Victor denied me that."

"Take a good look at yourself. You are a violent man, a killer just like your father. You dare to invade my house and threaten an old man and his loved ones. Bad genes are passed down from one generation to the next. Evil begets evil!" shouted the old man, his face turning bright red with anger, his body visibly shaking in the chair.

"Bag him!" screamed John in rage to his two accomplices.

CHAPTER FIFTY-THREE

"Do you think he will show?" asked Donna eyeing Jack. "I still think it's our best chance."

"It's Victor's drive to work that worries me most. That's where he'll be exposed. We'll have two Agents in the car with him. We'll be following them in our car, but will that be enough?"

"It has to be. Don't forget that half of Washington's police force is on the lookout for Fallon."

Donna's cell phone rang. She punched the answer tab and put the phone to her ear.

"It's Agent Dickson here. I have some information for you about John Fallon and Victor Luca. Archival material shows that John Fallon's birth father Dracul Antonescu was a Nazi collaborator and guard at a concentration camp at Pechora in Romania during the Second World War. Victor Luca and his mother were imprisoned at the same camp. They were Romanian Jews."

"Wow, you may have hit the jackpot!" exclaimed Donna.

"That's not all. I got to speak to one of the camp's survivors, who was just a child at the time. Seems Fallon's father was a right charmer. He was feared and hated by all the prisoners. He tortured and murdered several of them. He had a particular predilection for Jews. He raped and murdered several of the Jewish women. Victor Luca was just a child at the time. He was barely alive when the Allies liberated the camp. It's possible Fallon's father raped and murdered Luca's mother."

"Yikes, great work Agent Dickson. That's very helpful. I'll get back to you if we need anything else. Thanks again."

"Glad to be of service."

Donna gave Jack the details of the conversation.

"Certainly explains why Victor Luca might hate John Fallon, at least to go as far as ruining Fallon's career."

"It's sad when you think about it though. Why should anyone demand that children pay for the sins of their parents?"

"History recalls dozens of intergenerational feuds that lasted for decades, even including royalty. Revenge is certainly one of humanity's less attractive traits. It can stir incredibly powerful forces in some people."

"Workplace revenge, and revenge over harm to family and loved ones, must be close to the top of the list."

"There is one fact we are overlooking though. Victor Luca mentioned that he and Fallon were on good terms when they last met. He even went as far as stating they were friends. What makes you think Fallon knows anything about Luca's betrayal? Luca has betrayed him for years. Fallon has never taken an interest in his birth parents. He can't know about his father's extreme anti-semitic hostility and wartime history, or he would never have trusted Luca in the first place."

"For whatever reason, Fallon appears to be on a tight timeline in seeking retribution. Just look at his time-frame for murdering his Oxford Bridge University colleagues. It's patently clear he is no longer interested in his academic position at Harvard University. He is hell-bent on self-destruction. He has just one thing in mind, and that is revenge."

"You're right. Why give up a distinguished medical science career? He must realize he's eventually going to get caught. I just don't get it. He seems to have become mentally unbalanced"

"I bet he's probably recalled every instance he has been abused or harmed in some way, including his childhood in Romania. He's going to punish everyone responsible for doing him any harm. By now he has probably researched his birth parents, especially his mother who gave him away to the orphanage. I'm guessing that by researching his family's history, in particular his father's wartime history, John will have worked out that Luca has betrayed him."

"What about other members of the grant assessing panels that assessed Fallon's grants? That is, those other than his Oxford Bridge University colleagues. They could also be targets?"

"He may try to extract that information from Luca. I'm sure he will only want to punish anyone who repeatedly sabotaged the success of his grant applications. Hang on ... I just remembered Professor Brown mentioning something about a person who Chaired the meetings of the grant assessing panels."

"Isn't that the SRO's job?"

"Better get your colleagues to check that out," suggested Jack looking concerned.

Agent Dickson rang later that day.

"Back so soon, Agent Dickson?" Donna answered.

"Yeah, can't keep away," he replied grinning to himself.

"I can tell you that there is a separate Chair for those grant assessing panel meetings. Victor Luca almost always employed the same Chair, a Professor Nathan Schuller. Schuller was partly retired but still works at a University in Washington DC. He is also Jewish and attends the same synagogue as Luca. He lives in the same suburb not far from Luca, which could be of interest."

"Do you have his address?"

Agent Dickson provided the address.

"Can you get over to Schuller's place to check whether he is OK, and make sure his house is secure."

"No problem."

Donna turned back to Jack.

"A Professor Nathan Schuller chaired the grant assessing panel meetings. Luca played a more administrative role in selecting the reviewers. I've sent Agent Dickson over to Schuller's address to make sure he's OK. Looks like Schuller is a friend of Luca's, maybe his best friend. They are both Jewish, attend the same synagogue, and live close to one another. We may need to provide him with protection as well."

An agitated Agent Dickson phoned back an hour later.

"I'm afraid we were too late. Schuller is dead. His body is still warm. He is sitting slumped in a kitchen chair. He's been suffocated with a plastic bag. Same MO as used in the other murders. Looks like Fallon's work. There is no sign of forced entry."

"Damn, if only we'd got to him faster. No doubt about it now, Fallon is here in Washington DC. We need to beef up our security on Luca."

"Sure thing. I'll get onto it straight away."

Donna turned to Jack and repeated the conversation.

"Fallon is here in Washington DC. Schuller is dead. He's only recently been murdered. It's Fallon's MO all right. As you probably heard, I've requested extra protection for Luca."

"He's bound to try to get to Luca. This might be our best and only chance to apprehend him."

CHAPTER FIFTY-FOUR

John Fallon's headaches were becoming ever more excruciatingly painful. This was despite the transdermal patches he wore, which were medicated with increasing doses of fentanyl, a powerful painkiller. He was well aware that time was running out. Reluctantly, he felt he now had little choice but to trust the lawyers he had chosen. He transferred the bulk of his funds to their nominated Swiss bank account to be held in trust for the June Foundation. That at least gave him some satisfaction. Bringing Victor Luca to justice would be his last task. After that, he would take steps to end his own life. His death would be in his own time, and by his own hands. He aimed to end his life before the pain became uncontrollable. Or before the effects of the tumour caused some critical body function to fail and left him vulnerable as an invalid.

He needed Luca to confess before he killed him, just as Nathan Schuller had confessed. He had been lucky with Schuller. The old man had been left completely unprotected. He accepted that Victor Luca would be an entirely different kettle of fish. He would be protected by FBI Agents and the Washington Police Force.

Victor Luca was due to attend a committee meeting at the NIG Centre for Scientific Review. He had to make the necessary preparations. He was allowed to drive his late-model Lincoln Continental with one FBI Agent riding shotgun in the front passenger seat. Another Agent rode in the back passenger seat. Plainclothes FBI Agents in an unmarked black Chevrolet Tahoe escorted the Professor's car. Donna and Jack followed in their hire car. The cavalcade of cars safely reached the NIG building on Rockledge Drive off the Washington National Pike. Luca parked his car in his usual parking spot. The Agents surrounded Luca as they escorted him into the building. Donna acknowledged the two Agents stationed at the entrance. Once inside, the group escorted

Luca to his office on the tenth floor of the building. Two of the Agents positioned themselves outside the office door. They received specific instructions from Donna not to let anyone into the office unless they had appropriate authority and ID.

"Don't you think this is all a bit over the top?" asked Luca, eyeing Donna and Jack.

"You might think so, but we have just learned that your colleague Professor Nathan Schuller has been murdered," replied Jack, who had initially withheld this information so as not to scare the old man. "The murder scene has Fallon's signature all over it."

Victor Luca's face turned ashen white from fright, and then it became a picture of sadness.

"Poor Martha. She has gone to Philly for the week to help her granddaughter with her new baby girl," muttered Victor empathetically.

"Who is Martha?"

"Nathan's wife. How can I tell her about what has happened to Nathan? What can I say to comfort her?" groaned Victor.

Donna and Jack eyed one another, unable to find the words for an appropriate response to comfort the old man. They left Victor Luca sitting at his desk looking confused and forlorn.

CHAPTER FIFTY-FIVE

Victor Luca was escorted the short distance to and from his workplace at the NIG Centre for Scientific Review for a week. There was no sign of anything out of the ordinary during the five workdays. The only visitors he had were the occasional colleague, and the cleaning staff when he had to work late. Victor's wife packed him a lunch, which he ate each day in his office. Luca's house was closely guarded by the FBI and police officers both day and night. Jack and Donna checked in on the couple every evening. Donna warned her FBI colleagues not to get complacent. John Fallon remained at large.

On the following Friday, Victor was forced to work late due to NIG commitments. Luca told the Agents posted outside his door that he did not want to be disturbed. He had important business to attend to and would be working a bit late. Most of the staff had left work for home at 5.00 pm. A few cleaners arrived later to clean the offices. An old man in the cleaning company's green overalls pushed his cleaning cart towards Luca's office. He was clearly elderly with thin wispy white hair, a stooped posture, and smudged wire-rimmed glasses.

"My last office for the night," rasped the old man, holding up his ID card for the Agents to inspect.

They quickly glimpsed the ID.

"Don't take too long. It is Friday night," one of the Agents replied, thinking about how doddery the old man was.

The cleaner slowly nodded in agreement. They held the office door open for him and closed it once he had shuffled through. The door opened about fifteen minutes later. The old man shuffled out with his cart into the corridor, closing the door behind him. The two Agents watched as the cleaner shuffled slowly down the corridor, eventually pushing his cart out of sight.

"Bloody hell, I hope I never end up like that poor sod," confided one Agent to the other.

The other Agent nodded in agreement. The following hour passed without any further visitors. The two Agents became impatient when by 8.00 pm Victor Luca had not exited his office. By 8.30 pm they were becoming agitated and irate.

"I'm going to interrupt the Professor. I don't care how important his work is. I promised my missus we'd go bowling tonight," exclaimed one Agent to the other.

"Yeah, I know it's not for us to say, but he's been working long enough. I'm getting hungry."

"He did say he was going to work a "bit" late."

"Yeah, but his "bit" is a bit too long."

One of the Agents knocked on the office door. There was no answer.

"I'm going in," said the other, and pushed the door all the way open.

The two Agents stood in the doorway, and quickly scanned the entire room hoping that Victor Luca might magically appear from behind the furniture. They stood awhile dumbfounded.

"The room is empty," said one Agent to the other.

"Fucking no kidding," said the other, getting hot under the collar.

"It's impossible. We've been standing outside the office ever since we last saw him."

They both rushed to the outside window.

"We're ten stories up here. Nobody is going to get a body out that window. Let alone lower it to the ground floor without being seen. Besides the window is latched. It doesn't open enough to even pass a cat through."

"I just don't get it. We saw the Professor today at lunchtime. Remember, he asked for a coffee from the vending machine down the corridor. You fetched it for him. Then at around 6.00 pm, I got him another coffee. At 7.00 pm you escorted him to the toilet.

"The only visitor he has had since that time was that poor old sod of a cleaner."

"Oh, shit! It must have been him. Quick, check the GPS tracking device Agent Collins placed in the Prof's trouser pocket."

The Agent opened up the tracking app on his cell phone. He discovered the signal was stationary and coming from the NIG building. It was coming from Luca's office. Both Agents quickly searched the room. They located the GPS tracking device lying on the floor under Luca's desk.

"Shit, we could lose our jobs over this. I'll phone Agent Collins. She's not going to be happy."

CHAPTER FIFTY-SIX

D onna received the urgent phone call just as she and Jack were dressing to go out for dinner.

"Victor Luca has disappeared. He wasn't in his office when we checked in on him at the end of the day. Agent Murphy and I were stationed outside his office all day. As late as 7.00 pm we escorted him to the toilet. But he wasn't in his office when we checked in on him at 8.30 pm."

"Shit! You've got to be kidding me!" screamed Donna into the phone.

"Only wish I was," replied the Agent meekly and continued. "His only visitor after 7.00 pm was an elderly cleaner. The cleaning guy was at least eighty with white hair and stooped. I kid you not, he could barely walk. He has to be the one responsible. I don't know how he did it. He must have rendered the Professor unconscious somehow, and then smuggled him out of the office in his cleaning cart."

"Exactly when was that?"

"About forty minutes ago. Even worse, the cleaner must have found the GPS tracking device you planted on Luca. We found it lying under Luca's desk."

"Ohhh... crap! Get all the CCTV coverage you can. Let's hope it hasn't been interfered with, but maybe that's unlikely given it's a Government building. We need to know if he left the building and where he is headed. For your sake, you'd better hope Luca is still alive."

"I'm sorry. I'll get back to you about the CCTV coverage ASAP."

Donna, Jack, and the two Agents sat in front of the computer screen. The building's custodian played the CCTV videos taken from different cameras installed in and around the building. The video taken of the corridors on the tenth floor clearly showed the elderly cleaner exiting Luca's office. Other videos revealed that he took the lift to the underground parking area in the basement of the building. He stopped next to a dark blue van owned and operated by the cleaning company. A large man exited the van. With help from the cleaner, he lifted a large black bag from the cleaning cart into the van.

"That bag has got to contain Victor Luca!" shouted Donna.

"Some firms have GPS trackers installed in their vans," proffered Jack, taking out his phone and calling the cleaning company.

"See if you can make out the van's registration number."

Jack passed the phone to Donna.

"This is FBI Agent Donna Collins. I need you to track one of your cleaning vans. We believe it has been commandeered in the progress of a crime."

She gave the man the van's registration number and waited.

"That van should have left the NIG Centre for Scientific Review about thirty minutes ago. The van is supposed to be returning to our depot. .....Hang on, I have it here on our tracker. It seems to be heading in the opposite direction."

"Tell me where the van is!" shouted Donna into the poor man's ear.

"It's heading towards Bethesda on the Old Georgetown Road."

Donna took out her cell phone and requested an APB be posted to be on the lookout for the dark blue cleaning van.

"Send up a chopper," she demanded.

CHAPTER FIFTY-SEVEN

The police helicopter "eye in the sky" spotted the cleaning van, lit up by street and shop lights, as it headed along Old Georgetown road toward the suburb of Bethesda. The van reached a multi-story building in central Bethesda and disappeared down into an underground carpark. The helicopter pilot relayed the sighting and remained hovering nearby.

Donna immediately posted another APB.

"Suspect in blue cleaning van seen entering underground carpark. All Agents to proceed to multi-story building on the corner of Old Georgetown Road and Rockville Pike. Block off all exits and entrances from the carpark and building. Proceed with caution. There are at least two suspects. They are likely armed. They have an elderly man hostage."

Donna and Jack drove to the building and were met there by the Commander of the Washington DC Police Force, the FBI Special Agent In Charge, and his SWAT team who had arrived at the site.

"Luca may already be dead unless he can breathe inside that black bag."

"I'm guessing Fallon will want to extract a confession. There's family history to be thrashed out. I'm hoping they'll want to keep Luca alive, at least for a while."

"I suggest we send in the SWAT team for a floor-by-floor search, starting with the underground carpark," said the Commander to the FBI Special Agent In Charge.

At that moment the distant whirring of another set of helicopter blades could be heard, getting ever closer. The helicopter veered past the police helicopter, reached the building, circled above it, and hovered. It then slowly descended onto the roof of the building. Almost immediately, two men carrying a large black bag bolted across the roof. They placed the bag carefully into the cabin of the helicopter. They then also alighted. Immediately, the helicopter pilot lifted the collective control and twisted the throttle to provide lift and thrust. The helicopter slowly rose skyward. The pilot gently pushed the cyclic control causing the nose of the helicopter to tilt downwards and move forward. In response, the helicopter flew off in a northerly direction towards Baltimore and the large cities on the eastern seaboard.

"Stand down, don't shoot! There's a hostage on board!" screamed the SWAT team leader.

"Follow that helicopter!" yelled the Special Agent In Charge, and Police Commander in unison.

"Put another chopper in the air," yelled Donna.

Almost immediately another police helicopter appeared seemingly out of nowhere. The two law enforcement helicopters sped off after the retreating helicopter containing the hostage. Without further discussion, the SWAT team and FBI Agents raced to their vehicles to participate in the chase.

"Let's go!" screamed Donna at Jack.

"Fallon could still be in the building!" yelled Jack over the scream of the sirens.

"They're getting away!" yelled Donna.

"You go. Leave me with a couple of Agents to check the building," pleaded Jack, getting close to Donna.

"OK, agents Murphy and Flanagan, you go with Jack!" shouted Donna to the two Agents.

With that Donna jumped into her car together with other colleagues and joined the cavalcade of law enforcement vehicles. Their sirens blaring as they headed north in the direction of the chasing helicopters, which had the fleeing helicopter in their sights.

CHAPTER FIFTY-EIGHT

Inside the building a very groggy Victor Luca was sitting in a chair with his wrists tied tightly with nylon cable ties behind his back. Fallon was sitting directly in front of him, legs splayed apart, on a backward-facing chair. His arms were resting on the back of the chair. He was smiling as he studied the old man's face.

"Do you hear that Victor? There's nobody here now except us. Your rescuers have all abandoned you," mocked Fallon, referring to the receding noise of the sirens and helicopters.

"I thought we were friends? Why are you treating me like this?" mumbled Victor.

"Cut the crap! Your Jewish friend Nathan Schuller told me all about you and our supposed friendship. You couldn't help yourself, could you? You had to delve into my background, into my past. You discovered I was adopted from a Romanian orphanage, didn't you?"

"Yes, and I discovered that you are the son of a murderous anti-Semite. Dracul Antonescu, your birth father, raped, tortured, and murdered many women during the war. I witnessed it. I was there in the concentration camp in Pechora where thousands died at the hands of the Nazis and their collaborators like your father. Your father raped and murdered my beautiful mother. She was the kindest person in the world. Your father was pure evil. I almost died at that camp too. But guess what, here I am today, still alive to recount history, and settle the score."

"I never knew my father and mother. They gave me up as a baby to a Romanian orphanage. I had no idea of my parents' history until a few days ago. I was raised as a child in that Romanian orphanage. The conditions there were as bad as in any Nazi concentration camp. I too suffered. I was starved, molested, beaten, and neglected. I was as much a victim of my father, as you and your family were. Children cannot be held responsible for their parents' sins. You cannot blame me for the sins of my father."

"You are a replica of your father. I'm guessing it was you who ordered the killing of that Japanese family, including their children. They were all asphyxiated by the same means you used to kill some of your colleagues. What injustice did they do to you?"

"Shut your mouth! If you must know, my adoptive mother's brother was an Allied prisoner of war. He was forced to work on the Burma Railway, the "Death Railway", during the Second World War. He was tortured and starved to death, suffering the most horrendous of conditions. Let's just say, I got a little bit of justice for him. I picked out Masuda for the task of killing Bentley after remembering seeing the Japanese man giving a show of his martial arts skills at a cultural event when he worked at the Dana Farber Cancer Institute in Boston. It was a pure coincidence that he subsequently went to work with my ex-colleague Professor Kearney in London. What a test it was, the martial arts expert versus the talented Dr Bentley. I thought it would be no contest, but Richard proved me wrong. Still, he proved to be no match for my orphanage friends."

"Ughh..., you are no better than your father. You are just as vindictive. Those people were innocent of any crime. You said that children can't be blamed for the sins of their father, yet you condemned a whole family to death for what their father and grandfathers did during the war."

"Well hear this! I'm condemning you for what you did to me! You have no right to blame me for what my father did. Perhaps his Jewish neighbours wronged him in some way?"

"That says it all, doesn't it. It is so easy to blame the Jews when things go wrong. You have no idea of the true suffering that can result from cultural or religious persecution. Millions, yes I said millions, of Jews were starved, tortured, and murdered during the war. Collaborators like your father were among the torturers and executioners. They were the worst as they preyed upon their own countrymen. They willingly helped the Nazis do their dirty work. They were pure evil. Death followed them like night follows day. When I learned you were Dracul's son, I realized I had a chance, my chance, for revenge. There is no statute of limitation for crimes punishable by death."

"So you admit it? You made sure my grant applications were unsuccessful. You destroyed my career, my life."

"Of course, I don't deny it. Why do you deserve to be successful? What right do you have to lead a life of luxury and privilege because you were so lucky to be adopted into a wealthy family? You should have been left to die in that orphanage. Your father and his Nazi masters destroyed my family. Why shouldn't I want to destroy his? You have turned out just like your father. What do the English say ... "a chip off the old block". You are nothing but a cold-blooded serial killer. You systematically murdered your University colleagues."

"Shut your mouth! They all deserved to die. Like you, they ruined my career and my life. You are nothing but a vindictive old man forever entrenched in the past."

"You and your father are not innocent. Your father made my childhood a living nightmare. A living hell that is forever burned into my memory, and from which I can never escape."

"Well, it's your lucky day. I am here to put you out of your misery."

"Do you think I am afraid of death? I escaped death twice at the hands of the Nazis and your father. I have lived a long and fulfilled life. Unlike my long life, yours will be much shorter, and your death hopefully much more painful," sneered Luca, as he looked carefully for signs of a reaction.

"Do you think you can threaten me? What do you mean by that?" demanded Fallon menacingly.

"How is your health these days?"

"It is better than yours will shortly be."

"You may kill me now, but I began killing you years ago," scoffed Luca. "The poison I fed you at my home will soon reap its rewards. My prediction is that you will die quite soon, from either cancer or heart disease, I am not fussy which one. Yours will hopefully be a slow, lingering, and painful death," mocked Luca, grinning at Fallon.

John Fallon slowly stood up from the chair. He felt faint and began to feel dizzy. He tightly grasped the back of the chair for support. He struggled to stay on his feet after comprehending the enormity of what he had just been told. He bent over and held his head in his hands, and let out an ear-splitting cry.

"No!! You bastard! It was you who gave me this brain tumour!" as he realized for the first time the probable origins of the tumour that had been slowly growing in his brain. The tumour that would shortly end his life.

In a blind rage, he lashed out at the old man sitting in front of him. He bashed him repeatedly on either side of the head with closed fists, til blood began to ooze from his ears and mouth. The old man's battered and bloody head slumped forward. Still conscious, Victor Luca slowly raised his bloodied head and smiled.

John Fallon stared at the grotesque figure facing him, his hatred of the man now unquenchable. He would remove that haunting smile forever. He extracted the plastic bag from his jacket pocket. He carefully opened the bag and placed it over Luca's head. All the while Luca held his head stoically upright in a final display of defiance.

CHAPTER FIFTY-NINE

J ack and Agents Murphy and Flanagan entered the high-rise building, each holding a pistol for protection. They had no idea they were being watched by two of Fallon's accomplices still inside the building. The working day had ended. The building was deserted. The body of the building's custodian slain by Fallon's accomplices lay behind the reception desk on the ground floor.

"We don't know if Fallon is here, if he is alone, or if he has company," cautioned Jack.

"If he is here, which seems unlikely, then he is probably on one of the upper floors," suggested Agent Murphy.

"Agreed," responded Jack. "There are five floors including the basement. Let's check each floor in turn. Agent Murphy, you check the carpark on the lower ground floor, Flanagan you check the ground floor. I'll take the first floor. Take the stairs, not the lift. Meet me on the second-floor stairwell when you've finished your searches. Call for backup immediately if you sight or encounter Fallon or one of his accomplices. Don't challenge them alone. We don't want anyone being a hero," cautioned Jack.

The building was essentially a square box with outer and central offices connected by a long corridor. Jack and Agent Murphy walked to the stairwell to climb or descend to their nominated floor. Murphy raced through the carpark. It was mostly empty except for the cleaning van and a couple of cars that had been left in the building overnight. There was no sign of their owners.

Flanagan stealthily strode past the custodian's desk into the corridor on the ground floor. The corridor was dimly lit, presumably due to some power-saving system. He anxiously scanned the entranceway for any sign of movement, then proceeded slowly forward to the first office. But he failed to notice the janitor's cupboard on the right-hand side of the corridor just past the entranceway. It wasn't until he had passed the cupboard that he felt a hard thud in his back. He stopped immediately in his tracks. He stood motionless for a few seconds as if trying to comprehend why he wasn't moving. Then he slumped face-forward, lifeless, onto the floor. Pavel Covaci, one of John Fallon's enforcers, walked quickly forward, placed his foot on the dead man's back, leaned down, and recovered his bloodied knife. He cleaned the blade of the knife of blood by swiping it back and forth on the dead Agent's jacket.

Murphy completed his search of the carpark, finding nothing of interest. He began climbing the stairs, aiming to meet up with Flanagan on the ground floor stairwell. Flanagan wasn't there. After a brief wait on the ground floor stairwell, he proceeded to climb the stairs to rendezvous with Jack on the second floor. He focused his attention on the stairs in front, looking up now and then at the stairwell above. He failed to check his rear. Pavel Covaci silently opened the stairwell door on the ground floor. He steadied himself, aimed, then hurled his knife with great force upwards at the Agent climbing the stairs. The knife struck Agent Murphy between his shoulder blades. The FBI Agent staggered then tumbled uncontrollably backward down the stairs until finally landing at the feet of his assassin. Once again Pavel placed his foot on his dead victim's prone body, leaned down, and recovered and cleaned his bloodied knife.

"Two down. Just one to go," he whispered to himself in Romanian.

Jack opened the door on the stairwell to the first floor. Every nerve in his body was on high alert, with adrenalin surging from his adrenal glands into his bloodstream. He scanned the empty corridor and walked slowly forward. He searched for any signs of movement and listened intently for any foreign sound. The floor was poorly lit and eerily quiet, except for the low hum of the air-conditioning.

As Jack walked forward he noticed the janitor's cupboard just to his right. He pressed his body close to the wall immediately before the cupboard door. In one swift movement, he opened the door, his finger ready on the trigger of his pistol. He breathed a sigh of relief. The cupboard contained nothing but a collection of mops and brooms and other items that make up a janitor's cleaning inventory.

He moved on slowly down the corridor acutely aware that one of Fallon's men could be in any one of the offices or behind the bend at the end of the corridor. As far as he could tell, the door of the meeting room just to his left, and the doors of all the offices down this side of the corridor were closed. He would have to open each door in turn, exposing himself to considerable risk each time. He stood to the side of the door of the meeting room. As before, in one swift movement, he turned the door handle and flung the door open with considerable force. He charged through the doorway in a semi-squatting position with his pistol held forward, finger on the trigger, scanning the room. There was a startled cry, then a groan, as the door slammed into Vasile Popescu, one of Fallon's enforcers, positioned behind it. The man's pistol hit the floor with a thud and skittered across the highly polished vinyl floor to the wall. Regaining his senses, Popescu grabbed an available chair nearby, wielded it high above his head, and drove it down onto Jack's arms, causing him to lose his grip on his pistol. The weapon dropped to the floor and skittered to the opposite wall. Popescu flung the chair at Jack and raced to the wall to be the first to recover his weapon. Jack tossed the chair aside and tackled Popescu to the ground just before he reached his pistol. Popescu was a big, strong man, almost as big as Jack. He would not go down without a fight and would have to be subdued quickly. Jack placed Popescu in a headlock and employing the chokehold he compressed the man's upper airway blocking off the carotid arteries, slowly starving the brain of oxygen. Jack could feel the man's considerable strength as he fought to be released from

Jack's vice-like grip, his legs struggling against the floor to gain leverage. But after a couple of minutes, Jack could feel the man's strength ebbing away until at last there was no fight left and he went limp. Jack maintained the chokehold for a further couple of minutes just to be sure the man was dead.

"Damn, how many more of Fallon's men are in the building," cursed Jack silently to himself, as he picked his pistol off the floor.

Jack quickly, but cautiously checked every office and room on the first floor, but found nothing of interest. He opened the door to the stairwell leading to the upper floors. He was now ultra-cautious following his encounter with one of Fallon's men. He felt certain now that the helicopter chase must have been a ruse to mislead law enforcement. He was sure Fallon and his hostage had remained behind in the building. He kept his back to the wall and scanned up and down the stairs searching for the two FBI Agents. Nothing. Jack immediately had dark thoughts about the fates of Murphy and Flanagan given their failure to rendezvous with him. He walked slowly up the stairs to the stairwell landing on the second floor keeping his back to the wall. He repeatedly scanned up and down the stairwell.

"Damn. Where are Dickson and Flanagan?" he swore to himself.

He entered the second-floor corridor and stood aside the front of the janitor's cupboard. In one motion he flung open the door. His right fist was raised, aiming to plant it on anyone hiding in the cupboard. The cupboard was empty save for the usual janitor's inventory. Jack carefully and cautiously checked each room on the floor but found nothing of interest. He then carefully checked the rooms on the third floor and also found nothing of interest.

Jack was now certain Dickson and Flanagan had been compromised. They had not made the rendezvous and hadn't contacted him. He pulled out his phone and tried to contact both of them. Neither Agent replied. He was alone.

There was only one floor left to check. Fallon had to be on the top floor of the building. The immediate question was, how many of his men did he have with him? Were they armed with lethal weapons? Would Jack be walking into a trap?

Jack opened the door on the stairwell of the top floor and very cautiously entered. He carefully checked the janitor's cupboard, and rooms along the near corridor. Nothing of interest. He then opened the first door on the far corridor. There in the centre of the room stood a figure with his back turned. The figure was placing something on the bloodied head of a man seated in a chair. Jack immediately grasped the situation and dashed forward to save Victor Luca from a gruesome fate. But Pavel Covaci had raced up the stairs to protect Fallon after killing the two FBI Agents. He was hiding just behind the door as Jack entered. Pavel drove his arm down on Jack's hands, causing Jack to drop his pistol. He then lunged with his knife catching Jack on the left side of his body, just below his Kevlar vest. The knife sliced through Jack's jacket, and into his body. Jack swivelled. With lightning speed, he side-stepped to avoid being stabbed a second time. He parried another strike, sending the knife tumbling onto the floor. The two men faced each other, breathing heavily. An ominous red stain appeared on the side of Jack's jacket, and at the top of his pants. Pavel smiled at the sight of the blood, and lunged forward aiming to slam his fist into the open bloody wound in Jack's side. But Jack blocked the blow and smashed his large fist into his assailant's neck with all the force he could muster. The blow crushed Pavel's windpipe and severed his spinal cord. Jack turned, even before the body had hit the floor, and dashed towards Luca. He shoulder-charged John Fallon who was struggling to apply duct tape to the bag. The impact flung John Fallon across the floor. He came to an abrupt and painful stop against the far wall of the room.

Jack immediately went to the aid of Victor Luca. The old man's face was purple from anoxia. Jack lifted the bag off Luca's head and he instantly gulped in several large breaths of air, almost choking in the process. His face quickly began to regain its normal sallow complexion.

Meanwhile, John Fallon had taken the opportunity to make his escape. He dashed to the door, ran down the corridor, onto the stairwell, and climbed the stairs to the roof.

After seeing Victor was out of danger, Jack instructed the old man to remain where he was.

"I'll be back soon. Stay here!"

Jack collected his pistol and raced off after Fallon taking the stairs two at a time. He opened the door leading to the roof and did a quick broad sweep of the rooftop. He located Fallon perched and teetering on the side of the building. Fallon was staring down at the traffic moving below him, as if in a trance. Jack slowly approached Fallon and raised and lowered his hand with the palm held down in the universal body language for "get down".

"Don't come any closer or I'll jump. You'd rather incarcerate me, wouldn't you, than have to scrape me off the pavement?" shouted Fallon, almost delirious.

Jack didn't approach any closer, but slowly took out his cell phone, and phoned Donna.

"Get back now, I have John Fallon in custody," said Jack rather prematurely. "As I thought, he stayed in the building to interrogate and kill Luca. The helicopter chase was a red-herring."

"Ohh..., great. That's great news, Jack. How's Victor Luca?"

"He's alive. It was a close thing."

"Even better. See you soon. Our ETA will be about thirty minutes. I'll post an APB for all police units in the area to proceed to your building."

"Thanks, Donna. See you soon."

Jack faced Fallon again.

"Come down John. You can't escape. Police backup units are on the way," pleaded Jack, all the while aware of the warm and sticky fluid leaking from his wound and collecting inside his pants.

"I'm not going anywhere."

"Why did you do it, John? Why did you murder your colleagues?"

"Revenge, what else. They made my life a misery. They destroyed my career. They had me kill the only person I ever loved. The only person who ever loved me."

"What person? Who did they make you kill, John."

"My adoptive mother June. She saw me push her husband, my paedophile stepfather, overboard from our yacht. How could I leave her as a witness? How could I?"

"Was there anyone else left on your hit list?"

"I killed them all, except for Luca. You shouldn't have stopped me. That man destroyed my life."

"I hope it's all been worth it. Now you must face the justice system, John. Come down off there before you fall."

"Don't worry about me. I'm a dead man walking. Ask Luca. He said he fed me slow-acting poison while I was a guest in his home. Test my blood and tissues if you don't believe me. That bastard created a tumour that's growing inside my brain. Ooh.., my head aches so bad," said Fallon, bending over and holding his head tightly in his hands. Excruciating agony was written all over his face.

"We can get you the medical help you need."

"It's too late, I've seen several doctors, the best in the business. They all tell me I am terminal. Anyway the justice system will put me on death row. There's nothing that can be done.... I can't stand this pain anymore. It's so bad. I've had enough..... no more talking."

With his very last words, John Fallon raised and extended his arms out from his pain-racked body. Silhouetted against the now dusky sky he resembled the Rio statue "Christ the Redeemer". He turned and smiled at Jack as if in a trance, then leaned back, and slowly fell off the edge of the building. Jack lurched forward to grasp the man to prevent him from falling. But he was unsuccessful. Jack crumpled unconscious at the site where Fallon had fallen, bleeding profusely from the vicious knife wound inflicted by Fallon's enforcer. Just at that moment, police cars with sirens blaring raced to the building to apprehend Fallon.

CHAPTER SIXTY

When Jack Baron finally regained consciousness the first person he saw when he opened his eyes was Donna. She was sitting by his hospital bedside looking down at him with a concerned expression on her face. But her expression quickly changed to a broad smile when she realized Jack was conscious and had opened his eyes.

"Welcome back, Jack" she whispered to him.

"How long have I been here?' rasped Jack, looking slowly around the sterile hospital room in which he was a patient.

"You were brought here by ambulance last night. The surgeon said you had extensive blood loss due to a knife wound in your side. He said you wouldn't have made it if your rescue had been delayed by just another thirty minutes. You would have bled out. They had to employ a massive blood transfusion protocol to replace your total blood volume to prevent you from undergoing hemorrhagic shock."

"What about Murphy and Flanagan?"

"They never made it. Sorry. Their knife wounds were fatal."

"And what about Fallon?"

"Police officers first on the scene saw him fall from the building. He was killed on impact. His body has been taken to the morgue."

"And Victor Luca?"

"Thanks to you he is still alive. He's a tough old bloke. He has been checked out by hospital staff, given a clean bill of health, and sent home."

"You know Fallon said some crazy things to me just before he fell off the building. He said his colleagues had made him kill his adoptive mother. Apparently, she was the only person he had ever loved he said. She had witnessed him kill his adoptive father, so he killed her as well to cover up his crime."

"Yes, you'll recall the newspaper article that reported a wealthy industrialist and his wife had been tragically lost at sea in a violent

305

storm while yachting off the coast of Portugal. John Fallon was the only member of the family to make it safely back to shore. It does make you wonder whether he really killed them or whether he was just feeling guilty because he was the only survivor?"

"Maybe he deliberately murdered his adoptive parents to inherit their money. They were incredibly wealthy. Guess we'll never know the answer to that as the only person who can tell us is dead. Fallon also said something about his adoptive father being a paedophile, which could have provided a motive. That is if he had been sexually assaulted by his father as a child. He also said something else that was truly weird. He accused Victor Luca of poisoning him. He said the poison had given him a brain tumour, and that his cancer was terminal. He was in a lot of pain at the end before he jumped off the building, complaining that his head hurt."

"That's a bizarre accusation. Can you imagine Victor Luca committing murder? That's ridiculous. Even if Fallon's father had raped and murdered his mother during the war, children cannot be held responsible for the sins of their parents."

"Whatever is the truth, Fallon suggested we should autopsy his body for the presence of toxins in his blood and tissues. I think we should just in case."

"I suppose a brain tumour might explain a few things. Brain tumours can supposedly change a person's personality. Like drugs, they can change brain chemistry and make a person do horrendous things they might never otherwise imagine doing."

"Yeah, just look at how Alzheimer's disease shrinks and scrambles the brain and alters personalities. It can make pleasant, highly intelligent, and capable people aggressive and belligerent, or even turn them into confused child-like figures that can't even remember their names or if they have eaten that day."

Jack yawned and his eyelids closed from the exhaustion of having to recount the details of the case.

"Jack, I rang your brother in New Zealand to inform him that you are hospitalized so you may get a phone call from him. Also, the Bureau has put me on another case. I leave for Florida in a couple of hours. I have enjoyed working with you," said Donna softly, with sadness in her voice.

Jack hadn't heard a word she had said. He had fallen into a deep sleep. Donna bent down and kissed him softly on the forehead, and walked out of the room and out of his life.

EPILOGUE

Professor John Kearney returned to work at the Imperial Institute for Genomic Sciences. He had personally thanked his old friend Jack Baron for the assurance he was safe, and for identifying the killer. He was shocked to learn that it was John Fallon who had murdered so many of his old Oxford Bridge University colleagues.

"I guess you really never know a person and what they are capable of," he thought to himself.

John Kearney had learned that Tak had tried to save his family. But John Fallon and his accomplices had killed them anyway. If only he had gone to the police instead of trying to meet Fallon's demands. It must have been a huge dilemma for him, but it wasn't right for him to try to take a life. Nevertheless, members of the laboratory would gather over a shared dinner to remember Tak, to celebrate his life, and his contributions.

Katia had continued with Tak's lengthy experiments. On a personal level, she wondered how long it would be before John realized she was in love with him. Why else had she stayed in his group year on year, giving up the chance of establishing and directing her own laboratory? She had done everything he had asked. She would have to work even harder to impress him. She would show him that she was the equal of this mysterious woman friend Helen. This woman, who he very rarely mentioned, yet loved from his days as a student more than twenty years ago.

"Tak's mice have continued to age more slowly than their littermates. But unfortunately several now have benign tumours. In a few of the mice the tumours have become malignant," said Katia to John.

"Damn, that's something I had always worried about. We'll have to find some way of preventing tumours from forming," replied John.

He rushed back to his office to plan the next set of experiments, with a spring in his step.

Fallon's body was flown back to the UK to Oxford for burial, as instructed in his will. Very few mourners attended his funeral. Professor Brown fully intended to be there. But he was advised by Professor Collingwood not to attend, for fear of damaging the University's reputation. The only ex-colleague attendee was Professor Susan Jones. She spent the time pondering over what might have been.

Attempts by British and American authorities to trace the whereabouts of Fallon's fortune came to nothing. Favre and Mueller, the two lawyers, had both quit their jobs. They were now both very wealthy individuals who would never have to work again. They were holidaying at separate resorts in the Mediterranean. They had never entered the details of their meetings with John Fallon in their law firm's records. Instead, they invented a story about an entirely different transaction that had come to nothing. They had transferred Fallon's funding to their own untouchable and untraceable bank accounts once they had discovered Fallon's real identity, and that he was a fugitive from the law. The children of Romania would have to wait for another good Samaritan to pass their way. That said, they always began to sweat profusely whenever they heard someone in their vicinity speak with a strong east-European accent. So that they wouldn't feel too guilty, they had anonymously transferred a small sum to John Fallon's Uncle and Aunt. To uncle Florin the sum was a fortune. It almost made up for all the beatings he had received at the hands of his cruel older brother.

An autopsy of Fallon's body revealed he had died of extensive trauma to his body from his fall. A large malignant tumour had been found in his brain and smaller tumours in other organs. He would have had only a few weeks to live, given the size of the brain tumour. In addition, he had advanced ischemic heart disease that would have led to heart failure in the not too distant future. At Jack's request, the MET biopsied John Fallon's blood and organ tissues for signs of toxins. They did find higher than normal levels of toxic PCBs. Since PCBs are commonly present in the environment, it could not be concluded with certainty whether or not they had been deliberately administered. They might have naturally accumulated in the body due to environmental contamination. When Victor Luca was questioned if he had deliberately poisoned Fallon he categorically denied the assertion.

"Are you crazy? That is ridiculous. John and I were friends. As I mentioned previously, I invited him several times to my house for dinner. Would I do that if I disliked the man?"

"You did not know that John Fallon was the son of Dracul Antonescu, the man who raped and murdered Jewish women at the camp in Pechora where you and your mother were imprisoned during the war?"

Victor Luca shrunk back in horror, his head violently shaking back and forth.

"No that's impossible. I don't believe you. John Fallon was a proud Englishman raised in Oxford in the United Kingdom. He studied at many fine English schools and institutions. His resume says so. He was the son of a wealthy English industrialist."

"Then tell me why would he want to kill you if you were one of his friends?"

"I feel the utmost sympathy for my friend John. He confided in me only recently that he had a brain tumour. The cancer was terminal. He was no longer in control of his senses. That tumour had robbed the poor man of his sanity."

www.ingramcontent.com/pod-product-compliance
Lightning Source LLC
Chambersburg PA
CBHW020942260626
47169CB00006B/1774